Praise for the Nightkeepers Series

Blood Spells

"This series goes right to your heart! Jessica Andersen is a must read for me!"

—#1 *New York Times* bestselling author J. R. Ward

Skykeepers

"An exciting, romantic, and imaginative tale, *Skykeepers* is guaranteed to keep readers entertained and turning the pages." —Romance Reviews Today

"Will knock you off your feet, keep you on the edge of your seat and totally captivated from beginning to end."

—Romance Junkies

"A gripping story that pulled this reader right into her Final Prophecy series." —Romance Reader at Heart (top pick)

"The Final Prophecy is a well-written series that is as intricate as it is entertaining."

The Romance Readers Connection

"The world of the Nightkeepers is wonderful, and I love visiting it. It is intricate, magical, and absolutely fascinating. . . . Step inside the Nightkeeper world and prepare to be swept away!" —Joyfully Reviewed

"If you're looking for a book to read, one that has an intricate, inventive, and well-researched world with characters that are fully realized, might I suggest *Skykeepers*?"

—Romance Novel TV

continued . . .

D0171802

Dawnkeepers

"Prophecy, passion, and powerful emotions—*Dawnkeepers* will keep you on the edge of your seat begging for more!"
—Wild on Books

"This strong new series will appeal to fantasy and paranormal fans with its refreshing blend of Mayan and Egyptian mythologies plus a suitably complex story line and plenty of antagonists."
—Monsters and Critics

"This exhilarating urban romantic fantasy saga is constructed around modernizing Mayan mythology. . . . The story line is fast-paced and filled with action as the overarching Andersen mythology is wonderfully embellished with this engaging entry."
—Genre Go Round Reviews

"Using the Mayan doomsday prophecy, Andersen continues to add complexity to her characters and her increasingly dense mythos. This intense brand of storytelling is a most welcome addition to the genre."
—*Romantic Times*

"Action-packed with skillfully written and astounding fight scenes . . . will keep you on the edge of your seat begging for more."
—Romance Junkies

Nightkeepers

"Raw passion, dark romance, and seat-of-your-pants suspense—I swear ancient Mayan gods and demons walk the modern earth!"
—#1 *New York Times* bestselling author J. R. Ward

"Andersen's got game when it comes to style and voice . . . a mix of humor, suspense, mythology, and fantasy . . . a series that's sure to be an instant reader favorite, and will put Andersen's books on keeper shelves around the world."
—Suzanne Brockmann on Writers Are Readers

"I deeply enjoyed the story. It really hooked me!"
—*New York Times* bestselling author Angela Knight

"Part romance, mystery, and fairy tale . . . a captivating book with wide appeal."
—*Booklist*

"[A] nonstop, action-intensive plot. . . . Ms. Andersen delivers a story that is both solid romance and adventure novel. If you enjoy movies like *Lara Croft* . . . or just want something truly new, you will definitely want this."
—Huntress Book Reviews

"Intense action, sensuality, and danger abound."
—*Romantic Times*

"If *Nightkeepers* is any indication of her talent, then [Jessica Andersen] will become one of my favorites. . . . [The book] brought tears to my eyes and an ache in my heart. I read each word with bated breath."
—Romance Junkies

"[A] terrific romantic fantasy . . . an excellent thriller. Jessica Andersen provides a strong story that . . . fans will cherish."
—*Midwest Book Review*

The Novels of the Nightkeepers

BLOOD SPELLS

A Novel of the Nightkeepers

JESSICA ANDERSEN

A SIGNET ECLIPSE BOOK

SIGNET ECLIPSE
Published by New American Library, a division of
Penguin Group (USA) Inc., 375 Hudson Street,
New York, New York 10014, USA
Penguin Group (Canada), 90 Eglinton Avenue East, Suite 700, Toronto,
Ontario M4P 2Y3, Canada (a division of Pearson Penguin Canada Inc.)
Penguin Books Ltd., 80 Strand, London WC2R 0RL, England
Penguin Ireland, 25 St. Stephen's Green, Dublin 2,
Ireland (a division of Penguin Books Ltd.)
Penguin Group (Australia), 250 Camberwell Road, Camberwell, Victoria 3124,
Australia (a division of Pearson Australia Group Pty. Ltd.)
Penguin Books India Pvt. Ltd., 11 Community Centre, Panchsheel Park,
New Delhi - 110 017, India
Penguin Group (NZ), 67 Apollo Drive, Rosedale, North Shore 0632,
New Zealand (a division of Pearson New Zealand Ltd.)
Penguin Books (South Africa) (Pty.) Ltd., 24 Sturdee Avenue,
Rosebank, Johannesburg 2196, South Africa

Penguin Books Ltd., Registered Offices:
80 Strand, London WC2R 0RL, England

First published by Signet Eclipse, an imprint of New American Library,
a division of Penguin Group (USA) Inc.

First Printing, November 2010
10 9 8 7 6 5 4 3 2 1

Copyright © Jessica Andersen, 2010
All rights reserved

SIGNET ECLIPSE and logo are trademarks of Penguin Group (USA) Inc.

Printed in the United States of America

Without limiting the rights under copyright reserved above, no part of this pub-
lication may be reproduced, stored in or introduced into a retrieval system, or
transmitted, in any form, or by any means (electronic, mechanical, photocopying,
recording, or otherwise), without the prior written permission of both the copyright owner and the above publisher of this book.

PUBLISHER'S NOTE
This is a work of fiction. Names, characters, places, and incidents either are the
product of the author's imagination or are used fictitiously, and any resemblance
to actual persons, living or dead, business establishments, events, or locales is
entirely coincidental.
   The publisher does not have any control over and does not assume any responsibility for author or third-party Web sites or their content.

If you purchased this book without a cover you should be aware that this book is
stolen property. It was reported as "unsold and destroyed" to the publisher and
neither the author nor the publisher has received any payment for this "stripped
book."

The scanning, uploading, and distribution of this book via the Internet or via any
other means without the permission of the publisher is illegal and punishable by
law. Please purchase only authorized electronic editions, and do not participate
in or encourage electronic piracy of copyrighted materials. Your support of the
author's rights is appreciated.

To family

ACKNOWLEDGMENTS

My heartfelt thanks go to Deidre Knight, Kerry Donovan, Claire Zion, and Kara Welsh for helping me take these books from a dream to a reality; to J. R. Ward for her unswerving support; to my many other e-friends for always being there for a laugh or cyberhug; and to Sally for keeping me sane.

The card readings used in this story were adapted from *The Mayan Oracle: Return Path to the Stars*, written by Ariel Spilsbury and Michael Bryner. The stuff I got right is thanks to them. . . . The rest is on me!

Legend

Mayan lore and modern science warn that 12/21/2012 could bring a global cataclysm . . . a threat that is far more real than we imagine. Dark forces stand poised to overrun the earth and crush humanity beneath a vicious rule of terror and blood sacrifice. Our only hope rests with a group of saviors living in secret among us: modern magic-wielding warriors called the Nightkeepers. Now, in the last years before the 2012 doomsday, these magi must find and win their destined mates in order to defend the barrier of psi energy that protects humanity against an ancient and powerful enemy. . . .

CHAPTER ONE

December 16
Five days until the solstice-eclipse
Far south of the U.S. border

As the robed Nightkeepers formed a circle around the ancient stone sarcophagus, deep underground, Patience wanted to yell, *Cancel the ceremony. The omens suck!*

She didn't, though, because the others didn't give a crap about the omens or the Mayan astronomy she'd gotten into lately. Besides, when the prophecies said, "On this day, you will jump," the magi freaking jumped. And when they said the Nightkeepers had to enact the Triad spell at the First Father's tomb on the Day of Ancestors—aka today—well, it wasn't like they could put it off, sucky omens or not.

This was now-or-never, do-or-die time . . . or potentially "do *and* die" given that the spell had a two-thirds attrition rate: The Triad had been formed only once before in the history of the Nightkeepers, and of the three magi chosen back then, only one had survived unscathed. Of the other two, one had gone nuts and the other had died instantly.

Patience suppressed a shiver. The air in the tomb was cool and faintly damp, and the flickering torchlight made the carvings on the walls seem to move in the shadows, morphing from Egyptian to Mayan and back again as though echoing the Nightkeepers' evolution.

Sweat prickled down her back beneath the lightweight black-on-black combat gear that, along with the black, tattoolike glyph on her inner wrist, identified her as a warrior-mage. She was heavily armed—the Nightkeepers all were—even though it was questionable whether jade-tipped bullets and ceremonial knives would be any use today. The magi weren't going up against a physical enemy; they were asking the sun god, Kinich Ahau, to choose three of them to receive the Triad powers.

At least that was the theory.

Problem was, theory also said that the entire pantheon was supposed to choose the Triad . . . but at the moment, all the other gods were locked up in the sky, barred from the earth by the Nightkeepers' enemies. Which meant . . . well, nobody knew what that meant for the Triad spell, amping the "not good" vibe that had taken root in Patience's stomach early that morning when she'd charted the day's sun, sacred numbers, and light pulses, and gotten what amounted to a cosmic suggestion that she should stay the hell in bed with the covers pulled over her head until tomorrow.

Not that anybody wanted to hear *that* right now. The ceremony was starting.

Across the circle, Strike—wearing royal red robes and a scowl of fierce concentration beneath his dark jawline beard—ritually invited the gods and ancestors to listen up. He was speaking ancient Mayan, having memorized the spell phonetically. Beside him, Jade joined in to smooth over his occasional fumbled syllable; she was the only one there who knew the old tongue. Her human mate, Lucius, was fluent, but this was a Nightkeepers-only ceremony . . . which was why the circle consisted of a whopping ten magi when the legends said there should be hundreds, even thousands, for the gods to choose from when it came to the Triad spell.

Yeah. Not so much.

Beside Jade was blond, good-looking Sven, face pale and serious beneath his winter-bleached tan. On Strike's other side were the king's younger sister, Sasha, and her mate, Michael, who stood with a hunter's sharp-eyed stillness. Alexis was next in the circle—blond and Amazonian, a warrior to her core. She was nearly as tall as her lean, dark-eyed shapeshifter mate, Nate, who stood beside her, their fingers brushing.

That was where the alternating male-female thing broke down, though, because next to Nate stood interruption personified in the form of their youngest member, Rabbit. But although the sharp-featured young man's veins ran with a dangerous mixture of Night-keeper and Xibalban blood and he pretty much embodied Murphy's Law, Rabbit had earned his place on the team.

When he glanced over at Patience, seeming to feel her eyes on him, she mouthed, *Good luck.* Their early close friendship might have faded over the past two years, but that didn't mean she'd stopped caring. She couldn't turn her emotions on and off at will . . . unlike the big man who stood next to her, completing the circle.

She was all too aware of him standing beside her, perfectly balanced and poised to move, as if they were headed into a battle rather than a spell. The black-on-black combat gear and flickering torchlight darkened his hair to sable and robbed his brown eyes of the shimmers of gold that brought them to life. His attention was locked on Strike and Jade as they recited the first layer of spell casting; he didn't react to Patience and Rabbit's brief exchange, and his thumbs were hooked into his weapons belt, his fingers not anywhere near brushing hers.

Oh, Brandt, she whispered inwardly. They wore the *jun tan* marks of a mated mage pair and the wedding bands from their six-year marriage . . . but just now he seemed a million miles away, locked behind the detachment that came with his warrior's mark. Untouchable. Unreachable.

Part of her wished she could hide beneath the

magic like that. But although her warrior's talent had given her increased speed, reflexes, and magic, and blunted the terror of battle so she could fight through her fear, she still *felt* the fear and everything that came with it. Brandt, on the other hand, didn't seem to feel anything when he was in warrior mode.

This isn't about us. It's about the war, she reminded herself. *Focus.*

It was a familiar refrain.

As Strike and Jade finished the first of three repetitions of the spell, a faint hum touched the air. *Magic.* It began at the very edges of Patience's hearing and gained depth, swirling around the magi in waves that resonated as both noise and energy. It was more than just the usual Nightkeeper power, she realized with an uneasy shiver. The red-gold sparkle of magic was laced through with a white-light crackle that smelled faintly of ozone, warning that this wasn't like any other spell the team had cast before.

Her pulse thudded in her ears as the fear broke through, reminding her of what they were doing, the havoc it could cause. If the chosen magi survived the Triad spell, they would gain the powers of all their most powerful forebears . . . at the cost of sharing their skulls and souls with the ghosts of those ancestors.

She couldn't imagine it. Didn't want to. Yet the thought of becoming a Triad mage had been giving her nightmares for weeks now.

Don't choose me or Brandt. Please. The inner whisper broke through the bonds of duty. Even that much of not-quite-a-prayer went against the writs, but it wasn't the first time she'd been guilty of the sin. How could she avoid it, when the rules of the magi said she had to put the needs of the gods, her king, her teammates, and mankind ahead of those of her husband and children?

Then again, Brandt didn't have a problem doing that. He just pushed her and the twins into a mental box called "family" when it suited him.

Focus.

"Okay, gang," Strike said after wrapping up the first repetition of the spell. Red-gold sparks of Nightkeeper power haloed him, glittering in the torchlight. "Let's link up."

Along with the others, Patience drew the ceremonial stone knife from her belt and used it to slash her right palm along the lifeline. Pain bit, and then magic fizzed in her bloodstream as the sacrifice connected her more securely to the barrier of psi energy that separated the three planes and supplied the magi with their powers.

With the pain came a hollow ache, as the magic swirled through the void in the center of her soul where she should have been inwardly connected to Harry and Braden. Blood of her blood.

I'm doing this for you, she whispered to the bright, beautiful boys she hadn't seen in two long years. They were safe, hidden with Woody and Hannah, cut off from the magic and the war. *We'll be together again.* On the day after the 2012 end date, she would put her family back together.

Gods willing that they—and the earth—survived.

Switching hands, her grip going slippery with blood, she cut her other palm, then wiped the blade on her robe and returned it to her belt. Finally, unable to delay any longer, she dropped down to sit cross-legged on the cool stone floor, and held out her hands to the men on either side of her.

On her left, Sven linked up immediately, gripping her hand so they were aligned blood to blood. The contact brought a flare of heat and magic, increasing the champagne fizz of magic in her blood to an Alka-Seltzer bubble as he squeezed her hand in a show of support, or maybe more because he was nervous. It was hard to tell what Sven was thinking most of the time.

To her right, though . . .

When her hand hovered midair, unclaimed, ice frosted the hard knot in her stomach. *Don't do it,* she thought fiercely at Brandt. *Not here. Not now.*

It was her darkest unvoiced fear, that one day he would decide that, with the twins gone and the two of them living mostly separate lives, he didn't want to bother with a shared suite and matching rings, that he was sick of their strained politeness and the way both of them tried too hard to pretend things were getting better.

Once, their mated bond had been so strong that he would have heard her whispered thoughts even without the bloody handclasp of an uplink.

Not now, though.

She looked over at him, and their eyes locked, her sky blue to his gold-spangled brown gone dark and forbidding in the torchlight. The skin was tight across his high cheekbones, aquiline nose, and wide brow, and shadows ringed his eyes, but his hair was neat, his shaved jaw smooth, his eyebrows the matching curves of a gliding eagle's wings. She felt sweaty and desperate in comparison.

"Don't do it," she whispered into the silence that had fallen as the others waited for her and Brandt to complete the circle.

"What's wrong?" His voice rasped slightly, though she didn't know if the roughness came from impatience or something else. She couldn't read him when he was this deep in the magic.

The magic fizz went flat inside her. *Everything's wrong*, she wanted to say, but that was the answer of the woman she'd been for too long, the one who had turned inward and self-pitying, becoming depressed after he and Strike had sent the twins away. She wasn't that person now, though, which meant the quick, knee-jerk answer didn't fit anymore.

The woman inside her, the one who still loved the memory of the man she had married out in the human world . . . that part of her wanted to tell him to be careful, to stay strong, and even—gods forgive her—to reject the Triad power if he was chosen. She wanted to tell him to think of the twins, of her, of the future they had once imagined.

The warrior inside her, though, refused to go there. The spell wasn't about being careful; it was about fulfilling a three-thousand-year-old prophecy and maybe—hopefully—gaining the power they would need to defend the barrier during the upcoming winter solstice, when a total lunar eclipse would destabilize the hell out of the barrier.

What was more, both the warrior and the woman inside her knew that she couldn't turn her back on the war. Between now and the end of 2012 the Nightkeepers needed to hold the rapidly weakening barrier against the *Banol Kax*. If they didn't, her future plans wouldn't matter worth a damn because there wouldn't *be* a future, not for her, and not for mankind. The lucky ones would die outright in the first wave, when the dark lords broke out of the underworld. The rest would be horribly trapped as the *Banol Kax* first fed on their souls, and then used their half-animate bodies to create new armies aimed at conquering the sky itself.

She hadn't let herself imagine marching as part of that army, had forced herself not to think about the fact that twins were sacred to the old legends, and therefore a threat to the dark lords. But the knowledge haunted her nightmares with shifting shadows and luminous green eyes.

And because of all that, there was only one answer she could give Brandt.

Calling on her warrior self, letting the magic blunt her emotions and bring determination, she stretched out her hand to him, palm up, so the bloody sacrificial cut glistened dark in the torchlight. "The only thing that matters today is calling the Triad. The rest can wait."

It was the proper answer, the dutiful one. And the

warrior within her meant every word of it, even as the woman yearned to turn back the clock.

"We need to—"

"Uplink," she interrupted.

He exhaled. "Patience...," he began, but then trailed off and reached out to her in return, pausing just before their fingers touched. Magic curled between them, hazing the air red-gold. The hum changed pitch, inching upward as their eyes locked.

Desire flared, coming from the inextricable link between magic and sex, and the power of the *jun tan* marks that still joined their souls even though the connection of their minds and hearts had waned. She didn't feel the added power that had once come when the *jun tan* link opened fully, joining them heart and soul. But there was heat and need, and an ache of longing.

"Don't shut me out." She hadn't meant to say it, not in front of the others, and certainly not in the middle of the Triad spell.

Always before when she had talked to him about how he put up walls between them, she had gotten blankness edged with frustration, and his reminder that they had a job to do. This time, though, she caught a gleam of gold and a flash of pain.

The sight surprised her, leaving her slow to react when he leaned into her, whispered her name, and kissed her.

And oh, holy crap, what a kiss. The soft warmth of his lips was a shocking contrast to the hard control of the man who'd been facing her only moments earlier.

They touched just at that single point of contact, with nothing holding her in place; she could pull away, *should* pull away.

Instead, she leaned in and kissed him back.

Their tongues touched and slid, and his flavor caromed through her, lighting neurons that had been dim for months now. Years. She felt the vibration of his groan, though the sound was lost beneath the escalating hum of power that surrounded them as heat raced through her veins. Excitement heated her blood, coming both from sex magic and the thought that something had changed, that he was finally seeing her, finally connecting with her the way the other mated pairs joined up within the magic. Psi energy flared as he shifted against her, lifting an arm as if to pull her closer.

Instead he took her hand, pressed their bleeding palms together, and completed the circle of ten.

Power zinged through the uplinked magi, and the red-gold buzz of magic went to a bloodred shriek that drowned out Patience's cry of surprise. Frustration slashed through her, coming less from the interrupted kiss than from the fact that he'd used it—used *her*—to provide the final power surge they had needed to trigger the spell. The kiss hadn't been about them at all. It had been about necessity. *Damn him.*

The world lurched, and suddenly she was moving without going anywhere, her spirit-self peeling out of her corporeal body and caroming sideways into the barrier. Then there was a final wrench of magic as the Triad spell took hold, gripping her with an inexorable force that warned her there was no going back. Not now. Maybe not ever again. *Gods.*

She tried to take the anger with her, knowing that it was better to be pissed than depressed. But as gray-green mist raced past her, laced with lightning and the smell of ozone, all she could do was close her eyes and launch a forbidden plea. *Please, gods, don't pick us.*

You're a dick. The growl came in Woody's voice, filtering out of the blur of transition magic. Even though Brandt hadn't seen his *winikin* in two years, Wood remained the voice of his conscience. And it had a point.

He shouldn't have kissed Patience in the middle of the Triad spell, shouldn't have touched her beyond the necessity of the uplink. But for a second there, he'd felt a flash of their old connection, a spark not just of chemistry but of the simpatico they used to share, back when they made each other stronger rather than nuts.

And damn, it'd felt good, like old times. Problem was, she wanted old times all the time, and he couldn't promise that anymore.

Which meant he shouldn't have touched her at all, despite the lure of sex magic and the way their link had seemed suddenly stronger than it had in a long time, more alive than it ever was back at Skywatch. It wouldn't last, he knew. Never did. But still, he held on to the feeling of connection as he materialized in the barrier: a gray-green, featureless expanse of leaden skies above and ground-level fog below.

The magi zapped in a foot above the ground and dropped, landing on their feet and then fighting for balance when the ground gave a watery heave and rippled outward in concentric circles that were mirrored in the calf-deep fog. The water-bed effect was new . . . probably another sign of the barrier destabilizing as the countdown neared T minus two years.

Brain working on the multiple levels of a warrior, Brandt filed the detail and scanned the scene—fog and more fog, no surprises there—while another part of him double-checked that the others had made it through okay. Especially Patience.

She was right beside him. And she was pissed.

Pulling her hand from his, she broke their uplink. "If you didn't think we had enough power to trigger the spell, you should've said something instead of just leaning on me for sex magic."

"I didn't—" *Shit.* It might not have been a conscious decision, but that was exactly what he—or rather his warrior's instincts—had done. "Maybe I did. Sorry."

He knew it wouldn't matter to her that it had worked; she would care only that it hadn't been about *them.* She didn't want to believe that for the next two years and five days, they belonged entirely to the Nightkeepers and their blood-bound duties.

"Yeah. Well." She shrugged and avoided his eyes.

Wearing no makeup, and with her long blond hair tied back in a ponytail, she didn't look much older than the nineteen she'd been when they met. Which just made him achingly aware of how far they had drifted, how much momentum they had lost. He wished he knew how to *talk* to her. Everything used to be easy between them. So why the hell was it so hard now? "Patience—"

"We've got company," Rabbit interrupted. His eyes were locked on a section of the fog.

Brandt turned, annoyed, but also a bit relieved. It wasn't like there was anything new he could say to her. And even if he had something new to bring, this wasn't the time or place.

Following Rabbit's line of sight, he didn't see anything at first. But then the seemingly random curls of vapor took form, darkening to shadows and then coalescing into human-shaped figures that weren't quite human. He tensed and automatically took a half step in front of Patience.

She moved away from him, snapping in an undertone, "It's the *nahwal*. And I can fight my own battles."

"Keep your guard up." He wanted to tell her to stay safe, to duck the Triad spell, to . . . hell, he didn't know. The words kept getting screwed up inside him, which was why he stayed silent. That, and the knowledge that destiny and the gods didn't give a shit what the Nightkeepers wanted when it came to the endtime war.

The fog swirled as the *nahwal* approached. Brandt's pulse picked up a notch. The Triad codex had mentioned that the creatures, which held the collected wisdom of each of the Nightkeepers' bloodlines, would be needed for the second layer of spell casting, but the part of the accordion-folded text that had explained exactly how that was supposed to work had been damaged beyond recovery. For the next part of the spell, the magi were flying, if not blind, then with some seriously low visibility.

The nine naked, sexless, hairless humanoid figures formed an outer ring concentric to that of the Nightkeepers. As before, the creatures had black, expressionless eyes and were adorned only by the bloodline glyphs they wore in stark black on their inner forearms. But where the *nahwal* had been stick thin and wrinkled before, now they had layers of flesh beneath smooth skin.

This was the first time Brandt had seen the change firsthand, and it was a damned unsettling reminder that nothing stayed the same.

Two of the *nahwal*—those of the jaguar and harvester bloodlines—looked almost human now. The one facing Strike and Sasha had a single ruby winking in its left ear and the former king's personality, while Jade's *nahwal* had a young woman's curves and the attitude of her warrior mother. Lucius's theory was that as the countdown continued, the leadership of each bloodline *nahwal* was being taken over by the ancestor who had the strongest connection to the surviving bloodline member. He'd predicted that the *nahwal* would all have evolved in preparation for the Triad spell.

Only the others hadn't changed. They differed only in their forearm marks.

"Do you think Lucius was wrong about the connection between the *nahwal* and the Triad spell?" Patience said softly.

"That, or only those two needed to change." Brandt's gut tightened as he did the math. The jaguar and harvester *nahwal* were blood-linked to Strike, Sasha, and Jade. Was that it, then? Had the Triad magi already been chosen?

The hope that he and Patience might be in the clear came with an equal thud of guilt. If the chosen survived, they would spend the rest of their lives sharing skull space with their strongest ancestors. The power would be incalculable . . . but so would the chaos.

If he could have prayed, Brandt thought he would have done so right then. But praying had never come naturally to him, not even in the barrier, so instead he squared his shoulders and turned to face his *nahwal*.

He had seen his ancestral being only once before, during his talent ceremony. The other magi had all been formally greeted by their ancestral beings during the ceremony, and some had gotten messages from their *nahwal* in the years since. Brandt had gotten jack shit then, and now wasn't any different. The eagle *nahwal* just stared at him.

Say something, damn it. His parents and two older brothers had died in the massacre; they should be inside the *nahwal*. So why wouldn't they freaking *talk* to him?

"What now?" Strike asked the creature opposite him. The jaguar *nahwal* held out its hand, palm up, showing the white line of a sacrificial scar. The message was clear. The Nightkeepers would have to uplink with their ancestral beings, forming a conduit for the Triad magic to make the transfer.

Wishing to hell there was another way, one that didn't involve a two-in-ten chance of winding up dead or nuts, Brandt palmed his ceremonial knife from his webbed weapons belt and offered it hilt first as the others did the same.

Expression unchanging, the eagle *nahwal* took the knife and drew the sharp stone blade across its right hand. The unlined skin parted with an unnatural zipping noise, and dark red ichor oozed through the slash. A glob welled and dropped, and was quickly lost in the fog as the ancestral being returned the knife, then held out its leaking hand as though offering to shake on a deal.

Brandt braced himself against a power surge as they uplinked, but he got nothing beyond the squish of cold ichor and the cold clamminess of the *nahwal*'s flesh. He glanced over as Patience linked with her *nahwal*, but she ignored him.

Be safe, he thought to her, but the message didn't get through. The *jun tan* link was stone cold.

Strike and Jade resumed the spell casting, starting from the beginning of the spell in the second of three repetitions. After a moment, two other voices joined in: the jaguar *nahwal*'s baritone and the high, sweet voice of Jade's mother, both chanting in single voices rather than the multitonal descant typical of the *nahwal*. A chill shivered through Brandt. *That's it, then. It's Strike, Sasha, and Jade.*

But then Michael's *nahwal* joined in with its multitonal voice, creating an instant chorus and suggesting that maybe the choice hadn't been made, after all. Alexis's and Nate's *nahwal* took up the spell next, adding depth and texture and turning the chant into something more like a song, something haunting and gospel, though in an ancient tongue.

Then a new voice joined in unexpectedly, one that didn't belong to any *nahwal*. Rabbit. Brandt glanced over and saw that the younger man's gray-blue eyes were locked on his *nahwal*'s face, his expression lit with power and a restless, edgy energy. *He wants this,* Brandt realized. *Son of a bitch.* But it made sense. Rabbit was a mind-bender, and cocky enough to think he could handle the ghosts. And he was ambitious as hell.

Sasha joined into the spell, then Michael beside her, their voices firm, expressions grim. One by one, the others chimed in, until finally it was down to Patience, Brandt, and their *nahwal*. Hers took up the chant first, in a sweet, multitonal voice. His lip-synched.

An ache tightened Brandt's chest, but they didn't have a choice. The Triad spell was nonoptional; it was their duty as warriors, as Nightkeepers. So he steeled himself and added his voice to the echoless chorus.

After a moment, Patience did the same.

The magi and their *nahwal* sang together, voices swelling as they finished the second repetition, and red-gold power arced through the sky with a lightning-thunder crack that made the surface beneath them shudder and roll. Brandt steeled himself as the sky darkened to storm clouds that swirled sinuously, though there wasn't any wind.

Then, deep within the swirling clouds, a figure took shape. The size of a small airplane, shaped like a bird of prey, and plumed like a parrot, it glowed crimson, orange, and yellow. Fire dripped from its wings, beak, and talons, brightening the stormy sky.

"Kinich Ahau," Patience breathed.

The sun god had arrived.

Or rather, its emissary had arrived. The firebird's image was thin and translucent, not the god itself, but rather a projection of some sort, a vaporware version that had been sent into the barrier to choose the Triad.

Brandt's pulse kicked. This was it. They'd been prepping for the ceremony for weeks now. Whatever happened next would change history.

The ozone smell grew stronger and static electricity charged the air as Strike led them into the final repetition of the spell.

The god-ghost circled high above the chanting group, once, twice. . . . Then on the third circuit the image shimmered, flaring sun-bright in a nova that forced Brandt to blink away the afterimage. When his vision cleared, there were three smaller firebirds where there had been one before; they flew in formation, wings outstretched, gliding in a wide spiral opposite the movement of the churning storm clouds.

The hum of magic gained a new note, counterpointing the grumble of thunder that deepened as they reached the end of the spell's third repetition. Then Sasha, who had a closer bond to Kinich Ahau than the others, raised her voice and called, *"Taasik oox!" Bring the three!*

Lightning slashed as the god-ghosts screamed a clarion call of trumpets and fire. And then they dove, headed straight for the Nightkeepers.

Tension ran through the magi, a thought-whisper of last-minute hopes, fears, and prayers that turned to gasps as two of the ghosts shimmered . . . and disappeared.

"What the—" Brandt broke off as the remaining firebird locked its glowing gold eyes on his. *Oh, shit.*

He held his ground as the thing plummeted straight toward him, but he bared his teeth at the sky. *No, damn you. I don't want—*

The ghost veered at the last millisecond. And slammed into Rabbit.

CHAPTER TWO

The firebird felt like a godsdamned fifty-caliber round going in.

"*Fuck.*" Rabbit staggered back against his *nahwal*'s grip as pain howled through his body, starting at the point of impact and searing outward, then reversing course and arrowing to his head and heart, the two seats of a mage's power.

The white-hot energy poured into his heart unchecked, where it became Nightkeeper magic, red-gold and awesome in its intensity. But in his head . . . *gods.* Pain lanced through his skull, incredible pressure building to flash point in an instant when the flow of magic crashed into an immovable mental barrier.

It can't get through the blocks. Fuck. He'd installed the barriers on Strike's orders, to ensure that he wouldn't burn shit down or climb inside someone else's mind unless he frigging meant to. The blocks slowed him down, forced him to think stuff through before lashing out. Which was a good thing, usually. Now, though, the barricades went from benefit to liability in a flash.

The magic roiled within his conscious mind, knocking loose a spate of recent memories: flickering candles, a huge house in flames, a knife that dripped onto Myrinne's fixed, staring eyes. . . . He cursed viciously, rejecting the vision images that had haunted him ever since he'd let her talk him into the scrying spell and gotten nightmares instead of answers.

He wouldn't hurt her, couldn't. He loved her, even if the gods hadn't yet tagged them with their mated marks. She was on his side; she believed in him more than anyone else did, some days more than even *he* did. Hell, she was the one who'd guessed he would be chosen, the one who believed he could handle the magic.

So let's do this.

Steeling himself against the pressure and pain, centering himself within the deep-down excitement of so much fucking *power*, he focused on the outer layer of mental blocks, the ones that kept him from using his mind-bending on others. Whispering a short counterspell, he visualized the protective shields as a solar array, row upon row of high-tech panels that folded up, accordioning smaller and smaller until they finally disappeared.

The invading magic rushed inward the moment the mental barrier was down, swamping him with a tornado of memories that flashed and collided, flaring bright in his mind's eye for a second before disappearing.

In one of them, he was in a crowd of bare-chested, loincloth-wearing men and women who danced in front of a new-looking Mayan pyramid. In another, he lay bound to a stone altar as a hawk-nosed priest wearing an elaborate bone, feather, and jade headdress lifted a stone knife above him. In the next, he stood in the hallway of an earlier version of Skywatch, laughing as three kids raced past him, chasing a half-grown puppy that looked more like a coyote than a dog.

Rabbit hadn't danced that dance, been that sacrificial victim, or watched those kids chase a coy-dog through Skywatch, but those experiences were suddenly inside him, along with thousands of others that beckoned for him to accept the power he was being offered by a god that had picked *him*, not one of the others.

The Triad magic. Holy. Fucking. Shit.

Before, it had been a fantasy, the subject of more than a few "wouldn't it be cool if I got picked so I could kick some *major* ass" convos late at night. Now, though . . . now it was very real.

Rabbit's heart hammered off-rhythm as the magic slammed into the second set of mental filters, the ones that blocked his talents of pyro- and telekinesis. Working faster now, he pulled down the blockade. More magic flowed into him; more memories raced past, going too fast for him to glimpse his ancestors' pasts.

Then the power hit the final layer of shielding: a thick blockade made of repeating geodesic panels, each marked with a bloodred quatrefoil glyph like the one he wore on his inner right forearm. The symbol belonged to the Nightkeepers' enemies, the Order of Xibalba. His mother's people. It was the sign of the dark hellmagic.

Of all the blocks, this was the one he relied on the most. When it was in place, the darkness couldn't reach him; the Xibalbans' leader, Iago, couldn't touch him.

But neither could the Triad magic.

Oh, fuck. Now what? Rabbit's mind raced as bloody tears hazed his vision red.

The last time he'd probed Iago's mind, a week ago, the Xibalban had still been comatose, his soul deadlocked with that of the powerful demon he'd summoned and then lost control of. Which meant it should be safe to drop the hell-block to let the Triad magic through.

It was a risk, but a calculated one. And Kinich Ahau had chosen *him*. The swirling memories—and the Triad power—could be his. Excitement sizzled, driving him on.

He could do this. For the Nightkeepers. For himself. The prophecy was clear: If the Nightkeepers didn't call the Triad, the *Banol Kax* would have the upper hand next week, when the solstice-eclipse destabilized the barrier enough for the dark lords to punch through. The good guys needed the magic, and he could bring it to them.

Heart hammering, Rabbit whispered the counter-spell that made the final blockade fold in on itself and disappear. He braced for the magic to rush into the center of his psyche, for the Triad spell to flood him with souls, spells, and incalculable power.

Instead, the hell-link slammed open and dark magic spewed into him, brown and oily, rattling like a damned striking snake.

Fuck! Rabbit made a grab for the doorway, but an alien force locked onto him, digging sharp claws into his consciousness and paralyzing his thoughts.

He flashed briefly on a fluorescent-lit cinder block room seen through half-open eyes. He recognized the view Iago saw in his comatose daze, recognized the bastard's semiconscious mental pattern. And in the half second it took Rabbit to make those connections, Iago's power made a connection of its own: straight to the Triad magic.

No! Rabbit screamed the word, but no sound came out; no warning reached the others. They didn't have a clue that things had just gone way fucking wrong, didn't know he needed help. He was on his own, fighting desperately to get free as ropes of twisted darkness twined around the Triad power and began pulling it back through the hell-link into Iago.

Echoes of rage flashed through Rabbit's conscious-ness as his ancestors' ghosts were pulled along with the Triad magic. Panic slashed. Impotence. He had to do something, but he couldn't get away from Iago, couldn't overpower him, couldn't—

Make a new fucking block, idiot. He didn't know if the

order came from an ancestor or from inside himself, but he latched on to it with desperate terror. Summoning every ounce of magic he had left, he cast the spell, pouring himself into the high-tech portal that shimmered into being, open at first, then irising shut around the dark magic, pinching and then severing the greasy tendrils. Adrenaline surged as the Xibalban's grip faltered. It was working! It was—

New tendrils spewed through the opening, latched onto the doorway, and ripped it from its mental moorings.

No!

The Triad magic poured into Iago and the green-eyed darkness within him. Rabbit saw it, felt it, through their mind-link. And he got it.

Oh, holy shit. Iago was using the Triad magic to gain control over the demon king, Moctezuma.

Fuck. Oh, fuck. Oh, fuckfuckfuck. For a paralyzed, pussy-assed second Rabbit couldn't think, couldn't react, couldn't do anything.

Then, deep inside him, a spark of fire magic kindled. It was his first and strongest talent, the one he'd done the most damage with. Now it took on a mind of its own, growing from an ember to a blaze, then to a conflagration. The flames seared him, tore at him, then curled into an alien shape, something he hadn't conjured, didn't control.

Oh, gods. Oh, shit. It was the firebird.

The sun god's emissary shrieked a shrill battle cry within Rabbit's mind, trailing flames from its wings as it attacked Iago's mind-link, tearing at the dark magic with its beak and talons.

As it did so, it summoned the Triad magic. The power leaped out of Iago and funneled back up the hell-link to pour into the firebird, which began to glow and pulse with the recaptured energy.

No! Iago's rage flared through Rabbit, edged with the luminous green of demon vision. Tentacles of greasy brown magic lashed the god-ghost, only to wither and die when they made contact. The firebird's body shone brilliantly, going almost pure white as the last of the Triad magic left Iago.

With a trumpeting battle cry, the firebird launched itself out of the hell-link, which collapsed behind it, cutting off the telepathic connection without warning.

Agony slashed through Rabbit's skull as Iago's claws tore out of his consciousness, but that pain was welcome. The pain racing from his head and heart, outward, and then in again to concentrate in his chest, wasn't.

No, he shouted inwardly, reaching for the firebird. *Wait. I can—*

New pain cracked through his skull, a wordless lash of rejection that his heart translated as, *You had your chance, half blood.*

Power thundered and the firebird disappeared, taking the Triad magic with it.

And Rabbit was suddenly alone in his head once more.

Gods! His eyes snapped open; his mouth worked with a silent scream as he returned to full consciousness, senses reeling. He was on his knees, clutching his *nahwal*'s hand, screaming aloud as a cloud of red-gold power erupted from his chest and the firebird took form once again, back-winging away from him, eyes blazing with rage.

"Wait!" Heart hammering, he lunged for the apparition. "I can handle it. I can—"

But it was too late. The firebird gave a trumpeting scream, locked on to the man beside him, and dove.

It hit Brandt chest high. And disappeared.

Oh, shit. That was the only thought Brandt could formulate as agony hammered into his chest and red-gold power poured liquid fire into his veins, bloating his head and heart.

Oh, shit. He'd been nailed by a Triad ricochet.

Oh, shit. It hurt.

Oh, shit. What the hell was he supposed to do now? What—

Power exploded at the place where he and his *nahwal* were joined, searing his hand and sending currents of fire racing up his arm. Pain lanced through his chest and his heart skipped a beat; he'd heard the expression before, but he hadn't really understood the dissonance of the off-kilter *thudda-thudda* until then.

Despair tore his soul as his *nahwal* moved, not away, but *into* him, aligning itself so its front was to his back. He felt the chill of its flesh, the flow of ichor beneath its skin as its form overlapped with his, suffusing him with a clammy chill and an awful sense of invasion.

He heard Patience call his name in a raw, frantic voice. He wanted to reach for her, wanted to make everything better. But he couldn't.

"I'm sorry, sweetheart," he rasped, the words setting his throat aflame. "I wish—" But he didn't get to finish, because the Triad magic rose up like the cold, unforgiving water of an ice-fed river. And sucked him down.

"Brandt!" The name tore from Patience's throat as his eyes rolled back in his head and he collapsed into the fog.

Yanking away from her *nahwal*, she dropped to her knees and scrambled to find him through blinding tears and the knee-deep mist. She found a leg first, followed it up to his armored torso and higher, to his throat, where she tried to find a pulse. Couldn't.

"He's not dead. Not dead. Can't be dead." She repeated it over and over, babbling the words in a litany, petrified that if she stopped, he'd *be* dead. One dead, one mad, one survivor. *Gods, let him be the survivor.* Suddenly nothing else mattered.

She fought the ground's squishy roll as she hauled his upper body up across her knees, trying to get his head above the level of the mist. He was deadweight, limp and entirely unmoving, his skin cool and cast the same gray green as the world around them.

But then she felt a flutter under her fingertips. Another. He had a pulse. And he was breathing, though the moves were weak. She shuddered with relief, ready to take whatever little she could get.

"He's not dead," she said to the others, who had gathered close. Tears dripped from her face onto his, adding to the moisture of the mist, as she bent over him, touching his face, his neck, his damp hair.

Rabbit had pulled Strike off to one side, and was telling him something in a low, broken voice. She caught Iago's name, but couldn't think about that right now. Her entire being, both woman and warrior, was focused on Brandt.

He was alive, but only barely.

"Wake up," she whispered, taking his hand in hers and forming a blood-link. "Please wake up." She opened herself to him, offering him all the magic and strength she had left to give.

The connection formed on her end, but nothing happened on his.

Sick nerves drilled through her. "He's not responding."

"He is trapped inside the Triad magic," a multitonal voice answered.

Patience's head jerked up. Her *nahwal* stood there staring down at her. It was the only one left; the other ancestral beings had disappeared.

"Trapped how?" she demanded, heart thudding.

"The Triad magic cannot speak to the eagle until he makes peace with his ancestors." The *nahwal* seemed to be speaking from rote, its expression blank. But for a second she thought she caught a glimpse of something more.

The creature had spoken to her only twice before, and both messages had been frustratingly vague. She hadn't made much of an effort to improve the connection through ancestor worship, preferring to focus on the living. Now that was coming back to bite her in the ass.

It was too late to fix that now, though. All she could do was try to reach that spark of humanity, the hint that someone—some*one*—in there was trying to get through to her. "Please tell me how to help him," she said, her voice low and urgent. "Please. I'll do anything." Almost.

"You must help him become a Triad mage before the solstice-eclipse. The lost jaguar and the serpent have long, dangerous roads to travel, and he is the only one who can prevent Cabrakan from avenging his brother's death at the hands of Kali's children."

The *nahwal* took a step back, away from the group. Patience would have gone after the creature, but Brandt's heavy body weighed her down. "What am I supposed to *do*?" Her voice broke. "Tell me."

"Take him home." The *nahwal*'s form blurred as the gray-green mist closed around it. *"Help him remember the debt he owes."* Another step.

"Wait!" She stretched out her hand. "Don't . . ." She trailed off as it vanished. Reeling, she looked up at her teammates, whose expressions ranged from concern to gray-faced shock. "What the hell is it talking about?"

It was her *nahwal*, her message. But it was Strike who said in a ragged voice, "The lost jaguar and the serpent have to be Anna and Mendez. The other two firebirds must have gone to earth." Which so wasn't good news. Anna didn't want anything to do with the Nightkeepers anymore, and Mendez was a rogue mage, a loose cannon who'd spent most of the past three years behind bars.

"Why the hell would the god pick them?" Nate asked. "For that matter, why did it go for Brandt if he can't complete the spell?" He locked on Patience, expression grim. "What debt was it talking about?"

She wanted to weep and rage, wanted to curl in a ball and pretend the last ten minutes hadn't happened. But that was the woman she had been, not the one she was now.

Focus. Prioritize. Her warrior's buffer might not be as strong as Brandt's, but it would be strong enough. It would have to be. Calling on it to stem the panic and pump determination in its place, she tightened her grip on him. "I don't know about any debt. But I'm damn well going to figure it out."

She had already been forced to say good-bye to her sons and *winikin*. She wasn't letting go of her husband without a fight.

Skywatch

The magi materialized in the sunken center of the mansion's great room, in a big open space surrounded by wide, low-slung leather couches and ottomans. In the kitchen area that opened off the upper level of the two-level room, Jox, Leah, and Lucius were sitting at the marble-topped breakfast bar, waiting for news.

They were up and moving before the 'port magic

had cleared, but faltered when they saw that Michael and Nate were carrying Brandt's motionless body between them.

Jox headed for Patience. In his midsixties, fit, and trim, with long gray hair that he wore back in a Deadhead ponytail, the royal *winikin* was responsible for protecting and guiding several of the magi as well as running the day-to-day operations of the entire compound. Yet despite his already heavy workload, he had unofficially adopted Patience when her *winikin*, Hannah, had left with the twins.

"What happened?" he demanded as he ran a quick vitals check on Brandt, who was deathly pale and cool to the touch, his lips dusky, almost blue.

The walls of the high-ceilinged great room seemed to press in on her, but she fought the panic and made herself be strong, made her voice stay steady when she answered, "The god chose Rabbit first, but when the power flux woke Iago, the Triad magic bounced out of Rabbit and into Brandt. Now, according to my *nahwal*, he's trapped in the spell because he can't connect with his ancestors until I help him remember some debt he hasn't repaid. If we can't wake him before the solstice-eclipse, we're screwed. And Anna and Mendez are Triad numbers two and three." Like ripping off a wax strip, she said it all at once, quickly, to get the pain over with.

Only this pain was just beginning, wasn't it?

"Gods." Jox's face lost all its color. "*Anna.*"

"Yeah," Strike grated. Leah stood beside him, gripping his upper arm in support. He said, "I'll make the calls. We need to know if they're—well. We need to know."

As Strike and Leah headed for the nearest phone, Jox pokered up and went into crisis-response mode, though Patience could see the effort it cost him.

She could relate.

Moving to the nearest intercom, the *winikin* keyed the button that would transmit his voice throughout the compound. "The away team's back. All hands on deck in the great room, ASAP." Then he said to Nate and Michael, "Help Patience get Brandt bedded down." To her, he said, "I'll send someone with an IV setup for him and food for you." The magi all needed to rest and refuel after the amount of magic they had just pulled.

His orders were practical, a veneer of necessity slapped over a deep layer of shock. But that was what the Nightkeepers did, wasn't it? They took what the gods threw at them, dealt with the bad stuff, fought the battles that needed fighting, and lived their lives in between crises.

Or tried to, anyway.

Focus, Patience told herself. *Make a plan.* This wasn't a physical enemy she could fight, but she still needed a strategy. "Let's hold off on the IV," she said to Jox. "I'd want to try uplinking and—"

"Not a chance," the *winikin* interrupted. "You need to recharge."

"But—"

"But nothing. Promise me you won't do anything before you've at least eaten."

"I can't just sit here."

"You won't be any good to him if you crap out in the middle of the uplink."

"I'll help," a new voice interjected. Patience turned to find Lucius standing behind her. He was pure human, but he was also their Prophet, endowed with the magical ability to search their ancestors' library for spells and answers. Although the magic had made him nearly as big and strong as a Nightkeeper male, his half-untucked T-shirt, finger-tunneled sandy hair, and ratty sandals reminded her of the geeky grad student he'd been when he first arrived.

Oddly, that small piece of continuity in the middle of chaos helped center her. Inhaling a breath that was too close to tears, she nodded. "Thanks. What did you have in mind?"

"Jade said the *nahwal* mentioned a couple of gods, Kali and Cabrakan. I'll pull together info on both of them. But I was also thinking I could try to find a reboot spell, something that could get a mage out of misfired magic. Maybe we can reach Brandt that way."

Patience's chest loosened a little at the reminder that even though the *nahwal* had said she had to be the one to bring Brandt back, she wasn't entirely on her own. "That'd be good. And maybe look for a memory-enhancing spell."

"Right. Any ideas what the *nahwal* was talking about Brandt having forgotten?"

Disquiet tightened her stomach. "I can only think of one thing that neither of us can remember."

Lucius snapped his fingers, making the connection. "The night you met."

"Yeah." They had both been down in the Yucatán for spring break and awakened in bed together the morning after the equinox with no memory of what had happened the night before. Later, it had become obvious that they hadn't met by chance. Instead, they had somehow connected with the magic more than four years before the barrier fully reactivated. And they didn't have the faintest clue what had happened that night.

The Nightkeepers and *winikin* had thrown around various theories, but those discussions had dwindled over time because the "where, how, why" of their marriage hadn't seemed all that important in the larger scheme.

It did now, though. What had happened that night? What debt did he owe? And how the hell was she supposed to help him remember anything if he was trapped in the Triad spell?

"I'll see what I can find." Lucius pointed toward the residential wing. "Now go. Eat. Sleep. I'll call you when I've got something."

She meant to rest; she really did. But once she was alone in the suite, with Brandt stripped down to a black tee and bike shorts, lying too still beneath the blue coverlet of the bed they had once shared, she couldn't settle. Instead, she found herself pacing the five-room suite, glancing at the framed pictures that were hung on nearly every wall.

Some were of just her and Brandt—a few candids

and a posed portrait from their small wedding. Others were of the family foursome: her and Brandt with the newborn twins; the four of them out in front of the starter house they had bought right before Strike had called them back to Skywatch. A few showed just the boys: Braden feeding a brown nanny goat while Harry hid behind Brandt's jean-clad leg; Braden playing on an inflatable moon-bounce while Harry stood off to the side with a look of intense concentration on his face, as if trying to figure out how the thing worked. There was even one from Skywatch, an extended family portrait with the four of them, plus Hannah, Woody, and Rabbit.

But where those pictures were familiar, when she stalled in the bedroom door, the man she saw lying in the big bed looked like a stranger.

She wished she knew what she could have done differently. She had resented the hell out of him for backing Strike's decision to send the boys away and then distancing himself when she had wanted—needed—to talk it through. And when, in the worst of her depression, she had gone behind his back to break into the royal quarters in search of a clue to the boys' whereabouts, Brandt might have alibied her when Strike and Leah had caught her coming out of their suite, but later, in private, he had turned away from her. And stayed gone.

Now, as she stared at his motionless form, the *nahwal*'s words echoed in her mind: *Help him remember.* But how?

Giving in to the impulse, freed by the knowledge

that there wasn't anybody there who would hit her with a derisive snort or eye-roll, she pulled a small deck of oracle cards from the pocket of her combat pants, where she had carried them for luck. She shuffled them, taking solace in the small action; the cards were one of the few things that belonged only to her these days.

When the deck felt right, she stopped shuffling, cut the cards, and flipped the bottom one in the quickest and simplest of readings.

A shiver touched the back of her neck at the sight of a geometric glyph that looked like the outline of two flat-topped, step-sided pyramids that had been joined together at their crowns to form a ragged "X" shape.

It was *etznab*, the mirror glyph . . . and the harbinger of unfinished business.

CHAPTER THREE

In the pitch of night in the middle of freaking nowhere, a mangled streetlight hung off the bridge at a crazy angle, shining on a busted-through guardrail that dangled down to touch the cold black river. The light was getting smaller by the second, though, as the wrecked, once-classic Beemer traveled downstream, sinking as water gushed through the punched-out windshield to fill the empty front seats.

Strapped into the back, eighteen-year-old Brandt tore at his seat belt, which was jammed tight, hung up on the crumpled door on one side, just fucking stuck on the other. The driver's seat was off-kilter and shoved up against his shins, trapping his legs, one of which hurt like hell, even through the numbing cold.

He shouted as loud as he could: "Joe! Dewey! Anybody! For fuck's sake, help!"

There was no answer. Hadn't been since he'd come to, alone in the car and stuck as shit.

He was godsdamned freezing; the icy water was up to his chest and climbing. His head hurt; he was pretty sure he'd banged it on the side window when Dewey hit the slick patch and the car spun out. Or maybe he'd been whacked by one of the hockey sticks that were now floating around him, along with other bits of their gear. He shoved one of the sticks aside. Then he stared at it as inspiration worked its way through his spinning brain.

Hey, moron. Ever heard of leverage?

Almost sobbing now, he grabbed one of the sticks, jammed it against the opposite door handle, and pushed. The lock gave! His pulse pounded as he shoved against the inward press of the water. The door opened a few inches, letting in more water but offering a way out. He was so damned excited to see the exit that he forgot about the other problems.

He lunged across, got hung up on the belt, and screamed when his injured leg shifted and flesh tore. "Fuck!"

Gods, it hurt. He grayed out for a few seconds, groaning.

As he started coming back, the world sharpening back into place around him, he heard Woody's voice in his head. Don't just react, *the* winikin *had lectured time and again during Brandt's fight training.* For gods' sake, *think.*

As if remembering the winikin's *advice had thrown a switch inside him, the night got brighter, his vision clearer. He saw the bridge in the distance . . . and the splashing movement of someone swimming. Two someones. The others were okay!*

"Joe!" he shouted. "Dewey!" But they didn't react; he was too far away, the rushing water too loud.

Thinking now, he swung the hockey stick around, aiming it past the driver's seat. His motions were slowed by the water and the beginnings of hypothermia, but the same lack of air bags that'd made the crash so gods-awful helped him now. He managed to jam the end of the stick on the column, and the horn blared.

The distant heads jerked around; faraway voices cried his name. He hit the horn a couple more times before a fat spark arced and the noise quit.

The Beemer's back end was dropping faster than the front, thanks to the cinder blocks Dewey's dad had loaded into the trunk for traction. The water lapped at Brandt's throat, his chin. Touched his mouth.

"Brandt?" The shout was faint with distance.

"Here! I'm here!" Spurred by hope, he twisted, contorting yet again in an effort to reach the knife sheath that was strapped low on his good ankle. He had tried to get at it before and couldn't reach. This time, though, he got it. His hands shook as he slashed through the seat belt. He immediately floated up, then jolted against the tether of his lower legs.

He freed his good leg with a yank, but even that move brought a slash of agony from the other side. And when he tried to pull on his torn-up leg, he spasmed and nearly passed out.

"Help! I'm stuck!" He shouted the words, but they came out garbled as the water closed in on him, filling his ears. He couldn't hear Joe and Dewey anymore. He was pretty sure the car was all the way under, hoped to hell they'd be able to find him.

His consciousness flickered as he crowded up near the roof of the sinking car, tilting his head into the remaining air, which was leaking out in a string of silvery bubbles. On his next breath, he sucked water along with the air.

Don't panic. *But all he could think about was Woody's stories of the barrier, the Nightkeepers, and the end-time war. The* winikin *had broken tradition by raising Brandt with full knowledge of his heritage even though they were in hiding, living as humans. But in all other ways, despite his easygoing nature, Wood was strictly traditional. He'd taught Brandt the old ways, and made him promise that he would keep himself fit and ready through the zero date, that he wouldn't marry or have children before that time, and that he would keep the faith.*

As the final string of silvery bubbles escaped, and panic chilled to grim desperation, Brandt's mind locked on the last of Woody's expectations. Faith, *he thought.* When all else failed, that was what it came down to, wasn't it?

Tasting his own blood in the water he'd inhaled along with the last little bit of air, he searched for a prayer in the old language. When nothing seemed right, with grayness telescoping inward from the edges of his consciousness, he went with his heart, and said, "Gods. If you can hear this, please help me. I'll give anything. I swear it."

Then the grayness closed in. The cold took over. And—

The cold vanished, the car and the river disappeared, and Brandt found himself hanging weightless and immobile, completely deprived of all sensory input save for that created by his body: the pulsing whine of blood through his veins, the sensation of swallowing, the repetitive act of breathing.

His brain spun as he fought to shift gears.

As he did so, he was aware that this wasn't the first time he'd made the transition, or the second. More like the hundredth. Sick dread latched itself on to his soul as he realized all over again that the Triad spell had trapped him in his own private *Groundhog Day*. He was reliving that night over and over again, an endless loop in which he sank into a vision, became his teenage self and experienced the terror of that night, then switched back to his adult self, only then becoming cognizant of what was going on.

He didn't know how long he'd been cycling, but he knew for damned sure that he had to get out of this fucking loop, and *fast*, because it wouldn't be long before it started all over again.

This wasn't part of the Triad spell. By now, he should be fighting to assimilate—or be assimilated by—his ancestors. Instead he was reliving the night he'd almost died in that river. At the thought, though, adrenaline kicked. A near-death experience formed a link to the gods. The Godkeeper ceremony involved near death by drowning. Maybe the Triad spell did too.

But he was already having an almost-dead-by-drowning experience within the vision. What more did he need to do in order to complete the spell?

He didn't know.

And then it was too late, because the temperature dropped, chilling him to his bones.

For the last few seconds he was himself, he let his mind fill with a warm memory, that of Patience's face aglow with happiness as they swapped marriage vows in front of a JP and half a dozen friends, needing nothing more than each other, really. Even though they had both lied about why their godparents—aka *winikin*—couldn't be there, beginning the chain of small lies that had shaped the early, happy years of their marriage, the memory brought only a poignant ache.

No matter what had come after, that had been a good day. One of his best.

As the small peace dissolved, he closed his eyes and whispered into the blackness, "Sorry, sweetheart. I'm lost and I can't figure out how to get back."

Then the bottom fell out of his world, his soul lurched, and his consciousness regressed to that of a terrified, dying teen.

Skywatch

Just past dawn, Patience jolted awake with her heart pounding and Brandt's voice echoing in her mind.

"Hey," she said, a smile blooming as she rolled toward him, having finally crashed in the bed, albeit clothed and atop the comforter. "You're—" She broke off at the sight of his still form, the lack of animation in his angular features. "Not awake," she finished, disappointment thudding through her as she saw that he looked the same as he had when she'd fallen asleep—his breathing too slow, his skin gray despite the IV taped at the crook of his elbow.

After recharging, she and the others had tried everything they could think of the night before, from a joint blood sacrifice to a one-sided attempt for her to call sex magic and awaken their *jun tan* bond. Their mated link had remained stubbornly silent. Yet now she could swear his voice had awakened her.

Although the other mated pairs could share thoughts when they were uplinked, her and Brandt's bond had always been different. Their *jun tan* link had carried a magic of its own, one that allowed them to transmit power, pleasure, and thoughts, sometimes even from a distance. So it wasn't impossible that she'd heard him, but still . . .

"It was probably just a dream," she murmured, knowing too well how much false hope could hurt. But that didn't stop her from taking his hand, interlacing their fingers, pressing their scarred palms together, and sending part of herself into their *jun tan* bond, just to see. The mark on her wrist warmed momentarily, but that was it. His half of their mated bond didn't respond.

It wasn't a surprise. But it hurt with a dull ache that gathered beneath her breastbone and lay leaden, weighing her down. She didn't let go of his hand, though. Instead, she inched closer to his big, warm body and let her eyes drift shut. *I'll just lie here for a minute longer. . . .*

Shrieks and laughter pulled her out of sleep into the warm drowsiness of yellow morning sunlight and the weight of her husband's arm across her hips, the curve of his body behind hers, enfolding hers. Through the open bedroom door, she saw Rabbit spinning around in the main room, roaring demonlike while Braden clung to his shoulders and Harry battered at his knees, two miniature magi fighting to bring down one of the fearsome Banol Kax. With a final roar, Rabbit fell back onto the couch, flailing in pretend death throes while the twins pounced on him.

Hannah and Woody were making a big breakfast in the kitchen nook beyond, in what had become a weekend tradition, a way to carve some family time out of the daily demands of life at Skywatch.

Catching Patience's look, Hannah grinned and turned her palms to the sky in an "I tried to get them to keep quiet" gesture belied by the amusement that snapped in her good eye. She had a brightly patterned kerchief tied pirate-style over the other side, where six parallel scars trailed down her face, tugging her smile slightly off center as she pretended to whack Woody's knuckles for snitching an underdone pancake off the stove.

In the main room, Rabbit rolled off the couch to pounce on Harry with renewed roars and a growl of "Gotcha!"

Braden shrieked and dove into the fray, and the three of them went down in a laughing, squirming tangle.

"Welcome to chaos," Brandt rumbled against Patience's neck, his voice amused. Beneath the bedcovers, he slid his hand up from her hip to her breast and began a slow, seductive morning fondle that was all the more enticing for its semipublic nature. More, it said that he was in a good mood, not sharp or distant as he had been too often lately, stressed by the transition to their new lives.

Her blood fired as she shifted to fit herself closer into the curve of his body, so she could feel the heavy throb of his morning erection. "*Silence is overrated,*" *she whispered in return, keeping her voice low in the hopes of protecting a few more minutes together before the twins noticed that Mom and Dad were up.*

And Dad was most definitely "up"; he rolled his hips a little to seat himself more firmly into the cleft of her buttocks, then slid his hand down to press her into him, with his strong, clever fingers drifting across the very top of her mound, sending spears of sensation that left her breathless. His breath was hot on the back of her neck and the side of her face, air-feathers that sent shivers coiling through her, making her yearn.

"Breakfast is ready!" Hannah announced brightly from the kitchen, her voice pitched to carry. "Last one out to the patio gets rotten eggs!"

Rabbit lunged upward, roaring something about food, and slow-motion charged for the sliders leading out to the kid-proofed deck at the far side of the main room. Braden scrambled to beat him; Harry lagged and shot a look toward the bedroom.

"Your mom and dad will be with us in a minute." Woody hustled him along, kicking the bedroom door shut on the way by, with an amused "Or twenty minutes, half hour, no rush."

Brandt's chuckle vibrated through his body and into hers. "Points to the winikin." He slid her panties down but not off, so the waistband caught at the tops of her thighs, holding her legs together and creating deliciously wicked friction as he positioned himself to rub against her slick folds from behind, teasing them both. She purred and

arched against him, heating to his touch and moving rest-
lessly as urgency built. Then he shifted to slide into her,
stretching and filling her—

Patience's body shuddered, and the movement snapped her from her light doze, jolting her back to reality.

She opened her eyes to find herself in the master bedroom, lying beside Brandt as the yellow morning sun came in through the window to warm the cool blue room. But that was where the parallels stopped. She wasn't wrapped in Brandt's arms, and he sure as hell wasn't making love to her. He hadn't for longer than she wanted to count. Yet arousal ran through her, making her shiver hot and cold, and wish she had stayed asleep a few minutes longer.

"Damn it. That wasn't fair." She didn't know who or what she was pissed at, just that she was pissed. Frustrated. Sad. Depressed.

No. Not going back there.

Forcing herself to get moving, she headed for the connecting bath, then through to the boys' room, where she usually slept. There, she changed into clean jeans and a long-sleeved blue T-shirt, and dragged her long hair into a ponytail. Every few minutes, she looked through the bathroom to the master bedroom, where Brandt lay unchanged, looking as isolated as she felt.

Outside the bedroom window, the sun shone brightly, warming her chilled skin when she pressed her palms against the glass and rested her forehead for a moment. "I could use some help here, gods. I need more to go on than just 'make him remember.'"

She waited a long moment, hoping for a sign. A clue. Something. Anything.

Nothing.

Exhaling, she turned away from the window and headed through the suite, intending to grab some breakfast, check with the *winikin* to see how things were going in the outside world, and see if Jade and Lucius had gotten any further with the library research. But as she was passing through the main room, a flash of purple on the coffee table caught her eye and made her hesitate.

It was her first deck of oracle cards, part of a boxed set that she'd bought off Amazon on a whim, and maybe a bit of rebellion against the traditions that dictated too much of her life at Skywatch.

Mayan astronomy wasn't part of the old ways; hell, as far as she could tell, most of the shtick had been lifted straight from tarot readings, glossed over with a veneer of Mayan glyphs and concepts designed to appeal to the human world, where there was a growing awareness that December 21, 2012, might be more than just some hype and a couple of loud movies.

Over the past few months, though, she'd realized that just because the codices didn't mention the oracle, that didn't make it bullshit. More and more often, she was turning over cards that related to—or even predicted—what was going on in her life. In fact, she was starting to think that the oracle could tap into some type of magic, whether or not the others wanted to accept it. Which was why she didn't brush off the instinct that told her to cut the deck now.

She crossed to the low table and chose a card at random, without even shuffling. When she flipped it, she froze at the sight of a jagged "X" formed of two step-sided pyramid outlines, joined at their crowns.

It was the mirror glyph, *etznab*.

Again.

A shiver worked its way down her spine, and her heart picked up a beat. What were the odds she would cut the same card twice in a row from two different decks?

Glancing at the sliders, at the shining sun and the blue sky around it, she said, "I get it. Brandt and I have unfinished business. And apparently he has some with his ancestors too. But I don't know what else I'm supposed to take from this." She reached for the dog-eared book that went with the deck, figuring she should reread the entire entry on the *etznab* oracle.

But then she hesitated, staring at the card.

What if it wasn't signifying unfinished business? What if it was telling her something far more obvious?

"Mirrors," she whispered. "Holy shit."

The ancestors had held mirrors as sacred, believing they were doorways into the soul . . . and into memory.

Her hands shook as she fumbled out her phone and called the library. Thanks to a private cell covering the compound—Jox's doing—the call went through immediately, though canyon country itself was a dead zone. "Hey there," Jade said in answer. "Any news?"

"Brandt is the same."

"I'm sorry. Anna's in bad shape too." Jade's voice echoed with concern for her friend. "Strike and the others are at the hospital now."

"Gods." Patience closed her eyes and sent a quick prayer. She didn't know Anna well, but she was a teammate, estranged or not. And, apparently, a Triad mage. She had collapsed within minutes of the Triad spell being triggered, and had wound up rushed to the ER with an intracranial bleed.

Jade continued, forcing a businesslike tone into her voice. "And in the 'not sounding good' department, Mendez's *winikin* disappeared out of his locked mental ward yesterday right after Mendez dropped out of sight. Nate, Sven, and Alexis are up there now, looking for both of them." She paused. "But I'm guessing you didn't call for an update."

"No." Patience let out a slow breath and crossed her fingers that this was going to work. "Did Lucius's search for memory enhancers pull up anything related to mirrors, like a mirrored artifact or a spell that uses one?"

There was a beat of silence on the other end. Then Jade said, "There's a mirror-bottomed pot on the 'to be translated' pile. The magic led Lucius to it, but we moved it down on the priority list because a rough translation of the first few glyphs suggested that it's more aimed at breaking mental blocks than recovering actual memories."

Patience's heart drummed in her ears. "Translate it now. Please. I think it's the one I need."

CHAPTER FOUR

While she waited, Patience downed a couple of energy bars and a cup of coffee, and skirted gingerly around the coffee table, where the *etznab* card lay faceup.

She had defended her new hobby, but now she realized that she hadn't really believed—not deep down inside—that the cards had any true power. Now, though . . . she hesitated to pull another, fearing that she would turn over something way darker than *etznab*. When a tap came at the hallway door, she flinched.

"It's open," she called. But then, unable to sit still, she stood and crossed to the door as it swung inward. She stopped dead at the sight of Rabbit. He was carrying a brightly painted, three-legged clay pot, and had a plastic bag and a manila folder tucked under one elbow. And he hadn't been in the suite in a long, long time.

For a few seconds, the past and present ricocheted off each other, making her yearn.

"I volunteered to bring this stuff over and see if you want help with the spell," he said conversationally, like they were picking up in the middle of a discussion they'd been having only moments earlier, rather than the year-plus it had been since the last time they had hung out together. His blue-gray eyes, though, were wary.

It was the same expression he'd worn early on, when he'd watched the world from behind the insulation of an iPod and a teenager's sulkiness. Back then, his father had given him good reason to anticipate trouble. Now she didn't like knowing she had put that look in his eyes.

She reached out impulsively to grip his forearm. "I was just thinking about you."

He went very still. He didn't pull away, though, and when he met her eyes, he saw an echo of her own regrets. "I'm sorry about Brandt. If I didn't have the hellmark—"

"It wasn't your fault," Patience interrupted, tightening her grip. "Not even you can control the gods. And besides, I wasn't thinking about what happened today. . . . I was thinking about the breakfasts we used to have in here, the whole gang of us together."

Rabbit nodded, but he broke eye contact and his body closed up on itself, the way it used to. After a moment he pulled away from her and headed for the master, where he took a long look at Brandt before turning away to set the pot on the floor beside the bed, then crouching to put the folder and plastic bag beside it.

Those simple actions seemed to take forever.

Finally, he said, "I miss the rats." That was what he'd called Harry and Braden—his rug rats. "I miss those breakfasts." There was a long pause; then he glanced up at her. "I miss us being friends."

She had been looking at the clay pot. Now she looked at him. And, seeing a hint of vulnerability, she didn't cheat either of them with a knee-jerk answer of "We're still friends." Instead, she said, "Myrinne doesn't like me."

His lips twitched, and he glanced away. "She figured out that I used to have a huge crush on you."

She kept it light, sensing that was what he needed right now. "I can't say I mind the idea of a gorgeous coed wanting to scratch my eyes out over a younger man." Though really they were only a few years apart in age.

His expression eased a little, but his body stayed tight as he stood and turned to face her fully. "That wasn't . . . *I* wasn't . . ." He took another breath and tried again. "Did having me around screw things up between you two?"

Oh. Ouch. So much for keeping it light. Too aware that Brandt was lying a few feet away, she said, "You didn't screw up anything, Rabbit. At least not between Brandt and me." In other areas, he was notorious. "You just reminded me what it felt like for a relationship to be fun and easy. And there were moments when I saw a younger version of him in you, and realized how much I missed the guy he used to be, how much I wanted him back."

They both looked at the bed, where the older, tougher version lay motionless and stern-featured.

"Okay," Rabbit said after a moment. "Yeah. Okay." She got the feeling he wasn't totally satisfied, but he didn't pursue it. Just nudged the pot with the toe of his boot. "You should be all set. The folder's got the translated spell, both in phonetic Mayan and English, along with Lucius's interpretation. There's some incense and stuff in the Ziploc. I'm not sure what all's in there, but Jade said the spell itself wasn't anything too drastic. None of the old 'Draw the thorny vine through your pierced tongue' or 'Let blood from your foreskin.'" He gave an exaggerated shudder, but his sidelong look was one hundred percent serious. "I could help, you know. Unless you think the hellmark will fuck things up yet again."

"I don't—" That time, the knee-jerk almost made it out, but she stopped herself, narrowing her eyes. "You're still a manipulative little shit, aren't you?"

He shrugged, unrepentant. "Almost worked."

She pointed to the hallway door. "Out."

The order echoed back to the numerous times she'd banished him and the twins out to the patio, or the pool, or just about anyplace other than the suite, with its enclosed spaces and tight acoustics. This time, though, the echo brought a sense of the past and present connecting rather than moving further apart. And it eased something inside her, just a little.

He tossed her one of the panic buttons that were

hardwired into the Skywatch system. "Jox wanted me to remind you not to be shy about using it." He paused. "You want an earpiece? One of us could monitor—"

"No," she cut in, "but thanks."

He nodded, sent her a "good luck" salute, and headed out. Before the hallway door had fully shut behind him, she had cleared off the nightstand, dragged it into position beside the bed, and hefted the three-legged pot onto it.

The upper rim of the artifact had a wide, flattened section that was stained dark with char. The interior of the pot was painted glossy black and buffed to a shine around the sides; the bottom was inset with a perfect circle of black stone—obsidian, maybe?—that had been polished to a ruthless gleam that threw her own reflection back at her, even in the indirect bedroom lighting.

A brightly painted scene ringed the outside of the pot: Against a creamy white background, the black-outlined figures were painted in shades of earthy red, orange, and yellow, with vivid sea blue accents. The painting showed a ceremonially robed figure with the flattened forehead and exaggerated nose typical of ancient Mayan art—a king or a priest, maybe—inhaling curls of smoke from the small dish at the top of the three-legged pot, with a second pot turned on its side to show the interior . . . which was marked with a jagged "X" symbol. *Etznab.* More smoke billowed around the figure, its tendrils becoming strange, hunched figures—gods, maybe, or ancestors—who acted out unintelligible pantomimes.

"Okay," she said softly to herself. "Burn the sacrifice, inhale the smoke, look into the mirror, and see your past. I can do that." Question was, could she use what was left of the *jun tan* bond to bring Brandt into the magic? *Gods, I hope so.*

She prepped things per Lucius's instructions, removing Brandt's IV, folding their blood sacrifices into a blob of the Nightkeepers' claylike brown incense, and then lighting the sacrifice with a match and a dash of highly alcoholic *pulque.*

As she tipped the pot on its side, so the mirror reflected Brandt's image, magic buzzed in the air, touching her skin with phantom caresses that heated her body and made her ache with the memory of better days. But it was those memories she sought, so she didn't will them away as she normally would. Instead she thought about her dream-vision of earlier that morning.

She remembered how he had slipped into her from behind, locking her to him with a strong arm that banded across her body to her opposite shoulder, trapping her with pleasure as he moved within her, possessed her, loved her. Their *jun tan* connection had been wide-open, letting the sensations wash back and forth so she felt his passion as her own, and vice versa, binding them together in an escalating wash of heat that had put her over and left her shuddering against him, helpless beneath their shared orgasm.

Ignoring the moisture that blurred her vision, she stretched out beside him and clasped his hand, pressing their bloodied palms together and intertwining

their fingers in a familiar move that made her throb
with longing. She inhaled a deep breath of incense-
laden air, then another and another, until her head
spun with the mildly hallucinogenic properties of
the *copan*. Closing her eyes, she whispered the spell
words Lucius had given her.

The humming magic changed pitch, gaining a
high, sweet note, and energy brushed across her skin,
warming her. For a few seconds she hesitated, unable
to make herself look into the mirror and complete the
spell, fearing that the memories wouldn't meet her
expectations . . . or that they would exceed them. She
wasn't sure which would be worse.

Finally, she whispered to herself, "You can do this."
And she opened her eyes.

The glossy black mirror glowed silver, lit by magic.
It swirled with liquid ripples that ran across the surface, light chasing dark in ever-expanding circles that
shimmered . . . curved . . . curled . . . and began to
resolve into images, flickers of memory.

She saw Harry's sweet smile, Braden's devilish
gleam, Hannah's proud scars . . . and Brandt's glittering brown eyes gone gold-shot with love.

Going on instinct, she rose over him, pressed her
lips to his, and summoned every shred of magic she
could wrap her mind around. She gathered the power,
not shaping it into a fireball, a shield, or her own personal talent of invisibility, but rather collecting it into
a pool of pure energy that rippled in her mind's eye,
suddenly looking like a mirror itself. Then she focused
on the cool spot on her wrist.

And she sent the magic into it.

The *jun tan* tingled, then heated. Warmth washed into her, through her, making her feel whole and connected, like she was part of something larger and stronger than herself. But still it wasn't enough.

She kissed him again, only this time she held nothing back. She opened herself fully, sacrificing her self-respect and the barriers that had protected her, offering her magic, energy, and love. Then, whispering against his lips, she repeated the spell.

Time stalled for a second; the magic went silent, the air strung tight with anticipation. Lifting her eyes, she looked into their reflections and said, "Show us the night we met."

The mated link flared to life, her *jun tan* going from cold to warm, then to blazing hot as energy poured out of her and into him, draining through the uplink. She gasped as the magic left her. Her perceptions grayed, yet still the power flowed from her, into a seemingly bottomless sink within him.

Then the grayness detonated in a red-gold flash, and she was back in her own body—or rather, she was in a younger version of herself.

The warm, humid Yucatán night embraced her, grainy sand pressed underfoot, and a sea of coeds swarmed around her in various states of inebriation and undress. Fireworks arced overhead, celebrating the equinox; when they burst, they illuminated the looming bulk of Mayan ruins nearby, overlooking the ocean.

It was spring break of her senior year in college. She was nineteen, almost twenty. And she was staring at the biggest, most gorgeous guy she'd ever seen in her life.

She had done it. They were back at the beginning.

CHAPTER FIVE

Cancún, Mexico
Six years ago

Hel-lo, handsome, Patience thought *as a salvo of salutes flash-banged overhead, lighting the sky and shortening her breath. Or maybe it wasn't the fireworks driving the air from her lungs. Maybe it was the guy she'd just locked eyes with, picking him out of the crowd because he was a half a head taller than everyone else, and he wasn't looking at the fireworks. He was looking at her.*

It wasn't like she'd never been stared at before. She was tall, stacked, and blond, and years of fight training had honed her movements in a way that drew attention—especially that of the Y chromosomes. So yeah, she was used to being looked at, used to being wanted.

But she wasn't used to immediately wanting in return. She recognized the warm, liquid shimmy in her stomach as

*desire, but had never felt it like this before, as an instanta-
neous chemical response that lit her up and made her yearn
for an entirely unknown quantity. Always before, she'd
liked her boyfriends before desiring them, gotten to know
them before taking the physical plunge. But there was
nothing gradual about this; it was like being hit between
the eyes with a big cartoon hammer labeled* LUST.

He was built big, which was an instant turn-on given
that she towered over lots of the guys she knew. He was
flat-out, hands-down gorgeous, with spike-cut hair she
thought would be dark brown in better light, and eyes a
shade lighter. His dark, unadorned T-shirt was stretched
across a wide chest and ripped abs, and tucked into faded
cutoffs that were practically painted onto narrow hips and
massive thighs. His calves were corded with muscle, tan
and hairless, his feet encased in beat-up boat shoes. But it
was more than just the way he looked. He seemed to radiate
a quiet, watchful strength along with a punch of charisma
she wasn't used to from guys her age, or even a year or two
older, as he appeared to be.

Her body flashed from hot to cold and back; she felt
dizzy and a little drunk, though she'd had only two rum-
and-whatevers since dinner, holding off the serious tequila-
ing for later after the fireworks, when she was supposed to
be going barhopping with Casey and Amanda. Who, she
suspected, were going to be on their own now, because he
was coming over.

Normally, she would've felt a flare of feminine triumph
that he'd lost their eye-lock standoff by making the move.
Now, though, all she felt was anticipation.

As he came through the crowd toward her, the inebri-*

*ated human sea eddied. The women turned toward him,
faces lighting and then falling when he moved past without
noticing them. The men shifted to let him through while
they kept their eyes on the sky, subordinates giving way to
the alpha. Then he was squaring off opposite her with his
weight evenly balanced, leaving him ready to move in or
away with equal ease. A fighter's ready stance.*

Her pulse kicked higher. Oh, yeah. *Thanks to growing
up with Hannah, she was culturally programmed to want
herself a warrior. Not for keeps, of course. She'd promised
her* winikin *she wouldn't commit to anything until after
the end date. She hadn't promised not to sample the wares,
though.* And thank the gods for that.

He held out his hand. "Brandt White-Eagle." *His voice
was as rocking as his face and bod, smooth and masculine,
with an orator's resonance.*

She pressed her palm to his. "Patience Lazarus." *How
odd that, of the two of them, he was the one with an animal
in his name. Hannah had modernized her bloodline name
from "iguana" to "lizard," and from there to "Lazarus";
the* winikin *was a Heinlein fan. But White-Eagle . . . if he'd
been a Nightkeeper, his bird bloodline would've outranked
her terrestrial one. As it was, the name—and his looks—
suggested Native American blood, which was pretty damn
sexy in its own right. She'd take* Dances with Wolves
over Heinlein any day.

"Are you here with someone?"

*Casey and Amanda had noticed the exchange and were
openly gaping. When Patience glanced in her friends' direction, she got a quadruple thumbs-up. She looked back at
the guy.* Brandt. "What if I am?"

She got a long, slow smile with lots of eye contact. "Then he's out of luck." A pause. "Unless you're not feeling it?"

"I don't know what I'm feeling, but it's something." In fact, the air seemed to be buzzing with that "something." Her skin tingled almost to the point of itching, making her want to rub herself, touch herself, do something to ease a sudden surge of restlessness.

"You want to get out of here?" He tipped his head away from the water. "We could head up to El Rey."

Yearning tugged at Patience. Gods, yes, she wanted to go there with him. El Rey was the only major Mayan ruin located in the Cancún hotel district. Its original name and most of its history were unknown; the modern name, which meant "the King," came from the discovery of several royal artifacts. The small site encompassed the ruins and footprints of some forty structures, including a large pillared palace and a high, flat-topped pyramid . . . which nowadays offered views of the boat-clogged lagoon and the entire hotel district, and overlooked the Hilton's golf course.

El Rey wasn't as important—or impressive—as the ruins of Tulum or Chichén Itzá; it had held Casey's and Amanda's attentions barely long enough to justify the thirty-peso entrance fee. Patience, though, had visited the site every day since the three girls had arrived the week before, until it'd turned into a running joke among them, how she was hoping the magic pyramid—that was the rumor, anyway, that it was magical—would grant her three wishes.

The friends had discussed those wishes with sotted intensity, finally deciding that she should wish for wild success in her yet-nebulous career aspirations, a long, healthy life, and true love. They had figured if she had those three biggies covered, she could handle the rest. Privately, she'd amended one—maybe all—of those wishes to an inner prayer that the barrier would stay closed, that she would never need to know most of the things Hannah had taught her.

"Too fast?" Brandt asked when she didn't answer right away. "Or are you wondering if I'm a Creepy Stalker Guy?"

She didn't—couldn't—tell him what she'd really been thinking, but she'd had a lifetime of practice avoiding some questions, outright lying in response to others. "The park closed at dark."

"I paid one of the guides to show me the back way in."

So had she. That he'd done the same made her take another, longer look at him. "Are you trying to get me alone?"

A challenge glinted in his eyes. "Is that a problem?"

She shook her head slowly. "Not for me. But then again, I'm a fifth-degree black belt."

"Figured something along those lines." He tugged on the hand he hadn't yet let go of. "Come on."

Behind him, fireworks burst in chrysanthemums of red and yellow, and cometlike arcs lit the sky. She was dimly surprised to see that the show hadn't ended yet, that they'd been talking for only a few minutes. How was that possible, when she felt like they'd known each other for way longer than that?

Don't try to make this into more than it is, *she cautioned herself, hearing an inner echo of Hannah's warnings, which contrasted with Casey's and Amanda's recent lectures urging her to cut loose.* He's hot, you're horny, and it's spring break. Go with the flow.

"El Rey it is, then." She let him lead her through the crowd. Again, the men moved aside to let him through and the women turned their heads to appreciate the way he looked, the way he moved. Only this time, they noticed her too, with varying degrees of resignation, envy, and bitchy glares.

Eat your heart out, girls, *she thought in triumph.* He's mine tonight.

As they let the moonlight and fireworks guide them along the faint pathway used by the few who cared enough to sneak into the park, she was acutely aware of the leashed strength in his muscles, the heat of his body. His strides were powerful, almost gliding, except for once or twice when she noticed the faintest hitch of a limp.

The small imperfection of an otherwise perfect package made him all the more interesting—what was his story? Who was he?

A liquid shimmy radiated from low in her abdomen outward to her fingertips and toes, making her hyperconscious of the gritty surface beneath her sandals, the weight of her clothes against her skin, the touch of the moist, cool air, and the breathlessness that hadn't come from the fireworks, after all.

Pyrotechnics boomed at regular intervals, making the earth below their feet tremble as their bodies brushed together at shoulder and hip. Nerves flared through Patience—not over the advisability of sneaking off alone with a stranger who didn't seem at all unfamiliar, but over whether she'd be able to hold her own with him. She'd dated plenty of guys who were far more into her than she was into them . . . but this was the first time she was on the other side of the insecurity, the first time she'd found herself wondering if she was aiming at someone out of her league.

The sensation was disconcerting . . . and oddly exciting. Was her hand sweating? She'd showered after the beach, and crunched a couple of Altoids after her onion- and spice-heavy dinner, so she should be okay on those fronts, but—

Her mental train derailed as they passed through the last of the low trees that surrounded the site.

The ruins spread out in front of them, washed blue white in the moonlight and cast with splashes of color when the fireworks briefly brightened the night sky. They had approached from the back side of the pyramid, which was the size of a split-level ranch, flanked by a pillared temple platform on one side and a long building—possibly a market—on the other.

Always before, in daylight, Patience had felt a buzz of reverence, a sense of connection that she hadn't had at any of the other ruins. Now, in the darkness, the sensation of being someplace both ancient and sacred was heightened by the heat of sexual anticipation, and her awareness of the equinox.

Back before the massacre, when the magic had worked and the Nightkeepers flourished, the cardinal days had been times of celebration and sex. Now, as fireworks painted the ruins yellow orange, making her think of torchlight, it seemed right for her to turn toward Brandt and move in for the kiss they had been heading for ever since he'd taken her hand to lead her out of the crowd.

Except she froze midturn, her eyes locking on a dark rectangle outlined in silver moonlight.

There was a doorway in the lower tier of the pyramid.

Brandt whispered, "That wasn't there before. Was it?"

"I don't think so." Actually, she knew for a fact that it hadn't been, but didn't want to seem too sure. Nightkeepers were supposed to fly under the human radar. But her pulse kicked and her hands started sweating in earnest.

He glanced down at her, eyes alight. "Want to check it out?"

She hesitated. Of course she wanted to check it out—she was dying to get in there, her anticipation fueled by a combination of her inner adrenaline junkie and cultural conditioning—but logic said she should ditch him before she entered the ruin. If the doorway had opened because of some equinox-triggered spell put in place by the ancients, possibly one that required the presence of Nightkeeper blood, then she shouldn't let the human anywhere near it.

But what if it was something more banal, like a new passageway opened by a rock slide? If it didn't have anything to do with the magi, there was no harm in exploring it with her spring-break hookup.

Or, more accurately, there was no more harm than there would be for two full humans who had snuck into a national park with zero equipment, experience, or mandate to set foot inside the pyramid. But because of her warrior's blood, that caution quickly lost to the urge to explore. What was more, a glance showed that Brandt was full-on channeling his inner Indiana Jones, practically vibrating with the urge to get his ass through that door and see what was on the other side.

When she hesitated, though, he said, "We don't have to. We could just sit and watch the fireworks." But the energy between them changed when he said it, making her suspect that if she went with option B, she'd find herself back on the beach while he returned to El Rey alone. Which so wasn't happening.

Besides, she thought, her brain skipping from option to option almost faster than her consciousness could follow, if the door is Nightkeeper-made and keyed to the presence of mageblood, then it being open now is . . . She trailed off, not even daring to say it inwardly. But what if the barrier had reactivated, if only at this one small spot?

If the magic was back online, then theoretically, she should be able to put Brandt to sleep, and even make him forget what he'd seen. Granted, she didn't have her bloodline mark, but the sleep and forget spells were lower-level magic. She might be able to pull them off.

So either the door was magic, in which case she should be able to handle the damage control . . . or it wasn't magic, in which case she was about to go exploring with a seriously hot, mega-interesting guy, during the equinox, when her blood was already on fire. Win-win.

Digging into her pocket, she pulled out her key chain, unsnapped the little emergency light, and gave it a flash. "What are we waiting for?"

His slow, sexy grin was practically its own reward.

They crossed the moonlit courtyard hand in hand, and approached the pyramid. The doorway, which was set in the center of the lowest tier, looked like many of the others she'd seen over the years, with carved pillars on both sides and a lintel over the top. She barely glanced at the carvings, in part because she knew only a few of the ancient glyphs and these were badly weatherworn. The larger part of her haste, though, was the hot excitement beating in her veins, urging her onward.

Tangling her fingers with his, she used her pitiful little light to illuminate the darkness beyond the doorway. Behind them, fireworks pounded, the deep thuds reverberating in the heavy stones of the pyramid. In front of them, an ancient stone staircase led, not up within the pyramid . . . but down into the earth.

Her breath thinned with excitement. On some level, she was aware that one or both of them should probably be bringing up some what-ifs—what would they do if the penlight died? What if the tunnel was booby-trapped? She wasn't entirely sure if that sort of thing was fact or fiction. Was this really such a good idea?

On another, more visceral level, though, she knew that hesitating wasn't an option. If this was equinox magic, the doorway would shut in a few hours. And if it wasn't . . . hell, either way, she was dying to see where the staircase led, and to see it with this man. Call it the hereditary bravery of a warrior bloodline, call it hormones, call it equinox madness; she didn't care.

Glancing at him, she lifted an eyebrow. "You ready?"

He brushed his knuckles across her cheek in a soft, sensual caress. The warm glow of the penlight brought color to his face and lit his eyes, which were a deep, gold-flecked brown. He inhaled as if to say something, but stayed silent instead, and in that instant, she thought she caught a hint *of reserve in his expression, the question of whether he dared share the adventure with her. But those were her thoughts, not his, she reminded herself. And there was nothing but the thrill of the hunt in his face when he grinned. "I've been ready since the moment I spotted you in the crowd."*

She laughed. "Lame."

"Yeah, sorry. I'm pretty sad in the pickup-line department."

She didn't believe that for a second, but the exchange had dispelled some of the tension, putting them back where they had been on the beach, daring each other to make the move. Then, he'd been the one to pull her into the darkness, headed for privacy. Now it was her turn to lead the way.

Taking a deep breath, she stepped across the threshold. And started down.

The air around them cooled as they descended the curving stone staircase in a silence broken only by the sound of his boat shoes, her sandals, and their cadenced breathing. The interlocking stones that surrounded them were uncarved and unadorned, and slippery with a layer of moisture that grew heavier as they went. The air, though, stayed fresh, suggesting that there was an outlet nearby.

"I can taste salt," Brandt said from close behind her. She was very aware of the heat of his big body, the brush of their clothing, and the feather of his breath along her jaw as he looked over her shoulder, both of them depending on the small penlight.

"Maybe this leads all the way back to the lagoon." She tried to remember if there was a cliff along the beach, someplace where the native limestone base ran down to the water.

"Or an underground river," he suggested. "There's almost no surface water in the Yucatán—it's all subterranean except for where the cenotes punch through. The ancient Maya used to throw sacrifices into the cenotes, hoping to appease the gods, and—" He broke off. "And I'll shut up now."

She glanced back. "Archaeology student?"

He shook his head. "Architecture student. But a geeky one. Day one, when my buddies headed for the cantina, I hit the museum."

It was a perfectly reasonable explanation that didn't play, though she couldn't put her finger on what seemed off about it, or why the realization kicked her pulse higher in a good way rather than bad. Then her pitiful flashlight beam showed that they had hit the end of the staircase, and she couldn't think of anything except what might lie beyond, where the walls fell away and there was only darkness. She smelled brackish water and thought she heard a liquid drip up ahead, so when she reached the edge of the last step, she aimed the light down, making sure there was something solid for her to step onto.

Without warning or preamble, a crack-boom split the air, and fireworks lit an almost perfect circle far above them with yellow, orange, and red sparks. The illumination brightened the interior of what proved to be a high, arching cavern. Graceful stalactites dripped down, reaching toward a circular pool of rippling water. At the apex of the arched ceiling, a sinkhole had punched through, letting in the night sky, where blue-green pinwheels twirled outward in concentric firework rings.

"Holy shit." Brandt stepped past her, trailing his hand

across the small of her back as he moved onto the wide strip of soft limestone sand that separated the curving cave walls from the lagoon. He was staring up at the circle of sky. "I didn't know there was a cenote at El Rey."

"The door was hidden somehow. Maybe the sinkhole was too." She came up beside him, looking not at the sky but at the swirling water.

The Maya—and the Nightkeepers living among them—would have sacrificed their most prized possessions into the cenote, imbuing the water with a power all its own. She stared into the dark pool, trying to sense the magic, which Hannah had described as a humming red-gold haze. She didn't hear any hum, didn't see any red-gold, but there was definitely something in the air.

The equinox was in full effect, the fireworks were building to their finale, and she was standing beside a man who fascinated her, compelled her, made her want. And, as he took her hand and twined their fingers together, she knew he felt the same—knew it deep down inside, the same way she wanted to believe that the two of them being there at that moment, together, wasn't a coincidence.

He looked down at her, his eyes shining with the thrill of adventure and the heat that built between them. "It's beautiful," he said, his voice rasping on the words. "And so are you."

The simple statement curled warmth through her as she reached for him and he reached for her. They came together in unison for their first kiss, bodies flowing together naturally, aligning perfectly. When their lips touched, the fireworks reached their finale, lighting the sky red and yellow, and making the earth tremble.

Heat flared through Patience; her center turned to liq-uid warmth, her muscles to pulsing need. Oh, yeah, she thought. Or maybe she said it; she wasn't sure of any-thing beyond the feel of his body against hers, all hard muscles and a vibrant energy that called to something within her.

She heard a humming noise, though she couldn't have said which one of them made the sound; it seemed almost to come from the air around them as it gathered and grew, seeming to circle them, going faster and faster.

What the hell? *She grabbed on to Brandt, digging into his solid strength when the spinning buzz gained traction, becoming a vortex that sought to pull her away from him. She screamed and clung, but he was already gone. Then she was rushing, spinning, moving at incalculable rates of speed while somehow staying still.*

Gray-green whipped past her, scraping off the lay-ers of innocence and enthusiasm, and aging her six years in the space of a few seconds.

Not yet! Patience cried in her soul. They needed to know what happened next, how the two of them had gotten their marks when the barrier was sealed, the magic disabled. They needed to know about Brandt's debt, and why the Triad magic had stalled. What was more, she wanted to know what their first time had felt like, what they'd told each other in the aftermath. Maybe remembering the past would help her figure out what the hell had gone wrong in the present.

She didn't return to the vision, though. Instead, her body took shape around her with the tingle of neurons reawakening to the real world. But as it did, she realized that she had brought a piece of the vision world out with her: desire.

Heat raced through her veins, lighting her up, making her feel things she hadn't felt in what seemed like forever. Excitement thrummed through her as the memory of her and Brandt's first kiss morphed to the sizzle of a new one in the present. Her lips were locked to his, their blood, power, and heat mingling. Exultation flared as a shudder ran through his body and he awoke, a testosterone-laden Sleeping Beauty coming to life beneath her kiss.

Oh, thank you, gods. The *etznab* spell had worked.

Relief hammered through her, but before she could say anything, he deepened the kiss, going from participant to leader between one breath and the next. Flames danced behind her closed lids as his free arm came up to wrap around her, catching her in a hard embrace that lit her senses with urgent desire.

His taste was fresh and new once again, his touch wildly exciting as he dragged his hand down her body to the place where the hem of her long-sleeve tee had ridden up to bare the skin above her jeans, which were soft with wear and rode low on her waist. His big hand closed on her hip, his fingers digging in with the inciting pressure of a rough caress that was echoed in his ragged groan.

Her excitement flared higher at the sound. It had been rare for him to ease up on his vicious self-control, rare for her to be able to push him past that point. If he was teetering now, it meant that she wasn't alone in being caught partway between then and now, riding a wave of relief and sex magic.

She didn't delude herself by pretending that the magic wasn't part of what was happening between them. But at the same time, she couldn't make herself care. She wanted sex. With him. Now.

When oxygen ran low, they ended the kiss and drew apart, both breathing hard and fast. She opened her eyes to find him staring at her with a hint of the wonder that was rocketing through her, along with the sense of "*there* you are." It felt like they had been looking for each other for months now, years.

She knew the intensity was an illusion of the sex magic, making the joining seem like so much more than it would otherwise, but she didn't care. She wanted to lose herself in the moment and forget about all the rest. Most of all, she wanted to hold on to the warm glow of love and desire that lit his expression right now.

But even as she watched, the glow dimmed. "The Triad spell didn't work," he said in a low rasp.

"We know. The *nahwal* warned us." She braced for his withdrawal, the return to business-first Brandt.

Instead, he reached up and brushed his knuckles across her cheek as he had done that night. Until she saw the wetness, she hadn't realized there were tears.

"The vision . . . ," he began, then trailed off. Something shifted in his eyes; they heated with molten gold, turning to those of his younger self. "I saw you in town that day. You were coming out of some bar with your friends, but I didn't see them. I only saw you. I froze for a second, and it was too long—you were gone. I spent the rest of the day searching—hotels, bars, whatever. By the time it got dark, I was pr—hoping to hell you'd be on the beach for the fireworks . . . and that you would feel what I was feeling."

Oh, Brandt. New tears stung the corners of her eyes, but she willed them back. "I felt it too. It felt like this." Knowing she was probably making a mistake, that this was going to hurt when things went wrong again, she leaned in and locked her lips to his.

She didn't care. She wanted this, wanted him.

He kissed her back, openmouthed, in a blatantly carnal demand that she met and matched, her body vibrating with need and arousal. Heat slapped through her alongside wonder when she found that although it was morning and they were in their bedroom, the moment she closed her eyes, she was right back in the night-dark cave, being held in the arms of a stranger while fireworks lit the sky.

She kissed the stranger who was her husband, not letting herself think of yesterday or tomorrow, of marriage or magic. The only thing that mattered was that moment and the things they were making each other feel. She didn't care that the feelings were coming from the mirror spell or a backlash of the magic she'd poured into their mated bond to bring him back. She cared only that he was alive, that they had recovered a piece of their shared past . . . and that it was a memory worth holding on to.

Although she didn't know how their first kiss had ended, she imagined how it had gone from there, putting herself into the fantasy.

When Brandt reversed them in a smooth, powerful move, so he was above her, pressing into her, the yielding mattress at her back became the soft limestone sand at the edge of the subterranean pool. When she dragged his T-shirt up and off, so she could stroke the hard-edged leanness of his chest and abs, following the feathery line of coarse, wiry hair from the wings of his collarbones to the yielding elastic of his bike shorts, the long, masculine groan she elicited from him echoed off water and stone. And when they wrestled the remainder of their clothes off and shoved aside the bedding, leaving them twined together, fully naked and exposed, the excitement of skin on skin came with a hint of the forbidden when she imagined what it might have been like to be with him in that cave.

But although the fantasy came quickly, vividly, the man who slid his legs alongside hers was very real. Almost too real. So she held on to the fantasy, using it as a buffer when emotion threatened to break through the heat and make her think when all she wanted to do was *feel*.

Chasing sensation, she trailed her mouth down the strong column of his neck, pressing lightly with her teeth as she worked inward, headed for the spot just above where his collarbones joined, where a kiss could make him shudder. Before her lips reached that destination, though, he tunneled his fingers through her hair and gripped, anchoring her as he brought their mouths together for a hard kiss that was more heat than finesse, more demand than request.

The move put her off balance, with a sense of "Wait. That's not what comes next!" But that realization warned her she was falling into a pattern she hadn't been entirely aware of, one that had grown up in their years together, as she had figured out what he liked and how to give it to him.

This was different, though—*he* was different. His hands were fast and borderline rough as he cupped her breasts, kneading them and dragging his thumbs across her nipples, making her arch against him, her fingers fluttering against his shoulders as she lost herself momentarily in the pleasure. His mouth shaped hers and she came alive to the scrape of teeth and the slide of tongue when he mimicked the act of love, in and out, until her body throbbed in time with his thrusts.

Her breath went thin; her head spun with knife-edge arousal and she had the feeling of being at the lip of a precipice, balanced between safety and free fall. She didn't know this lover. Or rather, she suspected she had known him at one time, but they had lost each other along the way. She didn't know what came next, didn't quite know where to put her hands or how to move her body as old patterns gave way to nerves and the thrill of experimentation.

Refusing to let herself be taken without leaving her mark on him first, she twined herself around him, seeking the upper hand. He yielded, lying back with a growl that turned to a harsh, rattling groan when she dragged her teeth lightly across his ribs and down, trailing kisses and nips along his torso. The salt on his skin made her think of the ocean-fed lagoon; the hammer of his pulse reminded her of the heavy thud of fireworks.

He lay still, his muscles locking as she tasted the points of his hip bones and the taut skin between, but when she shifted to move lower, he uncoiled lightning fast; in a blink, she was beneath him once again, trapped under his superior strength and bulk as he looked down at her, his chest heaving, his eyes wild.

She expected him to slow things down. Instead, he grated, "More." Then he proceeded to give her more, taking it for himself in the process. He kissed her long and deep as he ran one hand down to hook her knee up alongside his hip, so his body settled tighter against hers while his hips moved in a slow, tantalizing rhythm.

Whimper-moaning with mingled need and satisfaction, she dug her fingers into the strong muscles of his back, and lower down, where the long muscles of his quads blended into the hard handfuls of his ass. There, she felt the same near gauntness she'd noticed earlier in his face. He'd lost weight—his muscle mass was the same, but what little fat he'd carried had burned away, distilling his body to its essence. And although he'd been far from soft before, she thrilled to his new hardness, and the fact that he was using his bulk to pin her in place and make her writhe with pleasure.

He rubbed his hard cock against her, bringing her to another precipice, not one of free fall this time, but of an orgasm that sparkled behind her eyelids, equal parts magic and sensation. The skin of her inner wrist warmed and pulsed as their *jun tan* connection cracked open and let a trickle of arousal flow from her to him and back again.

"Yes," she said with her heart, mind, and voice. "Yes, now." Her mouth found his and she poured herself into a kiss.

He went utterly still against her, save for the throb of his hard shaft against her center. Then he exhaled a pent-up breath on a whisper that she thought was her name. Shifting, he nudged the wide head of his cock against the initial resistance at the entrance to her body. She was wet and wanting, but tight because of how long it had been since they had given up the pretense of sleeping in the same bed. The pressure wrung a growl from deep within his chest as he thrust home on a strong surge.

He invaded her, stretched her, filled her. And when he was seated to the hilt, pressing up against the end of her channel and making her breath go thin with the intensity of it all, he went still once more. For a long moment, they lay joined and motionless as the counterpoint beat of their hearts echoed in the throb of his hard flesh, the pulse of her inner muscles. Unable to stay safe in the darkness behind her eyelids, she opened her eyes and looked up at him.

His gold-flecked brown eyes were entirely focused on her, on the moment. He wasn't the twentysomething grad student who had glimpsed her across a crowded *playa* and chased her down, but in that moment he wasn't the hard, remote Nightkeeper mage she'd been coexisting with for more than a year either. In his eyes she glimpsed the man who'd carried her over the threshold of their starter house and made love to her in every single room, including the laundry nook during the spin-dry cycle.

Her eyes prickled at the memory, warning that she'd fallen out of the safe refuge of fantasy and magic. The heat and need, though, hadn't dissipated. The *jun tan* sent incandescent energy through them both; he hardened further within her, stretching her and setting off chain reactions of inner fireworks. She focused on those bursts and slid back into the fantasy, remembering how her younger self had felt when she turned and found him watching her, how it had felt to lead him into the cave, to kiss him.

For a second, she could've sworn that the cool blue bedroom walls around them darkened and aged, turning to stone. Wishful thinking or not, it was enough to push away the tears and put her back in the moment, in the fantasy. Locking her inner muscles around him in a liquid squeeze, she said, as he had done earlier, "More."

His expression turned inward, went glazed, and his teeth flashed on a purely masculine grin that held

an edge of violence. "Hell, yeah, there's more." His
voice dropped to a husky rasp that sent frissons of
anticipation coursing through her body. "Hang on to
me and I'll show you just how much."

He pressed her flat with his body, stilling her small,
inciting movements. Then, although she would've
sworn he was seated as deeply as he could be, he rolled
his hips and went farther, startling a low moan out of
her as he hit her sweet spots inside and out. When he
withdrew fractionally, she moaned again, this time in
protest at the loss of that delicious pressure.

"Hang on," he repeated. "Let me take us there."
He pushed forward again, then eased back. Forward.
Back. And as pleasure vised her, locking her muscles
around him, beneath him, she did as he'd demanded,
clutching his wide shoulders, which became her anchor.

He was pulsing more than thrusting, his movements on the scope of fractions of an inch, but her
body lit as hard and hot as if he'd been pistoning
into her, driving them both beyond reason. What
was more, the deep, subtle thrusts left them almost
entirely joined throughout. He was inside her, almost
becoming part of her. His pleasure echoed through
the *jun tan* connection; she felt the satisfaction of each
thrust from his perspective, then felt it from hers and
sent the sensation echoing back to him. The feedback
loop joined them even more deeply than his flesh
within her, uniting them.

Nerves quivered, but she focused on the moment,
on the man, turning her face into his neck and press-

ing her lips to the hollow dip at his collarbone. He shuddered against her but didn't change his stroke or tempo, flexing his hips and withdrawing, flexing and withdrawing, bringing her pleasure inside and out, until the sum total threatened to overwhelm her.

Tears stung again, but she was beyond processing where they came from, or why. She could only feel what she hadn't felt in so long, if ever. Her orgasm hovered close at hand, as if waiting for some signal from him, under his spell just as surely as she was. But although he was in charge of their lovemaking, she held power of her own. She exerted it now, contracting her inner muscles to counterpoint his pulsing thrusts, beginning to work him as he was working her.

His breath hissed out and his fingers flexed on her hips, where he held her against his relentless thrusts. That might have been his only outward response, but she felt a surge in the *jun tan* connection. Pressure and aching, impossible arousal echoed along the bond, sparking red-gold behind her eyelids as orgasm drew near. His. Hers. *Theirs.*

She tightened around him, her body taking over the volition. It seemed that each muscle fiber sent a starburst of warm anticipation when it contracted, building a new layer of heat atop the desperate pleasure within her. She dug her fingers into his shoulders, finding purchase at the base of his neck and hanging on for dear life.

"Yes," someone said. "Yes, *there*!" She wasn't sure if the words had come from him or her, or if they were entirely internal, a cry of pleasure shared along the *jun tan* bond. She buried her face against his throat, reveling in the slick skin, the heat, the feeling of being there, with him. Not alone.

He must have quickened his pace and lengthened his strokes an iota at a time, because they weren't locked together anymore, weren't pulsing together, touching along every possible inch of skin. Instead, he was fully moving within her, thrusting an inch at first, then more, both speed and swing increasing faster and faster, as though he'd fallen off the edge of self-control.

Her blood burned in her veins and her body undulated in opposition to his building thrusts, creating crazy-hot pressure with the liquid slide of skin and sex. The cave fantasy disappeared and the room around them ceased to exist as her entire universe contracted to the sum of her body and his, and the energy they created together. He groaned her name and wrapped his arms around her, enfolding her in an embrace that made her feel simultaneously protected and vulnerable.

Her strung-tight muscles reached the warm, breathless numbness that presaged climax, leaving her almost helpless in the throes, with her mouth pressed to his throat, open in a silent scream. His body was rigid, hot, and sweat-slicked; their mingled scents ripened the air with an earthy, primal musk that seemed to connect her, not just to him, but to the earth itself, and all its inhabitants. Then that preternatural flash disappeared as the tingling numbness contracted suddenly, centering itself on her moisture-slicked channel and the hooded flesh just outside it, and the slap and slide of his body into hers.

"*Gods,*" she whispered.

He responded with a groan that might have been her name, might have been a denial of the gods themselves. Then even those thoughts were lost as he thrust deep and held himself there, pressed against her inside and out, his cock throbbing within her.

The world went still; she was wrapped around him, pierced by him, and filled with the red-gold energy of the *jun tan*. She hovered there for three heartbeats. Then she tipped over in a screaming rush of pleasure. Her gut wrenched on an orgasm so powerful it was almost terrifying. She cried out on a shuddering breath and clutched at him, vising her legs around his hips and digging her fingers into his back as he bucked against her, groaning her name.

He pushed against her, counterpointing the rhythmic pulses of her inner flesh, which sent ecstasy radiating outward, washing the world behind her eyelids red-gold. His pleasure rushed through her, and hers transmitted to him in return, echoing between them through the Nightkeepers' mating magic, as they clung shuddering together, her face buried in the crook of his neck, his cheek pressed to the crown of her head.

Pulse led to pulse in a magic-amplified climax that echoed long past human-normal, long past the point where it ceased being just sex and became far too important.

Eventually, though, the waves of sensation leveled

off and subsided, the *jun tan* bond faded to background, and they became nothing more than a man and a woman wrapped around each other, their bodies cooling together in the aftermath.

Only they weren't just a man and a woman. And as the seconds ticked by in silence, Patience's postcoital bliss gave way to the knowledge that they couldn't stay like that much longer.

And didn't that just suck?

She didn't want to go back to their real lives . . . and she *really* didn't want to talk about what had just happened. The sex had gotten way too intense, made too many new memories. And she ran the risk of wanting to burrow in and cling, which hadn't been part of the deal.

They had gone into each other's arms with the unspoken agreement that they were acting on the vision magic, burning off the impulse she'd created by channeling herself into the *jun tan* bond.

The closer she stuck to that truce, the better it would be. They couldn't afford to add more complications, not now.

So she took a deep breath, channeled her warrior self as best she could, given that she was lying naked in Brandt's arms, and said, "Okay, here's the deal according to my *nahwal*. You can still become the Triad mage, but only if I help you settle some debt and make peace with your ancestors. And we've got four days to do it."

CHAPTER SIX

"I have to . . . Wait—*what?*" Brandt stared at Patience.

In the aftermath of their lovemaking, her face was soft, her lips kiss-stung, her eyes the blue of a Caribbean lagoon. But rather than looking well loved and dreamy, she looked . . . businesslike.

Not that he could blame her, given what she'd just hit him with. His thoughts churned. What debt? What peace with his ancestors?

But on a far more primal level, he was aware of the warm tingle at his wrist, the tangle of their bodies, the fading echoes of the sex they had just shared, and the hint of vulnerability beneath her outer calm. She had come into the magic after him, risking herself to save his sorry ass. He wanted to reach for her, wanted to kiss her and put himself back into the *jun tan* connection, the one place where they still synced up perfectly.

Before the impulse could fully form, though, his warrior's talent came online.

He gritted his teeth and tried to stop the shift, but the fighting magic ran so strong in the eagle bloodline—along with arrogance and egotism, at least according to Woody—that he damn well couldn't stop the change. Which pissed him off. The other magi had found ways to balance the needs of their magic and their mates . . . so why the hell couldn't he? Why didn't—

Pain lanced through his skull. *Shit*, he thought, pressing his fingers against his closed eyelids. The headaches had come with the talent . . . or, rather, they came whenever he thought about going against his warrior's mandate.

Frustration roughened his tone. "Tell me everything."

"The message came from your *nahwal* via mine . . . because apparently you and yours have a communication problem."

"'A communication problem,'" he repeated. "That sounds like something you would say, not a *nahwal*."

She stilled against him. Then she pulled away from their postsex tangle and climbed from the bed. Her shoulders were tight as she collected her clothes and started pulling them on.

He cursed himself thoroughly. "I'm sorry. That was an asshole comment. I'm . . . shit. I'm sorry." He pinched the bridge of his nose. "Headache."

She nodded without looking at him. "Your head's been through a lot in the past twelve hours or so."

Twelve hours. He glanced to the other side of the bed and saw his reflection in the glossy black bottom of a tipped-over pot. *Magic.* "You found a spell that could bring me back."

"With help from Lucius." Her expression took on a glint of defiance. "And the oracle."

He stifled the instinctive wince, not wanting to get into another back-and-forth about her wasting time on a pointless hobby when they had more important things to worry about. "Thanks. I owe you one."

It sounded pitifully inadequate, but what the hell else could he say?

"Nobody's keeping score. So here goes with the 'while you were sleeping' recap . . ." She leaned up against the bureau with her arms crossed, in a semi-casual pose that made her look like a guest in the bedroom they had once shared, as she took him through the events of the past twelve hours.

He started getting dressed, but by the time she got to the part about Anna and Mendez being the second and third Triad magi, he was sitting on the side of the mattress in his jeans, with a T-shirt wadded in one hand, forgotten, while she described her card-sparked hunch on the *etznab* spell, and using it to put them both into the vision of their first night together.

"I don't know why we didn't stay through to the end," she finished. "I didn't see anything that had to do with owing anybody anything." She paused. "Or am I on the wrong track? Do you think there's something else you're supposed to remember?"

How am I supposed to know if I've forgotten it? He

stifled the sarcasm, though. It wasn't her fault he'd lost twelve hours that felt like days, just like it wasn't her fault that he couldn't wrap his head around the way she was acting.

He'd spent the past two and a half years wishing she would let them concentrate on being Nightkeepers. Now that she was doing exactly that, he found himself wanting to hash out the sex, and why it'd felt the way it had. What they could do to keep that connection.

He really was a dick sometimes.

Focus. Exhaling, he pulled on the T-shirt, then stood to tuck it in. He caught a hint of her scent—*their* scent—but didn't let himself acknowledge the tug it brought. "I don't know what debt the *nahwal* was talking about, but I think you're right. It makes sense that it'd be something about that night." He paused. "The thing is . . . when I was stuck in the Triad magic, I kept looping through a different memory."

Her eyes narrowed. "Something you had forgotten?"

He shook his head. "No. It was there all along, just not in the front of my brain. But the thing is, there were debts owed. I thought I handled it right . . . but maybe not."

"Was it—" She held up a hand, cutting herself off. "Wait. This shouldn't be just the two of us. Let's go get Jade and Lucius, and see if the others are back yet. And you should get some real food into you."

Part of Brandt wanted it to just be the two of them, the perfect team they had once been. He didn't understand why a relationship that had worked so right out in the human world had gone so wrong inside Skywatch. It didn't make sense.

And he had to get his head back in the game. "Yeah. I could go for a breakfast meeting."

But as they left the suite and the last dregs of warmth from the vision-memory drained away, he found himself wishing he could go back to being the man he'd been on the beach that night, hunting down the blonde he'd glimpsed earlier in the day because somehow, deep down inside, he had known that she was meant to be his mate.

"Shit." He pinched the bridge of his nose. "Headache."

Keeping her tattered version of a warrior's detachment wrapped tightly around her heart, Patience led the way to the main mansion.

When they came through the arched doorway leading to the great room, her steps hitched slightly at the sight of the packed kitchen. Strike, Leah, and Jox sat at one end of the breakfast bar, looking tired and strung out. Lucius, Jade, Rabbit, and Myrinne were at the other end, deep in conversation, while Izzy, Shandi, and Tomas moved around the kitchen.

At the sound of Patience's and Brandt's footsteps, Strike's head came up and his cobalt eyes lit briefly. "Brandt. Thank the gods."

"Hold that thought. I don't have the magic yet."

The king's expression flattened, but he said only, "You're still better off than the other two."

Patience's stomach clutched. "Is Anna . . . ?"

"She's alive." Strike scrubbed both hands over his face, which did nothing to erase the strain etched in the deep lines beside his mouth and the dark circles beneath his eyes. "The neurosurgeons relieved the pressure and repaired what they could, but . . ." When he trailed off, Leah reached over and took his hand; their fingers interlaced, caught, and held. "If Sasha hadn't been there, I don't think she would've made it through surgery. She and Michael stayed behind to keep an eye on things." His lips twitched. "Rabbit did a little mind-bending on Anna's husband, retroactively intro-ing him to the family. He thinks he's known Sasha and me for years." The smile drained. "He was psyched to leave Sasha with waiting-room duty and bugger off."

"Dick." The word came from Lucius, and was both the man's name and a comment on his character.

Oh, Anna. Sometimes Patience had envied the other woman for having an outside life, a choice to make, and the guts to make it. Sometimes she had resented her for it. But she had never, even in the deepest depths of her blackest moods, wished for something like this. "The *etznab* spell helped me bring Brandt around. It might be worth trying on Anna."

Strike shook his head. "We can't do anything until she's medically stable. Magic can only go so far . . . at least within our tenets." His lips twisted in a bitter smile as he quoted from one of the codices Lucius had recently finished translating. "'A Nightkeeper shall not raise the dead, lest the barrier rift asunder.'"

Leah tightened her grip on him. "She's not going to die. Sasha's going to help her find her way back."

"Gods, I hope so." Strike nodded to Carlos as the stocky ex-wrangler *winikin* slid him a plate of scrambled eggs and toast. While the others dug into their breakfasts, he continued: "As for Mendez, Nate and Alexis found him unconscious in his flop. They're bringing him back now. There's still no sign of his *winikin*."

"So the Triad spell not only didn't give us any Triad magi—it hurt Anna and is forcing us to bring Mendez into the compound," Brandt said sourly. "If that was the will of the gods, then the gods are—"

"Sit your butt down and eat," Carlos interrupted, fixing Brandt with a look.

Brandt exhaled and sat. After a moment, Patience took her place beside him. The breakfast bar wasn't designed for so many people, which meant that the two of them had to sit very close together, bumping at hip and thigh.

Seeming unaware of the warmth that gathered at those points of contact, Brandt said, "After the firebird's ghost nailed me and the *nahwal* did its overlapping thing, I blacked out. When I woke up, I was eighteen years old, and I was trapped inside a crashed BMW with a busted leg, screaming my fucking head off as the car sank in Pine Bend River."

Patience frowned at him. "When I asked you about the scars on your leg, and why you limp when you're really tired, you said you were in an accident in college, that it was no big deal."

He didn't meet her eyes. "I might've downplayed it. Wasn't something I liked remembering."

Another lie, she thought. There had been so many of them back then, when they had both been playing human. "Go on."

"It was my freshman year at Dartmouth. Joe and I stayed with Dewey and his parents during winter break, because they were local and we could get back to campus from his house. Joe and Dewey were both on the football team and wanted to get in some extra workouts, play a little hockey, and I . . ." He paused. "I guess I just wasn't ready to go home yet. College was . . . different."

That part Patience got. She remembered the freedom of being on her own for a change, with no *winikin* telling her to be better, to try harder, that her parents had died saving the world.

Brandt continued: "Dewey's dad let us use his Beemer—it was sweet, borderline vintage, and could go like hell on the straightaways. Dewey was a good driver, though. The accident wasn't his fault. The bridge was fine when we went out, and it wasn't even that cold . . . but there was a slick spot at exactly the wrong place. The car spun out, went over the railing, and we ended up in the river. I must've blacked out for a minute, because I don't remember going over or hitting the water. Everything cut out after we hit the pylon. Anyway, I woke up alone, headed downstream in the Beemer, saw the other guys in the water and started yelling for help."

He described using the hockey stick to hit the horn,

then the ensuing race between his rescuers and the water level in the car while he fought to free himself, nearly ripping his leg off in the process. "I blacked out again, and the next thing I remember is waking up, lying near a boat landing. Alone." His voice was flat, his expression unreadable. "I was so fucking cold, and my leg hurt so bad, that I wanted to curl up right there and go to sleep. But I heard Wood's voice in my head, telling me to get my ass up, that I was too damned important to die like that. So I busted a branch off a piece of deadfall to use as a crutch, and hauled myself up to the road, where I flagged down a car and got help."

When he paused, Patience swallowed hard, trying to ease the tightness in her throat. "What about your friends?" she said, not letting herself ask the other questions that rattled around inside her. Questions like, *Why is this the first time I'm hearing this story?* And, *What else aren't you telling me?*

"Searchers found their bodies a quarter mile further downstream. The pathologist said they both drowned, but even after dredgers found the car and hauled it back up, nobody could tell me whether they died getting me out." He paused. "I think that's what happened, though. They died saving me. And that creates a debt." He spread his hands. "Woody had saved up to get me started after college, in grad school or whatever. We used the money to set up a scholarship instead, in their names. I talked to their parents, tried to apologize, but they wouldn't let me take the blame. They just kept saying it was just a terrible accident."

"Why . . ." Patience trailed off, not sure if it was the woman or the warrior asking, or if it mattered either way. This wasn't about the two of them, even if it felt that way to her.

"Why didn't I tell you the whole story before now?" He shook his head. "It just . . . I don't know. Until last night, it wasn't something I thought about, ever. Which, given the *nahwal*'s message, makes me wonder whether I'm supposed to remember something about the accident, instead."

Patience knew it was stupid to be hurt by the possibility that they might not need to remember the rest of their first night. "According to the *nahwal*, you need my help. If the Triad spell dropped you straight into the river vision, then that's not what you need to remember."

"Maybe, maybe not." Jade shot Patience a sympathetic look before she continued. "We don't know how the *nahwal* communicate with each other. We have to assume that they *do* communicate, given that Patience's *nahwal* relayed information from Brandt's, but if you think about it, there wasn't much time for them to confab. Maybe once Brandt's *nahwal* merged with him, his ancestors realized that they could help him access the river memory directly, without needing your help."

Brandt frowned. "But if my *nahwal* knew I couldn't use the Triad magic, then the gods should've known about it too. So why the hell did Kinich Ahau pick me?"

"For the same reason it picked me first," Rabbit said. He twirled a finger next to his ear, but his eyes were serious. "Maybe its brain—do gods have brains?—got screwed up while it was being held in that Xibalban pit. Maybe the *Banol Kax* implanted a mind-bend, programming it to screw us over when the opportunity presented."

"Damn it, Rabbit, that's—" Jox broke off, paused, then exhaled before finishing, "—not the dumbest thing you've ever said. Entirely sacrilegious, but not the dumbest. Shit."

As the others went back and forth trying to interpret Kinich Ahau's actions, Patience felt her magic flicker. It wasn't her warrior's talent, though; it was her other talent, that of invisibility, kicking into gear as the conversation flowed past her, making it seem that she didn't need to be there, that the others would all be fine without her.

You want to make me feel invisible? her magic seemed to say. *What if I just disappeared? What would you do then?*

But that was the sort of thing the old Patience would have thought and done—something self-pitying and pointless. So instead of sitting there and stewing, she broke into the debate and said bluntly, "No offense, but we have four days to make Brandt into a Triad mage. I think we should focus on that rather than quibbling over abstracts."

"Figuring out how I pissed off my own dead ancestors is pretty damned abstract," Brandt pointed out, but he nodded. "But you're right. We need to figure out what this debt is all about." His thigh pressed more firmly against hers as he shifted to face her. "I think should try the *etznab* spell again."

Her breath went thin, her blood heating with sensory memory and the mingled anticipation and unease that came with the thought of connecting with him again on that level. *We won't have to use the* jun tan *the next time*, she reminded herself. "We could also try visiting the actual places where the visions took place, and jacking in," she suggested.

"Good idea," Strike said. "Get me a satellite picture or something, and I'll 'port you two whenever you're ready."

Brandt turned away from her to say, "I'd rather go solo. It's not safe out there if Iago's awake and fully joined with Moctezuma's demon."

The flash of anger caught Patience by surprise. She was halfway off her stool before she was aware of moving, getting right in his face to snap, "It's not my job to stay safe. And whether you like it or not, we're still stronger together than apart—magically, at least." Suddenly becoming aware that she was on the verge of causing major a scene, where before she had been careful to keep things so private between them, she lowered her voice a notch. "I'm your partner. You can give me that much, damn it."

Their eyes locked. She sensed his anger, not through the *jun tan*, but in the set of his jaw and the tense lines of his body. She didn't back down, though. Not this time.

After a few heartbeats of standoff, he exhaled. "I'm not trying to be a dick here."

"I know." In a way, that made it all worse, because both of them kept trying to do what they thought was right, and it kept not meshing. "But you're not going to win on this one."

"Yeah." He smiled humorlessly. "I got that." But when he met her eyes, instead of the dark frustration she expected, she glimpsed a hint of gold. More, she saw *him*—the man, not the warrior—for just a second before the shields slammed back down.

Unexpectedly, energy sparked in the air between them.

Help him remember. The *nahwal*'s order echoed through her soul, and her pulse jumped as a new thought occurred. It was far too tempting to think that he was supposed to remember how to be her husband, her lover. She wasn't sure what that theory had to do with debts and ancestors, but it certainly jibed with how the magic worked. The closer their emotional ties, the stronger their magic.

What if he'd had it backward all along? What if they weren't supposed to table their marriage for the duration of the war? What if they were supposed to *fix* it instead?

Don't go there, she warned herself. They had tried too many times before to patch up their relationship. She was sick of trying, sick of failing. And there was no reason to think anything had changed, really.

Unless it had.

"Given what the *nahwal* said and the way the *etznab* spell seems to work, I want the two of you teaming up on every aspect of this. Find a way to make it work,"

Strike said in his "end of discussion, the jaguar king has spoken" voice.

Brandt faced front. "Like I said. I got it."

Patience sent him an edged look, but said to the king, "We'll do what needs to be done."

Strike didn't look totally satisfied by that answer, but he let it go and turned to Lucius. "Moving on. What have you got on the two gods the *nahwal* mentioned?"

Lucius had been frowning over something on his laptop. At the king's question, he looked up, blinking around at the group as though he'd forgotten they were there. "Kali and Cabrakan." He cleared his throat. "Right. The *nahwal* said that if—when—Brandt becomes the Triad mage, he'll be able to prevent Cabrakan from avenging his brother and finishing what Kali began. Which gives us two gods to work with. Starting with Kali, there's some debate on whether he—and this god is most definitely a 'he,' enormous schlong and all—is allied with the sky or Xibalba. Either way, he's the god of leadership. Nightkeeper leadership, in particular."

"That's why it sounded familiar," Strike said. "The Manikin scepter is carved in Kali's image, enormous schlong and all." The scepter, which resided in the barrier with the jaguar *nahwal*, was the symbol of his rulership. "Which I suppose makes us Kali's children, and means that Cabrakan is going to come after us." He paused. "So who or what is Cabrakan?"

"The lord of earthquakes."

"Shit," Brandt muttered. "Not good."

"Uh-oh," Patience whispered. Up until now, the *Banol Kax* had been able to send only relatively minor demons to test the barrier during the cardinal equinoxes and solstices. The earthquake lord, though, didn't sound like any minor demon.

Strike held up a hand to quell the rising buzz in the room. To Lucius, he said, "Go on."

"The ancients knew how to track the movement of the stars and predict basic weather patterns, which allowed them to make the proper sacrifices and feel like they were in relatively decent control of their environment. In contrast, earthquakes struck without warning, and could be absolutely devastating. Because of that, Cabrakan was one of the most feared of the *Banol Kax*. When an earthquake struck, the priests would hustle to throw together massive rituals of appeasement, in the hopes of mitigating the aftershocks."

"In other words," Brandt said, "this particular *Banol Kax* isn't something we want to fuck with."

Lucius nodded. "Problem is, we already have . . . and in doing so, we messed with the legends." He paused. "Cabrakan's brother is—or *was*—Zipacna."

Strike growled, "Son of a bitch."

Patience drew in a breath as the dots connected. Two years earlier, Strike and Leah had joined together with the creator god, Kulkulkan, to defeat the winged crocodile demon, Zipacna, in a fierce aerial battle. In the process, Zipacna's essence had been destroyed rather than being returned to Xibalba as part of the Great Cycle.

"According to the legends," Lucius continued,

"Zipacna was destined to make it through to the end-time war, when he and Cabrakan would fight the Hero Twins. The outcome of that particular battle was to be pivotal in determining whether the barrier falls completely, giving the *Banol Kax* total access to the earth plane. But now . . ." Lucius spread his hands. "We're off the map here, people."

Patience's heart clutched. "If Cabrakan is supposed to fight the Hero Twins . . ." She trailed off, unable to finish the thought.

The half-human deities starred in many of the old legends. In the stories, the young boys—one brave, the other studious—got themselves into and out of numerous adventures, eventually winning their ways through Xibalba itself in order to rescue their father, who had been captured by the *Banol Kax*.

Harry and Braden had never been bound to the barrier, and therefore couldn't be tracked by magical means, but the parallels had always unnerved Patience. Now they terrified her, especially given that the twins weren't babies anymore, not really. At five years old, if they had been growing up inside the old system, they would have their bloodline marks and be practicing their first small spells. *Gods.*

"Hannah and Woody won't let anything happen to them," Jox said. "They know how to stay out of sight. And how to raise good kids."

Patience smiled faintly at that. "Yeah. They do." She sobered. "But . . . I don't know. Every time the Hero Twins come up in conversation, my fight-or-flight response goes into overdrive."

"Mine too," Brandt said, surprising her. His expression was set and uncompromising, but for a change she found the steeliness comforting. "We won't let anything happen to them. Whatever it takes is what we'll do. Whatever they need from us is what they'll get." He met her eyes. "Even if it isn't what we really want."

It was the closest he'd come to talking about the boys being gone in a long time. It was also, she thought, an offer of a truce in Brandt-speak.

She slipped off her stool and held out a hand. "Come on. Let's see if the *etznab* spell can get us any further into either of the visions."

The most frustrating thing about the magic was its unpredictability. At first, the magi had ascribed the problem to lack of info and proper training, but the more they learned from the library, the more it seemed that the magic was a closer to an art form than a defined set of actions and reactions. Given the increasing volatility of the barrier, which was ramping up both light and dark powers in spurts, with lull periods between, the magic was rapidly becoming a crapshoot.

Rabbit's mind-bending talent, which had faded to almost nonexistent for a while, had rebounded in the past few months, while Lucius had lost his onetime ability to form barrier conduits. Which meant there were no guarantees when it came to the mirror spell.

Still, when Brandt took her hand, the contact brought a kick of anticipation.

"If the mirror pot doesn't work this time, don't be

afraid to try the cards again," Lucius put in. When Strike shot him a "what the hell?" look, the human held up his hands. "Don't hate the messenger. She said she needed a spell that involved a mirror, and 'abracadabra' or *'et voilà'* or whatever, I put paws on the spell she needed. That's not a coincidence."

"It was—" *just a hunch,* Patience started to say, but broke off because it had been more than that.

"Look at it this way," Jade put in. "The magi have always adapted themselves, and their powers, to their local environment. When they lived in Egypt, they worshipped cats and crocodiles. With the Maya, it was maize and chocolate. The core beliefs were the same: The astrology, the pyramids, the sun worship, and the hieroglyphic writing, those pieces of the religion were all there. But the trappings changed. Maybe something similar is happening here."

Brandt frowned. "So you're thinking—what?—that the Mayan Oracle is a divination ritual that leaked to the human world somehow?"

"Actually, I'm thinking the reverse: that it's a fully human invention that resonates with Nightkeeper power, or at least with Patience's power." Jade paused. "There were *itza'at*s in her bloodline, you know."

Strike's head came up; his eyes narrowed on Patience. "Really?"

Patience's pulse tapped a quick, syncopated rhythm at the thought of being able to see into the future, but not change anything she saw. "I wouldn't know. I'm not big on genealogy."

In fact, she hadn't learned more than the basics

about her parents and bloodline. As far as she was concerned, Hannah was her mother, and Brandt and the boys were her family. It wasn't that she resented her parents for dying, or anything complicated like that. She just didn't feel much of a connection to the prior generation of Nightkeepers.

Or rather, she hadn't until the day before. Now she realized that, without her even really being aware of it, she had been subconsciously digesting her interaction with the *nahwal*, replaying the message and that moment when she had seen a spark of life within the creature . . . and thinking about where—or *who*—it had come from. Her mother might be in the *nahwal's* collective consciousness; her father definitely was. Her uncles, grandfather, great-grandfather . . . an entire patriarchal iguana lineage were represented within the creature. And, apparently, an *itza'at* or two.

Strike nodded slowly. "All right. Use the cards. But do what you did with the mirror spell, and get some sort of independent confirmation before acting on what they tell you."

"They won't 'tell' me anything," she said with some asperity. "They're just a tool, a way to—" She broke off as magic rippled along her skin and the background power sink that surrounded Skywatch decreased sharply and then kicked back up over the span of a heartbeat. "What was that?"

Brandt put himself between her and the front door. "Something just came through the wards." Moments later, a shrill alarm blatted three short blasts to warn that someone had keyed in the combo to get through the front gate of the compound. Which meant it was one of them.

Strike uncoiled from his stool, but nobody else moved. They all held their places as the front door swung open and Nate's voice became audible, saying, "—fucking deadweight. Thought the pilot was going to shit himself when we showed up. Lucky for us he knows Jox, and will do just about anything for a bonus."

Heavy footsteps sounded in the short hallway that ran past the dining room turned war chamber, and then the small group came into sight. Alexis led the way, schlepping a battered black duffel bag. Behind her, Nate and Sven carried a folding stretcher between them. On it lay an unconscious man who was immobilized beneath a cocoonlike layer of cargo straps that might have seemed overkill if it hadn't been for the sheer size of the guy, who was huge even by Nightkeeper standards. His head wore the stubble of a week-old skull trim, and his features were wide and strong, with a prominent beak of a nose that made Patience think of ancient carvings, Mayan kings and gods.

Even in repose, he emanated an aura of power on both the physical and psi levels, one that seemed to announce, *Here I am. What are you going to do about it?*

Seeing that most of Skywatch was standing there, gaping, Nate stopped and raised a sardonic brow in the king's direction. "Guest suite or basement?"

Strike didn't hesitate. "Basement. Do not pass go. Do not collect two hundred." What the lower-level storerooms lacked in amenities, they made up for with the absence of windows and the presence of heavy doors that could be securely locked with dead bolts and magic.

Nate nodded. "No argument coming from me."

As the two men hauled their deadweight cargo in the direction of the stairs leading down, Sven called back, "This guy gives off a major 'don't fuck with me' vibe even when he's barely breathing. You think that's the Triad magic?"

"Nope." Strike shook his head. "That's one hundred percent Mendez. Be warned. And for fuck's sake, don't turn your back on him."

CHAPTER SEVEN

December 18
Three days until the solstice-eclipse
Skywatch

For Patience, the thirty or so hours after Brandt re-awakened passed in a blur of fruitless *etznab* magic, failed hypnosis, and an uncomfortable trip to New Hampshire, where visits with the dead boys' families and a trip to the scene of the long-ago accident succeeded only in turning Brandt's mood dark.

Mendez and Anna were both still deeply comatose, and there was still no sign of Mendez's *winikin*. Fortunately, there hadn't been any sign of Iago either. Lucius speculated that the Xibalban would be physically weak after his long period of stasis, so was probably recuperating. Even given the accelerated healing of a demon-human hybrid *makol*, he might be out of action through the solstice, gods willing. With the time ticking down, Rabbit and Myrinne were down in the Yucatán, trying to open the passageway beneath the El Rey pyramid, but so far that was a no-go. Which left the Nightkeepers with three days until the solstice and no idea how they were supposed to stop the earthquake demon.

Worse, earth tremors had hit Albuquerque and northern Honduras almost simultaneously the prior evening. They'd been below four on the Richter scale, but left little doubt that Cabrakan was stirring.

The threat permeated Skywatch, making the air tense and tight, and driving Patience outside in search of some fresh air . . . and some privacy.

Even though Strike had asked her to see if the cards could provide another clue like they had with the mirror spell, she hadn't been able to bring herself to start laying spreads in the kitchen or great room, or even in the suite where Brandt was brooding. Or maybe—probably—it was *because* she was under orders that she couldn't settle to the task. There was pressure now. Expectations.

She had been planning to hunker down in a corner of the training hall, where she'd put in hundreds of hours drilling the others on hand-to-hand and evasive maneuvers. But as she pushed through the glass doors at the back of the great room and started across the pool deck, her eyes lit on the pool house that stood off to one side.

The small building—just a single room with a tiny attached bathroom—had been Strike's chosen quarters when they had all first gathered at Skywatch. Once he moved into the royal suite with Leah, the pool house had become one of the twins' favorite hangouts, a grown-up-sized playhouse of their very own.

They hadn't been allowed there unsupervised, of course, not with the pool right there. But Hannah had brought them there often, as had Patience. Best of all—at least as far as the twins had been concerned— was when they had been able to persuade Rabbit to bring them to the pool house, shut the door . . . and tell them the Hero Twin stories.

Back then, Patience hadn't been able to figure out what made Rabbit's stories so cool for Harry and Braden; they were more or less the same legends she and Hannah told. Now she wondered if Rabbit's nascent mind-bending ability had been starting to break through even that early on, allowing him to paint word pictures in the boys' minds.

Regardless, as she pushed through the door into the pool house, she was hit with a vivid memory of one particular night when she'd peeked in to check on her boys, and found them there with their "uncle Rabbit."

They had dragged cushions off the daybed and sat on the woven rug-covered floor, with lit candles providing sufficiently creepy flickering light. Harry had been neatly cross-legged, his hands folded in his lap, his eyes locked on Rabbit, his only movement that of one thumb tapping atop the other in the perpetual motion of a three-year-old boy. Braden had been sprawled on his belly nearby, toes drumming, face rapt.

Rabbit had looked so much younger than he did now, lean and rangy with only his bloodline and fire-talent marks on his forearm; he hadn't worn the hell-mark back then and hadn't yet grown into himself. But the same wild intensity had burned in his gray-blue eyes as he shaped the air with his hands and described how the twins, Xblanque and Hun Hunapu, had gotten trapped in Xibalba while searching for their father, and hid from the *Banol Kax* by making themselves very small and hiding inside Hunapu's blowpipe.

That's right, Patience thought now. *They can't see you if you make yourself disappear.*

Slowly the image faded, leaving her alone in the pool house. Everything was clean and neat, but the air smelled sterile and unloved, like she was in a guest room rather than an integral part of the compound. Which she supposed was true now. The magi had more important things to do these days than hang out by the pool.

The room looked the same: The daybed was there with the same pillows and throw, and the same woven rug covered the floor. The half-open bathroom door revealed a large mirror, fresh towels, and a loaded soap dish. Another mirror hung in the main room, this one full-length and showing her wide-eyed reflection. Logic said the big mirror was a hold-over from when the little playhouse had functioned as a changing area, but still . . . *There's no such thing as coincidence; it's all just the will of the gods.*

"Okay." She blew out a breath. "I get it."

She closed the door and crossed to the daybed, where she sat cross-legged with the pillows at her back. She didn't let herself dwell on the knowledge that Harry and Braden had napped on those pillows and wrestled on that bed. Still, the knowledge warmed her with a gentle ache of sorrow. She opened herself to the emotions, knowing that it was all too easy to block the flow of magic, and that foretelling was one of the most fickle talents of all.

She fanned the large purple-backed deck, and set the accompanying book off to the side, in case she wanted to check herself on anything. She had memorized the major connections for each glyph card, but there were also subtler associations listed for each: symbols, numbers, flowers, scents, stones, and elements. In addition, each glyph had a shadow aspect, a darker set of foretellings. She would need the book for those readings.

Figuring more magic was better than less, she used her ceremonial knife to nick her palm, and murmured, *"Pasaj och."*

The power link with the barrier formed instantly; the magic skimming across her skin was far stronger than it had been even three months earlier, during the autumnal equinox. Things were changing so fast, and they were still two years out from the end time. What would the world look like in a year? Two years? Three? *Gods help us get this right so Harry and Braden will have a world to grow up in.*

Feeling the power wrap around her, warming her and making her yearn—for her sons, for the future—she whispered, "How can I help Brandt become a Triad mage?" Then she selected three cards from the fan, held them for a moment, then laid them side by side in front of her.

There were numerous types of spread, ranging from the single-card quick-and-dirty reading she had done when she pulled the *etznab* cards, to a full array of stars, lenses, and oracles, placed in intricate patterns of meaning. For this reading, she had chosen a simple three-card line called the "tree of choice." Trees were sacred; their roots tapped the underworld, their trunks lived in the realm of mankind, and their canopies touched the sky and protected the villages. In the oracle spread, the three cards represented, in order from right to left, the root of the problem implied by her question; the core—and potentially flawed—beliefs surrounding the problem; and the branches through which the answer could be achieved.

At least that was the theory.

Taking a deep breath, she flipped the first card. On it, four parallel yellow curves crossed a maroon square that was outlined in black. Behind the square rose a yellow, rayed sun. "Imix," she said, pronouncing it "ee-meesh" in the ancient tongue. The Divine Mother card, it symbolized trust, nourishment, maternal support, and receptivity.

Her stomach flutter-hopped, because she pulled Imix almost every time she did a reading for herself. It was her totem card.

But pulling the card now made her grimace with twisted amusement. "Great. *I'm* the root of the problem."

She couldn't sustain the self-directed humor, though, because that seemed all too likely. Brandt had tried to get her to back off the family stuff and focus on her magecraft, but she hadn't been able to make that switch. Loving him and the twins wasn't something she could step away from, and it pissed her off that he'd done it so seamlessly. If they needed to work together to regain his lost memories, then it was certainly possible that her negative emotions could be blocking things.

Taking a deep breath, she reached for the book. Flipping through the worn pages, she found Imix, and read down its associations. Most of them didn't seem related to the issue at hand, but one pinged: Imix was connected to the earth element, and they were racing to counter the earthquake demon. It wasn't exactly a neon sign, but it was something.

Then again, in the outside world she'd been a champion at reading deep meanings in her fortune cookie fortunes.

Moving on, she skimmed over the light aspects of Imix, which she knew by heart. The card was a call for her to look below the surface of her life, to give and receive love. She was *trying* to do that, damn it.

She paused, though, when she got to the first line of the next section.

"'The shadow aspects of Imix are issues of trust and survival, feelings of being unsupported or unworthy, and the need for outside validation,'" she read aloud, feeling a tingle run through her body. Except for the validation part, that described the person she'd been during her depression, and the temptations she still had to fight against.

The reading seemed to say that her thought processes were at the root of the problem. Which sucked. But at least that was something she might be able to fix. "Okay, fine. Be that way. So what's the core belief I need to use or get past in order to move forward?"

Not letting herself hesitate, she flipped the second card. It showed a royal blue square in the middle, with yellow circles at each corner. In the center of the blue square, a diamond-shaped cutout showed a starscape beyond. Behind all of that was the same yellow sun as on the first card. The continuity of pulling two sun cards in a row seemed to point at the involvement of Kinich Ahau, which played. This particular card, though, wasn't familiar. She didn't think she'd ever drawn it before.

She read the single word at the bottom: "Lamat." A quick search through the book revealed that Lamat was the card of the One Who Shows the Way. Okay, then, it symbolized leadership. She didn't think it referred to Strike, though. She didn't see how the king could be at the core of Brandt's inability to become a Triad mage.

Moving on to the light aspects, she read: "'Lamat indicates harmony, clear perspectives, and the creation of beneficial combinations.' Meh." She shrugged and moved on. "'The shadow aspects of Lamat are disconnection and the belief that there is only one right way, one exclusive system that can bring harmony.'" That resonated. More, when she added it to the concept of leadership, she came up with the distant, rigid, system-based former architect who had been prophesied to lead the magi against Cabrakan. *Brandt.*

Unfortunately, identifying Brandt as the core of the problem wasn't news either. Disappointment gathered as she skimmed through the rest of the information, finding little of note except for the animal and elemental associations of Lamat: the rabbit, and fire. That suggested that Rabbit was involved with the core issue, or maybe its solution. But beyond that, she wasn't seeing anything nearly as concrete as the mirror card had been, in terms of giving her a clue of what she was supposed to do next.

"Have faith," she murmured. And she flipped the third card.

The image was unfamiliar, and very different from the first two, done in a watery blue green, with white accents, showing none of the yellows and blacks that were on the other cards. It was a moon card, with a white disk in the background. In the foreground was an arrangement of lines and shapes, just as on the others. But on this one, the combination of downward-arching lines at the upper corners and a circular pattern at the lower center combined to form the image of an angry, scowling face with a strange twinkle in its eyes.

"Chuen." She flipped to the proper page in the book, and frowned when nothing connected. Chuen was the Monkey Trickster. Its light aspects were celebration, innocence, joy, and laughter; its shadow aspects were the destruction of old, useless patterns, the upending of known life, and the creation of a new one. Disappointment kicked. Frivolity sure as hell wasn't going to connect Brandt with the Triad magic, and she didn't see how mixing things up would help either. "Come *on*. Give me something to work with here!"

Frustrated, she paged to the front of the book, where it described the spreads. Maybe she had missed something, or made a mistake.

But when she figured out what she'd done, she just stared for a long moment. "Oh. Oh, gods." This wasn't good.

The tree-of-choice array was supposed to be laid out in a line from top to bottom, canopy to roots. She had laid her cards from left to right, which wasn't the tree-of-choice spread. It was the past-present-future spread, which had nothing to do with the question she'd asked, and had everything to do with the person who had pulled the cards—namely, *her*.

The Divine Mother was her past.

The rigid, rule-following leader was her present, and he had put her world in disharmony. Brandt.

And her future was chaos and upheaval . . . leading to a new life.

She didn't want a new life, she thought on a surge of pure self-pity. She wanted her *old* life back, damn it. She wanted to be a wife and mother first, with everything else coming after that. She wanted to be back in the pretty kitchen of the Pittsburgh house, with Brandt snoozing in their shared bedroom, the boys napping down the hall. Or, rather, with Harry napping and Braden planning world domination, toddler-style. She wanted to know that if she headed into the bedroom, her sleepy-eyed husband would snag her hand and pull her back into bed with him.

But that life was already gone, wasn't it? She wasn't just a wife and a mother anymore; she was a warrior. And even if the magi won the war and everything went back to so-called "normal," she wouldn't ever get her old life back. On some level she knew that. But that didn't mean she wanted to think about what her new life was going to be like.

"Did the oracle work?"

She jolted at the sound of Brandt's voice, the sight of him filling the pool house doorway. "Oh! I didn't hear you come in."

He wore black cargo pants and a black tee with square-toed boots. The outfit was almost, but not quite, combat gear, suggesting that it was time for their next and almost last option. Her heart thumped, but with an aching wistfulness rather than surprise. When he raised an eyebrow, she realized she hadn't answered his question about the oracle.

"No. It didn't give me anything."

He got points for not even hinting at an "I told you so." Or maybe her success with the *etznab* spell had made an impression. Instead of commenting on the cards at all, he said, "Strike's ready to 'port us down to El Rey. He'll leave us there to poke around for as long as we need." He paused. "Jox suggested we should try getting a room at the same hotel or one like it. We could spend the night and see if it jogs some memories."

"That makes sense." It also made her want to weep. Instead, she carefully gathered her cards, stacked them atop the book, and cradled the small pile against her as she unfolded herself from the daybed. She didn't look back at the pillows or the memories they brought.

She did, however, catch sight of herself in the big mirror beside the door. And for a second, she didn't recognize the person staring back at her.

The Patience who had come to Skywatch with her sons and been shocked to find her husband there already—instead of on the business trip he'd claimed— had looked younger than her twenty-three years, soft-faced and bouncy despite her fighting credentials and Nightkeeper upbringing. The woman in the mirror had lost the softness and gained an edge that said she wasn't just trained to fight; she had fought for real and emerged, if not victorious, then at least alive.

On some level, though, "alive" was about all she could claim. She wore jeans and a practical shirt, sturdy shoes, and a ponytail. And all she wanted to do was get through the next solstice, the next year, the next two years, and hope that tomorrow would be better than today.

Gods. Was that the person she had become?

"Patience? You okay?"

There was honest concern in Brandt's eyes, but

that was it. Chest gone suddenly hollow, she nodded. "Yeah. Let's go."

She headed for the door, but instead of giving way, he caught her hand. And pulled her into his arms.

As she stiffened in shock and fought the too-tempting urge to burrow into him, he wrapped himself around her, enfolding her within the curve of his body and the strength of his arms. He splayed his hands, one spanning her waist, the other buried in her hair, holding her face tucked into the hollow between his neck and shoulder, with her lips almost touching the sensitive spot at the base of his throat.

She tried to pull away, but he held her fast, not squeezing too hard, but not letting her go either. "Hush," he whispered into her hair, though neither of them had made a noise. "Just give me a moment here, and take one for yourself."

If she fought, he would let her go, she knew. And she *should* fight. She should yank away and tell him that it wasn't fair for him to reach for her now, when he'd pushed her away so many other times before. She should tell him to make a godsdamned choice, that he either wanted her or he didn't, that she couldn't handle seeing desire in him one moment, distance the next.

She should tell him that she would be his partner in whatever way he needed her in order to gain the Triad magic, but only because it was her duty, that if it were up to her, she would walk away, not look back, because he was the root of her problem, not the branches of its answer.

Instead, she burrowed in. And for a minute, she let herself hang on tight.

Chiapas Mountain Highlands
Mexico

Rabbit whooped and grabbed the holy-shit strap as Cheech—his and Myrinne's driver-slash-guide, who was in his midteens and drove like a death bat out of hell—gunned the battered Land Rover over a mogul-sized bump and caught some air. The dirt track flattened out on the other side, and Cheech revved along the one-laner, which was barely holding its own against the fuzzy undergrowth and the vines that hung down from the overarching trees.

In the cramped backseat, Myrinne cheered.

They flashed past scatterings of goats and pigs being herded among ancient stone stelae by little kids wearing everything from T-shirts and hip-hanging denim cutoffs to hand-loomed textiles in a dizzying array of bright colors and loud patterns. When they turned a corner and Cheech eased up on the gas, so they rolled past a cluster of homes at slightly under warp speed, Rabbit saw the same juxtaposition of modern and traditional materials, with some of the round pole buildings capped with *huano* thatch made of palm fronds and grass, others roofed in tin.

"Upgrades?" he said, nodding to the metal roofing.

"Nonoptional," Myrinne corrected. "The contractors building the so-called 'green' resorts have clear-cut so much of the native vegetation that several of the major palm species have wound up federally protected."

"Thank you, *Fodor's Guide to Mayan Villages*," he intoned, but grinned at her from the front, where he rode shotgun.

"It's called 'Google' and 'getting the lay of the land.' You should try it sometime." She smiled sweetly, but her dark brown eyes sparkled in challenge.

Her dark hair was slicked back in a twist that left her neck and shoulders bare above a skimpy tube top, though the goods were modestly covered—sort of—with a filmy white button-down that she'd tucked into a pair of low-riding cutoffs. They had started out as jeans, but she had scissored and frayed them midthigh when she and Rabbit had wound up staying down south a couple of days longer than originally planned. For today's adventure, she had skipped her sexy woven sandals in favor of lace-up boots more suitable to bumming around the mountains, but even though Rabbit couldn't see it, he knew she was wearing the ruby red toe ring he'd bought her the other day.

And, as always, she wore the promise ring he'd given her the year before. He got a hard charge out of that, one that was admittedly harder because of all the looks she'd been getting on their little working vacation. He knew it made him a "guy"—in his head he heard the word in her voice, with a sneer—but seeing the way other men looked at her, and knowing she was with him, heart and soul . . . that mattered.

"Gods, you're hot." So hot, in fact, that he was starting to sweat in the lightweight long-sleeve shirt he'd worn to hide his forearm marks. He hadn't exactly forgotten how flat-out gorgeous she was, but when they were at Skywatch, it was easy to lose track of how much exponentially hotter she was than most everyone else in the universe. Any second now and he'd be drooling.

Her teeth flashed, but she raised an eyebrow and shifted her eyes in Cheech's direction, as the Rover cleared the little village and the pedal hit the metal once again. "Going polytheistic on me?" In other words: *Watch yourself. We're supposed to be normal gringos.*

He covered the wince with a chuckle. "More like going native. This place feels . . . familiar. Like I wouldn't mind staying for a while."

That earned him a tolerant-seeming "stupid-ass tourist" look from Cheech, but it was the gods' honest truth.

Rabbit had been to dozens of centuries-old ruin sites, ranging from tourist traps to magic-shielded Nightkeeper temples, but although he'd gotten power buzzes from plenty of the sacred sites, he'd never stepped into one and thought, *I know this place. I belong here.* Yet ever since they'd told Strike a couple of half-truths and set out from Cancún for San Cristóbal, and from there up into the mountains, that sensation had been growing steadily.

It was like he could *breathe* up here in the mountains.

Like things made sense. He'd barely needed the directions they'd gotten in San Cristóbal to reach the foothill village, not just because the road system thinned out to few options, but because he'd instinctively known where to go.

The same thing had happened in the village itself. He'd parked the rental, ensured its safety with a couple of bribes and some low-grade mind-bending, and then led Myrinne out into the strange mix of old stone and bright cloth like his feet knew where they were going, even if he didn't.

Myrinne had gawked and lost herself in the first market they had come across. She had haggled delightedly over a brightly patterned scarf and a pair of rope-and-leather sandals, using a stumbling mix of the Spanish she'd picked up quickly at UT and the old-school Mayan trading language she'd absorbed at Skywatch, which bore zero resemblance to the modern dialects. Most of the locals had understood the Spanish far better than the other, but Rabbit had stood back and paid attention, picking out three men and one woman who had all gopher-popped their heads when they heard the ancient words.

A quick sift of their minds—very low-level, tight-beam magic he didn't think Iago could sense—had revealed that two of them had studied the trading language as part of the new revival movement. The other two, both men, recognized a few of the words from a dialect spoken high up in the mountains, in a small hamlet called Oc Ajal.

It wasn't exactly the "Ox Ajal" Jox had remembered

Red-Boar mentioning as the name of the village where he'd stayed around the time of Rabbit's birth, but it was damned close. More, some discreet questions revealed that there were rumors of dark magic connected with Oc Ajal. Which made sense if Rabbit—half Xibalban, half Nightkeeper—had been conceived there.

It might've seemed like a terminally stupid idea for him and Myrinne to travel alone to a remote village that could be enemy territory. But although Rabbit's old man might've been a PTSD-zonked asshole, he'd been a company man. He wouldn't have visited the place—or left it standing—if it had been dangerous or against the tenets of the Nightkeepers.

And besides, Rabbit had already mentioned Oc Ajal to Strike—not in relation to Red-Boar, but because of the potential connection between the Triad magic and the village's name, which meant "thrice manifested." He'd even passed along the rumors that the villagers worshipped Xibalba.

Strike had filed the info with a "thanks, we'll put it on the to-do list," and Rabbit had figured his ass was covered. He and Myrinne were just going to look around, anyway. If there was anything doing up at Oc Ajal, they had promised each other they would call for backup, pronto.

Of the two men who had known of the village, one had been far too interested in Myrinne. The other had been Cheech, who had been perfectly happy to overcharge a couple of gringos to take them up to Oc Ajal and play translator.

Rabbit had stuck pretty close to the truth, saying

that his father had recently died, and in going through his things they had discovered notes suggesting that he might have family up in Oc Ajal. Technically, Red-Boar hadn't kept any souvenirs of that period of his life, unless Rabbit counted himself. But the rest was pretty accurate. And it had a fist of nerves riding low in his gut, tightening with every passing mile.

"Hey." Myrinne leaned forward against her seat belt to give his arm a reassuring squeeze. "Don't freak. Whatever happens next is out of our hands. We've just got to let it play out, you know?"

He took a deep breath that did zilch to quell his urge to have Cheech pull over so he could barf in the undergrowth. "Yeah. Thanks."

Cheech had been following the exchange but staying discreetly silent. Rabbit knew it was intentional because he'd kept a light link with the kid, so he could pick up big thoughts and emotions but not details, and hopefully get some warning if their driver—or his friends—were planning to roll the gringos for their wallets. So far, so good, though. There was no hint of duplicity as Cheech said, "We will reach the village soon, in five or ten minutes." His English was schoolroom-perfect and a little stilted, but it was still way better than Rabbit could do in anything other than English. He knew a few dozen spell words by heart, and that was about it.

"Thanks." Rabbit glanced at Myrinne, and took a deep breath. "Well, here goes nothing."

"I've got your back."

"That's one of the few things I've never doubted."

The backup was way more than figurative too; her shoulder bag held a pair of lightweight nine-millimeter ACPs loaded with jade-tipped bullets, along with spare clips. One of the many benefits of 'porting over the border rather than flying was the ease of getting arms down south. Granted, it meant they would have to 'port back, because customs tended to get pissy when U.S. citizens tried to reenter the country without there being any evidence of them having ever left. But he and Myrinne both had their satellite phones and panic buttons, so they were covered there too.

He'd done his best to think things through and be smart about this. Now, like she said, they would just have to let things play out.

A few minutes later, Cheech eased up on the gas as they came to a bend in the narrow dirt track, then braked to coast into a wide, tree-flanked circle of packed dirt where the road dead-ended. Two seventies-era F-150s and a VW Bug—the old kind—were parked in a neat row. Cheech added the Rover onto the end.

When he cut the engine, the world seemed to go preternaturally silent for a few seconds. Then there was a series of birdcalls—not the parrot screeches typical of the lowland rain forests, but rather the high, challenging cries of raptors: hawks, maybe, or even eagles.

The sound shivered along Rabbit's skin, kindling his blood and touching his warrior's talent. His surroundings snapped into clearer focus as his senses expanded.

He could feel Myrinne's nervous optimism on his

behalf, Cheech's idle musing on whether he could soak his passengers for a second fee to drive them back down to the market village . . . and in the near distance, a few dozen people he perceived as pinpoint glows of consciousness.

To his surprise, he didn't feel the hum of energy that would indicate the proximity of a power sink, whether natural or man-made. Both dark and light magi tended to live near power sinks; Skywatch itself was built near the remains of a Chacoan pueblo, and Iago's hideouts had gravitated to well-hidden ruins and modern sacred sites. Oc Ajal, though, didn't seem to follow the pattern.

Which meant . . . hell, he didn't know what it meant. Maybe nothing. Maybe everything.

"I take it we're hiking in from here?" he asked Cheech.

"Yes. These people are very traditional, very spiritual. They don't want cars disturbing their earth connection." The driver hopped out, then paused and turned back. "No cameras either."

Myrinne slung her bag over her shoulder and held up both hands. "No problem. We're not here to take pictures."

Rabbit was ready to step in with a mind-bend if the convo turned to weapons, but Cheech's thought process didn't go there. He just gave a "come on, then" wave and started heading up one of three trails that led away from the parking area. Myrinne glanced at Rabbit, who nodded to indicate that their guide was on the level. As they fell into step on the pathway, she whispered, "You getting any buzz?"

"Not really."

She took his hand, threading their fingers together and squeezing, so he could feel the hard bump of the ring he'd given her.

They hiked uphill through the trees for five minutes or so, picking their way over rocks and roots. Although the mountain trees were much lower growing than their giant rain forest cousins, their leafy branches wove together overhead, and the under- and middle growth was thick, giving the hikers little hint as to what was up ahead . . . until they reached two high stone columns that were topped by a crude archway held in place by a lintel stone.

The construction wasn't up to the ancients' standards and didn't resonate with power on the dark or light level, but it definitely marked a boundary.

Cheech paused to let Rabbit and Myrinne catch up. Then he waved them through the archway. "Oc Ajal."

Rabbit took a deep breath. Then, tightening his grip on Myrinne's hand, he stepped through.

He was braced for almost anything. What he got was a village that looked pretty much like the others they had driven through on the way up, with the exception that the pole buildings were made entirely of natural materials, with no tin or fiberglass. The villagers weren't total purists, though: Two denim-wearing kids and a couple of skinny mutts wrestled over possession of a dingy volleyball off on one side, and although the four women clustered near a central fire pit were hand-grinding maize on traditional millstones, they were dumping the resulting cornmeal into brightly colored plastic bowls.

As he and Myrinne stepped through the archway with Cheech right behind them, the women looked up, their eyes bright and interested.

All too young to be her, Rabbit found himself thinking, even though he'd tried to talk himself out of expecting too much. He just wanted some info on the other side of his bloodlines . . . and to check out Myrinne's theory that the only way his old man would've slept with a Xibalban and schlepped along the resulting bastard child was if that Xibalban had been part of a sect separate from Iago's red-robed sociopaths.

But although he'd told himself not to have any expectations, he went a little hollow when their only reaction was for one of the women to call what he assumed was the equivalent of "Got company!" to someone inside a nearby building. Then the women went back to grinding, while the kids and the dogs— which were barking now, belatedly warning of the intrusion—headed around the back of the hut circle and disappeared.

So much for the return of the prodigal whatever.

Fuck it. Forcing himself to focus on the here and now, he leaned closer to Myrinne. "Why didn't they hear us?" he said in an undertone, though what he really meant was, *Why didn't they sense me?* He could've sent the thought straight into her mind through the touch link of their handclasp, but she didn't like him inside her head. As she put it, there had to be *some* boundaries between them. So he whispered, and kept it general, trusting her to translate his real meaning.

"Can you 'hear' them?"

He shook his head. No. He hadn't sensed any magic—light or dark—on the way up the path, and he didn't sense any now. "Maybe Jox remembered wrong, or my old man lied to him about the name of the village."

But that didn't totally play either, given the rumors about dark magic in the village, and the way Cheech and the other guy down in the market had connected the trading language with Oc Ajal, even before Rabbit asked about the village by name.

What was more, he realized with a click of connection, the whole place was arranged around powerful numbers and symbols.

There were two rows of thirteen huts each, arranged in a three-quarters circle around a central fire pit, with the archway centered in the gap. Seven flattened millstones surrounded the fire pit. And he'd bet a minor body part that the spiral designs incised, row after row, into the poles that made up each building would, if he counted them, add up to plays on 13, 20, 52, 260, and various other numbers that had been central to the ancient calendars.

More, with the central fire pit surrounded by concentric circles of millstones, huts, and then trees, the village's whole layout symbolized the entrance to Xibalba, which was located in the dark spot at the center of the Milky Way galaxy.

The symbols didn't prove anything, though, he reminded himself. Plenty of modern Maya were spiritual without being magic users. And the villagers they had seen so far looked indigenous. Given that the Order of Xibalba had been a splinter sect of the original Nightkeepers, the descendants of the order should have retained the size, coloring, and charisma of the magi. Iago sure had.

Which meant . . . hell, he didn't know. And he didn't know what he was hoping for, just that he was hoping for *something*.

As if in response to that thought—or, more likely, the woman's call—a man emerged from the building directly opposite the archway, and started toward the visitors. He was wizened and white-haired, though given the living conditions, Rabbit couldn't guess his age any more accurately than "somewhere over fifty."

The elder wore battered jeans and a patterned serape; his eyes were bright, his mouth nearly toothless as he flashed a smile and said, *"Oola."*

It was a standard greeting that had been adapted from the Spanish *hola* because many Mayan languages lacked the typical "Hello, how are you?" pleasantries of other cultures.

Rabbit sensed other people nearby, some in the pole buildings, others in the forest beyond. None seemed threatening; if anything, they seemed unusually mellow, without the spiky discord he usually felt from at least a few people in any given group.

Cheech stepped up and returned the greeting, followed by a spate of words that seemed to be a patois combining the most common modern Mayan dialect, Yucatec, along with equal parts Spanish and the ancient trading language.

Rabbit caught the semiderogatory Yucatec term for American tourists, which literally translated to "white odors," followed by the ancient honorific for "mother" and the word for "rabbit," which in Yucatec sounded like "tool." He didn't let on that he'd caught that much, though. He just stood there with his senses wide-open, waiting for a ripple in the barrier's energy—something, anything, that would indicate they were in the right place.

He got fucking nothing.

"This is the leader of Oc Ajal," Cheech said formally. "His name is Saamal."

Tomorrow, Rabbit thought, translating the name, which itself was a powerful spell word. Still, that didn't prove anything. Symbols and words weren't the same as magic.

"Is he willing to talk to me about my   " Rabbit stumbled over the word "mother," and wound up going with, "About what my father's note said?"

"I told him what you told me. He will answer your questions."

Rabbit wasn't sure if it was Cheech's English or Saamal's answer that made that one feel off, but he kept going, speaking directly to the elder while Cheech translated. "The note my father left said he met my mother while staying here in Oc Ajal, twenty-two years ago. He would have been my age when he came here. He looked like me, but with darker eyes and a sad soul." Which he figured was better than saying "off his fucking rocker over his dead wife and kids."

When the translation ran down and Saamal didn't say anything, Myrinne nudged him. "He said he'd answer your questions. I'm guessing he meant that literally."

Oh, for fuck's—"Fine. Do you remember my father?" Rabbit unbuttoned his right sleeve and flipped the cuff, baring his forearm. "He had marks like these, only all black. He wore the peccary, the warrior, and the *jun tan*." He watched the elder, but the guy didn't show any outer—or inner—sign of recognizing the marks.

He did, however, nod and answer in a few words. Cheech translated: "Yes, I remember your father." For a second, Rabbit thought he was going to have to pull the info twenty-questions-style, but then Saamal continued, and Cheech fell into rhythm, echoing a few words behind the elder. "He only stayed a few days, though, and he was alone. He was lost." Cheech paused. "Not wandering lost, but lost in his head. You understand the difference?"

"Yeah. Trust me, I get it." Rabbit exhaled through his nose. "Do you know where he went when he left here?"

Saamal shook his head. *"Ma."* Cheech didn't bother translating the obvious negative.

"Not even what direction? Uphill? Downhill? Anything?" Rabbit did his best to keep the frustration out of his voice; Jox had dinged him often enough for whining, and Saamal reminded him of the royal *wini-*

kin. Impatience flared inside Rabbit, though, bumping up against power, anger, and all the other things he'd learned to control. More or less.

"He left in the night," Cheech translated. "We didn't see him go."

"Do you remember him asking about any ruins, any other villages? Anything that would give me an idea where to look next?"

"Ma."

Fuck it. Deciding it was worth the risk, Rabbit hit the air-lock doors, sent the outer blockade folding back in his mind, and touched the barrier with an inner whisper of *Pasaj och.* Nightkeeper power flowed into him, blooming red-gold and firing his senses and talents, heating his skin and bringing a whiff of smoke.

"Easy there, Sparky," Myrinne said softly. She might not have Nightkeeper magic in the traditional sense, but she could perceive the ebb and flow of his power. According to Lucius, her experiences as Iago's prisoner two years earlier had left her sensitized.

"Sorry." He throttled it back, then leaned on the mind-bend and opened himself to Saamal, keeping the power in careful check, and making sure the inner blocks guarding the hell-link remained intact. Addressing the elder once more, he asked, "Why did he come here?"

"He was looking for his sons. He said his wife had been murdered, but he'd never seen the boys' bodies. He suspected they were still alive."

"Oh." *Ouch.*

That explained why Red-Boar had nearly killed Jox before disappearing into the highlands. He'd been trying to erase the only living person who had seen the bodies of the children killed back at Skywatch, in the second wave of the Solstice Massacre.

In years past, Rabbit would've been seriously pissed about learning that Red-Boar had fathered him while on a quest to find his full-blood sons. Now it just made him want to go home and get back to work, in the hopes that the Nightkeepers would eventually hit on the right alchemy, the right combination of sacrifice, magic, prophecy, teamwork, and sheer fucking luck that would allow them to seal the barrier tightly shut when the zero day came.

If they didn't, the Solstice Massacre was going to look like a warm-up act.

Saamal said something more, and Cheech translated: "You were one of those sons?"

"No." *Hell, no.* "I came later."

"Did he find what he was looking for?"

Rabbit shook his head. "He knew they were dead. He just didn't want to believe it."

The elder spread his hands and looked to the sky, and for the first time since their arrival, Rabbit felt a shimmer in the barrier. It wasn't magic, though, or at least not the kind he was looking for. It was the gentle warmth that came from Saamal's prayer.

When the elder finished and returned his attention to Rabbit, his eyes were sad. He said something, and Cheech translated: "He said they were twins."

And therefore so much more valuable than their

younger half brother, Rabbit knew. Anger kindled, bringing a whiff of smoke that he tamped down even before Myrinne touched his arm in warning. Coiled way too tight, he paced away a few steps, fisting his hands so tightly that his fingernails dug in and drew blood.

Dial it down, he told himself. It wasn't Saamal's fault that Red-Boar hadn't left a forwarding addy, or that Rabbit had gotten his hopes up.

"Down the mountain, in the village, they say the people of Oc Ajal worship Xibalba," Myrinne said. "Is this true?"

Cheech shot her a look, but translated her question and Saamal's response: "This is true, but not the way I think you mean it. We worship the gods of Xibalba, the *Banol Kax*, but we do not revere darkness or evil deeds."

Rabbit's head came up. "How is that possible? Xibalba is the underworld."

"But not as the Christians perceive it, as a place of hellfire and damnation. To my ancestors and my people, the sky and underworld are simply the residences of the gods. Some of them oversee positive things, such as science, medicine, and justice; others negative things like cruelty, greed, and addiction. Most, though, are a mix of dark and light, just as we are." Saamal paused. "Xibalba is where the dead are challenged, yes, but it is not perdition. It is simply another plane, one that balances the sky."

"But the—" Rabbit broke off, not wanting to reveal how much he knew about Xibalba—as in "been there, got the tee." Instead, he opened his mind to the elder's and skimmed off what he could about the religion of

Oc Ajal, which proved to be almost identical to that of the Nightkeepers, except turned upside down.

In other words, the trip was a bust. The villagers might worship the gods of Xibalba, but they weren't members of the Order of Xibalba. He hadn't found his mother's village, and he hadn't found new allies for the magi. *Please hang up and try your call again.*

Shaken and more let down than he wanted to admit, Rabbit said woodenly, "Thank you for answering my questions."

Cheech translated the elder's response as "Good luck," but Rabbit was pretty sure the literal word-for-word was more along the lines of "May the future go well for you."

We can only hope. He sketched a wave to the old man and turned away, tugging Myrinne with him. Cheech followed a moment later.

They were at the archway when Saamal called, *"An. Tool!"*

"That is *so* not my name," Rabbit grumbled, but he turned back. "What?"

He didn't follow the elder's quick words, so cocked his head back for Cheech, who said, "He says the peccary is a fine animal—clever, fierce, protective, and ambitious. But it was a rabbit that helped the Hero Twins save their father from the underworld."

Rabbit's throat closed, but he managed to get out, "I know the story."

It had been one of Harry's and Braden's favorites. He had a sudden memory of sitting in the pool house with them, telling them that very part of the story—

the savior-rabbit part—while Patience leaned in the doorway and watched her sons with a small, soft smile. The expression on her face, a mixture of love and contentment somehow coexisting with fierce possessiveness, had reached inside Rabbit and imprinted itself within him.

Nobody had ever looked at him that way, not before or since. And maybe he'd been fooling himself coming out to Oc Ajal, trying to pretend he was looking for allies when what he'd really wanted was to see if there was someone up here who could look at him like that.

Shit. Like father, like son, he was searching for something that was long dead.

Swallowing heavily, he jammed his hands in his pockets and headed for the archway, closing off his mental air locks as he walked.

Behind him, Cheech started in on Myrinne about the ride home, and she squeaked an indignant protest and geared up to haggle.

Without looking back, Rabbit said, "We'll pay. Just get us down as fast as you can without killing anyone."

He didn't care what it cost. He just wanted to go home.

CHAPTER EIGHT

Cancún, Mexico

The sky was bloodred with the sunset as Patience and Brandt left El Rey and headed back into town. They didn't speak as they walked. He held her hand, their fingers twined together like a promise. And although he knew he couldn't keep that promise, he couldn't make himself let go.

Because this was their spot.

Over the past couple of years, he had put his boots on the ground at hundreds of sites south of the U.S. border. He'd fought the Xibalbans in the Yucatán and Honduras. He'd let blood in Guatemala. He'd climbed sacred temples in Belize. And throughout the former Mayan territories, he'd patrolled the ruins, both continuing the search for a new skyroad and shoring up weak spots in the barrier as 2012 approached.

He'd breathed the air of rain forests, cloud forests, ancient mountain strongholds, modern cities and towns. Zap him into an empty warehouse with no contact with the outside world, and he could tell if he was in a former Mayan city-state, because all those places felt a little bit the same to him . . . except for this small section of Cancún.

Here, the air danced across his skin as it did nowhere else. And here, he and Patience *worked*.

They had been back only once since becoming full-fledged magi, on a fact-finding trip that had turned into an unexpected second honeymoon, a seventy-two-hour sexual marathon that had wrung him out, lit him up, and left him hoping that they had made a breakthrough.

Unfortunately, once they were back at Skywatch, reality had returned and they had continued growing into their roles and away from their marriage. And no matter how hard they had tried to keep it together, the connection they had shared in El Rey had slipped away and disappeared.

Until now.

Technically, the day had been a bust. As Rabbit had reported, there was no sign of the doorway. There was also no hint of a concealment spell at the base of the main pyramid, at least not that he or Patience could detect. Jade would have the final say on that; her spell caster's talent included the ability to sense and manipulate magic-hidden pathways. She and Lucius were off chasing down a lead on Cabrakan, but would be there the next morning to check for evidence of a concealment spell, when Strike did a 'port bounce through the Yucatán, gathering the scattered magi.

Which left Brandt and Patience alone for the night, in the place where they had begun, surrounded by air that danced across his skin and left him aching. The sizzle wasn't one-sided either; he saw it reflected in the sidelong glances she shot him as they left the park, felt it when their bodies brushed as they walked side by side.

He knew it wasn't fair for him to want her one moment and push her away the next. But he was having a hard time holding on to that logic now that they were in their own personal paradise, a place out of reality where they could steal a few hours of the past.

That was their mission, after all. Finding memories.

He paused outside the restaurant where he'd taken her for their first real date. "Can I buy you dinner?" It was a feeble joke; with access to a bankroll intended to fund an army, money was one of the few things the Nightkeepers didn't need to stress about.

"Looks like it's come up a few notches in the world." What had been a midpriced joint offering a tourist-friendly selection of Tex-Mex and burger-and-fries staples the first two times they'd been in town now offered Mayan-themed fine dining with handwoven tablecloths and a had *Zagat* review in the window. She slanted him a look. "Think we're underdressed?"

His jeans and button-down were casual, his boots

practical, his weapons concealed. She, too, was subtly prepared for action in cargo pants, lace-up shoes, and a tight tank that accented the strong lines of her arms and torso, the generous curves of her breasts. Over that, she wore a clingy blue shirt against the cooler air of the rainy-season night. It clung to the contours of her body and was very soft when it brushed against him.

"Let's find out."

He tried not to think it was destiny that there was a cancellation in an otherwise booked night, allowing them to slip right in. He wanted to deny that it was fate when they were led to a table for two by the window, in the same spot where they had sat during their first date, and overlooking the place where he'd been standing the very first time he saw her.

"Want to start with a bottle or two of tequila?" she asked, her eyes lighting with wry amusement.

He snorted. "Getting drunk's not the worst idea you've ever had."

They didn't, though. Instead, they shared *tamalon tutiwah*—round, flat corn cakes with bean and pumpkin-seed filling poured into thirteen indentations evenly spaced around the circumference, representing the thirteen-month calendar of the Maya—followed by flavorful spiced snapper wrapped in banana leaves and baked in a clay pot. Dessert was fresh fruit swimming in lightly fermented pineapple juice, leaving them satisfied but not weighed down.

The conversation, too, stayed light, not because they were working to keep it that way, but because they just freaking *clicked* here.

They left the restaurant and headed toward the hotel with his arm across her shoulders, hers looped around his waist. "I wish—," she began, but then broke off, shaking her head. "Never mind."

"Yeah." He tightened his arm in a half hug. "I know." He wished too. He wished he knew why things seemed so different here than they did back at Skywatch, wished he knew what kept going wrong between them, and how to fix it. He paused, looking up at a storefront that looked familiar, yet not. "This was the bar I saw you coming out of." Thanks to the *etznab* spell, the memory was fresh and new.

"Now it's a souvenir shop." A bell above the door tinkled as she pushed into the colorful, crammed space, tugging him along with her. "Come on. Let's check it out."

It was a night for bringing things full circle, after all.

They wandered through the shop, took turns trying on a blinged-out, green velveteen sombrero, and picked out a couple of hot sauces to add to Jox and Sasha's collection.

As they headed to the counter, Patience paused at a display of brightly colored textiles, her face lighting as she touched a vivid purple scarf. "You go ahead. I'm going to look for—" She broke off, animation draining. "Never mind."

Purple was Hannah's favorite color, Brandt remembered with a dull twinge of regret, the kind he didn't usually let himself feel. "You could get it anyway," he said. "Save it for the day after." That was what they used to call it, back when they still talked about being reunited with their sons and *winikin* on the day after the zero date.

Two years and four days. The number was never completely out of his mind, even when it was buried deep.

She turned away from the display. "If I went with that theory, the suite would already be crammed."

"Yeah. Between birthdays and the *wayeb* festivals, it's tempting to go a little crazy and fill the gap with stuff." He didn't bother pointing out that anything they bought now would be outgrown long before they saw the boys again. No need to twist that knife. He gestured with the hot sauces. "I'll go pay out. Think about the scarf. She'll always love purple."

But as he moved past her, she gripped his biceps, digging in. "Wait."

He paused. "Problem?"

"I didn't know you thought about them like that." Her expression hovered between wariness and confusion.

Although something deep down inside told him it was a bad idea, that given the uncertainty of the Triad magic, they should keep the status quo between them, he met her eyes and said, "There's a midgrade book about coral reefs on the shelf near the door, packaged with a snorkel, mask, and fins. That would be for Harry, because he'd love the book so much that he'd want to get out in the water and see all the critters for real. I'd get Braden one of the make-your-own Mayan drum kits in the back. We could sneak in some history while putting it together, and he'd be into the potential for making noise." He paused, throat thickening. "I miss them too."

A single tear tracked down her cheek. "You never say anything."

"Talking about it didn't seem to help either of us. If anything, it made things worse."

To his surprise, she nodded, accepting that. Or if not accepting it, then accepting that was the way he'd seen it. With a small, defiant chin tilt, she took the purple scarf off the display and headed for the checkout desk.

She didn't say anything when he added the snorkeling gear and the drum kit to the pile on the counter.

In fact, neither of them said anything, really, as they left the store with their purchases and headed for the hotel. But he was entirely aware of her, of the way her body moved with a fighter's economy of motion, but was still utterly feminine. The neon-lit darkness cast her face in light and shadow, making her look fierce and capable. Like a fitting mate to an eagle warrior. Like the woman he fell in love with, but had somehow lost along the way.

She glanced at him. "You're staring."

He should let it go. But he didn't. "I wish I knew why we get along so much better here."

Stopping, she turned to face him. "You know why. We both do. And we don't have to talk about it. Truly."

She was offering him an out. They could check into the hotel, go upstairs, and they would probably make love, because the two of them made sense together in El Rey.

But he didn't want the out. Not tonight. "Things went to hell after I got my warrior's talent."

According to Woody, his eagle ancestors had been tough, loyal, and almost always brilliantly successful at their jobs, as long as they stuck within their skill sets of math and engineering. They had also been workaholics, and had the highest rate of broken matings among the magi, largely because their talents so often took over their lives.

"You're not the only warrior in the family."

"Your bloodline is different. It didn't affect you the same way."

It was the simplest answer. And although it wasn't comfortable—none of this was—it made sense within the magic, and gave him reason to hope, deep down inside, that he'd be able to put his life back together once the war was over.

But Patience shook her head. "Unfortunately, there's another explanation." She paused. "Why else would we have been crazy about each other from the night we met, right up until our talent ceremonies?"

Brandt frowned, not seeing it . . . until he did.

Oh, holy crap. The bloodline marks they had both gotten on that first—and forgotten—night had formed their initial link with the barrier. Their talent ceremonies had formed the second link, bringing them into their full powers. And in between those two events . . .

"Bullshit." He didn't want to think their marriage

had been nothing more than an extended case of pre-talent hornies.

"Is it? The timing fits." Her expression was closed and sad. Resigned.

As part of their transition from childhood to full-fledged magehood, Nightkeeper youngsters experienced wild hormonal fluctuations in the weeks leading up to their talent ceremonies. Most of the current magi had gotten their bloodline marks as adults, followed two weeks later by their talent marks. During those two weeks, they had paired off in some serious sexual marathons, trying to burn off the horns.

All except for him and Patience, who had gotten a contact high off the others, but hadn't really experienced the same sexual urges. Maybe because they'd been living with those urges for the the past four years and mistaking them for love?

No. Impossible. Closing the small distance between them, he took her hand in his, feeling the kick of warmth, the soft strength of her, and the faintest of tremors that told him she felt the heat too, despite all their problems.

Her eyes met his, darkening as he unbuttoned her cuff and pushed back her sleeve, trailing his fingers up the smooth skin of her inner wrist to touch the stark black *jun tan* glyph.

"This didn't come from hormones, damn it." His voice was low, rough. "It means that we're gods-destined mates. It wasn't a coincidence that we met on that beach, and it sure as shit wasn't by accident that we found our way into that cave. The gods chose us for a reason; they put us together for a reason."

"Maybe this is it." Eyes shadowed, expression unreadable, she linked their fingers, stepped away, and tugged him in the direction of "their" hotel, where Jox had reserved them a room. "Come on. We've got a job to do."

The hotel was way tackier than Brandt remembered. Way, way tackier.

The formerly understated mission style had been replaced with brightly patterned serapes, velveteen sombreros, and lacquered castanets tacked to the walls, along with drink advertisements and prominent signs pointing to the cantina, and some decent prints that leaned heavily on festival and mariachi themes.

It wasn't until they got up to the desk and he saw a stand-up display of brochures that he realized the prints had something else in common: They all had brides and grooms in them. The place had been turned into a wedding factory.

"'Mariachi wedding packages,'" Patience read, sliding him a look. "Seriously?"

Her expression invited him to lighten things back up. More, it practically begged him to. *I'm trying to be strong*, her look said. *Help me out.*

His chest tightened at the sight, and at the realization that for all the times he had wished she could be more like an eagle and focus on her duties, the change saddened him, and made him very aware of the souvenirs he was carrying.

But she'd had a point—they had a job to do. So he played along.

He flicked one of the brochures. "The economy's in the crapper. If the shtick works, more power to them." Still, it was disconcerting that their hotel had gone from three-star anonymity to a chapel-slash-reception-hall that offered four different themes that he read off the brochure. "Sexy Spanish, Enduring El-vis, Beach Bash, and Mayan Adventure. Guess they couldn't come up with anything alliterative to go with 'Mayan.'"

"Mayhem?"

"Works for me. Not sure if that was quite what they were going for, though."

Her relieved grin not only thanked him for fol-lowing her lead; it quashed his fleeting urge to bag it and head for more romantically neutral territory. So when the couple in front of them moved aside, he exchanged plastic for a couple of key cards.

In the elevator, the Muzak was mariachi, the post-ers pimped the cantina, and the wall-to-wall was a muted tan with a pair of red footprints smack in the center in a faux-Mayan pattern. Brandt avoided standing on the prints, as did Patience. To the Maya, those woven footprints had symbolized leadership. When the king had stood on the footprints, it meant "Listen up. I'm about to say something important." That the symbol had been transferred to an elevator seemed—

"Tacky," commented Patience, finishing his thought as the doors opened on their floor and they headed for the end of the hall.

"No kidding. I'm almost afraid to see what the room looks like." He stuck one of the key cards into its slot, and pushed open the door. "What do you think? Are we going to get a heart-shaped bed, a full champagne-and-strawberries spread, or maybe—?"

He flipped on the lights and broke off when their reflections blazed back at him. Swallowing hard at the noncoincidence of it all, he finished, "Or maybe mirrors."

There were mirrors on three walls, windows on the fourth. The dressers were glossy black with mirrored edging, glass tops, and reflective knobs. Even the headboard was mirrored, though with beveling—to make a stab, he supposed, at taste. Neutral-colored drapes hung at the corners of the room, looped back with tasseled gold braid.

From the looks of the curtain rods, the drapes could be pulled across the walls, dampening the effect of the mirrors, which was pretty damned startling when his and Patience's images were reflected back at them from what seemed like a hundred different surfaces.

As Brandt stared into his own eyes, the faint background hum of magic—the one that sounded different to him there than anywhere else in the Mayan territories—quivered slightly and increased in volume.

"Let me guess—they got the ceiling too," she said from half a step behind him, her voice betraying a faint tremor, though he wasn't sure if that came from nerves or half-hysterical laughter. Or both.

Overhead, mirrored ceiling tiles gave way to a huge mirror hung over the king-sized bed. Swallowing at the thought of what the mirrors were meant to show, he nodded. "You know, we should probably be laughing about this. It is *way* tacky."

But it wasn't laughter that heated his blood as he turned to face Patience, and it wasn't amusement that lit her eyes.

It was heat. Desire. *Magic.* And a certain sense of inevitability.

There was power in the air, in their reflections. And when she lifted her hands to frame his face, there was magic in her touch, and in the brush of her breasts against his chest when he gripped the curves of her hips to draw her closer still. Their bodies fit together perfectly, bringing an ache of memory. *Yes,* said something deep inside him as his blood fired and his body hardened. *Oh, hell, yes.*

Their images were reflected at dozens of different sizes and angles. She was light to his dark, lean to his bulk, but as he angled down and she rose up to meet him, their reflections merged and blended, becoming one intertwined blur of light and dark as they kissed.

The first touch of their lips drew him tight and sent flames rocketing through his body. The second kiss, coming with a gentle slide of tongue, eased some of the hollowness within him even as a new, far more demanding urge built. His fingers dug into her hips, latching her body to his as he went in for kiss number three, taking it blatantly carnal with a thrust of tongue and a slow grind that said: *Here. Now. Mine.*

After that, he couldn't count, couldn't think. He could only feel and react, and take what she offered him, then demand more. He kissed her throat as she caught his earlobe in her teeth and sent heat hammering through him. His hands raced over her clothing, then under to find soft skin.

She hissed and tugged at his shirt, and then they were wrestling out of their clothes on their way to the bed, while his head spun with lust and the relief of finally being where he was supposed to be, there and then, with her.

Naked, he pressed her up against the bedpost, which ran all the way to the ceiling and was bolted firmly in place. Not letting himself think too hard about what acrobatics might have prompted *that* engineering decision, he cupped her breasts up against his face as he pressed butterfly kisses between them.

The past and present collided and then meshed, becoming a singular "now" composed of sensations and moves that were familiar yet not.

He knew the taste of her skin and the way she arched against him as he spiraled soft, licking kisses inward along one breast, knew the fascinating transition of textures where velvet skin went exquisitely smooth at the edge of her areola, then became crinkled as he worked ever inward. He knew her gasps of pleasure, the rhythm of her hands as they slid to his shoulders and trailed across the ticklish spots along his rib cage. And he knew the aching pleasure-pain of being hard and full to the point of bursting, throbbing and dying to pound himself into her, yet holding back, knowing it would please them both more to wait and take it slow. Even if it killed him.

But then she fisted her hands in his hair and tugged, raising his head from her breast, and he didn't recognize the gleam in her eyes. It called to the hard, hot thud of "want to hit that *now*" resonating through his system, tempting him to put her up against the nearest wall, mirrors be damned.

He didn't, though. She deserved better than the hard, fast rut his body demanded, and he knew she liked it slow and easy.

"Too fast?" he asked, voice grating from deep in his chest.

She shook her head. But the ripple of surprise brought by that negative was nothing compared to the hot, greedy shock that pounded through him when she turned around, bent slightly at the waist, and braced herself against the bedpost. The mirrored headboard gave him a delicious view of her round breasts, her taut belly, her parted thighs, with a neat triangle of darker blond between—and his own expression going from a dropped jaw to fierce heat when she looked back over her shoulder, eyes smoldering, and said, "Let's take one for ourselves before we try the magic."

His body tightened on a howl of *yes, yes, yes, hard and fast, yes!* But he held himself in check as he moved up behind her, curled his body around hers, and went still for a second, absorbing the sensation of her skin against his. He knew he should stroke her, knew he should take care of her before himself, but he was already on a knife-edge of control.

Gritting his teeth at the effort it took to move slowly, he reached down to rub the head of his hard, aching cock against her moist opening, hissing at the spear of sensation that pierced him, making his stomach muscles tighten against the press of her round, firm buttocks. He'd meant to move up and forward to tease the soft flesh at her front, but she shifted as he did, rolling her hips to accept the blunt tip of him.

Wet warmth slid around him, surrounded him with a sledgehammer of pleasure that had him surging forward with a harsh, primal growl. He thrust once, hard and deep, seating himself fully with zero thought for her, only for himself.

Slow down, damn it, said the gentleman within him, the one who knew how she liked it. Realizing he had one arm banded across her stomach, the other pressed flat against that enticing blond triangle, in a hold that pinned her back against the pressure of his hips, he eased up. "Sorry."

"Don't be. And don't hold back."

The husky, unfamiliar timbre of her voice had his eyes opening. It took him a moment to focus, surrounded as they were by reflections of themselves from all different angles, the blend of his skin against hers, and the shadows they made together. Her face was flushed, her eyes gleaming. Belatedly, he noticed that her arms mirrored his, snugged tight atop his grip, holding him tight against her.

Their eyes met in the reflection, and hers blazed. "Take what you want. It's what I want too."

Lust roared through him like fury, but he managed to rasp, "Tell me you mean that."

In answer, she fisted her inner muscles around him, so hard that the pleasure edged toward pain when she shifted back against him, inviting him to do more, to do everything. A whole-body shudder rose up from the soles of his feet as he locked his arms around her, his body into her. And he began to move.

The first stroke wrung a groan from his chest and battered his defenses with lightning-bolt lust; the second blitzed through the tattered remainder of his analytic self and left him in the throes of instinct, and the blind quest to possess the woman in his arms, and the power that sang in the air around them.

He held her, surged against her, pounded into her in a frenzy that went beyond emotion to pure action and reaction. He wasn't fucking her, wasn't making love to her; this was mating, pure and simple, the primal drive to lose himself in her, fill her with his seed. Even the distant knowledge that all the magi had undergone fertility-blocking spells to avoid complications in the final years before the end time didn't diminish the imperative to plant part of himself inside her and mark her as his own in a place beyond marriage and the *jun tan* mark.

On some level, he was aware of her escalating cries, the graceful curve of her neck as she pressed her face to her arms and gave herself up to his hold and thrust. Her hand atop his urged him inward, until his fingers were tight against the hard bud of her clit as he rode her from behind.

Her pleasure, though, was far secondary to the need that consumed him, the pressure that built within him, tightening the muscles of his abdomen and ass. One second he was breathing hard and deep; then in the next he stopped breathing entirely, as oxygen became so much less important than the rushing tingle that started at the bottoms of his feet and the tips of his fingers and raced upward and inward, warming and tensing each individual muscle until his whole body felt the pleasure that had previously belonged solely to his cock.

A groan reverberated in his chest as he bowed his body to match hers, thrusting again and again in search of the pinnacle, helpless to do otherwise in the face of a gathering orgasm of unparalleled intensity.

Patience shuddered against him, said his name in a passion-strangled voice, and went over the top of her own climax.

He felt the hot, moist pulse on every inch of his skin, felt her pleasure as his own. Sinking himself deep within her, beyond all thought of control or finesse, he stroked again and again, then roared as his vision went white and he locked himself against her and came.

He flashed outside himself with a lurch of magic, and suddenly he was *above*, looking down on the two of them, suspended in a vision, yet not.

He saw them surrounded by a pearlescent gray dome, a shield unlike any other he'd ever sensed before. Within it, their images were strangely distorted, refracted, as though together they formed the pieces of an incomplete whole. Somehow he was certain—gut-deep certain—that the pieces they were missing could be found just beyond the dome, that he and Patience could be whole again if he could only breach that gleaming shell.

Then the vision shattered and he was back inside himself, losing himself to the rush of pressure and pleasure, the pulsing throb of ejaculation as he emptied himself into her. He held her tightly, binding them together as his vision grayed and time seemed to slow, measured only in the pulse of their joined flesh.

Even after the intense wave passed, he stayed still, absorbing the moment, the sensations.

Then, inhaling a huge draft of air, he pressed a kiss to her nape, where damp tendrils had escaped her beleaguered ponytail. As he eased out of her, he was all too aware that he'd taken her standing up. And he'd do it again in a heartbeat.

Feeling that he needed to say something profound, he started with, "That was . . . wow." Okay, not so profound after all. Magic danced invisibly across his skin, making him conscious of the warmth of his *jun tan* mark, the faint sense of connection where they had been apart for so long. Trying again, he said, "I think—"

Dropping her braced-arm stance, she turned and

silenced him with a soft brush of her fingertips across his lips. "Don't think. For right now, let's just leave it at 'wow.'"

Instead of arguing, he kissed her.

He set a soft, slow rhythm that was the diametric opposite of the hard and fast, borderline-rough sex they had just shared. He'd meant the gesture to soothe, to wordlessly apologize if that had been too much for her, to thank her for the gift. To his surprise, she met him more than halfway with an inciting nip of teeth and tongue, and a shudder-inducing drag of her fingernails down his ribs.

Heat flared as he took the kiss deeper. Magic hummed anew, wrapping around them both and making him think of the shell that had surrounded them in his vision-flash, and the sense that good things were waiting outside that shell, that things would get better, not worse, if he could manage to break through the barrier blocking him from the Triad magic.

Or was that just wishful thinking?

It doesn't matter, his conscience warned. *You don't have a choice. And it's time.*

So he ended the kiss, stepped back, and held out a scarred palm. "Lie down with me?"

Her eyes held a shadow of resignation as she took his hand, but she smiled. "With a brothel bed like this, how can I say no?"

"At least it's not heart-shaped. And I'm pretty sure it doesn't vibrate."

"Color me disappointed."

It *was* a ridiculous bed, all mirrors and black lacquered wood, topped with a scarlet brocade bed-spread edged with gold braid, and a huge pile of gold-edged red pillows.

Somehow, though, it didn't seem ridiculous. Instead, the red-gold of the bedding blended with the hum of magic that touched the air, intensifying as she stretched out on her side near the center of the plush mattress with one hand behind her head, one leg slightly bent, goddesslike in her nudity.

He stretched out opposite her for a kiss, then rolled onto his back and drew her with him, so she was cuddled up against his side with her hand over his heart, the two of them fitting together, puzzlelike. Their legs twined and he brushed his scarred calf along the softness of her skin.

Then, in unspoken agreement, they looked up into the big mirror that hung suspended over the bed. As their eyes met in the reflection, they touched the magic that hung thick around them, and together invoked the *etznab* spell.

The mirror wavered; the world around them went thin. And they slipped into memory together.

CHAPTER NINE

El Rey
Six years ago

*Holy hookup, Batman. That was about all Brandt's brain
was capable of managing as he lay beside the underground
lagoon, intertwined with Patience while their bodies cooled
in the aftermath of some seriously hot sex.*

*How much of that had been about the two of them, and
how much of it had been about his bloodline connection to
whatever the hell was going on beneath El Rey? He didn't
know, couldn't even begin to guess.*

*According to Wood, sex had been part of the magic
on almost every level. In another lifetime, he might have
thought the gods had meant for him and Patience to pair up
like this. But he was out of that loop now, which meant . . .
hell, he didn't know what it meant, except that something
had drawn him to her, and it was no coincidence that they*

had found the underground cave together, or that they had gotten down and dirty beside the sacred lagoon.

But what did it all mean?

When she stirred and let out a small, satisfied sigh, he tightened his arm around her and cracked his eyelids, trying to come up with an awkward-moment-after line that didn't sound totally cheesy.

Then he got a good look around them, and all he could come up with was, "Holy crap."

The fireworks were long gone, but the air still sparkled red-gold.

Magic.

Patience's body tightened. "Oh. My. God." Her voice was tinged with the wonder he saw in her face when their eyes met. Then her expression clouded. "I'm sorry," she said softly. "I can't let you see this."

Reaching out, she cupped his cheek and whispered three words in a language that should have been unfamiliar.

Except it wasn't unfamiliar at all. It was a fucking sleep spell.

Shock hammered through him. Her expression fell when he didn't go narcoleptic, and he could almost hear her thinking, Why didn't it work?

If he could've formed a coherent sentence, he would have told her it was because lower-level stuff like the sleep spell didn't work on magi. But his thoughts were racing too fast for that. The questions bombarded him: Where the hell had she learned the spell? How had she known what the glitter-dust effect meant? She obviously wasn't Maya, but—

Whoa. *He stared at her as the litany ran through his*

mind: The Nightkeepers had been big, fast, smart, and char-ismatic. And they were extinct. He was the last of them.

Unless they weren't extinct.

And he wasn't the last.

Excitement knotted low in his gut. What if that ex-plained everything? What if he'd been meant to see her, meant to follow her and bring her to El Rey just in time for them to discover the doorway?

Granted, the chances of that were pretty fucking slim given his history. But the gods were low on options. And if the magic was coming back online now, with eight years to go before the zero date . . .

Holy. Shit.

His blood hammered as he held out his hand, cupping it palm up, and whispered the spell to call a foxfire. There was no surge in the magic, no kindling of the blue-white glow he had tried to summon, but in the wan illumination of Patience's tiny, dying flashlight, he saw her eyes go wide.

She eased away from him. But she didn't go far.

He sat up, conscious of the way the red-gold sparkles followed the motion, swirling on unseen currents. He held his breath, barely daring to hope, afraid that there was—had to be—some other explanation.

Hell, for all he knew, he'd gotten trashed and this was a really vivid dream. She could easily be his subconscious's projection of his dream girl, all blond and blue, with a kick-ass, can-do attitude wrapped in a glossy package. And ever since he'd been a kid, he'd pictured himself wielding the magic of his ancestors, and imagined finding someone else like him.

The shock in her expression was giving way to specula-tion . . . and hope. She moistened her lips. "You're not NA, are you?"

NA? Oh, she'd guessed he was Native American from his name. He shook his head. "Nope."

"Then what are you?"

Her quiet question hung on the air, echoing in the vaulted cave and counterpointed by the slow drip of wa-ter falling from stalactites to the water beyond them. The world seemed to hold its breath—or maybe that was him, because he had the sudden sense that what he said next was going to change both of their lives. This was no dream, he knew; it was the real thing.

He said, "I'm the sole mage-born survivor of the Solstice Massacre." He paused. "At least I thought I was."

Tears shone in her eyes. "Me too."

An unfamiliar pressure expanded in his chest. This was real; it was actually happening. Patience was a survivor, just like him. "What's your bloodline name?"

"Iguana." The word wasn't even a whisper, more a shaping of the lips. "My winikin changed it after the mas-sacre, in order to keep us safe."

His voice rasped when he asked, "Are there others?"

"Hannah thought we might be the only ones. The way the drop box for contact info is set up, she couldn't tell."

He nodded. "Woody said the same thing. I wanted him to crack the box and see if there were others, but he refused. Said he was sworn to keep us hidden until he was con-vinced it was time to reunite the Nightkeepers."

It was the first time either of them had said the word, and it hung in the darkness, echoing in the sacred space.

Nightkeepers. *Their people. Their magic.*

He'd been programmed from birth to believe in the unbelievable, to take it on faith that he had a higher destiny and the potential for magical skills that might or might not be needed, depending on whether the barrier stayed shut through the end of 2012. But belief and faith suddenly seemed insubstantial now that he was face-to-face—and naked—with another full-blood survivor, one who knew what he knew, who'd been raised, as he had, by an actual winikin.

It was impossible. Unbelievable.

But somehow it was true.

They stared at each other for a long moment, speechless. Finally, he swallowed hard. "I—" *Wow, he didn't know what to say to her, how to deal with the sudden realization that they were connected far more deeply than by the sex they had just shared.*

Patience's eyes darkened. "Gods. This must mean that the massacre didn't seal the barrier after all."

"Maybe." *He cupped his palm and watched red-gold swirl.* "Maybe this is just . . . I don't know. An anomaly." *But he had a feeling neither of them believed it.*

She exhaled slowly. "I was supposed to leave this morning for a two-day island hop to Cozumel. Something told me I shouldn't go."

"I was supposed to leave yesterday for Chichén Itzá. Didn't feel like it."

"The gods wanted us to meet."

It was a tempting thought—very tempting—but he shook his head. "I think it was more the equinox magic pulling us here. The gods aren't my biggest fans."

Her brows drew together. "For real?"

"For real." He rubbed the numb patch of scar tissue high on his inner calf. *"I'll tell you about it, but not here, not now."* He paused. *"I think we should try to jack in. If the power is back online and pulled us here together . . ."*

When he trailed off, she nodded. *"Yeah. We're here for a reason. Which means I'll let you get away with the not-so-subtle subject change. But don't think you're going to get out of explaining that little comment about the gods."*

"I won't." He'd never told another soul the whole wretched story, not even Woody, but he had to tell her. That was suddenly very necessary.

Reaching for her piled clothing, she dug in a pocket and withdrew a matte black handgrip that flipped open to reveal a five-inch combat knife. *"You have a blade?"*

He nodded, excitement sparking at the sight of the knife, and the challenging gleam in her eyes. *"You didn't check that with your luggage, did you?"*

"Bought it when I got here. You?"

"Ditto." He fished through his clothes and pulled out a butterfly knife that had looked cool at the pawnshop where he'd picked it up, but had taken some practice getting used to. Now, though, he was able to open it with decent flair to reveal a blade about the same size as hers, though his was edged on both sides and narrowed to a wicked point, while hers was wide and serrated on one side.

It wasn't their potential as fighting weapons that mattered, though; it was their ability to draw blood sacrifice. No Nightkeeper walked around without a knife. It just wasn't done—at least according to Woody. And apparently according to her Hannah as well.

He grinned at her and she grinned back, and magic hummed faintly in the air.

It hit him then, that his life had changed forever the moment he'd caught a glimpse of her coming out of that bar with her friends.

They weren't just lovers. They were about to become teammates. And to a Nightkeeper, a fighting partner was so much more than lover.

Setting their knives aside, they dressed in unspoken accord, staying close to each other, not seeming to need words to communicate the basics. He was achingly aware of her, attuned to the way she moved like both a fighter and a woman, capable yet feminine, and entirely at home in her own body.

The fading penlight emitted a muted glow that made her look like an angel, while the fact that she carried a combat knife, and the suppressed excitement he saw in her eyes, called to something inside him.

Red-gold power flared, this time inside him, filling him with hot, hard purpose and an unfamiliar, almost atavistic possessiveness. We're meant for each other, *said something deep inside him, with a certainty that swept aside all other considerations.*

Closing the small distance that separated them, so they stood toe-to-toe at the edge of the underground lagoon, he took her hands and lifted her knuckles to his lips in a gesture that should have seemed foolish, but didn't.

"Before I saw you, I didn't believe in—" Love at first sight, *he was going to say, but the "L" word jammed in his throat, blocked by the part of him that knew he couldn't go there.*

Fuck me, he thought as his emotions revved. *What the hell did he think he was doing?*

On one level, his analytic self knew he'd been caught by a surge of sex magic, and that he needed to freaking watch himself. On another level, though, he wished, more than ever before, that he could go back and undo what he'd done. But he had scoured the myths and magic of a dozen cultures looking for a way, and come up empty. There was no way out. And if the magic was coming back online, that was going to be a big fucking problem.

"You don't believe in what?" She was gripping his hands, forming a link he didn't want to break . . . but had to.

He lowered their joined hands, easing his hold. "I don't think I really believed I would ever meet another mage, or that the barrier might come back online. We don't know what's going on, or what's going to happen next . . . but I want you to know that I'll do my damnedest to get us both through it safely." *Because the two of them being there together, on that night, couldn't be a coincidence.*

They both knew that wasn't what he'd originally intended to say. She didn't call him on it, though. Instead, she crouched to retrieve their knives, which lay side by side on the sand. Straightening, she offered him the butterfly knife, holding it by its two-edged blade. "That goes both ways, bucko. You've got my back. I've got yours. Deal?"

Their eyes locked and he nodded. "Deal." *But he intended to make damn sure he took the brunt of whatever came next. He'd been raised human enough to want to protect his lover, whether or not she wanted to be protected.*

His lover. Gods.

*He moved to take the knife from her, but instead of let-
ting go, she closed her grip around the blade as he pulled
it back.*

*He jolted. "Are you okay?" He reached for her, then
stopped himself. "Shit. Dumb question." He'd blooded
himself dozens of times. But he'd never blooded anyone
else.*

*She opened her hand to show the double slices where
both edges of the blade had cut her, freeing blood to well
up, looking black in the darkness. With her other hand, she
offered her knife, this time blade first.*

*He shook his head and lifted the butterfly knife, which
was wet with her blood. "I'll use this one."*

*Setting the point to his palm, he gouged along his life-
line. Pain flared in his hand and up his arm, morphing to
a buzz of heat. There was something erotic about sharing
her knife, her blood. And that was the Nightkeeper in him
talking, not the human veneer.*

Meeting her eyes, he grated, "Well, here goes nothing."

*"Forget that. Here goes everything." She faced out
over the black lagoon.*

*The flashlight had finally died, leaving them lit only by
the starlight that came in from up above as he stood beside
her, so they were hip to hip, shoulder to shoulder. They held
their hands out over the swirling pool and let the sacrificial blood fall into the water. When the first droplet hit, the
buzz in Brandt's veins altered its pitch, seeming now to
hang in the air around them.*

*A glance at Patience showed that she felt it—heard
it?—too. He nodded back with what he hoped was an expression of reassurance rather than the greasy nerves that*

had sprung up at the realization that this was it. This was what he'd spent his entire life preparing for, without really believing it was going to happen.

He was about to bust his magical cherry. Holy shit.

He took a deep breath, aware that Patience was doing the same thing beside him. Together, they said the magic words: "Pasaj och."

Warmth bloomed in his chest and rocketed outward, suffusing his body. His senses expanded: He heard the imperceptible lap of fresh water against stone and smelled how it went slightly brackish near the tunnel, where a submerged conduit must run out to the ocean. His skin prickled, sensitizing to the warmth of Patience's body on one side of him, the chill of the night air on the other. He tasted their lovemaking and smelled the tang of blood that hung between them, around them. His night vision sharpened too, making him squint against the sudden gleam of starlight. It reflected off the water and sand, and off the stones around them, where tricks of the light formed strange patterns.

But that was all that happened.

He didn't leave his body to enter the barrier, didn't see or feel a change in the faint red-gold sparkle.

Disappointment thrummed through him. "Shit. I guess we can't jack in without a proper bloodline ceremony, after all."

As babies, their lack of connection to the barrier had saved their lives. Now, though, it meant that the magic didn't recognize them.

"Maybe not, but something *happened." Patience's attention was fixed on the back of the cave.*

He followed her gaze. "I don't—" He broke off as the

reflected starlight and shadows rearranged themselves in his mind, and excitement jolted. "Holy fucking shit."

What had been light and shadows moments earlier had become the silver-limned outline of a doorway: two heavily carved pillars connected by a linteled archway, with stygian blackness beyond.

The carved details were obscured by distance, but there was no doubt that the doorway was Mayan-Nightkeeper in style . . . and it hadn't been there before. Even as lost in each other as they had been, they would've seen it by the light of the fireworks. Which meant they had called it with the spell words, even though they lacked their bloodline marks.

The magic—at least that much of it—was working. Wonder thrummed in his veins. Anticipation.

He stared at the doorway, wanting more than anything to get his ass through it and see what was on the other side. "What do you think?"

Her teeth flashed, reflected starlight. "Stupid question."

"Sorry." And she was right; it was their duty as Nightkeepers—trained or not, bloodline marked or not—to figure out what the hell was going on, and whether it signaled the beginning of the end. More, they were programmed for this shit, bred and born for it. No way either of them was turning away from the adventure.

Given his choice under human ethics—and, hell, as a Nightkeeper male whose body was still warm from hers— he would've left her behind in the cave. But he didn't have any reason to think she wouldn't be able to handle herself. So despite his natural inclination to protect the shit out of her, he nodded. "Let's go."

Excitement kindled in her eyes. "I've got your six." She patted his ass. "And a delightful six it is."

"Don't let the ogling distract you."

"I'm a chick. We multitask." But she was all business as they set off, skirting the lagoon to approach the silver-limned doorway, knives at the ready.

As they approached, the starlight and shadows resolved themselves into a pair of gape-mouthed serpent carvings forming the pillared uprights, with an intricate text block incised into the arch above them.

"I can't read the glyphs," he admitted. "You?"

"The dots and lines are numbers." She indicated two geometric glyphs that looked like a pair of dominoes. "As for the rest, you've got me. Hannah said the hieroglyphs were dropped from the curriculum a few generations ago because most of the modern-day spells were either memorized phonetically or had more to do with mental powers than spell words."

"Woody too. Let's hope it doesn't say 'abandon all hope, yadda yadda.'" Catching a whiff of something funky, Brandt narrowed his eyes, trying to make out a lumpy variation of the shadows just inside the tunnel. "No shit."

"What?"

"Flashlights. Sort of." He reached in, felt around, and came up with a couple of torches, a flint, and a striker. "They're pretty low-tech, but should do the job."

Once lit, the torches proved to be artifacts in their own right. They were made of glyph-carved bones—he tried not to wonder if they were human—that had been hollowed out and packed with a hardened, crusty substance that smelled faintly like rancid grease and flowers. The business ends were loaded with a flammable combination of plant matter he couldn't begin to identify, glued together with a dried-out, resinlike substance.

It was all pretty crusty, but it took only a couple of tries with the flint to get the first one started, and once they were both going, they gave off decent light, very little smoke, and an earthy, not unpleasant incense.

Patience eyed hers. "How old do you think these things are?"

"No clue. Somewhere between two decades and two millennia?" There was really no way to tell right then whether the torches were ritual pieces that had been used by their parents' generation, or if the tunnel was a relic from before the conquest. And wasn't that a hell of a thing to think? "My gut says they're old, though."

"Mine too." She lifted the slow-burning brand; the light revealed a tunnel leading away from them. "But I'm going to file that under 'things I can't think about right now,' because I'd way rather see where this goes."

At his nod, she moved through the doorway, taking point even though she'd promised to watch his six.

No hardship, Brandt thought, and followed her in. He kept his senses wide-open, including the unfamiliar, buzzing level of the magic, and stayed focused as Woody had taught him. Beneath that, though, ran the thrill of finally doing what he'd trained for all these years . . . and the sick fear that something would go wrong and Patience would pay the price.

Not this time, he thought grimly. Never again.

The limestone walls of the tunnel were marked with softly rounded ripples, suggesting that it had originally been the track of an underground stream. The floor was wider than the arched ceiling, with tool marks showing where the surface beneath their feet had been widened and flattened. The walls were uncarved, but the ripples made them seem decorated nonetheless. A footpath was worn smooth along the middle.

"Lots of traffic," Patience said.

"Makes you think it leads somewhere cool, doesn't it?"

"Gods willing." She glanced back at him, eyes firing. "What if—"

"Sh! Wait." He held up a hand when, at the edges of his perception, the magic fluctuated.

"I felt it." Her eyes went unfocused. "Up ahead. It's . . ." She frowned. "It doesn't feel the same."

"Like we're experts?" But he wasn't arguing. "It's . . . darker. Greasy, almost."

"You think it could be the Banol Kax trying to come through the barrier?"

"We'd better hope to hell it's not." The last time a couple of the dark lords had made it fully onto the earth plane, they had wiped out most of the Mayan Empire before the Nightkeepers—or rather one Nightkeeper, a member of the legendary Triad—had forced them back behind the barrier.

His gut fisted at the knowledge that if the dark lords had managed to tear a gap in the supposedly sealed barrier, the world was in very deep shit.

And nobody knew about it except the two of them.

He wanted to invent an excuse and send her back up to the cave, but knew she wouldn't go. More, that was the man and the human talking. A true Nightkeeper would never put a lover above his duty.

"I'll take point," he announced, and moved past her.

She caught his arm. "Wait. What do we do if it is . . . you know. Them?"

Her eyes were wide with mingled excitement and nerves. She wasn't going to back down from this fight, or any other. And in another lifetime, she would have been his mate. Damn it all to hell.

Ignoring the warnings that blared from his subconscious, he went in for a kiss. She met him halfway, gripping a fistful of his shirt to hold him close. His lips slanted across hers; their tongues touched and slid as the kiss went from hot to gentle and back again. He gathered her against him, trying to imprint the feeling in his sensory memory just in case.

Hard, hot pressure built in his chest and tightened his throat, and for a moment the buzz changed pitch and red-gold sparkled in the air.

Then he broke the kiss and eased away to meet her eyes, which had gone stormy with passion. "The gods put us here, right? I'm willing to have faith that they've got a plan for us."

Or, rather, for her. They wouldn't sacrifice her for his sins.

He hoped.

She released his collar and touched his lips with her fingertips, with a brush reminiscent of their kiss. "Then why did that feel like good-bye?"

"Not good-bye," he lied. "Good luck." As in, they would be damned lucky to both walk away from this if their worst fears were confirmed. But if only one of them was going to make it out, he'd make sure it was her. Given his status *with the gods, she was the one the world was going to need. Not him.*

She didn't believe him; they both knew it. But they also knew this wasn't the time for their first fight.

Instead, they got moving. She led the way, walking soft-footed. He did the same, and they ghosted along in silence for a few minutes, carefully watching for booby traps as the strange, oily-feeling magic grew stronger with every step.

In the back of his head, he was thinking, What the fuck are we doing? There's no way that two untrained, un-marked college kids can take on a *Banol Kax* with a couple of five-inch blades, two torches, and a piece of flint.

But the rest of him was entirely in the moment, testing the limits of his senses, the placement of each footstep. That part of him knew that their lacking bloodline marks wasn't entirely a negative. It meant that whatever was pumping out that strange power wouldn't be able to sense them, at least not on the magical level.

In theory, anyway.

The tunnel curved, then curved again, and they saw a light up ahead, beyond the next bend. Brandt snuffed his torch against the tunnel wall, working not to sneeze against the puff of incense-laden smoke. Patience did the same, plunging them into a near blackness that made him acutely aware of how long the tunnel stretched behind them, and how late it was getting. How far past the actual moment of equinox would the doorway stay open? He didn't know, didn't have any basis for guessing, but they couldn't turn back now.

Patience's hand found his in the darkness. He squeezed

back, trying to let the gesture convey affection, attraction, respect, reassurance, and all the other things he wanted to surround her with. The handclasp stung, then flashed sudden warmth up his arm as his sacrificial cut aligned with hers and blood spoke to blood.

Mine, he thought as he had earlier in the day when he'd first laid eyes on her. *You're mine.*

Except she wasn't. Not in this lifetime.

Pulling away, he got ahead of her as they moved on. He might not be able to claim her or keep her, but he damn sure wasn't letting her be the first one into a fight.

As they silently closed in on the corner, and the light beyond, his heart beat double time while his brain churned. Even if it wasn't one of the Banol Kax up ahead—and he hoped to hell it wasn't—the dark lords commanded many ur-demons, like the *boluntiku*, six-clawed lava creatures that moved as vapor and went solid the instant before they attacked, and the *makol*, damned souls that could possess human hosts, turning their eyes a luminous green.

Without warning, a man's voice rose over the humming buzz of magic, chanting in the old tongue. It sounded human, but how could they be sure? This wasn't exactly a "know thy enemy" situation—they were making it up as they went.

When they reached the corner, Brandt's pulse thudded in his ears as he took in the scene: Beyond the curve, a straight section of hallway ended in a sheer wall with an arched, open doorway that was set at a right angle, giving them some hope of approaching without being seen right away. Both the chanting and the light—flickering yellow-orange firelight—were coming from within.

Holding up a hand to warn Patience back, Brandt eased down the last straight stretch and popped his head around the corner, staying low.

His brain snapshotted the scene: Beyond the door was a circular chamber that looked natural, as if there had been another lagoon, now gone dry. There were two other entrances. The one opposite their position opened to another tunnel, while the middle doorway was shut with a carved stone panel. Torches set into holes in the wall provided light and incense, and a plain altar sat against the wall, little more than a square block of stone with a shallowly curved top.

A lone man stood before the altar.

A . . . Nightkeeper?

Brandt risked another look, confirming his first impression. The guy was tall, wide-shouldered, and fair-haired. Wearing black, insignialess paramilitary gear, with a carved stone knife stuck in his leather belt, he could've stepped right out of one of Wood's stories. From the looks of him, he was a good decade older than Brandt . . . and he knew his shit. He was holding his bleeding palms out over the altar, letting the blood fall in the shallow depression. His chant rose and fell with ancient intonations, the syllables seamless.

Yet the power pumping out of the room jarred dissonantly against the red-gold hum within Brandt.

His mind raced as he returned to Patience and briefly described the room and the stranger. Were they wrong about the rattling power being dark magic? The Nightkeepers were the only earth-borns capable of using the barrier's power, and this guy sure as shit looked earth-born, not Banol Kax or boluntiku. Which left only two options.

So what was he, mage or makol? *Please, gods, let him be a mage, Brandt thought, mind plunging ahead to the hope of there being more survivors, older warriors who could teach him and Patience what they lacked . . . and who might know how he could fix his cosmic fuckup.*

Behind him, the chant switched to English, startling him. Brandt turned as the stranger said, "By nine times nine chants and our shared blood, I call on Werigo, son of Okom, father of Ix and Iago."

Magic rattled in the air, hard and abrasive, but that wasn't the worst of it. He saw Patience's eyes widen, saw the understanding dawn.

Because oh, holy shit, nine wasn't a sacred number of the Nightkeepers. It belonged to the underworld.

"Lords," the stranger continued, "release my father's soul, so he can continue working on your behalf."

Brandt's gut twisted as his fantasy of more Nightkeeper survivors imploded beneath the realization that this was no mage. It had to be a makol, a possessed human whose demon rider was trying to bring another like it through the barrier.

Kill it! his gut screamed. Acting on instinct, not fully aware of what he was doing, he summoned the red-gold power from the thin barrier connection he and Patience had formed.

"Wait!" she said urgently.

But it was too late. Like a striking rattlesnake, the dark magic lashed out into the tunnel and struck sparks off the red-gold. The makol howled a curse as it sensed the intruders.

Brandt didn't hesitate. He lunged through the doorway

and swung his torch like a Louisville Slugger, aiming for the thing's head.

He had a bare second to register that its eyes were a murky hazel, not luminous green. It was a man, not a ma-kol. Was he a Nightkeeper after all?

Shit! *He pulled the blow and deflected the swing. The other man ducked; the bone torch glanced off his shoulder, smashed into the limestone wall, and splintered at its end.*

"Who the hell are you?" Brandt demanded.

Without any change in expression, the stranger yanked a nine-mill from his belt and fired at Patience.

She dove out of the way, but her torch and knife went flying as the other man tracked her with his weapon.

No! *Rage poured through Brandt, possessed him. He teed off and swung again, and this time he didn't pull a godsdamned thing.*

The splintered end of the torch hit the guy in the temple. The impact sang up Brandt's arms and left his hands vibrating.

The blond man staggered, gun hand sagging. He cursed when Patience kicked his wrist, sending the weapon flying. Brandt wasn't thinking or planning, didn't have any thought in his mind aside from stopping the bastard. He roundhoused the torch and slammed it into their enemy's skull with a sickening crunch.

Blood and brain spattered into the shallow sacrificial bowl as the other man slid to a heap on the floor.

Brandt froze. His pulse throbbed sickly in his ears as he stared at the gore. At the body.

He had just killed a man without really knowing why, or who he was.

"He was going to kill us." Patience was breathing hard, her eyes wide and white. "We had to—"

A terrible rattling roar split the air, drowning her out as the wall behind the altar shimmered and went strange and flexible, turning a sickly muddy brown-green color. Brandt shouted and yanked her behind him when the surface bulged obscenely, as though something was fighting to be born through the membranelike surface of the dark magic.

Oh, holy fuck. The dark mage's death had punched a hole in the barrier.

"Go!" He shoved her toward the doorway. "Get all the way out, call your winikin, and tell her to crack the drop box."

She spun back. "I'm not leaving you!"

He knew she wouldn't leave unless he made it good, so he gripped her wrists and met her eyes. "Think about it. One of us needs to make sure nothing comes through this gap. I'm bigger. I've got more blood to sacrifice. I'll meet you as soon as the equinox is over. Now go!"

It was only partway a lie; he would try to hold the barrier with bloodletting. If it came down to it, though, he could only hope that since a dark mage's sacrifice had opened the connection, the sacrifice of a Nightkeeper, even one like him, would close it back up again.

Woody would understand, even approve.

Patience hesitated, then spun for the doorway. But she was too late. The membrane tore with a wet ripping sound that amped the rattling magic to a maniacal chatter. Smoke poured through the opening, unrelieved black save for two pinpoint glints of luminous green. A makol!

The dispossessed demon soul arrowed straight for Patience, moving fast.

"Run!" Brandt dove for the billowing presence, trying to grab it and keep it away from her. He passed right through it, though, catching nothing but air. He landed hard, rolled, and lurched back to his feet just in time to see Patience dodge the smoke and make a dive for the altar.

She snagged the stone knife from the corpse's belt, slashed both her palms and thrust her hands into the mess atop the altar, crying, "Gods help us!"

A soundless detonation rocked the chamber, thumping deep within Brandt and making his ears ring. The dark-magic rattle modulated, becoming underlain by the buzzing hum from before. The undulating membrane went from muddy brown to pure silver, shot through with rainbow hues, like the surface of a bubble seen from an angle.

Patience's expression turned radiant; she seemed to glow from within as she turned to him. But then her face blanked with horror, and she screamed, "Behind you!"

Brandt lifted the bloodstained torch and spun—straight into a roiling cloud of black smoke. He caught a flash of fluorescent green and smelled char, and then he was seeing the world in fluorescent green, and his brain was impossibly split in two.

He was himself, but he was someone else too; he caught kaleidoscope images of terrible blood rituals designed to prepare the living for resurrection. He saw two boys, flashing images of them growing, one into the guy he had just killed, the other into a younger, auburn-haired version. He saw them carve their father's beating heart from his chest and make the sacrifices that would ensure his immortality as a demon soul. The dead brother had been stone-faced, the other in tears.

He was Werigo, ex-leader of the Order of Xibalba, a group even more deeply underground than the surviving Nightkeepers. He was also Brandt White-Eagle. And the part of him that remained Brandt would be fucked if he was going to let a dark mage turn him into a makol.

Forcing his body to move, he lurched for the altar. "Give me the knife!"

Patience tossed it and he caught it on the fly. The second his fingers closed around the hilt, the dark magic that had been used to baptize the blade rose up within him, giving Werigo the upper hand. Seeing the light of the gods inside Patience and recognizing the power her sacrifice would generate, the makol wrested control of their shared body away from Brandt and reached for her.

Panic slashed through Brandt. Using that fear, he managed to regain enough control to shout, "Kill me. Do it now!"

Her eyes flashed. "No way. I just found you."

She closed the distance between them, dodged Werigo's knife slash, and grabbed Brandt's wrist in a numbing, twisting grip. The knife clattered to the floor as she kissed him, grabbed his bloodstained hand in hers, and connected them, blood to blood.

Brandt howled in his soul when he felt part of Werigo leave him and enter Patience through the kiss, felt the makol gather his magic and inwardly begin a spell that would kill the two Nightkeepers and use the sacrifice to reanimate the dead man as another makol. Brandt struggled to pull

Werigo back but couldn't, fought to push Patience away, but she held on to him, not letting him end the kiss.

Against his mouth, she whispered, "Please, gods."

Without warning, power jolted into him, through him, in a screaming rainbow that flayed his soul raw in an instant, leaving him bare.

He sensed the gods within Patience, and knew they were saving her because she deserved it, and were saving him solely because he and Patience were connected. Collateral salvation instead of collateral damage.

His inner right forearm burned at the spot where the magi had worn their bloodline marks.

Then the makol *howled as the gods tore it out of Patience and aimed its essence toward a rainbow funnel cloud that spun midair above the blood-spattered altar.*

Werigo's old, angry soul dug claws into Brandt's consciousness, tearing deep furrows in his psyche. The gods might be saving Brandt, but they sure as shit weren't protecting him from the fallout. Patience was trying to, though; she held him tighter, kissed him harder, sharing her blood, her strength, and the grace of her gods.

Brandt howled and fought to free himself from Werigo. Triumph flared when he felt the makol's *grip give and sensed the bastard's realization that he was going to be trapped once again behind the barrier. But he also felt Werigo's determination not to let them escape with the knowledge that the barrier was friable within this sacred spot, which had access points for both light and dark magic, or that the Order of Xibalba was real, not just a bedtime story used to frighten Nightkeeper children.*

Before Brandt could block the move, if he had even

known how, Werigo reached through the connection of blood and sex magic that bound him and Patience together. The demon soul locked on to both of their consciousnesses as dark magic rattled harshly.

Brandt shouted curses as oily brown power clouded his mind, blocking off memory after memory, and doing the same to Patience.

He saw the images parade past in reverse: him and Patience creeping through the tunnel; them intertwined in the aftermath of lovemaking; his elation at finding her on the beach; the first moment he saw her. Then Werigo went back further still, to another time, another encounter with the gods. Brandt howled, tried to fight it, but he didn't know what to do with the magic, didn't know how to defend himself as his past was torn away from him.

Then Werigo was gone. But so were the memories.

"No!" Brandt croaked the word aloud, surprised to realize that he could speak, that he was back in control of his own body again. Deep in his bones, he felt it the moment that the equinox faded and the barrier solidified.

The air above the altar went still. Silence filled the chamber. And the magic snapped out of existence, leaving him utterly empty.

He sagged against the altar, retching against the awful, sickening spin of his head. Patience lay unmoving on the floor, but a fumbling vitals check reassured him that she was breathing, her heartbeat steady. Gray fog clouded his vision, his thoughts; it was all he could do to light her torch using one of the wall sconces. He wanted to pass the hell out, but he didn't dare. His gut told him that their exit wouldn't be open much longer.

He had to get them out of there.

Dizzy but determined, he picked her up, staggered out of the chamber, and started back up the tunnel.

With each step he took, the gray fog got thicker, obscuring his memories of the—what was it again?

"Doesn't matter," he rasped through a thick-feeling throat. Channeling Woody, he said, "Focus on your priorities." Knowing he was losing it, that he wasn't far from shutting down entirely, he fixed a single priority in his mind: I've got to get us both back to the hotel.

He repeated that over and over again as he carried her through the tunnel. By the time he reached the lagoon cave and dropped the burned-out torch at the edge of the water, he didn't know how he'd gotten there, didn't know the name of the woman in his arms or why they were both wearing ripped, dirty clothing that stank of blood. Instinct had him washing away the worst of the gore in the lagoon before he carried her back up the stairs and out of the pyramid, which looked solid once again when he turned back, looking for . . . what?

He couldn't remember. He just knew that they couldn't stay in the park after dark, so he followed the path out the back way, and trudged up the beach, past a scattering of motionless partyers who had passed out after the fireworks.

When he hit the street and a couple of guys loped up to make sure they were okay, gut instinct had him playing "still drunk from last night." He wobbled and slurred, "I've got to get us both back to the hotel."

One of the guys—red-eyed and hovering on the borderline between last night's drunk and tomorrow's hangover himself—offered to help.

By the time Brandt and the blonde were up in his room, and he'd thanked the Samaritan with a twenty to buy himself a few rounds, he was barely conscious. It was all he could do to strip them both, crawl into bed beside her, and fall the hell asleep.

If he was lucky, everything would make sense when he woke up.

CHAPTER TEN

December 19
Two days until the solstice-eclipse
Cancún, Mexico

Patience awoke with her cheek pillowed on Brandt's shoulder and one leg thrown over his. As always, his body temperature had crept up to "furnace" overnight, making her too hot, but she hadn't moved away as she slept, didn't want to move away now. Instead, she cuddled into him, pressing her lips to the smooth, tough skin of his upper arm as she slid her leg higher along the satin-slick sheets and—

Satin?

Pulse jolting, she opened her eyes to find herself looking into a wall of mirrors that showed her initial surprise, then the way her eyes clouded as memory sledgehammered her with so many long-forgotten truths that she wasn't sure what to think about first.

She made herself roll away from him, not letting herself feel the loss of warmth. "Wake up, big guy. We fell asleep."

"We wh—? Huh?" He blinked awake and locked on their reflection over the bed, and his face went through the whole surprised-then-remembering sequence she'd just been through. He cleared his throat. "Oh. Well."

"We should get dressed," she said too quickly, latching on to the practical details when the thought of dealing with the other, larger pieces of the puzzle made her palms sweat. "Jade and the others will be here soon."

Taking the slippery top sheet with her, she headed for the shower, trying not to make a big deal about snagging her scattered clothes along the way.

"Patience."

His quiet word stalled her in the bathroom doorway. Taking a deep breath, she turned back.

She lost the breath she had just taken.

He sat cross-legged in the center of the mattress, bare-chested, with the bedspread tossed casually over his lap. His hair was tousled, his eyes still carried a blur of sleep, and the mirrored reflections behind him showed the strong curve of his spine. Her body still hummed from their raw sex of the night before; the thought of it brought a clutch of desire low in her abdomen, a blush of moisture to her cleft.

But last night hadn't been about them; it had been about the place, the magic, and the memories. Loving him now, in the light of a new day, would be something entirely different.

He held out his hand, but she took a step back, shaking her head.

"I can't," she whispered, the words little more than a breath.

His expression tightened. "I just want to talk." But he let his hand drop.

Her heart twisted. "We knew," she said softly. "From almost the very beginning, we knew we were both Nightkeepers."

"Yeah, we did. Until Werigo blocked the memories."

She told herself to focus on the pieces that mattered to the next forty-eight hours. But the words slipped out. "It was such a relief to think that I wasn't going to be alone anymore."

"We were together after that," he pointed out. Which was true—instead of an awkward morning-after walk of shame, they had ordered breakfast. Three months later, they were married.

"Not the way we should have been." As magi. Partners.

"Maybe not. But they were good times."

It hit her then, what knowing all along would have really meant. They would've come clean to their *winikin* right off the bat, might've even gotten married, not in the furtive-feeling ceremony they'd had, but with full Nightkeeper pomp. Then after that, they would've been in training, fully immersed in the world of the magi. And, knowing firsthand that the barrier wasn't completely sealed and the end time was a real threat, she probably wouldn't have gotten pregnant . . . and Harry and Braden wouldn't exist.

"I—" She broke off, pressing a hand to her stomach. "Oh, gods." She was sorely tempted to take the bathroom escape route, but they owed each other better than that. She didn't look at him, though, as she said, "If it hadn't been for Werigo's spell, we probably wouldn't have had the boys. And, gods forgive me, sometimes I think it would've been easier if we'd come into this as strangers, or as lovers but not parents. I don't regret having Harry and Braden, never that. I just wish . . ." She trailed off. "I wish I knew which parts have been pieces of the gods' plan, and which have been our choices."

"I would've picked you out of the crowd with or without the magic," he said softly. "You dazzled me then, both as a man and a mage. I'm still dazzled by you now. More so, even, because you gave us Harry and Braden."

Patience swallowed against the hard, hot lump of emotion that narrowed her throat. "But will you still feel that way back home?"

To his credit he didn't lie. But the regret in his eyes hurt just as much as the lie would have.

The burble of her phone was almost a relief at that point. She pawed through her clothes, pulled out her cell, and checked the new text message. "Jade and the others are downstairs."

"They're early. You want to tell them to grab a table someplace quiet and we'll debrief while we eat?"

She shot off the return text and fled to the bathroom, where she took a quick shower and pulled herself together.

Ten minutes later they left the room with only a messy bed and steamed-up bathroom to show that they had been there. She paused for a last look back as he held the hallway door for her. The mirrored decor wasn't any less cheesy than it had been the night before, but she felt a pang at leaving it behind.

"We won't forget this time," Brandt said quietly.

"No, we won't." But as they headed downstairs to meet the others, she found herself wondering whether it would be enough for them to remember that first night. She felt so far removed from the person she'd been back then, so far away from the awestruck wonder of discovering the magic and fighting at her lover's side, that she couldn't see how the memories could help fix a damned thing.

Their teammates had snagged a private room at the back of the hotel restaurant, which was mercifully low-key on the themed-wedding kitsch, instead leaning toward a trellised indoor-garden feeling, with skylights that were wide-open to the sunny morning.

Patience hesitated slightly at the sight of not only Strike, Jade, Rabbit, and Myrinne, who she'd been expecting, but also Alexis, Nate, Sven, Lucius, and Leah. "Wow. The gang's all here. Almost, anyway."

It shouldn't have made her claustrophobic to step into the room or take one of the two empty chairs and have Brandt's arm bump hers as he did the same. But the walls closed in on her nonetheless.

"Sasha stayed with Anna, and Michael's on Mendez duty," Leah said. "The rest of us figured we'd tag along and boost Jade, on the theory that the cardinal-day spell concealing this doorway of yours could be tough to unravel on a noncardinal day."

And also, Patience knew, because the Nightkeepers were one-hundred-percent adventure junkies. Just look at how easily she and Brandt had talked each other into exploring the tunnels below El Rey.

The good news was that, in doing so, they had discovered something the Nightkeepers badly needed. Without preamble, she said, "The doorway leads to an intersection."

There was a short pause; then Sven whooped and the others started firing questions, the mood in the room shifting abruptly to one of "Oh, holy shit. Finally something might be going our way!" Ever since Iago had destroyed the intersection beneath Chichén Itzá, the magi had been searching for another sky-road, a place where the barrier was thin enough to allow the gods to contact them directly.

Rather than trying to field the questions, Patience held up a hand. "Hold on. It's complicated. I think we should start at the beginning." She glanced at Brandt. "Do you want to tell it, and I'll jump in where I've got a different perspective?"

He nodded. "Sounds like a plan." He didn't look at her, but beneath the table, he shifted, looping his foot around hers and pressing gently in an unseen half hug. "We used a mirror in our hotel room to trigger the *etznab* spell," he began, then went on to summarize the events of that long-ago night, with her adding details as they seemed relevant. They were forced to pause several times as the waitstaff filled their orders. By the time he had described Werigo's banishment by the gods, and the final spell he'd cast, the room was dead quiet.

When he was done, there was a moment of silence that wasn't so much stunned as it was a case of nobody knowing what to tackle first.

"Are you guys okay?" Leah said finally.

"We're coping," Patience said, not wanting an open forum on her and Brandt's relationship, then or now.

Leah's nod seemed to accept the evasion more than the answer.

"If it's an intersection—" Strike began.

"There isn't any question about that," Brandt said, "at least not in my mind. It channeled both light and dark magic, and let both demons and gods reach through. Hellroad plus skyroad equals intersection." He paused. "But there's a problem. Given that Ix knew about the El Rey intersection, then we have to assume that Iago does too."

Patience hadn't really been thinking in that direction, but now her mind leaped ahead. "But if he had access to a functional hellroad six years ago, why didn't he use it back then?" A cold knot twisted in her stomach as she answered her own question. "Unless what happened that night destroyed the El Rey intersection."

Brandt nodded. "There has to be some reason why the site hasn't pulled anyone else in since then."

"But we—" She broke off as disappointment tugged. "Damn it, you're right. We've scoured the area. We wouldn't have missed something pumping that much magic."

"You might if it's not using the power you're looking for." That came from Lucius. "Let's not jump to conclusions. You said there were two other doors leading out of the chamber, right? What else was different from the old intersection beneath Chichén Itzá?"

Brandt said, "This one was very plain, unadorned. The outer doorway was carved, but not the tunnel or the chamber itself. The sconces were strictly functional, and the altar was just a square chunk of stone, not a *chac-mool*." He paused. "Anybody got a pen?"

When Nate tossed him a ballpoint, he got busy sketching a napkin schematic. Meanwhile, Patience put in, "The torches we found just inside the tunnel were carved, but not with glyphs. Patterns, mostly." She went on to describe the slow-burning resin and unfamiliar incense.

When they were both finished, Lucius studied the napkin map, added a couple of notes from her description, and then lifted a shoulder in a half shrug. "No guarantees, but based on the lack of carvings, and there being none of the tricks that were part of the intersection at Chichén Itzá—the sliding doors, the elevator-type mechanism, and such—I'd guess that this is a very early site, maybe the first few centuries after the Nightkeepers came to this continent."

Understanding shivered through Patience. "Back when they were still using *muk*, you mean?" That was what he'd meant about it not being the power they were looking for: *Muk* was the ancestral magic that combined the light and dark aspects of the power. Among the magi, only Michael could use *muk*, and at that, he wielded only a small piece of its total power. Yet even that much was devastating.

Lucius nodded. "Up until the Nightkeepers came to this continent, they managed to maintain the balance between light and dark spells, but something about being here ramped everything up." He made a *boom* noise and pantomimed an explosion. "The magic increased by the century, permeating the emerging Mayan culture."

Jade put in, "Which is why the culture on this continent resembles that of the original Nightkeepers so much more closely than any of the civilizations our ancestors lived with before or after."

"Right," Lucius said. "Eventually the boar-blood-line king couldn't maintain the balance anymore, the darkness corrupted a dozen of his strongest magi, and"—he snapped for emphasis—"the wielders of light and dark magic split into the Nightkeepers and the Order of Xibalba." He paused. "Before that, though, the biggest rituals were split between light and dark . . . sometimes even with separate entrances to the ritual sites."

"That would account for two of the doors," Patience said, hope kindling at the inner click of connection that suggested they were on to something. "The one we came through was keyed to light magic, while Ix came in through the other one. Which probably means there's a dark-magic entrance hidden somewhere in the ruins of El Rey. But that doesn't account for the third door."

"You said it was a closed stone panel." Lucius thought for a moment. "Maybe it's not even a doorway at all, just carved into the stone, which would mean it would be more of a symbolic entrance . . . maybe for the gods?" He frowned. "Except that if that's the case, then there should be one for the dark lords as well, in order to keep the balance."

"Not if the site dates back before the Nightkeeper-Xibalban split." Surprisingly, the comment came from Rabbit, who usually kept his mouth shut during meetings. He continued: "Back then, there wasn't the same good-versus-evil distinction between entities that lived in the sky versus the underworld. They were all considered gods."

Strike scowled. "Bullshit." He inhaled to keep going, but subsided at Leah's warning glance. Patience had noticed several such exchanges in recent days, with Leah checking Strike's temper against not only Rabbit but Jox and Sven as well.

Rabbit bristled, but it was Lucius who said, "Actually, it's not BS. There's some evidence in the library that the ancients viewed the sky and Xibalba as locations rather than moral barometers."

Strike's jaw flexed. "There was nothing fucking balanced about what the *Banol Kax* did to our parents."

Rabbit looked away and said nothing, but Patience

could guess what he was thinking: *Your parents, not mine.*

"None of this explains why Iago didn't use the El Rey intersection to activate the barrier," Brandt put in. But where before Patience would have been annoyed by his overfocusing on the job rather than the people around him, now she saw it as a redirection of the conversation. The press of his foot on hers said that he too had noticed the growing tension between Strike and Rabbit, and didn't like the looks of it.

"Maybe he knew about it but couldn't make it work," Lucius offered. "It sounds like Ix had connected enough to split off the dark magic he wanted to use to open the barrier—which, in turn, summoned you guys via the leftover light magic. But he hadn't managed to punch through. . . . It took him dying to fully activate the hellroad."

Patience nodded. "If Iago didn't know to try a human sacrifice, he wouldn't have been able to open the intersection." She paused. "Will *we* need a full-on sacrifice?" Human sacrifice wasn't an aspect of most light-magic spells . . . but they weren't talking about strictly light magic anymore, were they?

"I think it's time to find out." Strike signaled for the check. "Let's go. If we can reopen the skyroad during the solstice-eclipse, we should be able to take out Cabrakan even without a Triad mage."

Brandt's expression flattened. "Patience's *nahwal* seemed pretty certain that it's going to be up to me. Problem is, we don't have a fucking clue why my ancestors can't reach me."

Patience frowned. "Yes, we do. Don't you remember—" She broke off at his look of utter confusion. Then her pulse started bumping unevenly as it connected. "Oh, shit. It was Werigo's spell."

"What was?"

"That night in the tunnel, you hinted that the gods had turned their backs on you. When I pressed, you said you'd tell me the whole story later. Then when the skyroad opened, their power came through me, not you, even though you were the one fighting Werigo. I thought it was because I was the one was touching the altar, but what if that wasn't it? What if it was because the gods couldn't—or wouldn't—reach out to you?"

"I don't remember saying anything about the gods."

"You never do, do you?" Lucius said, eyes narrowing.

"I don't what?"

"Call on the gods. You never say 'gods know' or 'godsdamn' or anything like that. And it's not the 'I'm a daddy. I don't swear' thing. You swear plenty, but you don't blaspheme. What's more, although I've heard you talk *about* the gods, I don't think I've ever heard you talk *to* them." Lucius paused. "Do you pray?"

Brandt scowled. "That's between me and—" Breaking off, he muttered an oath that had nothing to do with the sky. "It's not my thing."

Surprise rattled through Patience. "Why didn't I ever notice that?"

"Because of Werigo's spell," Lucius answered. "It

screwed with your perceptions. He must've blanked not just your memories of what happened in that chamber, but all your memories of experiencing magic up to that point in your lives. In Patience's case, that meant everything from the moment she saw Brandt on the beach. But in his case, the spell not only back-tracked to earlier in the day when he first laid eyes on Patience; it also went back further to a previous event involving the magic."

"The car crash," Brandt said flatly. "That's the only other missing memory I'm aware of."

"Oxymoron alert. But, yeah. I'm willing to bet that your near death by drowning could have had enough magical oomph to punch through the barrier, even that far back." Lucius paused. "Did it happen the night of the winter solstice?"

"It was early during winter break, before Christmas. It could've been. . . ." Brandt trailed off, frowning. "Yeah, it was the night of the solstice. But . . . I didn't remember that until you asked, just like I never thought about the accident."

Patience's thoughts raced. "Werigo's spell blocked us from remembering that the magic works. If the gods intervened that night and something happened to create a debt and make them turn against you, the spell would've blocked all of it."

And deep down inside her, a new thought exploded through her mind: What if Werigo's magic had also messed with their mated bond? It wouldn't have bothered them out in the human world . . . but the effects could have manifested once she and Brandt were bound to the magic and started functioning as mates within the Nightkeeper milieu. Which was exactly when things had started going wrong between them.

Question was, would that change now that they had broken at least part of the spell? Gods, she hoped so.

"Regardless, the central issue remains," Brandt said. "I can't fix the problem until we know what I did wrong."

Patience caught the bleakness at the back of his eyes. She touched his hand. "The gods didn't shut you off because you somehow sacrificed your friends to save yourself. That's not what happened."

"You don't know that."

"I know you," she said firmly.

"Michael's magic got screwed up because he came into his powers with too much of a sin burden on his soul. The same thing could be happening to me."

"There's a fundamental difference between being in an accident and being an assassin." She didn't think she would've had the guts to put it quite that bluntly if Michael had been there.

For a second she thought he was going to pull away from her. But he didn't. Instead, he nodded. "I hope to hell you're right. But hoping and theorizing aren't going to be enough here. I need to see the rest of that vision."

Sharp relief kicked through Patience when he didn't go back into shutdown mode on her. But it didn't count until they managed to keep things working back at Skywatch, where loving each other wasn't nearly so easy.

Telling herself to deal with one crisis at a time, she said, "It seems to me that the *etznab* spell doesn't just need the words and props; it also needs the right atmosphere. I don't think it'll work again here at the hotel."

"Maybe not. But what about our cave?"

At the thought of going back down there—with him—her stomach tightened. "That might work."

He stood and offered her his hand. "Then let's see if we can find the way in."

CHAPTER ELEVEN

As the others headed out of the restaurant, Rabbit hung back and signaled for Strike to wait up. Myrinne stalled too, so the three of them wound up alone just outside a pair of restroom doors bearing sombrero-wearing stick figures of either sex, and labeled SE-NORS and SENORITAS in case the pictures weren't obvious enough. *Duh.*

"Problem?" Strike asked, cutting a look between them.

Rabbit hesitated, but then went ahead and said it: "I've been feeling funky ever since we touched down here, kind of itchy, or like I'm coming down with something." That wasn't likely, though; the magi didn't get sick, at least not from germs.

Strike stilled. "You didn't feel it when you were here two days ago?"

"No. Just this time. I wasn't even going to say

anything, just figured I was tired from all the running around." After leaving Oc Ajal, he and Myrinne had driven to three different ruins that had included sacrificial skull platforms—*tzomplanti*—dedicated to Cabrakan, but had come up dry in the clue department. Since they'd needed to do the two-day trip in one, in order to make up for the time they'd spent up in the mountains, they were both pretty short on sleep. "But between Brandt saying that this place buzzes different for him and Patience, and then us figuring out that there might be a dark-magic intersection entrance somewhere in the area, I figured you should know."

"Does it feel like dark magic?"

Rabbit glanced at his forearm, at the scarlet quatrefoil above the black glyphs. "It doesn't feel light or dark, really."

"Please tell me it's not *muk*."

"Nah. I'm not even sure it's magic. It's more like— I don't know, an itch between my shoulder blades, maybe. Like something's going to happen soon."

"You're not going prescient on me, are you?" Strike tried to play it like he was kidding, but they both knew he wasn't.

Nightkeeper males occasionally envisioned their destined mates before meeting them, but that was where Y-chromosome foretelling left off. What was more, precognition tended to have nasty-assed repercussions within the magic. So while the approach of the end date continued to increase the scope of the Nightkeepers' powers—for example, allowing the warriors to cast shield spells at greater distances for longer times—there were some talents, like prescience, that they were hoping wouldn't go on the rise.

Forcing aside the memory of the things he'd seen the night Myrinne had tried her foretelling spell on him, Rabbit shook his head. "It's not prescience. It's just . . . I don't know. An itch." The more he talked about it, the dumber it sounded. He wouldn't even have said anything, but didn't want to jeopardize the team by being a dumbass and keeping quiet about something that was probably nothing.

Strike thought for a minute. "Could you be sensing the solstice-eclipse ahead of the rest of us?"

"Maybe. Or maybe I'm getting paranoid because my ass is dragging." Myrinne had pointed out—rather acerbically—that fatigue sometimes triggered his old patterns. And gods knew the whole "the world is out to get me" thing used to be one of his fallback modes.

"How are your blocks?"

"My head's locked down tight." He'd made damn sure of it after they left Oc Ajal, and again this morning. No way he wanted Iago breaking back through. "And I'm not trying to bag out on you. Myrinne almost never gets to see me do my thing, and I'm totally jonesing to get inside the pyramid." At the thought, the itch between his shoulder blades got worse. "I just thought it should be your call whether I stayed behind or not."

"Yeah. It should be." Strike didn't seem as grateful as Rabbit would've expected, though. If anything,

he looked more annoyed than before, though that
sort of seemed to have become *his* fallback recently.
Finally, after a long enough pause that Rabbit's stomach had started to think about sinking, the king said,
"I have a feeling we're going to need your oomph to
get this doorway open. But"—he shot Rabbit an "I'm
way fucking serious" look—"if the itch gets worse or
anything else changes, you pull out of the link immediately, and tell me what's going on." Before Rabbit could nod, Strike transferred his glare to Myrinne.
"Same goes for you. If you see him doing anything
you don't like, you tell me. Got it?"

She played it cool, nodding and saying, "Will do."

Inwardly, though, Rabbit knew she was doing a
boogie-woogie victory dance. She was grateful to the
magi for taking her in—on Rabbit's say-so and with
Anna's support—even though she had been raised
by one of Iago's allies. Strike had given her a place to
stay, spending money, an education, and some small
jobs within Skywatch. But being grateful didn't stop
her from wanting more—not financially, but in terms
of getting in on the action. She was dying to be out on
the front lines with the other warriors.

Rabbit sure as shit knew how that felt; he'd been
there, done that, and eventually earned the king's
trust. Now it was her turn . . . he hoped.

"Was there anything else?" Strike asked.

Rabbit shook his head. "I'm good if you are."

"Then let's go."

They met the others outside the hotel and headed
for El Rey. There, they all went in through the main

gate, paid the entry fee, and joined the scattering of other park visitors, who were being desultorily watched by a couple of attendants who wore uniforms but no sidearms.

Once they were in, Strike gave a little finger wiggle. "Let's spread out. We'll meet up in five at the back of the pyramid."

Although the magi could conceal themselves with a chameleon shield or by uplinking with Patience when she went invisible, the spells would be a power drain, so they stuck to more conventional camouflage to start with, splitting up to wander into the park, flying casual.

At least most of them did. Rabbit stopped just inside the main gate and took a long look around.

Most of the old buildings were little more than stone footprints, lines in the limestone outlining where the village's market buildings, houses, temples, and palace had once stood. It all looked exactly the same as it had two days ago . . . but the air carried a subsonic whine he didn't remember from before, one that made him want to work his jaw and pop his ears.

Myrinne had initially moved off with the others, but now backtracked and put herself in front of him. "What's wrong?"

"It's not wrong, so much. I'm just getting a strange buzz off this place. It's probably just the same thing Brandt was talking about." He resisted the almost overwhelming urge to scratch the back of his neck. "I'm probably feeling it because we're almost on top

of the solstice-eclipse. I bet the others will start noticing it soon."

She looked dubious. "Should we tell Strike?"

"Not yet." When she opened her mouth to argue,
he warned, "Don't cry wolf on me, babe."

She made a face at him. "You're just pissed that
when he finally gave me something to do, it turned
out to be babysitting you."

"Ouch." But he snorted, amusement smoothing
out some of the itchiness. "Witch."

"Pyro."

They grinned at each other like a couple of idiots
in love—which they pretty much were—then linked
hands and headed for the pyramid. But even as he let
himself be distracted by the bounce in her step and
the excited gleam in her eyes, he stayed very aware
of the angry-mosquito buzz that plagued him just below the audible level . . . and the feeling, deep in his
gut, that he was missing something.

At the back side of the square pyramid, out of sight
of the tourists and the park attendants, the magi gathered near the center point of the lowest tier.

Brandt flattened his hand on a section of stonework
that looked exactly like its neighbors on either side.
"It was right here." Beside him, Patience nodded.

They were standing closer together than usual,
Rabbit saw, and when Patience caught his eye and
sent him a "hope this works" look, she didn't look as
tight as she had for the past few months. He hoped
that meant she and Brandt were putting things back
together. He didn't like them being out of whack, be-

cause if those two couldn't make it work—hell, he didn't know. It wasn't good.

Jade stared at the stones, her eyes going blurry with the inward-looking expression she wore when she used her spell caster's talents. After a moment, though, she shook her head. "I'm not sensing any sort of concealment spell. Let's try uplinking and see if the power boost helps."

To be on the safe side, Alexis cast a thin chameleon shield that would obscure them from view, making them seem to blend into the surrounding stone. Michael had discovered the variation on the warrior's traditional protective shield, and Alexis had picked up on it through her connection to Ixchel, the goddess of weaving and rainbows; she said it was like weaving light.

They were the only two who had mastered the magic so far, though. Most of the others could only cast the protective shield. Rabbit had managed to alter his, but instead of going into stealth mode, it turned the deep, vibrant orange found at the heart of a fire, and grew bitching hot to the touch. Which was neat, but not exactly subtle.

Once the chameleon shield was in place, perceptible as a wall of blurriness separating them from the human world, Nate passed out the combo earpiece-microphones the warriors wore to keep in touch on ops. The reception wasn't totally reliable underground, but the earbuds were better than nothing, and although this wasn't an official op and they weren't wearing full combat gear, they were all on guard, and most of them were carrying, concealed in some form or another.

At Strike's cue, the magi pulled their ceremonial knives and blooded their palms on both sides. Rabbit *pasaj och*–ed his way into a barrier connection, and grinned when Nightkeeper power flared to life within him. Gods, he loved magic. The energy level kicked higher when the others started joining up, linking blood to blood, with the three non-Nightkeepers standing outside the main circle.

With his senses amped, Rabbit smelled blood and the mingled scents of his teammates' soaps, colognes, and perfumes, along with the sharp edge of rich Mexican coffee and breakfast grease. He heard the trill of a sugarbird and the sigh of a gentle breeze, and saw subtle imperfections in the seemingly smooth spots on the pyramid face. But he didn't see a doorway, not even with the inner senses that followed the flow of magic.

Then the energy flow fluctuated as Jade leaned on the uplink. Because the magi were all blood-linked so deeply, Rabbit picked up on the shimmer of her normally intangible magic as it spread across the stone surface, seeking a concealment spell.

And finding one.

Seeing the magic trace the contours of an arched doorway, Jade bore down, pulling magic from the whole team as she whispered a counterspell.

For a second nothing happened. Then the pyramid face shimmered and changed, revealing the doorway as a dark square leading inward.

Beside him, Patience gave a low gasp, and pain echoed through their handclasp.

Rabbit said in an undertone, "You okay?"

She nodded. "I'm fine," she said, equally quietly. "It's just that—"

Without warning, the mosquito buzz in Rabbit's head ratcheted to a shriek and dark magic smashed through his mental blocks like they were fucking newspaper.

The hell-link slammed open and a terrible presence entered him, swelling inside his skull and seizing control of his body.

Before, Iago's mental pattern had felt like those of the other magi. Now it was ten times stronger, faster, and more complex, with his and Moctezuma's thoughts and memories twisted into a single entity controlled by the mage's consciousness. And the bastard dug in and hung on tight. Agony ripped through Rabbit, but the Xibalban didn't let him cry out in pain or yank his hands away from the blood-link and jam them against his temples. More, the bastard blocked Rabbit's magic, not letting him transmit any sort of warning through the uplink.

Rabbit's inner vision kaleidoscoped inward, spinning with fractured images, most unfamiliar. He caught impressions from Iago's current lair: a cement-slab tunnel lit by strings of bare bulbs with a time-worn yellow sign hung on the wall. Those images were mixed with Moctezuma's memories: scenes of sun-drenched pyramids, bright feathers, blood pouring onto sand as his Aztecs fought their Spanish enemies. Over it all lay a night-vision overcast of luminous green.

But then, a few frantic heartbeats later, the kaleidoscope reversed. It stopped showing him memories, and started taking his instead, lifting them wholesale from his mind.

Oh, holy shit. The bastard was fucking *downloading* him.

No! Rabbit screamed inwardly as information gushed out of him, Iago focusing on the Nightkeepers' recent highlights: the Triad spell, Patience and Brandt's visions, the breakfast meeting, Ix's death. Iago roared with rage over that last memory; he hadn't known what had happened to his brother, or who had been responsible. He dug deeper, probing Rabbit's memories of Patience and Brandt, and what he knew of Ix's death. The information sped faster and faster, going to a blur that left Rabbit with no idea of what he'd divulged.

Howling inwardly, sick with the knowledge that he was giving up his teammates while they stood around him, unaware of the danger, he hammered against the bastard's hold, trying to break free, trying to keep some part of himself locked down, but not managing to do either.

"Rabbit? What's wrong?" Myrinne's voice seemed very far away.

Help! He didn't know what had tipped her off, or whether she caught his desperate cry, but suddenly she was shouting Strike's name.

He was barely conscious of the magi converging on him, their mouths opening and closing as they asked him questions he couldn't hear. All he could do was stare at them while his vision flickered from green to normal and back again, like a hard drive rebooting.

Then Iago vanished from inside him.The invading presence disappeared. The green disappeared. The mental blocks reappeared, seeming strong and solid, like there had never been a problem.

But there was a big problem. His brain was in a fucking shambles.

Rabbit writhed as his body tried to tear itself apart from the inside out, like that was going to make up for the weakness it had just displayed. Memories hammered through him—his own, someone else's; he didn't fucking know anymore. Tremors racked him; he couldn't breathe, couldn't do anything except clutch himself and groan, wishing to hell he'd paid more attention to that twitchy feeling.

Then he couldn't even do that, because the seizure got worse. He staggered away from the pyramid, and passed the fuck out.

As Rabbit went down, a headache came out of nowhere to nail Patience behind her eyeballs, washing her world white with sudden agony. She reeled sideways, grabbing for her temples, as the others bolted for Rabbit.

Brandt spun back. "Patience!"

She waved him off as the sharp pain subsided,

leaving a dull ache behind. "I'm fine." Or if not exactly fine, she was doing better than Rabbit.

The others were trying to keep him from hurting himself as he thrashed wildly, his eyes rolled back in his skull, his lips drawn back in a terrible, silent scream. Strike had his shoulders and was wrestling to hold him flat on the ground, while Nate, Sven, and Lucius grappled with his flailing arms and legs, and Jade tried to get something between his teeth.

Then, as quickly and unexpectedly as the convulsions had begun, they ended. Rabbit went limp and utterly still.

Too still.

"He's not breathing," Myrinne cried.

Patience's heart clutched at the sight of Rabbit's sharp features gone lax, his bristly haircut and beard shadow forming a dark contrast against his too-pale skin.

Without a word, Brandt shouldered his way through the small crowd and dropped down beside Rabbit. Moving with grim efficiency, he checked vitals and then started CPR, snapping, "Myrinne, get in here and breathe for him. Pinch his nose. On my count, *breathe*."

Patience's initial surprise quickly morphed to the realization that he must have learned the first aid after the accident, thinking that maybe he could have saved his friends if he'd known how.

She dropped to her knees opposite him. "What can I do?"

"Pray," he said raggedly.

Almost before the word was out of his mouth,

Rabbit jerked and shuddered. She gasped, afraid it was the beginning of another seizure. But then he rolled partway onto his side and dragged in a rattling breath. He tried to say something, but the words devolved into a painful hacking cough.

"Thank the gods," she whispered, and the sentiment was echoed by several of the others.

Brandt didn't call on the sky, but he did rock back on his heels, his expression easing slightly. When Rabbit struggled to speak, he pressed on the younger man's shoulder. "Take it easy. There's no rush."

But Rabbit shook his head furiously, finally managing to get out, "It was Iago. He came right through the blocks and saw everything. He knows exactly what we're—"

A rattling roar split the air, drowning him out.

A millisecond later, twenty warriors materialized within the confines of the chameleon shield.

The men were in their twenties and thirties, lean and muscled, their arms and legs marked with scars and tattoos that ranged from crude letters to intricate, high-tech art. But although the ink was modern, their outfits and weapons were pure Aztec.

They wore bulky quilted shirts and intricately wrapped cotton loincloths that were knotted at the front, leaving the decorated ends to dangle at knee level. Most of them carried long, flat wooden staves that had rows of sharpened obsidian blades inset along the edges, turning them into crude but effective swords. The lone exception carried a long, obsidian-tipped spear and wore a blue-painted wooden helmet that left his face visible through the gaping mouth of a terrible horned creature with a pug nose and sundisk eyes.

Their eyes glowed luminous green.

Strike roared, *"Makol!"*

The Nightkeepers reacted instantly. Red-gold magic sang in the air as the magi brought their talents online and ranged themselves around where Brandt, Patience, and Myrinne still crouched over Rabbit.

At first the obsidian-edged staves didn't seem like much of a threat, but then the demon-helmeted leader barked an unfamiliar spell, dark power rattled in the air, and the obsidian blades spun into magic-wrought motion, whizzing chain-saw-like. At a second command, the sword tips became spear throwers that launched spinning, razor-sharp blades toward the Nightkeepers.

"Shields!" Strike ordered, though most of the warriors already had their protective spells online. The first barrage bounced off those shields, except for a single blade that caught Sven in the shoulder, sending him to his knees as blood splashed the rock behind him. He clamped his lips on a cry.

Alexis dropped down beside him, yanked his shirt off, and worked it into a passable field dressing as the others launched a salvo of fireballs and jade-tipped bullets. Within the core of the defensive formation, Patience brought up her shield magic and spread it out, forming a protective globe that encompassed a groggy Rabbit, and Myrinne, who hadn't left his side. Brandt did the same, so together they cast a double layer of protection as Rabbit struggled up, eyes wild. He pointed to something behind them. "The doorway!"

Patience's heart lurched as she spun and saw that two of the Aztec *makol* were headed straight for the tunnel mouth, both loaded with heavy satchels. *They are headed for the cave!*

As one, she and Brandt started after them. Behind them, Rabbit shouted, "Iago got right into my head. He knows about the light-magic entrance."

Brandt cursed. "If he sent the *makol* to breach the inner doorway, he must not have known how to get into the intersection, after all."

"And watch your backs," Rabbit said, his voice now coming from their earpieces as they crossed to the pyramid. "He knows you two killed Ix. He'll be gunning for both of you."

"Roger," Brandt said. He paused near the darkness of the doorway. The two *makol* were gone. When he glanced at Patience, she saw the warrior in his eyes, but there was something more there too. Something worried. "You should stay up here and make sure none of the others get through."

Which was logical enough. But it was also bullshit, and they both knew it.

"You're not leaving me behind." This was their cave. Their intersection. She wasn't letting Iago have it.

But at the same time, part of her liked that Brandt was suddenly acting more like a mate than a mage. On impulse, she stood on her tiptoes and brushed her lips across his.

When she drew back, his eyes were dark, without a hint of gold. But they weren't cool. Not by a long shot. His voice was rough when he said, "They'll pin us down in the tunnel if they sense us. We'll have to sneak in. Which means no shields."

"Then that's an even better reason to bring me along. They can sense spells, but not talent-level magic." She held out her hand.

He took it. And she turned them both invisible.

They dropped their shields and headed through the doorway and down the stairs. As the cool darkness closed around them, Patience felt naked, partly because she couldn't use her shield and partly because going invisible always made her feel strangely insubstantial even though her mass didn't change. But although she didn't need direct contact to maintain Brandt's invisibility, he didn't let go of her hand.

Instead, he tightened his fingers on hers as they rounded the first curve, and whispered almost soundlessly, "I've got your back and you've got mine. Deal?"

The words echoed back to that first night, warming her and making her feel more solid. *Focus,* she told herself. But the warmth lived alongside her warrior's battle tension as they continued downward, trailing the fingers of their free hands along the tunnel wall to help guide them in the pitch blackness.

Then, suddenly, the darkness lightened: Up ahead, she could see where the tunnel opened up to the cave, which was lit from sunlight coming down from above.

"Can you guys read us?" Brandt breathed into his throat mic, but got static back. They were on their own.

As they moved closer, the air gained a hint of salinity and freshness. The combination was a potent memory trigger, but Patience kept the lid on her emotions as they took high and low positions and eased around the corner to check out the situation.

"Oh, dear gods," she whispered almost soundlessly as she got her first real look at the cave.

It was beautiful.

The ancient cathedral had been impressive at night, lit by fireworks and starlight. In the daylight, illuminated with yellow sunlight, it was magical. The perfectly circular skylight dripped with lush green vines that hung down from up above. Sunlight streamed through, casting the lagoon water in vivid blues and greens that contrasted with the white limestone and the richer tans and browns of soil and other stones.

But even as one part of Patience locked on to the beauty of the subterranean pool, her inner warrior focused on the situation: There was no sign of the doorway that led to the inner chamber, but the two *makol* were positioned right where it had been. One of them stood guard with his buzz sword at the ready, staring through them. The other one was hammering something into the wall.

"Looks like the bastard's not going to bother with magic," Brandt breathed. "He's just going to blast his way in."

"Not if we take out his *makol*," she said, equally softly, though her stomach churned.

She hated killing *makol*. Even though their human hosts were chosen based on evil, and couldn't be saved once the possession was complete, she was all too aware that each of those hosts had once been someone's child.

Taking a deep breath to settle the quease, she pulled her ceremonial knife. "You're on point. I've got your six."

He squeezed her fingers. "Stay safe." Then he broke their handclasp, drew his knife with an almost inaudible rasp, and moved out.

With her warrior's talent going full blast, Patience mirrored his movements, monitoring his position by the faint sounds he made as they entered the cave and skirted the outer perimeter, where the shadows largely concealed their growing trail of footprints in the sand.

When they got within a few feet of the *makol*, Brandt moved in for an invisible attack. All Patience saw were the consequences: The guard jerked, his luminous eyes going wide and his mouth gaping in a gurgling cry as his throat opened in a gruesome line of blood that quickly became an arterial spray.

The second *makol* spun and shouted, then slashed out wildly with his buzz sword. Patience ducked the attack and used an invisible foot sweep to send him sprawling, then followed him down, planted a knee in the middle of his back, and pithed him.

Her bile surged as the cartilage, tendons, and muscle at the back of his neck resisted and then gave, and her blade slid home. She twisted, and the *makol* convulsed and went still.

Exhaling, she reminded herself: *Head incapacitates, heart banishes.* These lesser *makol* didn't require the complicated cardinal-day ritual it would take to banish a powerful *ajaw-makol* like Iago had become, but she still needed to make sure her enemy was dead.

As the Nightkeepers' powers had increased, so had those of their enemies.

A few feet away, the other *makol's* protective tunic ripped off its chest, seemingly of its own volition, revealing a heavily tattooed, thickly muscled chest and abdomen. When a long slice appeared out of nowhere, she gagged and dropped the invisibility spell.

Brandt appeared, grim-faced and covered in blood. He met her eyes over the *makol's* body. "I'll take care of both of them. See what you can do about the bomb."

Adrenaline spurted anew. *The bomb. Oh shit.*

Bolted securely to the stone very near where the light-magic doorway had appeared, the device was marked only with a bar of light that flashed through a building sequence from dim to bright and back again, on a repeating cycle that sped up incrementally as she approached.

Her heart hammered against her ribs. It was a timer, but without a countdown, she didn't have a clue how long they had left. It could have ten minutes left on it, or ten seconds. Her gut-level instincts said to haul ass out of there. Her DNA said they had to protect the light-magic intersection. An explosion wouldn't hurt the magic, but it could block the hell out of the tunnel.

"If we can get it off the wall—" She reached for the device, heart racing.

Dark magic spat a fat spark, pain cracked through her body, and a booming electric shock flung her backward. Brandt lunged forward and caught her against him; she clung for a second, grateful when he called up his shield magic to protect them both.

"Are you okay?"

"Tenderized." But the magic had given her an idea. "We can shield it ourselves and contain the blast," she said quickly, pulse hammering as the light blinked faster by the second.

Working together, racing against the barely flickering light, they cast a pair of double-thick shields, one around them, the other around the bomb and part of the rock wall behind it.

A high whine split the air.

"Close your eyes." Brandt put his body between her and the danger, pressed her cheek to his chest, and buried his face in her hair.

She wrapped her arms around him and splayed her hands across his back in a feeble gesture of protecting as much of him as she could. That wasn't enough to stem the panic that threatened to punch through her warrior's determination, though. She needed to do something more, say something more. *Don't say anything you'll regret later*, she warned herself, knowing that her emotions were far too close to the surface.

So instead she rose up on her toes and locked them together in a kiss. She meant to hold herself back, to find the strength of sex magic without giving away too much of herself. But she was too aware of the sacred lagoon behind them, the drape of green vines, and the yellow warmth of the sunlight coming down from up above. Power hummed around them, coming from the shield spells, from the cave itself. And from the heat that sparked at the first touch of her lips on his.

Yes, she thought. This was their place. This was where they clicked, where they made sense.

He groaned at the back of his throat and answered her kiss, pulling her up into his body and sliding his tongue against hers. And she gave him everything, holding nothing back. Desire poured from her to him and back again through their *jun tan* connection, turning their shields red-gold, so they were surrounded with the sparkling magic that they made together.

They twined together, held on to each other.

And the bomb blew.

The brilliant flash of the explosion flared through the cave, strobing her vision even through her closed eyelids. The shields muffled the roaring *boom*, but the spell sucked mad power as they fought to contain the shock wave, concussion, and shrapnel spray.

Patience clung to Brandt, who tightened his arms around her, anchoring them both as they poured their combined magic into the shield, which bucked and shuddered, threatening to give way.

It held, though, remaining intact as the conflagration within it crested and drained. The terrible pressure on their joined magic eased . . . and they opened their eyes, still nose to nose, their lips touching.

Although their cave visions had skipped the interval between their first kiss and the end of the lovemaking that had followed, those memories filled her now as she looked up and saw tenderness in the gold-shot depths of his brown eyes. And now, as then, she was filled with the utter certainty that the two of them had been meant to find each other that night, that they had been meant to fall in love.

Now, though, she realized that she didn't know whether they had been meant to *stay* together.

A deep-seated fear that the answer was no had her wanting to hold on too tight. So instead, she made herself step away from him, drop her shield, and take a look at the damage.

She stared. "Holy crap."

The shield had contained the explosion exactly within its sphere, carving a scoop out of the stone behind where the bomb had been attached. If the wall had been solid, there would have been a missing half-moon of limestone.

Instead, there was a perfectly circular opening, with darkness beyond.

"The tunnel," she whispered as her heart stuttered in her chest. They had punched through to the tunnel. "We can get to the inner chamber before the solstice-eclipse." And maybe—hopefully—call on the gods.

A sudden blast of static made both of them wince,

and then Strike's voice, broken up by interference, said, "Almost . . . we're . . . *shit*."

Patience and Brandt exchanged a look and bolted for the surface.

By the time they got topside, though, the fight was over, the *makol* gone. The air stank of char and vibrated with magic, but the coast was clear.

Patience's adrenaline flagged quickly, fatigue threatening to take over, but there was triumph, too, as she said, "The cave is clear . . . and the tunnel is open."

The announcement was met with a ragged cheer. The magi were beat-up, dirty, and fight-worn, but they had won the intersection.

"Don't get too excited," Rabbit warned in a low voice from the edge of the group, where he sat on a boulder, slumped and boneless. Myrinne stood beside him, her hand on his shoulder. Patience hadn't always loved how much influence the younger woman had over Rabbit, but now she was glad to see her there, the two of them forming a united front against Strike's scowl.

"The blocks didn't work," Rabbit continued. "Iago got everything. He knows what I know about Ix's death, the Triad spell, Anna and Mendez being chosen, how Brandt is linked to Cabrakan. . . ." He trailed off and looked at Patience, eyes hollow. "Once he realized you and Brandt killed Ix, he focused on you guys. He pulled everything he could about you. . . . I'm not sure what he got out of me, but he has to have seen the twins."

"The—," she began, then broke off when the oxygen drained out of her lungs. She wasn't even aware that she'd started swaying until Brandt grabbed her arm to keep her from going down. "No," she whispered, leaning on him. When he started to say something, though, she held up a hand to stop him, and then pushed away to stand on her own when she repeated, louder: "No."

Rabbit looked suddenly eighteen again. "I'm sorry—"

"I mean 'no' as in 'I'm not going to let this screw me up,'" she interrupted. "The whole point of having Hannah and Woody take them away was so nobody—not even Iago or the *Banol Kax* themselves—could find them if our enemies learned of their existences, right?" Strike had even gone so far as to have Rabbit use his mind-bending to make it impossible for a teleporter to lock on to any of them. They were off the grid. Safe. *Please, gods, let them be safe*, she thought, knowing she was beyond lucky that Rabbit didn't know the one vital clue that Iago could have used to find them.

"She's right," Brandt said, stepping up beside her so their fingertips brushed. "How much does it really matter that Iago knows who was chosen for the Triad? I'm already watching my back, and the other two are protected. He wants a piece of me and Patience because we killed Ix? Well, we want a piece of him right back. As for the intersection, we won the first round of that fight." He gestured to the tunnel entrance. "So I vote we get down there and see about protecting our newest asset."

Sven's eyes fired. "Hell, yeah. Let's—"

A roaring *boom* cut him off as a violent explosion detonated beneath them. The ground shuddered and bucked, sending Patience reeling. She grabbed on to Brandt, screaming as a huge gout of debris erupted from the pyramid's doorway in a giant shotgun blast of dust and shrapnel.

There was no time for a shield spell. Brandt turned them so he took the brunt; she felt the impacts shuddering through him, and cried out when pain slashed across her upper arm on one side, her calf on the other. A series of crashes followed the first detonation, sounding like the earth was tearing itself apart.

As the noise faded, the others started shouting questions and raging at their enemy, but Patience couldn't make out words over the low-throated rumble of stone and earth resettling itself, and the ringing in her ears.

Heart hammering, she pushed away from Brandt, took two steps in the direction of the pyramid, and stopped dead.

"No!" The word ripped from her throat in a scream. She pressed the back of one hand to her mouth, tears flowing at the sight of a huge pile of rubble where the pyramid had been.

It had collapsed in and down, toppling into the deep, circular depression that had appeared behind and under it. *Their cave.*

"He planted a second bomb," she said numbly. Her own voice sounded strange in her ears, though the ringing had subsided.

Brandt gripped her hand, squeezing hard, his eyes dark with anger. But then he tugged her away from the wreckage to where the others were gathering. "Come on. We need to get our asses out of here and regroup."

He was right. The chameleon shield had held through the blast, but the humans would be incoming, rushing to see the damage that they would undoubtedly blame on one of the miniquakes that were part of Cabrakan's warm-up act. And the magi were banged up: She had deep cuts on her arm and leg. Brandt was favoring one side of his torso, his face drawn in pain; Sven was cradling his arm; the rest of their teammates were variously bloody and battered. Not to mention that they were all starting to sag with postmagic fatigue.

Patience stared at the rubble for a long, yearning moment, not wanting to believe that the beautiful blue-green lagoon, with the flowered vines and the pretty white beach where she and Brandt had first made love together, where they made sense together, was gone. But it was.

After a long moment, she turned away and headed to join the others. And she didn't let herself look back.

CHAPTER TWELVE

Skywatch

When Patience had finally resigned herself to the twins being gone, one of the few things that had helped was knowing that Hannah and Woody were taking care of them, raising them. But when the banged-up team materialized back at Skywatch and the other *winikin* descended on their charges, she would've given almost anything for Hannah to be there too.

Then Patience would have had someone to fuss over her, someone who would be focused on helping her bounce back as quickly as possible, with no other agenda beyond that. And although part of her beating the depression had involved being responsible for her own well-being, just then she would've given a body part to duck that load for an hour or two.

Sighing, she dropped onto the nearest couch and

let the chaos of fragmented explanations and *wini-kin*-led triage flow around her. She would get up in a minute, she thought. Already, her accelerated healing powers were dulling the pain of the cuts on her shoulder and leg, expelling the debris, and knitting the flesh. But right now, she didn't want to have to take care of herself.

"What do you say we head for the suite, so we can get cleaned up and survey the damage in peace?"

It took a moment for Brandt's words to penetrate the cottony numbness that surrounded her, another moment for her to focus on him.

He was leaning over her, holding out a hand that was crusted with blood, dust, and ash, as was the rest of him. His hair stuck up in gluey clumps, and blood seeped from a cut above one eyebrow, but she was struck by the way those red-rimmed eyes were entirely focused on her. She saw grief and anger in him, and frustration that Iago had beaten them and destroyed the cave.

But she didn't see the hated distance, the detachment. He was still there, totally with her in the moment. They were back at Skywatch . . . but he still had gold in his eyes.

Hope fluttered in her chest, cautiously unfurling. Had El Rey changed things between them after all?

She didn't know. What she did know was that, just then, she needed someone to fuss over her, and he was offering.

Putting her hand in his, she said, "Lead the way."

He pulled her to her feet and they set off toward the residential wing, leaning on each other.

"You two want some help?" Jox called across the great room.

Patience smiled at the royal *winikin*, but shook her head. "No, thanks. We can take care of each other." And for the first time in a long, long time it didn't feel like that was wishful thinking.

Two hours later, the residents of Skywatch gathered in the great room. Michael was there, having left Mendez, still zonked out in one of the basement storerooms and guarded by Carlos and a double-barreled shotgun loaded with jadeshot. Sasha was there too; Strike had 'ported her back to the compound so she could quick-heal Sven's busted arm, Brandt's cracked ribs, and a few other blast injuries, and also to give her a break from watching over Anna, whose condition was stubbornly unchanging. Nate and Alexis, posing as members of the extended family, had taken over at the hospital.

Patience felt loose-limbed and relatively well rested, thanks to a long shower and a huge shared bowl of pasta that Brandt had made while she was washing up. And if it had seemed once or twice that he'd been trying too hard, at least he was making an effort.

As Strike called the meeting to order and did a quick "this is where we're at" to bring the *winikin*, Michael, and Sasha up to speed, Patience pressed her sneakered foot against the side of Brandt's boot and received a return nudge that meant more to her than it probably ought to. But she let herself have the moment.

Strike finished his rundown with, "Obviously these new developments raise a shitload of additional questions and issues, but our priority needs to be finding a way to get our asses into the intersection for the solstice-eclipse. We can't use the light-magic tunnel. Even if we could come up with a spell to move that much rubble, the area's going to be under some serious human scrutiny. Which means we need to find another way in." He looked at Rabbit. "Do you think you could find the dark-magic entrance?"

"Maybe. Could I open it once I found it? Probably. But that'd lay me wide-open to Iago, and I don't—" He broke off, flushing. His voice was tight with guilt and frustration when he said, "At this point, I don't know what the fuck to do except stay here inside the wards for the rest of the war. It doesn't make any godsdamned *sense* for me to go outside where Iago can read me whenever the hell he wants. It's like I'm an enemy spy, only I'm not. I'm just . . . fuck. I'm not strong enough to block him anymore." He fell silent, scowling miserably. Myrinne, who sat beside him on the far love seat, touched his arm in support; he nodded acknowledgment, but his expression didn't lighten.

"I keep wondering *why* Iago didn't know about the intersection already," Patience said. She'd been going over it in her head, partly in an effort to *not* think about the cave, or the fact that they were running out of time.

"I've been thinking about that," Lucius said. "The Order of Xibalba split off from the Nightkeepers, right? But then it developed its own characteristics, which we're pretty sure parallel the Aztec culture. Well, in the Aztec world, the boys who were destined to be soldiers were raised under really rough conditions. When they hit fifteen, they entered military training camps, where knowledge was power and an elder son always had a much higher status than his younger brothers. Based on that, I could see Ix keeping the intersection's location a secret from Iago, especially if they were the only two surviving members of the ruling bloodline. It was all about competition, even between brothers."

Rabbit didn't look entirely convinced. "If that was the deal, why was Iago so pissed when he found out how Ix died?"

"Because they were blood," Strike said flatly.

"And because we're Nightkeepers," Brandt put in. "Not to mention that we prevented his father's reincarnation as a *makol*. It doesn't matter how he felt about Ix—he's going to be bullshit."

A shiver crawled down the back of Patience's neck. "'What has happened before will happen again,'" she murmured, quoting from the writs. When Strike gestured for her to continue, she said, "Everything cycles. Cabrakan and Iago both blame Nightkeepers for killing their brothers. And they both want revenge." But she frowned when that jarred. "Except if Iago wanted to kill me and Brandt, why didn't he blow the cave while we were inside? He had to have seen us through the eyes of the *makol*."

"He might have decided he couldn't risk killing the two of you right at the light-magic entrance," Lucius pointed out. "There's a good chance the sacrifice would have opened the skyroad for good."

There was a beat of silence as they absorbed the near miss.

In that moment, though, Patience had an idea. To Rabbit, she said, "I know you said you're not strong enough to block Iago anymore, but do you think you could direct him to certain pieces of information? Or hide other pieces so he can't get to them?"

A faint spark kindled in his eyes. "Maybe. Yeah. I think I could figure out a block that looks like my normal background mental pattern, sort of camouflaging some stuff."

"No," Brandt growled. "Don't even think about it."

Which meant he already had. Pulse bumping with a mix of nerves and adrenaline, she turned to Strike. "Iago didn't come after us today because he's too smart to waste the power he could gain from our sacrifice. We can use that to set a trap."

"No," Brandt repeated, jaw set. "Abso-fucking-lutely not."

Strike flicked him a look. "That's not your call."

Brandt glared. "I'm not saying we shouldn't try it. Set me up all you want. Douse me in ketchup and tie a fucking bow around my neck. I don't care. But she doesn't get used as bait."

Patience's inner warrior wasn't buying that one, but the woman within liked the steel in his tone. *To new beginnings,* she thought. "We don't have to decide the details now. The immediate question is whether Rabbit can figure out a way to show Iago only what we want him to see."

Brandt turned back to her. "I'm serious; if we set a trap, I want you waiting with the others, not down in the hot zone with me."

But instead of the gold-shot concern she expected to see in his face, she saw cool distance.

Her heart plummeted, and her pulse bumped off rhythm when she realized that he wasn't present anymore. He was . . . gone. "That didn't last long, did it?" she said softly.

Regret flashed briefly in his eyes. Instead of answering, though, he turned to Lucius. "Is there anything in the library about major dark-magic spells that are specific to a solstice-eclipse? It'd help if we knew what Iago could be planning for tomorrow night."

"He might not be planning anything," Rabbit pointed out. "I think he's still pretty weak, at least physically. He might hold off until the spring equinox, when he's at full power."

"You willing to bet on that?"

"No. I'm just saying."

Patience let the conversation move around her while she tried to make the inner shift from "this is our new beginning" to "I'm responsible for my own emotions." She'd gotten pretty good at the latter, but it sucked to realize how quickly she had fallen back into old patterns based on a few good days.

Damn it, she knew better. But she was weak when it came to him, too ready to give things between them a second chance. Or a fifth. A twenty-fifth.

A noise from the far side of the great room jerked her from self-recrimination.

Jox stood white-faced in the arched doorway leading to the *winikin*'s wing.

Strike bolted to his feet. "What's wrong? Is it Anna?"

"There's been an earthquake in Mexico City. I'm not sure how bad—it just hit the CNN crawl."

The room went dead silent. *Oh shit*, Patience thought as her heart nose-dived and her and Brandt's problems suddenly felt a whole lot smaller.

"Fuck." Strike grabbed the remote, powered up the big screen that dominated one wall, and clicked over to one of the Mexican news stations they monitored.

The audio came on first, in Spanish. Patience had to wait for the image to clarify and the closed-captioning to come online. The picture steadied first; it showed people thronging a street, milling and gesturing.

Moments later, words scrolled along the bottom of the screen: *". . . the quake, which reportedly registered 6.1 on the Richter scale, shook buildings and sent people out into the streets, but no injuries have been reported. Many of the people you see standing outside their homes and jobs remember twenty-five years ago, when an 8.1 earthquake leveled much of the city and killed upwards of ten thousand people."* The screen switched to a montage of twisted steel and crumbled cement against a background pall of gray dust.

They watched for a few more minutes, the tension in the room leveling off as it became obvious that the quake could have been far worse.

Finally, Strike killed the volume and tossed the remote. "Cabrakan's letting us know that he's coming for us."

But Brandt frowned. "If that's the case, why hit Mexico City? That was Aztec territory. Why not aim for a Nightkeeper site?"

"Mexico City is built over Moctezuma's capital city, Tenochtitlán," Lucius pointed out. "Maybe it's a message for Iago, not us." He paused. "It's not like Iago and the *Banol Kax* are allies anymore. We've got a three-way fight shaping up: Iago wants to finish the conquest Moctezuma began in the fifteen hundreds, the *Banol Kax* want to conquer the earth plane and use it as a staging area to attack the sky, and we're trying to hold the freaking status quo."

Patience was only partway paying attention; she was focused on the closed-captioning and the images that flashed on the TV screen, partly because she was numb and heartsore over Brandt's withdrawal, partly because of what was showing on the screen.

In the absence of any real damage from the current quake, the new ghouls were rehashing the earlier quake atop a montage of film and still shots showing rescue efforts, stadiums turned into morgues, and tent cities of dispossessed survivors. *"Even though the epicenters of both the 1985 earthquake and today's quake were located some 350 kilometers away, in the Pacific Ocean, Mexico City is particularly vulnerable to seismic activity because of its location atop a dry lake bed. The lake was filled during the expansion of the Aztec city of Tenochtitlán, but the fill isn't stable, creating a drumhead effect that amplifies low-frequency waves . . . like those of seismic activity."*

"Ten thousand dead," she said to herself, not really realizing she'd said it aloud until the others fell silent.

Jox, who had taken a seat near Strike, said, "Some of the upper estimates were over fifty thousand fatalities. The Mexican government ordered a news blackout after the quake, so there's no real confirmed number. Internationally, the general sense was that ten thousand was a low-end estimate."

She couldn't conceive of those numbers. Or rather, she could, and the thought of it tightened a fist around her heart. "We can't let the next earthquake come," she whispered. "People are going to die. Lots of people." Hundreds. Thousands. Tens of thousands. She looked at Brandt. "We have to stop it."

He grimaced. "You said it yourself: The *etznab* spell needs more than the words." He didn't say that he wasn't sure they had "more" just then. He didn't need to.

Despair pricked, but she didn't let herself give in to it. Instead, she reached into a pocket and pulled out the small, well-worn star deck. "These led me to the *etznab* spell. Maybe they'll help us figure out what comes next."

Realizing that the room had gone silent and she had become the center of attention, she looked around, flushing slightly. "Sorry. I'll go—"

"Stay." Lucius shoved a coffee table across to bump against her knees, making Jox wince at the scraping noise the hardwood made. "Show us how it works."

"No, really. I'll just—" She stopped herself. "Scratch that. Sure, I'll show you."

Knowing that her focus was scattered, she began with a prayer that defined the reading. *Please, gods, help me to help him earn the Triad magic.* That had to be her priority. After that . . . she didn't know.

She shuffled the cards until they slid freely, then cut the deck three times—once for the past, once for the present, once for the future.

Setting the deck on the coffee table, then said, "Given the nature of the *etznab* spell, I'm going to use a spread called the 'hall of mirrors.'"

She took the top three cards off the deck, then arranged them facedown in a triangle, with the top card at the lower left, the middle at the lower right, and the last forming the pinnacle of the two-dimensional pyramid. Then she tapped the lower left card. "This one is called the smoky mirror. It represents the shadow darkening my present state of being, making things unclear or asking to be revealed. The one next to it"—she touched the lower right card— "is the clear mirror. It offers truth, guidance, and vision. Finally, the card at the top shows me how to step through the mirror into self-awareness and reach an answer."

Taking a deep breath, she closed her eyes, centered herself, and tapped into her magic, which responded sluggishly. She kept working at it, though, seeking added power. Hearing the rustle of movement, she assumed the crowd was thinning. So she was startled when a hand touched her shoulder and her magic surged. She opened her eyes to find the magi gathered around the couch where she and Brandt were sitting. Sasha was touching her shoulder; she was connected to each of the others by a touch, forming a linked circle all the way around to Brandt.

He waited until she looked at him, until their eyes met. Then he extended his hand across the short gap separating them. His expression was all warrior, but she told herself that was the way it should be. This wasn't about them; it was about the Triad magic and the war.

Still, her heart ached. *Oh, Brandt.*

Nodding as much to herself as to any of the others, she took his hand and felt the team's joined power swell through her. Without blood sacrifice it was a gentler magic, one that warmed rather than energized, centering her rather than pushing her beyond her normal limits.

"Okay." She exhaled slowly. "Here we go." She flipped the lower left card. A sense of inevitability skimmed through her at the sight of a burgundy and black glyph against a yellow sun sign. "This is Imix, the Primordial Mother. It's the card I almost always draw in positions representing my needs."

"Which means that the magic's working," Jade offered.

"I think so. The question is going to be whether I can correctly interpret the cards I pull. Getting Imix in the smoky-mirror position suggests that I need to reveal myself, or that in the past I've been my own worst enemy."

"Which could apply to most of us," Brandt pointed out.

Trying not to read too far into that, she turned over the card on the lower right, and jolted at the sight of a deep blue-black design with a starscape in the center and the sun behind it. "Lamat. Wow."

"What is it?" Lucius pressed, seeming fascinated.

"I drew the same two cards in the same order the other day. That can't be an accident." Exhaling to settle the sudden churn of her stomach, she continued: "I think of Lamat as Brandt's card." She didn't elaborate; there was no need to broadcast that it was his card because its shadow aspect was disconnection and a rigid adherence to dogma. "For his card to appear in the clear-mirror position means that he holds the answer we're looking for. Which is a given, really, since he's the only one who knows—consciously or not—why the gods won't speak to him."

"Could the Lamat card refer to anything else?" he asked. She couldn't quite read his expression.

"Possibly. Maybe the third card will help clarify things." She flipped the apex card, and her stomach sank at the sight of a jagged "X" symbol. "*Etznab.* Shit." She shook her head as disappointment rolled through her. "We already know we need to step through the mirror. That's what we're *trying* to do, damn it. But what mirror? Where?" Looking up at the others, she made a helpless gesture. "I'm sorry. It's a real reading—there's no way I could accidentally pull a reading that says Brandt and I should step through the mirror. But it doesn't tell us anything new."

They all stared down at the triangle of cards for a long moment. She was surprised when Brandt was the one to break the silence. "What if it's trying to tell you something new, but you're not listening?" When her head snapped up, he held up his free hand. "Whoa. Not trying to start a fight. I'm just wondering whether you're making assumptions here based on past readings. What if you—I don't know—try to look at this with completely fresh eyes? No preconceptions."

"Right. Because I'm my own worst enemy."

"I didn't say that."

"No. The cards did." And as much as it sucked to admit it, he could be right. She stared down at the spread, trying to blank her mind and start over. "Okay. Imix is the mother figure, period. In the shadow position, it deals with issues of trust and revelation. I'm confident of that interpretation." She'd been through the book so many times in the past week that she didn't need to look anymore. She knew the aspects by heart. "But you might have a point about Lamat. Not everything about it connects to you. The shadow aspects are a perfect fit, but this isn't a shadow card." Thinking fast, she recalled, "In its light aspects, Lamat is the One Who Shows the Way. He's a leader who seeks to harmonize disparate things. He's connected to the rabbit, fire, and the path of destiny." Light dawned; she turned to Strike. "Hell. *You're* Lamat here. I would've thought you'd be Ahau, the king's card, but you're not, at least not in this spread. Here, you're the clear mirror."

"Keep going," Brandt urged.

Thinking out loud, she said, "Strike holds the clarity I'm seeking. To reach it, I need to reveal myself. In doing so, I'll step through—" She broke off as dismay rattled and her stomach knotted. "Oh." *Oh, shit.* The cards had practically been beating her over the head with it, but she hadn't seen it until now.

In the end, it was all about the hall of mirrors.

Brandt tightened his grip on her hand. "You've figured it out." It wasn't a question.

"I think so." And in revealing herself to her king, she was going to have to out Brandt as a coconspirator, when the incident in question had been one of the few times he'd really come through for her at Skywatch.

Then again, she thought, revelation, like sacrifice, wasn't supposed to be easy.

She released Brandt's hand. As if that had been a signal, the other magi dropped their touch links. Taking a deep breath, she stood and faced Strike fully. "Brandt and I need to use the shrine."

"The ceremonial chamber?" Strike said, referring to the sanctified room near the center of the mansion, where a glass roof let in the sun and stars, and the ashes of their ancestors provided a power sink. "Of course. No problem."

"I'm not talking about the chamber. I'm talking about the shrine in your suite. The one with the torches, the *chac-mool*, and the obsidian mirror on the back wall."

A mirror that, as she'd stood there, heart pounding with the fear of being discovered, had created the illusion of her being in a torchlit hall of mirrors instead of a tiny closet hidden within the royal suite.

Jox and Leah looked startled. The rest of the magi and *winikin* looked confused with the exception of Strike, whose expression darkened. "That's a private room. Why would you—" He broke off, looking disgusted and rapidly heading for pissed-off territory. "My laptop. You've got to be fucking kidding me."

Patience glanced over at the muted TV, which was back to cycling through the destructo-montage of images from the big quake. *Ten thousand dead,* she reminded herself. *Brandt can stop it from happening if he becomes the Triad mage.* And to do that, they needed access to the king's hall of mirrors.

Taking a deep breath, she said, "Earlier this year, I snuck into your suite and searched it, looking for information on where Woody and Hannah were hiding with the twins. I figured you'd have it on a nonnetworked computer, so I kept looking until I found it."

"In the shrine." The words came from Jox, who was glaring at Strike. "Thanks for the fucking vote of confidence."

Although the royal suite was off-limits to the others without invitation, the royal *winikin* had free access to Strike and Leah's living space. He wouldn't have gone into the mages-only shrine, though . . . which was why Strike had hidden the laptop there, removing the temptation. At least, that was what Patience had guessed when she had found the machine, and now it seemed that Jox had made the same leap.

Strike's lips thinned. "I thought it would be easier that way. You took it so hard when Hannah left."

The *winikin* drew himself up to his full height, which suddenly seemed much more than his actual five-nine or so. "Right. So you figured that I might jeopardize, not just her safety, but also that of Woody, who I respect the hell out of, along with Harry and Braden, who are the last Nightkeeper twins on the earth plane—by tracking her down and . . . what? Popping out for a visit?" Jox's face had gone a dull, furious red. "And this was based on what? The way I turned my back on her during the massacre, and got you and Anna to safety, even though Hannah was *screaming my name*? Or how I *didn't* go looking for her over the next two decades so I could focus on raising you kids and keeping Red-Boar as sane as possible?

"Or maybe it was because of the way I kept my distance from her once we were all back here, or how I lectured her, like a pious little twerp, on how us *winikin*—especially me—needed to put duty and responsibility ahead of personal feelings? Was that it?" The *winikin* was shaking, but his voice was razor sharp, his eyes cold. "Well, fuck you. I deserve better than that after everything I've done for your kingship and this fucking place." He waved a hand around Skywatch, and maybe even the earth plane itself.

"Wait. Jox." Strike held up a hand. "Please."

"Screw that." Jox looked around, expression edging toward wild, as if he'd just realized that he'd gone off on his king in front of his subjects, and contrary to everything the *winikin* stood for, he wasn't sure if he gave a shit. "And screw this." Wheeling, he stalked off.

"Jox!" Strike called, his voice caught somewhere between a royal command and a plea. The *winikin* didn't look back as he headed down the hallway that led to the huge garage.

In the stunned silence that followed his exit, Patience realized she'd stopped breathing. She was afraid to keep looking at Strike, but couldn't look away from the grief and guilt written on his face, knowing she had helped put it there.

Oh, shit. Now what?

Leah started after Jox. "I'll go talk to him."

"No," Rabbit said. "Let me." At her startled look, he lifted a shoulder. "I owe him. He put up with my old man for all those years so he could make sure things didn't get too bad for me. He did that even after—" He broke off. "I just owe him. Okay?"

Leah held up her hands in surrender. "Okay. You go. But tell him . . . tell him we were trying to make things better, not worse."

Rabbit's lips twitched, but with zero humor. "Yeah. Been there." He sketched a wave at Myrinne and disappeared in the *winikin*'s wake.

When he was gone, Strike fixed a glare on Patience. "I thought the cards said you were supposed to reveal yourself to your leader, not fuck him over."

She opened her mouth to answer, but nothing came out. What could she say? "I'm sorry" was far too weak, but it was all she could come up with.

"Maybe what the cards mean is that we need to reveal the shadows to each other." To her surprise, the suggestion came from Brandt. To her further surprise, he stood and moved to her side, so they faced Strike together. "Whatever made the gods turn away from me, it can't be good. That's my shadow. Patience betrayed you, and in doing so, she violated the writs. That's her shadow, and it's partly mine too, because I alibied her."

Strike's expression sharpened over the ragged dismay. "That day in the hallway. You said you were looking for us, but Patience was coming the other way, from the suite. You were covering for her."

Brandt nodded. "I haven't always been there for her, but that time I managed it."

"Strange time to come through," Strike said flatly, "given that she'd just committed treason."

Treason. The word slapped at Patience, carrying, as it did, a death sentence under the old laws.

But Brandt snorted. "You've played fast and loose with the rules from day one, and we're living with the consequences. Don't even try to pretend that Patience going through your sock drawer is on the same plane as you breaking the thirteenth prophecy."

And there it was. She sucked in a breath at Brandt's having the balls to throw down something that had previously gone unsaid, lurking among them as an undercurrent.

In taking Leah as his mate, Strike had broken the final prophecy leading to the end-time countdown. And ever since then, the Nightkeepers' luck had flat-out sucked. They had lost the skyroad and the three-question *nahwal*, and for every step they fought forward, it seemed that they lost the same amount somewhere else.

In a world ruled by destiny and the cycle of fate, the magi would've had to have been idiots not to think their bad luck was connected to Strike's defying the last of the First Father's prophecies. They weren't idiots . . . but none of them had openly voiced the theory. Until now.

Strike bared his teeth. "Do you really want to go there?"

Brandt shook his head. "No. I want to use your fucking shrine so I can get my memory back and figure out how to fix whatever's broken between me and the gods. We've got less than two days until the solstice, so we're going to have to table some of the other stuff until after that."

Patience had a feeling that was at least partly aimed at her, but she couldn't argue the point. Especially not when Brandt had stood up for her and redirected the brunt of Strike's wrath onto himself.

And the king was furious. She didn't think she'd ever seen him this angry before, not even after Rabbit accidentally torched a good chunk of the French Quarter. He was so furious that when Leah touched his arm, he actually snarled down at her, his eyes firing. "Not now, damn it."

She glared back. "Yes, now, damn it. I know you're pissed. You're also worried about Jox, and feeling guilty about playing that one wrong. But like it or not, Brandt is right. We're running out of time." She nodded to Patience. "The shrine is yours. Do whatever you need to do."

"*Damn it, Leah!*" Strike surged against her gentle hold, then subsided. "That room belongs to the jaguars," he grated. "It's *ours*."

"It still will be when they're done with it," Leah said, but she didn't sound like she totally believed what she was saying.

Patience swallowed a surge of misgivings. "The cards led me to the *etznab* spell," she said softly. "Let them give us the Triad mage we need." Her heart cracked and bled a little, though, at the knowledge that this would be it—the last of the visions, and potentially the last thing Brandt would need from her in order to fulfill his destiny.

And after that? She didn't know, damn it.

Strike nodded shortly, a muscle pulsing at the edge of his jawline beard. "Fine. Use the room. And you'd better hope this works."

"Trust me, I do." Because if it didn't, they were screwed.

Without another word, she headed for the archway that led to the royal suite. Brandt stayed a half step behind her, as though covering her retreat. As they passed through the archway into the royal hall, with its plaster-and-beam mission-style decor, heavily carved sideboard, and ornate wooden doors, she

tried not to think of how she'd crept along that hallway six months earlier. Stealing information from her
king had been the lowest point for her; after that, she
had fought her way out of depression. But that didn't
change the fact that she had betrayed two people she
respected, teammates she needed to trust and have
trust her in return.

Yeah. Like that was happening after this.

"Hold up," Strike said from behind them.

Patience's heart thudded sickly against her ribs as
she stopped and turned. It helped that Brandt was
right there, and that he was on her side in this matter,
at least. But for all that Strike was a good guy, he was
their king. And he had a temper.

He stood alone, framed in the archway with his
arms crossed and a serious, intense look on his face.

She lifted her chin. "Yes?"

"I did what I thought was best. I still think it
was—and is—best to have your sons away from all
this, so they're safe and you two can focus on your
own magic." He paused. "But at the same time . . .
I'm sorry I broke up your family." His tone suggested
that he wasn't just talking about the boys and the *winikin*. He was talking about her and Brandt too.

Her throat closed, locking on a choked-back sob.
Having the king talk about their family like it was
over and done with made the possibility far too real.

Worse, Brandt didn't say anything. He just stood
there beside her, there for her, but not *there* for her,
just as he had been for so long.

Swallowing hard, she said, "I'm sorry I broke into

your suite. If it helps any, that was what made me turn things around, realizing that I had become a sneak, a liar, and a thief. I've been working on it since then. And you were right. . . . The boys are safer where they are. I'm sorry it took me so long to believe that."

He didn't say anything else. He just nodded and turned away.

Taking a deep breath, telling herself to stay focused, she turned back and reached for the doorknob of the normal-sized door inset into the larger, carved panels that opened into the royal suite. She glanced at Brandt. "You ready?"

He met her eyes. "Does it matter?"

"No," she said softly. "I guess it doesn't." Ready or not, they needed to connect him to the Triad magic.

CHAPTER THIRTEEN

Brandt followed Patience inside the royal shrine, which was the size of a large closet, and had gas-powered incense-burning torches at the corners and a large *chac-mool* altar taking up the wall opposite the door. Above the altar hung a highly polished obsidian disk that reflected their images from the minute they entered the room and shut the door. A woven footprint mat took up the small floor space, and a laptop was tucked in the corner.

She followed his eyes to the computer, and grimaced. "Yeah. Looks like the same one." She waited for a three count, as if to say "I'll tell you if you ask." He didn't, though, and on the count of four she exhaled and nodded. Palming her knife, she faced the altar. "Okay. Let's do this."

He stared at the laptop a moment longer, wanting to know whether she had found out anything about where Woody and the boys were hiding, yet unable to ask, just as he couldn't reach out to her the way he wanted to, or be the man he'd been before, the one he'd rediscovered in El Rey.

He knew he was hurting her. And he couldn't fucking stop doing it.

Sometimes being an eagle warrior sucks, Woody had said to him a few months after they all moved to Skywatch, when he'd stopped being able to pretend things between him and Patience were okay. The *winikin* had gone on to say, *But for the next few years, we need warriors more than we need good husbands.*

And right now, they needed a Triad mage.

He took his place beside Patience and nodded. "Ready."

The torches filled the small space with the scent of ritual incense, and the flickering light outlined their reflected images in a haze of orange yellow that made them look like negatives projected onto the sacred black stone.

She glanced at him, and he had the sense that she was waiting for him to say something, only he didn't know what.

Then the moment passed and she said, almost to herself, "I think we're supposed to try the *etznab* spell here partly because it's a power sink, and partly because it's a place I associate with the twins. And it's tied to me too, I guess, because breaking in here was me hitting rock bottom. After that, I knew I had to change what I was doing, who I was becoming."

Brandt's throat was tight. "I'm sorry I didn't help

you more. I should have . . . I don't know. Done something." Even now, with guilt gut-punching him, he couldn't reach out to her the way she needed him to. What the hell was *wrong* with him?

Dull agony pounded behind his eyes. Fucking headache.

"I had to figure things out on my own, I think." She paused. "Before, someone else was always around to tell me who I was. Hannah taught me that I was a Nightkeeper, and the color of my belt told me how far I had gotten as a fighter. In school, depending on who you asked, I was a straight-A student, a princess, a tease, or all of those things. Then I met you, and I became a girlfriend, a fiancée, a wife, a mother . . . but at the same time, I was still a Nightkeeper, which made me unique, at least as far as I knew. Special.

"Then, when we came here, I got a whole new set of labels. I wasn't the only Nightkeeper anymore, but I was part of the only mated mage pair, and the mother of full-blood twins. My talent manifested before most of the others', and it was my job to teach everyone hand-to-hand combat skills. . . ." She trailed off. "But then Hannah left with Harry and Braden, and you and I drifted apart. Over time, my talent didn't prove all that useful, and the fight training petered out. Suddenly I wasn't special anymore. I was just *me*."

He couldn't argue the chronology, but she was mistaken about one thing. "If you don't think you're special, you're dead wrong. Trust me. . . . You're special. You're—" But he couldn't do any better than that. All the love words he'd once used freely with her stayed jammed in his throat.

She didn't seem to notice that he'd locked up. Or more likely, she was way too used to it. "I'm starting to figure it all out," she said. "The good news is that I don't need your sympathy or your help. I'm doing okay on my own." She shook her head. "And I didn't mean to get into any of this right now. Sorry."

"Don't be." He met her eyes in the mirror, and wished with all his heart that he could snap his fingers and make everything better between them. "I'm the one who's sorry. For all of it."

She nodded, but didn't say anything more. Instead, she pulled her knife and bloodied her palm, then held out her hand for the uplink. *Being sorry isn't enough,* the action said. *Not if you can't be what I need.*

And it wasn't like he could argue with that either. So he drew his knife, slashed his palm, and took her hand.

"Focus on the accident," she said. "But keep your eyes open. Keep looking into the mirror."

Werigo's magic made the memory slippery and hard to pin down, but he made himself remember the sinking Beemer, the blaring horn, and the sound of his own voice screaming for help. His skin crawled with a sudden chill and the imagined press of frigid water. Swallowing hard, he nodded. "Let's do this."

They chanted the spell together, as they had in the mirrored hotel room. But this time as the world spun around him and his consciousness lurched sideways, he was acutely aware that she wasn't with him, not even as a tingle feeding through the *jun tan* bond.

He was entirely on his own, which wasn't nearly the relief his warrior self thought it should be.

Then even that sadness disappeared.

The world went black and cold.

And he was dying.

He crowded up near the roof of the sinking car, tilting his head into the remaining air, which was leaking away by the second. He watched the bubbles rise up, silver in the darkness, and longed to follow them. On his next breath, he sucked water along with the air, and had to fight the gag reflex that threatened to double him over.

Don't panic. Think! *But all he could think about was Woody's stories about the Nightkeepers, and the end-time war, and how important it was for him to work hard, train hard, and have faith. As the final string of silvery bubbles escaped, his mind locked on the last of Woody's expectations.* Faith, *he thought.* When all else failed, that was what it came down to, didn't it?

Tasting his own blood in the water he'd inhaled along with the last half breath of air, he searched for a prayer in the old language. When nothing seemed right, and the grayness started to telescope inward from the edges of his consciousness, he went with his heart, and used the last of his oxygen to say: "Gods. If you can hear this, please help me."

He spat blood into the water, though that seemed redundant given how much he'd already lost from his leg. Then he thought, deep down inside, I'll do anything. I'll give anything. I swear it on my soul. Just get me out of here.

A soundless detonation ripped through him in a shock wave and the world exploded around him, lighting the blackness with a rainbow flash that coalesced to fiery white light.

A voice boomed in his head, somehow sounding like flutes, drumbeats, and a man's voice all at once. "Son of eagles, your offer is accepted because the earth cannot lose a Triad mage in this era. But to keep the Triad intact, a triad must be sacrificed. Two will be taken as tradition holds, but one will come later. The last sacrifice will have both power and your love, because there is no sacrifice without pain."

Brandt convulsed as his body fought for air. He was distantly aware of movement, a rush of water and bubbles, a hand grasping his wrist. Panic clawed at him. His terror that the voice might be real was equally balanced by the fear that it was nothing more than a delusion, the light at the end of the tunnel, a final salute by his dying brain.

Which was it, a god or biological death?

"Son of eagles, do you accept?"

Accept what? He couldn't follow, couldn't think, couldn't do anything but crave oxygen. With his free hand, he clawed at his throat, his chest. Both of his legs were pinned now, by a heavy weight that yanked at him in return, pulling until he felt muscle and tendons tear. A jolt of adrenaline cleared his perceptions slightly and he realized that Joe and Dewey were in the car with him, trying to get him out.

Gods, yes! Pull! he shouted, *but didn't make any noise.* Yank the fucking leg off. I don't care what happens. Just get me out of here!

The voice came again, saying, "If you do not care

what the cost, then take the oath mark and carry it willingly until the balance is restored."

Out of nowhere, glyphs streamed through his head, symbolizing words in the language of his long-ago ancestors. He didn't know how to read the symbols, but somehow the syllables were right there in his head.

"Kabal ku bootik teach a suut!" *he gasped, parroting the syllables that danced in his spinning brain. New pain flared in his injured leg, but he was beyond screaming, beyond caring. The white light went dim, the pain receded, and the world grayed out.*

Then, blessed gods, he was breathing again!

He coughed out water, sucked in biting cold air, and shuddered as it burned his lungs. Slowly, the world came back into focus. Sort of.

He was hanging on to something solid, pointy, and buoyant, and the bitingly cold current was carrying him along. For a minute, all he could do was concentrate on breathing—in and out, in and out. Then his other senses started coming back online: He could hear the rush of the river and feel his ribs hurt with the effort of moving the air. His throat burned and his injured leg throbbed with dull, cold agony. But he was alive!

He went weak with relief. Hell, he was weak, period. It was all he could do to hang on.

"Fucking A," he croaked. "I can't believe you guys got me out of there." His voice sounded strange in his ears.

Even stranger was the silence that followed.

Jarred fully awake by a sudden slash of fear he couldn't pinpoint, he opened his eyes and squinted, trying to make sense of the shadows and moonlit reflections.

He was hanging on to a piece of deadfall; the nubs of broken branches dug into his ribs and stomach, but at least the thing was keeping his head above water. He was floating along, carried by the river's current, paced by other flotsam from the wreck. He saw a couple of hockey sticks and what looked like the unopened package of gym socks he'd had in his bag.

Then the reflections shifted and the white flash stopped looking like a lumpy plastic bag and started looking like something else entirely.

His already freezing body iced further and his heart stuttered. "No." The word came out chattering and broken. "NO!"

That wasn't Dewey's face, open-eyed and fixed in death. The shadows around it weren't a body that moved limply with the current.

No. Impossible. He wouldn't believe it. His buddies were alive, they had gotten him out, they had—

Suddenly, he heard his own voice saying, "Kabal ku bootik teach a suut." And although he didn't know the old tongue, the words somehow translated themselves inside his head: The gods pay; you return the price.

The ice inside him shattered as the rest of it came back— the god's voice, the bargain it had offered. "The sacrifices will be taken as tradition holds," it had said. He hadn't thought about what that meant; he'd been starving for oxygen, fighting to live.

"Joe? Dewey?" His voice wobbled on the word. "Come on, you two, answer me!"

A soft touch of cloth brushed his arm as something heavy, solid, and yielding bumped into him from behind. He didn't want to look, but he couldn't not look.

A harsh sob caught in his throat at the sight of a moon-silvered face and shadowed, lifeless eyes. "Joe." The word turned to a groan when he saw that the white splash had drifted nearer and definitely wasn't a bag of socks. "Dewey."

Grief broke over him like a storm, filling him with a huge, terrible anger.

"No!" He lashed out, hammering at the water that surrounded him, at the deadfall that had saved him. "Damn you, that wasn't fair! I didn't know! I couldn't think!" He lost his grip and went under, then fought his way back up, screaming, "I didn't mean it. I didn't fucking mean it!"

He thrashed and fought until he was bruised, bleeding, and exhausted, clinging limply to the floating wood as tears streamed down his face, feeling barely warmer than the water surrounding him. He sobbed for his friends, and for himself, and when his body went increasingly numb and his grip slipped, he was tempted to let go, tempted to even up the gods' precious balance on his own terms.

He didn't, though, because the sacrifices had already been made, and because Woody had taught him better than to quit.

The sound of a car's engine punched through the shock and misery. He jerked around in time to see a pair of brake lights disappear around a turn in the middle distance. Adrenaline gave a cold-numbed kick at the sight of a light farther downstream, shining on a small building and a dock.

The black riverbanks rose high everywhere else, ominous and impassable.

"Okay," he said through teeth that had stopped chatter-

ing as he passed from cold to the beginnings of hypothermia, despite his hereditary toughness. "You can do this."

Using one leaden arm to paddle, he turned the deadfall, angling to hit the shore pretty far upstream of the dock; he was too damn weak to fight the current, so he would have to use it instead.

Making sure that the floating bodies were securely snagged on the trailing branches, he looped his arm around a sturdy protruding branch and gave a huge frog kick.

He screamed hoarsely, and nearly passed out when his bad leg awakened from warm numbness to raw agony. His cries echoed off the water and the high riverbanks as he convulsed against the deadfall. He clutched the worn branches to keep his head above the water, but his struggles shifted the floating tree, causing it to spin in the frigid current, seeking a new balance.

The branch he'd been holding on to snagged his shirt and dragged him under as the log rolled, taking him with it.

No! His heart hammered as he yanked with fingers weakened by cold, shock, and pain. The fabric tore and gave, and then snagged again, pulling so tightly that there was no way he could get free. He was trapped, pinned helpless mere inches away from air. Flailing, he tried to roll the tree, snap the branch, tear the fabric, to do something, anything, to break free.

Please gods, please gods, please gods! The mantra cycled in his head, though with a sick sense of inevitability now that he knew what the gods were capable of.

His lungs ached with the now-familiar pain of oxygen deprivation. Adrenaline flared through him, giving him a final, desperate spurt of strength that he used to twist *himself into a painful knot. He brought up his good leg, jammed it against the tree trunk, and pushed with everything he had left.*

The shirt cut into him; the collar tightened across his windpipe with a pressure that made his instincts say, Stop. You're choking. *But choking didn't matter when there was no air left to breathe, so he bore down and wrenched against his bonds.*

For a second nothing happened. Then the shirt tore, and he was free!

He tumbled away from the deadfall, spinning head over ass underwater, not sure which way was up. Terror clawed at him alongside pain and the reflexive need to breathe. Then his head broke the surface, more by accident than anything. Cold air slapped his face as he sucked in huge gulps of air, keeping his head above water with spastic churns of his arms and one good leg, while the other hung useless, dragging in the current.

He wasn't going to be able to tread for long. He had to get out of the water.

He blinked into the darkness, taking too long to focus, then even longer to comprehend the sight of the deadfall some twenty feet farther downstream, with Dewey grotesquely snagged and pulled partway out of the water, so his arms were draped over a couple of branches, his head cocked the way it did when he was about to fire off one of his killer put-downs.

Brandt's heart lunged into his throat and even though he knew it was an illusion, he yelled, "Dewey! Hey, Dewey!"

There was no answer, of course. Dewey was dead. Which

was what he was going to be if he didn't get his ass out of the water.

He was just upstream of the boat landing now, and would pass within twenty or thirty feet of the dock. From his vantage, it looked like a mile.

You've got to do it, *Woody's voice said inside him. Brandt hesitated, looking downstream at the deadfall and the pale splash of Dewey's face. Then he turned away and started struggling for the dock with weak strokes of his leaden arms and feeble kicks from his one working leg.*

He almost didn't make it.

The current nearly pulled him past the dock, but he closed the distance with a last violent, muscle-tearing surge. His fingers banged into the cold, slimy wood of the dock pilings. He grabbed, missed, grabbed again, and this time got a good grip on the slippery wood.

He just hung on for a minute, breath burning in his lungs as he absorbed the feeling of being attached to something solid once more. Then, muscles screaming, he dragged himself up onto the dock. Once he was on solid ground, he collapsed, went fetal, and just lay there, shirtless, banged up, and stunned.

What little he knew about first aid said he was fucked unless somebody drove down to the boat landing and found him, because there was no way in hell he was going to make it up to the road. But even as he thought that, he felt the strength of his heritage trickling back through him, warming him a few degrees and getting some of his systems back online.

With those inner reserves came a thrum of basic sur-

*vival instincts that drummed through him with the beat
of his heart, a throbbing refrain of,* Get up. Get moving.
Get help.

*Rolling partway up with a groan of pain and effort, he
took stock in the light of the single overhead bulb. It was solar powered and threw off dim, half-charged illumination.
But that was enough for him to see that his right foot stuck
out at an odd angle from his jeans, which were chewed back
to his knee on the inside, leaving the limp, wet fabric plastered over his calf.*

*He didn't want to look. But he had to. Steeling himself,
he pulled back the fabric. And stared.*

*It wasn't the deep, swollen slash in his leg that fixed
his shocked attention, though. It was the sight of a strange
marking a couple of inches above the injury: three curved
triangles inside a round-cornered rectangle. It was stark
black and looked like an inch-by-inch-and-a-half tattoo he
didn't remember getting.*

*It was a glyph like the ones Wood wore on his right
forearm.*

*A hypoxia-jumbled memory leaped out at him, that
of the god's voice saying,* "Two will be taken as tradition holds, but one will come later. The last sacrifice will have both power and your love, because
there is no sacrifice without pain. . . . Take the oath
mark and carry it willingly until the triad balance is
restored."

*Horror dawned. He still owed another sacrifice. And it
would be someone he loved, someone who carried a connection to the magic.*

Woody.

"No." He didn't scream it this time, didn't rail against the gods or the cruel bargain they had demanded. Instead he went cold, deep down to his very core.

The answer crystallized in his brain, coming from that cold, rational place: The god had said for him to carry the oath mark willingly until the balance was restored . . . which implied that if he rejected it, the oath would be broken.

His entire universe suddenly contracted itself to the sight of the god-mark on his leg and the burning need to get rid of it. He didn't know how the knife got in his hand, hadn't even fully grasped that it'd been in his pocket, shoved there after he'd cut his way free from his seat belt what now seemed like a lifetime ago.

All he knew was that the blade was there. His bloodied leg was there. And he had to get that fucking mark off.

"Son of eagles, do not shame your ancestors." The voice was familiar, yet not. It could have been a delusion; it could have come from the sky.

"You killed them," Brandt grated.

"You made the oath."

"Now I'm breaking it." Clenching his jaw, he set the knife point to his flesh, nearly an inch beyond the border of the mark, like it was a cancer and he had to take enough to be sure he got all of it.

"Do not do this, or the gods and your ancestors will be lost to you until you willingly retake the oath."

"Fuck that." Brandt's consciousness grayed around the edges, tunneling until all he could see was the stark black mark.

And he started to cut.

Without warning, the images kaleidoscoped inward, contracting to a point, and the royal shrine took shape around him once more; he sensed torchlight and incense first, then the pressure of Patience's fingers twined through his. He blinked and swayed, then turned and sagged back against the altar, partly so he wouldn't fall, partly so he would be looking at Patience, not her reflection, when he told her everything.

But then he met her eyes and saw shock. Grief. Maybe even revulsion. *She knew.* She must have followed him into the vision after all, though he hadn't sensed her there.

He would've thought he couldn't possibly get any colder inside. But he could. "Patience." He reached out.

She backed away, expression stark. "Oh, gods." A trembling hand lifted, pressed to her mouth.

The walls of the tiny room closed in on him; the world telescoped to her horrified expression. "I—" He broke off as he got it—he fucking got it. His legs gave out; his ass banged down on the altar. His mouth worked, but he couldn't get out the words that would make it better, because there weren't any. *Oh, holy hell.* The thick incense burned his throat, his lungs. "Werigo made me forget."

And in doing so, the Xibalban had unknowingly struck a hell of a blow for his team.

"Why didn't Woody say anything?" she whispered almost soundlessly.

"I didn't tell him. I couldn't. He would've been . . ." Horrified. Disappointed. Worse, he would've insisted that Brandt retake the oath and finish it. That was how deeply Wood's faith ran. Brandt gripped the edge of the altar so hard his fingers shook. "I made a blood vow to tell him all about it if the barrier came back online and the countdown rebooted."

Only he hadn't, because Werigo had made him fucking *forget* it.

"You knew." Her eyes were red, like she'd been crying, even though she hadn't shed any tears. "That first night, you knew that you were under this, this *curse*. And you didn't warn me, not even once you realized I was a Nightkeeper."

Things had been so crazy that night. He'd been wrapped up in the magic, hooked on the adventure. "I would have told you later."

"Right. Just like you were planning on telling Woody later." She took a step toward him, eyes flashing. "You came up to me, made love to me, knowing that we couldn't be together."

It was just supposed to be a spring-break hookup, he thought, but didn't say, because she was right. He'd done what he wanted to do that night. But his decisions back then weren't the *point*. Once again she was getting stuck in her emotions when they needed to be dealing with the practicalities. Frustration knotted his gut. "Don't you get what this means? *You're* at the top of the fucking list now." His throat locked, but he got it out. "You and the boys."

Her expression iced to the "don't mess with my sons" look he had seen only once before, when Strike had told her they had to send Harry and Braden into hiding. "I'm not an idiot. I get that. But what I also get is that this has all happened because you're so godsdamned convinced you know everything, that you have the right to make decisions for the people around you."

"Bullshit." His head hammered with his pulse. "That's just bullshit. And can we please focus on what's important here? We'll deal with the relationship stuff later."

"On your schedule." Her voice was chill, but her reddened eyes were full of pain.

"Patience." He held out a hand. "Please. Let's not do this right now. We need to concentrate on figuring out how to get at the Triad magic safely."

To his surprise, she took the hand he'd offered. But instead of twining their fingers together, she turned his palm up, so torchlight shone on the half-healed sacrificial cut. "Don't you get it? Everything's connected." Something new moved in her expression, a hint of grief existing beneath the anger. "None of this has been a coincidence."

"You want me to have faith." He said the last word like a curse.

She tightened her grip on his hand. "I want you to *let me in*. I want you to tell me everything, and listen to what I have to say. I want you to trust me. I want you to trust all of us." Her voice went low and urgent. "You've got to stop making decisions for other people. And you've got to let us be your teammates. That's the only way we're going to be able to figure out how to fix this. As a team."

"There's no way *to* fix it," he said harshly.

"You don't know that for sure. Lucius might be able to find something in the library, or one of the others might have an idea." She tugged on their joined hands. "Come on. Let's go tell them what happened."

But he stayed rooted. "I can't."

She let go of his hand. "Can't or won't?"

"I need time to think it through. An hour. Give me an hour to figure things out, so we can go in there together."

"So you can tell me what we decided, you mean." Her smile was bitter. "That would've worked six months ago, but not anymore. You don't get to be the leader of a team within a team anymore. You either come out there with me now or I go on my own." And with that, her request became an ultimatum. *Come with me now, or don't bother coming out at all.*

"Fifteen minutes." Pressure vised his temples, pounded behind his eyeballs, but he couldn't give her what she wanted. And he didn't know why.

He glimpsed tears as she turned away and pushed open the door. With her back to him, she said, "Woody once told me that it was impossible to change an eagle male, that I had to either learn to live with you the way you are or cut my losses."

She paused for a moment, giving him a chance.

He opened his mouth to tell her not to go, to tell her that he would go out there with her, that he would try harder, but a surge of pain grayed his vision and took away the words. He put his face in his hands, digging his fingers in at his temples. *Son of a bitch.* He sensed, deep down inside, the moment that she gave up, the moment that she stepped through the door and let it swing shut behind her. But he couldn't move. Nausea rose as the torchlight speared through him, gone suddenly far too bright.

The headaches were getting worse, but why? What was—

Oh, shit. He got it. He fucking got it.

And the moment he did, the headache snapped out of existence.

He didn't wait around to enjoy the relief, though. He straight-armed the door and went after her. "Patience, wait!"

CHAPTER FOURTEEN

Patience marched down the hallway outside the royal suite, intent on telling the others what she'd seen in the vision . . . and, in doing so, making a clean break. She hadn't planned it that way, hadn't consciously decided to issue an ultimatum, but it was long past due.

Maybe he had a point that the timing was wrong, that they should table the personal stuff until after the solstice-eclipse. But, deep down inside, she didn't believe that. The magic of a mated pair came, not just from the sex, but from the love they shared. Without that love, they were just exes who occasionally slept together.

And oh, gods, how that thought hurt.

"Wait," his voice said from behind her. "Please."

Her heart thudded and she told herself to keep going. Instead, she stopped and turned back, because she was weak when it came to him. Weak, weak, weak. She got even weaker when she saw the hint of gold in his eyes, the suppressed excitement that said he'd figured something out. *Be strong*, she told herself, not even sure she knew what that meant anymore, but sure she couldn't keep going on the way things had been between them for so long.

She lifted her chin. "What?"

He closed the distance between them with long-legged strides and stopped opposite her, so they stood face-to-face very near the heavily carved sideboard that was one of the few pieces of furniture in the hallway.

It was almost exactly where and how they had stood while he'd chewed her out for breaking into the royal suite six months earlier.

"You're right that it's all connected. But not the way you mean." He reached to take her hands, hesitated, and hooked his thumbs in his pockets instead. "We were right that our problems dated back to the talent ceremony, but we were wrong about why. My warrior's talent wasn't trying to screw things up between us. . . . It was trying to *protect* you."

It took a second. But then, like the last few pieces of a three-dimensional puzzle slipping into place, her perceptions realigned themselves, and she saw it. *Of course.* Understanding seared through her, paralyzing her. She couldn't breathe.

"The talent ceremony must have punched partway through Werigo's spell." He paused, his voice going rough. "My subconscious knew I was cursed, and that I had to drive you away, but my conscious self didn't know why. All I knew was that I was making you miserable and I didn't know how to stop. And when I tried to fix things, it felt like my head was ripping itself apart."

"And now?" Her mouth had gone suddenly dry.

"The second I figured it out, the headache quit. I know what's going on now, so my protective instincts don't need to clash with my wanting to be with you."

"Gods," she whispered.

"Everything's going to be different from now on. I promise." He held out a hand. "Come on. Let's go brief the others. You're right—we need to work together to come up with a plan."

But as she took his hand and let him tug her into his arms, let herself rest her cheek on his shoulder for a moment, part of her held itself away. She had spent a long time telling herself that everything would be okay if they could figure out what had gone wrong, and how to fix it. Instead, things were more complicated than ever. And she wasn't sure she trusted any of it.

Tired and sad, Patience mostly sat back and listened while Brandt brought the others up to speed. That was, until Lucius asked Brandt to draw the mark he'd cut out of his leg, and he sketched out a glyph that was reminiscent of a sailboat on the ocean, with seagulls flocking around the mast, all contained within a round-cornered square.

The air went thin in her lungs and the low-grade

nausea in the pit of her stomach kicked up several notches. She leaned in, touched the picture. "Akbal."

"What?"

"It's the name of the glyph," Lucius said. "Akbal. It symbolizes the third day of the everyday calendar of the ancients. Literally translated, it means 'darkness,' because it was associated with . . ." He trailed off, then finished, "Eclipses. Okay. That's relevant." He looked at Patience. "It means something to you?"

"Akbal is the Abyss card." She paused. "I told you guys how I almost always pull the Mother card, Imix, when I'm putting myself in the light position of a spread. Well, when the card representing me is in the shadow position, I almost always pull Akbal. Its negative aspects are issues of internalization, poor self-image, depression, and fear of change." She had to remind herself to breathe, as if her body had suddenly forgotten how. "I guess I was destined to be the third sacrifice all along, huh? And I guess we know when it's supposed to happen."

She kept her voice steady, but her thoughts spun with an inner litany. *Oh, gods. Why me? Why now? Why like this?* She had thought she was through with the tears, all cried out for the day. She was wrong.

The glyph symbolizing Brandt's last sacrifice was the one that represented her shadow self.

"Fuck that." He surged to his feet. Once he was up, though, he didn't go anywhere. He just glared down at her, eyes hard and wild. "I drew the glyph wrong. It's something else."

She shook her head. Swiping at her cheeks and

trying to breathe past the churning fear to find her warrior's strength, she said, "Akbal fits too well. It's connected to dark caves, obsidian, water, and access to dream worlds and memories, all of which symbolize your visions and what we've been through over the past few days. What's more, pulling the card is a call to step into the unknown . . . or the afterlife."

"I won't do it," he said flatly.

"I don't want you to. But we can't let Cabrakan get loose." She stood and faced him, refusing to let her legs shake. "You saw those pictures. You heard the numbers. Ten thousand people died in the Mexico City earthquake, and that was a year after the massacre sealed the barrier. How much worse will it be with the barrier wide-open? What's more, the miniquakes haven't just been confined to Mexico." She paused, fear tightening her throat. "He could hit anywhere in the world. *Anywhere*."

Anywhere . . . as in where the twins and *winikin* were hidden. And she wouldn't even know they were gone.

A muscle pulsed at the side of his jaw. "We'll go somewhere safe, dig in, and hide. That's what we should've done in the first place." He cut a steely look at Strike. "Sometimes a man has to put the woman he loves above the writs."

The king didn't say anything. But he didn't order Brandt to retake the oath either.

Heart aching, Patience took his hand, not caring that they were laying things out in public this time, where before they had always tried to keep a layer of privacy intact. "Once upon a time, I would've given anything to hear you say that."

His gold-flecked eyes radiated raw pain. "But not anymore?"

"It still matters. But running away isn't an option, and you know it. Cabrakan is going to come after the Nightkeepers. Even if we hide, he'll find us." She turned their joined hands so their marks faced the sky. "He'll be able to track us the same way the *boluntiku* tracked our families."

He looked away. "I fucking hate this."

"Finally, something we agree on."

"Shit." He let out a long, drawn-out sigh and let his forehead rest on hers. "This sucks."

They stood there for a moment, leaning into each other while their teammates watched in silence.

Finally, Strike said, "Okay, you two. Go get something to eat, and take a few hours of downtime. If you're not ready to crash yet, you will be soon."

She was dully surprised to realize that it had grown dark out.

"Want me to pull something together for you?" Sasha offered. In her previous life out in the human world, she had been a highly trained chef.

Patience grinned humorlessly. "Normally I'd be all over that offer. But it feels a little too last-mealish right now. Maybe tomorrow, okay? Or, even better, next week. No offense."

"None taken."

"Come on." Brandt pulled Patience away from the group. But instead of heading straight for their suite, he detoured them to the main kitchen. At her side-long look, he said, "Don't know about you, but I'm starving. And I'd like some privacy."

But where for so long when he'd said "privacy," he'd really meant "time alone," now he meant "time alone with you."

Swallowing against the sudden press of emotion, she nodded. Together, they raided Jox's supplies for enough food to fix a simple meal of the sort they had cooked together back in Pittsburgh, in the pretty starter house with the chrome toaster and Formica countertops. She was aware that the meeting contin-ued on in their absence, with Strike and Leah discuss-ing contingencies for the solstice-eclipse, while Lucius and Jade conferred with Rabbit about something that lit the younger man's expression with a wary hope that was mirrored in Myrinne's face.

But although she was aware of those things, she was also very aware of Brandt, and the way he moved around the kitchen and nearby storeroom and walk-in cooler, juggling the veggies and packaged chicken breasts she'd handed him while cruising the small wine selection and picking a chardonnay.

A small bubble of privacy seemed to separate them from the others, just like it used to out in the outside world, when—especially before they had Harry and Braden—they had often shopped like this, not even really talking about what they were going to make, partly because they were letting it evolve from their choices, and partly because they had been so in tune that they hadn't needed the words. They might not have recognized it as magic back then, but it had certainly been magical.

Now that same sense of simpatico bound them together as they finished "shopping" and headed for their suite.

Was it love? She wasn't sure anymore what that felt like. But for the first time in a long, long time, she didn't feel a pinch of grief when she opened the door. Instead, there was building anticipation.

As they cooked, they shared a glass of wine a sip at a time. The suite's kitchen nook was a tiny space, but instead of that being an irritation as they bumped into each other, it increased the sense of intimacy that grew as they traded off the wineglass, or reached around each other for ingredients and utensils. As they built a meal of chicken stir-fry, fresh vegetables, tortillas, and cool garnishes of the guac and sour cream variety, they traded "remember-whens" about the boys, making them seem very near.

When the food was ready, she carried their plates to the dining table, which hadn't been used for anything but clutter since Harry, Braden, and the *winikin* had moved away. Brandt had cleared it off and set two places, complete with candles. As she set down the plates, she saw that he'd added an off-center centerpiece: a framed photo he had taken of Harry, Braden, Hannah, and Woody all working on one of the Lego fortresses that had been the boys' shared passion—Harry's because of the engineering involved in building them, Braden's because of the fun in knocking them down.

Her eyes filled as she sat.

Half filling a second wineglass for himself, Brandt handed over the one they'd been sharing, then held his glass out to her, inviting a toast. "To family."

She blinked back the tears as she clinked her glass to his. "To family."

They ate largely in silence, but it wasn't an uncomfortable quiet. It was more that they were both tired of talking about the situation, tired of thinking about it. For the moment, they were both content to just *be*, and to do it together.

Patience suspected that the soft, intimate sense of calm probably came from a strange, delayed sort of postmagic crash, one that smoothed over the rough spots rather than making them sleepy. Or maybe this was what it felt like to be a true warrior couple, bound together in danger, yet able to compartmentalize and focus on each other when time allowed.

Later, after they had tag-teamed the dishes and showered in comfortable sequence, they met without prearrangement at the foot of the big bed in the master bedroom. He had pulled his jeans back on after his shower, and wore unbuttoned one of his old work shirts, a tailored oxford gone soft with age. She had thought about wearing one of the sexy nightgowns he used to love, but instead had gone with the silky, comfortable robe she'd bought recently to please only herself.

His eyes fired at the sight of her in the pale amber robe. His lips curved as he closed the small distance between them, and swept her up into his arms.

Letting herself fall for the moment, she sank against his strong body and slid her hands up beneath his open shirt as he carried her around to his side of the bed, bringing his lips to hers as he lowered her to the yielding mattress. He followed her down without breaking the kiss, and they twined together atop the covers partly clothed, partly naked, and fully involved in each other.

Their lovemaking was a mix of fast and slow, rough and gentle, new and old, and entirely in the moment . . . because neither of them wanted to think about the future.

December 20
One day until the solstice-eclipse

Brandt woke alone to find that Patience's side of the bed was cool to the touch, and the sun was bright beyond the blue curtains. There was no fuzzy transition between asleep and awake, no moment of wondering what day it was or what he had on his to-do list. Instead, he snapped to consciousness acutely aware that, in sleeping as long as he had, he'd burned through hours he could've spent in the library, trying to find a way around the Akbal oath . . . or spending time with Patience.

It was a surprising reality check that those two options were equally tempting. He had a feeling this was what she wanted from him: not for him to subsume his duties as a Nightkeeper so much as for him to put her equal to those responsibilities.

In the outside world, she'd been fond of saying, *I'm a chick. We multitask.* Maybe it was his turn to figure out how to do that. If they made it through tomorrow . . .

His thought process ground to a halt, hung up on that "if."

"We'll make it," he grated with the force of a vow. He didn't know how, though, or what it might cost them.

And he wasn't going to figure it out lying in bed.

Hauling himself upright, he hit the can, pulled on the jeans and oxford she'd peeled him out of the night before, along with his boots and knife, and headed for the main mansion. He found her in the great room, along with most of the team and the *winikin*, all scattered over chairs and couches with coffee cups at their elbows, wolfing down an army's worth of chocolate-chip pancakes. Sasha and Michael were up in the kitchen, working on another batch. Michael sketched a wave in Brandt's direction. "Go sit. I'll hook you up."

"Thanks. And may I say you wear your apron well? For an assassin, that is." The apron in question belonged to Jox; it had dancing chili peppers on it and came down to approximately the level of Michael's crotch.

"Don't push it."

"I take my coffee light. Keep it topped off and I'll double your tip."

"Here's a tip for you: Stuff a jock in it, or you're not getting shit."

"Ha." Satisfied, Brandt turned for the conversation pit. And stopped when he found pretty much everyone staring at him. "What?"

Patience set aside her plate, stood, and crossed to him, then faced the group with a sardonic grin that briefly lit the stress shadows in her eyes. "I'd like you all to meet my husband, Brandt White-Eagle." She paused. "Brandt, this is everyone."

He got it then. "Have I been that much of an asshole?"

Sven shook his head. "Not an asshole so much. You've just been . . . preoccupied. Or maybe 'absent' is a better word. You do the job and then some, but you don't connect. Didn't connect, I mean."

He stood there for a moment, feeling like a complete dick, hating that the others had been affected by the disconnect, and wondering just how much he had screwed up team morale. "Shit. I'm sorry."

"A man can't be himself when he's fighting something inside him," Michael said from up in the kitchen.

"You would know." That wasn't a joke, either. Michael had fought through his own hidden demons not long ago.

"Yeah. And I'm here if you ever need to decompress." The other man grinned evilly. "We could go out to the range. That usually works for me."

The offer was strangely appealing, though there was no question that Michael would kick his ass on the target course. "Thanks. I'll keep it in mind." Aware that the others had gone back to their conversations,

Brandt lowered his voice and said to Patience, "How are you doing?"

She looked away. "I'm okay. Hoping we can figure something out."

He scanned the room. Nate and Alexis were still off guarding Anna, and Rabbit and Myrinne didn't seem to have made it up yet. The others were all present and accounted for, though. "Anybody had any brilliant ideas yet?" he asked.

"We're still at the pancake stage. I only just got out here myself." She still wasn't looking at him.

"I figured you'd been up for a while."

"I took a cup of coffee out on the patio and watched the sunrise." She hesitated. "It's part of my morning routine."

It was also something they used to do together. Now she did it alone. More, he thought he knew why she hadn't woken him. There had been too many fresh starts over the past two and a half years, too many times when he'd promised to be there for her, only to revert. Was it any wonder she hadn't wanted to wake him, in case he'd turned back into that guy overnight? Gods knew it'd happened before.

"Maybe I could meet you out there tomorrow morning," he suggested casually.

Her lips curved. "It's a date."

It was also, he thought, a start.

"Sit," Michael ordered, coming up behind him. "Unless you'd rather wear this?"

Seeing that he was balancing two pancake-piled plates and a couple of cups of coffee—one light, one black as tar—Brandt relieved him of a plate and the non-paint-peeling coffee, and followed Patience to the love seat.

As Michael and Sasha settled themselves, Strike asked Brandt, "Anything you want to add to what you told us last night?"

"Wasn't that enough?" But Brandt knew what the king was asking. He shook his head. "I've got all the memories. Now it's going to be a case of figuring out what we can do with them. If anything gels, I'll tell you."

"Do that." Strike turned to Lucius, who was hacking away at something on his laptop, fingers flying. Seeing that he was in full-on glyph-geek mode and oblivious to the outside world, the king threw a balled-up napkin, bouncing it off his forehead. "Yo, Doc."

Lucius straightened and looked around, blinking in surprise. "What? Oh, sorry. This glyph string is . . . right. Never mind. And don't call me Doc. My thesis defense was a train wreck."

"Largely because the head of your committee was Xibalban." But Strike waved the point off. "What have you got for us?"

"Is Rabbit coming?"

Strike shook his head. "He and Myrinne didn't crash until like an hour ago. He was up late working on disguising the classified stuff in his head."

Lucius said, "Well, send him my way when he wakes up. I think we found something that'll help him block the mind-link." He dug under his chair, came up with a wrapped bundle, and shook off the T-shirt wrapping to reveal a circlet of pale jade that was worked so thin that it was almost translucent.

Patience leaned forward. "What is it, some sort of necklace?"

"You're about a foot too low." Holding the delicate artifact carefully between his palms, Lucius said, "Turns out the tinfoil-hat wearers aren't that far off; they're just using the wrong material to protect their brain waves. They should be wearing jade. With this"—he set the circlet on his head, where it perched awkwardly—"the hellmagic shouldn't be able to get through to him."

"Nice work," Brandt said.

Lucius removed the diadem and stared at it for a moment. "I'm still figuring out how to be an effective Prophet, obviously. Now that I've got this thing, it seems ridiculously obvious. You guys use jade-tipped bullets and jade grenades to neutralize creatures of dark magic, so it makes sense that something like this could work." He paused. "We'll need to field test it, of course. I can't guarantee it'll work against Iago, given that he's got a demon riding shotgun in his skull."

"We'll set something up once Rabbit's awake," Strike confirmed. "How did you guys do on the Akbal oath?"

Brandt was aware that Patience's fork hesitated halfway to her mouth, then slowly lowered to her plate. He almost said, *Don't get your hopes up.* Now that the memory block was fully demolished, he remembered the hours he'd spent online and in the library, researching all the religious oaths he could find, looking for a way to break them.

Lucius shook his head. "Sorry."

Patience let out a long, slow breath. "Did you find *anything*?"

"No. And that doesn't make any sense." Lucius patted the laptop fondly. "Think about it: Akbal is an incredibly common glyph—it's a day name, and the ancestors were all about their calendars. So going into the library search, I was figuring on getting Google bombed like whoa and damn, because even specifically asking about the 'Akbal oath' should've pulled hits from most everything related to the concepts of fealty and the calendar." He paused and spread his hands. "Instead, I didn't get shit, not even a bunch of random hits. Nothing in the library appears to have the words 'Akbal' and 'oath' together."

Strike narrowed his eyes. "Does that mean the oath magic postdates the hiding of the library?" Because their ancestors had folded the library into the barrier to keep its contents safe from the conquistadors, its knowledge cut off in the mid-fifteen-hundreds.

Lucius tipped his hand in a yes-no gesture. "Maybe, but that wouldn't explain the lack of random hits."

"You think the ancestors actively avoided using the term 'Akbal oath,'" Brandt guessed.

"Yeah. Sort of a 'he who shall not be named' thing." Lucius paused. "Unfortunately, knowing that doesn't help us figure out how to deal with the oath." He paused. "I'll keep looking." But his voice warned, *No guarantees.*

Brandt grimaced. "Thanks for trying."

Patience threaded her fingers through his and squeezed. "Don't give up."

"I'm not—" His voice broke, went ragged. "Damn it."

"We have today and part of tomorrow," Strike said. "Something's got to break. It doesn't make any sense that the gods came to Patience's aid against Werigo only to turn their backs on her now."

Brandt badly wanted to get up and pace, but he made himself stay put, next to Patience, the two of them forming a team within the team, as it should have been all along. Gripping both of her hands in his, he took a deep breath and looked at Strike. "Okay, we've got a day and a half. What's the—" *Plan*, he was going to say, but an air-raid whoop split the air, drowning him out and kicking his adrenaline level to red alert in an instant.

The loudest, deepest sound came from the mansion intercom, but each of their pocket units emitted smaller, shriller versions of the alarm, which was keyed to the panic buttons carried by each of the residents at Skywatch.

All of who were in the room . . . except for two.

As the others flew to their feet, Jox lunged for the intercom cutoff, killed the alarms, and slapped the button to activate alarm device's two-way feature. "What's wrong?"

Myrinne's voice came over the system, edged with hysteria. "You've got to hurry. Something's wrong with Rabbit!"

* * *

Oc Ajal was burning.

The yellow-orange bloom of fire, usually so beautiful to Rabbit, was monstrous as it clawed at the pole buildings, eating away the thatch roofing and carved markings, then down through the skeletons of the structures, to the bones of the village itself.

The flames curled horribly around blackened human shapes. Other bodies were sprawled where they had fallen: A brightly dressed woman lay facedown, clutching a blood-spattered grindstone that suggested she'd died fighting. Several men lay unmoving in front of the central dwelling. A boy's foot stuck out from behind it, and a half-grown pup lay dead nearby.

Six Aztec makol *were spread around the village, carrying shields and long buzz swords across their backs as they hunted their prey.*

Dark magic spat in the forest, followed by a scream that cut off abruptly. The makol *didn't react to that, just as they didn't seem interested in the female sobs and harsh rutting noises coming from inside Saamal's hut.*

Rabbit writhed in his bed. *It's a dream,* he told himself. *Wake the fuck up!* This wasn't happening, couldn't be happening. It had to be a dream. Iago couldn't mind-link him through Skywatch's wards.

Only he wasn't seeing the carnage through Iago's eyes.

"Let me go!" he shouted, railing against the nightmare's grip as his vision went bouncy with forced motion. But the words came out in a stranger's voice, in a stranger's language, shocking Rabbit into the realization that he was seeing things through Saamal's eyes, experiencing the attack through his perceptions.

Four makol *dragged the village elder to the fire pit at the center of the village, pulled him spread-eagled, and dumped him on the coals from the morning's cooking fire.*

He screamed as the hot embers burned through his tunic and into his skin, then again when the makol *lifted the heavy mortar stones from the corn-grinding stations and dropped them onto his hands and feet, pinning him in place. But those physical agonies were far eclipsed by the agony of knowing that he'd failed his people, failed his gods. Failed his destiny.*

Movement flashed in his peripheral vision as the soldiers' leader, wearing the blue demon mask and a red-feathered cloak, moved into his line of sight and lifted a carved ceremonial knife—

"Rabbit!" The sound of his name in Myrinne's voice was followed by a jolt of *chu'ul* magic, a lifeline that lassoed his consciousness and dragged him out of Saamal's head, out of the nightmare.

He came awake screaming, "No!"

He lay spread-eagled, but his hands and feet were suddenly free of the crushing weight of the mortar stones, his back unburned.

Heart hammering, he lunged upright, saw a flash of blue and red, and hurled himself at the *makol* leader. He hit the bastard hard; they went down in a tangle, smashed into something wooden and sharp cornered that didn't jibe with the fire-pit image that was locked in his brain, and landed on a hard, flat surface that wasn't highland dirt.

As Rabbit grappled with the disconnect, his enemy flipped him onto his back. And sat on him.

The familiarity of a move that had ended untold wrestling matches during Rabbit's youth—and the sudden lack of oxygen as all the air left his lungs under pressure from two-hundred-plus pounds of Nightkeeper—cracked the barrier between nightmare and reality and brought him slamming back into himself. He lay still for a moment, gasping through sinuses that were full of the stink of smoke, charred flesh, and blood.

Strike's face swam into view, looking concerned as hell.

Rabbit managed to get out a word: "Uncle."

The king's expression eased some, though it stayed worried as he shifted his weight off Rabbit's torso and rose to crouch over him. "What the hell happened? That was no dream. We had to send Sasha in after you."

Vision clearing as oxygen scrubbed away the last lingering shreds of confusion, Rabbit saw that most of the magi and several *winikin* were crowded into his and Myrinne's bedroom.

Urgency beat through him with the cadence of running feet and the screams of the hunted as he blurted, "We have to get our asses to Oc Ajal, right fucking now."

A strangled, startled noise came from Jox.

Strike turned on him. "You know what he's talking about?"

"Not exactly." But the *winikin*'s face flushed.

"We're wasting time," Rabbit interrupted. He held out his hand to Strike. "I'll show you." When Strike hesitated, he pressed, "No tricks, no lies. I promise."

"Which means you've tricked and/or lied to me recently." The king's expression darkened, but he reached out and took his hand.

"You need to see this." Through the touch link, Rabbit sent a compressed thought stream straight into Strike's head.

He started with Myrinne pointing out that his old man wouldn't have slept with the enemy and suggesting that his mother's people might be a different sect of the Xibalbans, that they might be potential allies. Then he showed Strike how Jox had dropped the name of the village, moved on to his and Myrinne's visit to the village and the whole-lot-of-nothing they had found. He finished with the images of the burning village, the bodies, and the village elder spread out for sacrifice in the central fire pit that symbolized the entrance to the underworld.

When the download ended, Strike blinked at Rabbit for a few seconds. Then his features flooded with a rage so profound that Rabbit flinched away from him, ducking a little.

Strike's voice went deadly cold. "I'm not going to punch you out. I'm tempted as all hell, but I want you awake for this . . . and I want you to remember, every fucking second, that whatever happened in that village was your fault."

"Hey!" Myrinne got right in his face, eyes flashing. "Back off. He was trying to do the right thing."

"Oh? And what's your excuse?" But then Strike held up a hand. "Fuck it. Later." Refocusing on Rabbit, he grated, "That dream punched through the compound's wards, but it wasn't Iago sending it. How could you see all that through the old man's eyes?"

"How can I do half of what I do?" Rabbit said, voice raw. "I'm a freak." His stomach churned on a sharp-edged mix of grief and anger, coated over with a huge, crushing load of guilt—because, godsdamn it, Strike was right. Iago must've found out about the village from being inside his head. But why bother to send the *makol*? There hadn't been anything in the village worth the effort.

Unless there had been, and he'd missed it.

Shit. Making himself meet Strike's glare, he said, "Are we going or not?"

"We're going. Let's hope to hell it was just a nightmare." But Strike's expression suggested that he didn't think they were going to get so lucky.

Rabbit didn't hold out much hope either.

"It could be a trap," Michael pointed out. "We can't be the only ones thinking in terms of using something—or some*one*—as bait."

"Then we spring the trap," Strike said, expression grim. "And we give Iago hell."

CHAPTER FIFTEEN

Oc Ajal, Mexico

It wasn't a trap. In fact, by the time the Nightkeepers 'ported in, wearing full battle gear and armed to the teeth, there was no sign of the *makol*. But it wasn't a false alarm either.

The village didn't just look as bad as Rabbit had feared; it looked worse.

All but two of the pole buildings had collapsed to smoldering cinders of wood and flesh, and the stench of charred meat permeated the air. The village was silent save for the sputter of smoke and ash. Even the surrounding forest seemed to have been struck dumb by the slaughter. And there, in the center of it all, Saamal lay splayed out in the fire pit with his hands and feet weighted by millstones, his head lolling on one of the large rocks that had probably been used for seating, and his chest laid open, ghastly and broken-ribbed where the *makol* leader had ripped out his heart.

Myrinne made a sound of distress and moved closer to Rabbit's side. Strike hadn't suggested leaving her behind; he was punishing both of them.

Michael, Sasha, and Sven moved off to secure the perimeter and search the forest, while Patience, Brandt, Lucius, Leah, and Jade headed off to search the few buildings that remained intact.

Strike started toward Saamal's body, gesturing to Rabbit and Myrinne without looking at them. "Come on."

Rabbit wished he could overload to numbness, as he had done when he'd stumbled over his father's body lying in the tunnels beneath Chichén Itzá. Instead, he remained painfully aware of the sound of Myrinne's quiet sniffles, and the heavy weight of grief and guilt that pressed on him, making it hard to breathe.

Breathing got even more difficult when they got close enough to the corpse to catch the stink of blood, entrails, and fear. The funk made Rabbit's skin itch. Flies had found the corpse; the rattle of their wings sounded like— *Shit.*

"Stay back," he snapped. "The body is covered with dark magic."

Strike, who had been reaching out to close the elder's half-mast eyes in a gesture of respect, yanked his hand back, then scowled. "I don't feel anything."

For that matter, Rabbit hadn't caught on until he was practically on top of the corpse. Concentrating on the faint rattle, he stretched out his hand to probe the spell. "It's not the same as the stuff Iago uses," he said after a moment. "It's . . . I don't know. Softer, maybe. More passive."

"I thought Lucius said the thing on your head was supposed to block hellmagic."

Startled by the reminder, Rabbit touched the circlet Lucius had given him just before they all left Skywatch. He'd forgotten he was wearing it, largely because the moment he'd put it on, light magic had flared and the stone had gone fluid and soft. When the magic faded, the crown had become a thin, flexible strand that was shaped perfectly for his skull and lay almost invisibly along his buzzed-down hairline.

"He said the circlet blocks mind-bending at a distance," he said. "I can use my other talents, but Iago can't get through to me as long as I'm wearing it."

"We hope."

"Yeah." Rabbit stared down at the corpse. *I'm so fucking sorry*, he thought. *I didn't mean* . . . Shit, this was no time for excuses. It was time to respect the dead. And, gods willing, avenge them.

The elder's face was slack, his skin gray. But there was something strange about the body's waxy stillness. Who had he been, really? He had denied using dark magic, but he had put himself inside Rabbit's mind despite the protective wards around Skywatch, and now his corpse was enshrouded in power.

A quiver ran through Rabbit. Had the elder somehow left him a message using the dark magic?

"I need to take a closer look at the spell," he said

into the strained silence that surrounded the grisly scene.

He halfway expected the king to no-fucking-way him. But Strike just looked at him for a moment, expression unreadable. Then he nodded. "Go ahead. But be careful, and pull the hell out if it feels wrong."

"Will do." He glanced at Myrinne. "You'll keep an eye on me?"

She smiled crookedly. "Always."

But Rabbit didn't tap into the strange-feeling dark magic right away. Instead, he took a deep breath and faced Strike squarely. "We were wrong to go behind your back, and we're going to have to live with the consequences of that. But you're wrong to put the rest of it on us. Iago sent the soldiers. He's the enemy. Not Myrinne and me."

A muscle pulsed at the corner of Strike's jaw, but he said only, "You went looking for Xibalban magic in the highlands. You found it. Now fucking do something useful with it."

Raw, hurting anger flared deep in Rabbit's gut, but instead of lashing out, he tamped it down, nodded stiffly. "If that's the way you want it."

Taking a deep breath, he centered himself, making sure his magic was turned inward rather than outward, and he wouldn't accidentally open the hell-link. Then he stretched out his hand and laid it flat on the outer edge of the dark magic that surrounded the elder.

Power, brownish and faintly greasy, prickled along his skin and rattled through his body . . . but it didn't invade him, didn't force its way inside and try to take over. It was just . . . magic.

Letting his mind sink into the spell, he followed the power flow as it encircled Saamal's body and swirled down into the open chest cavity, where it pooled, pulsing in an asynchronous rhythm.

Rabbit let his hand follow the path his mind had taken, skimming along the old man's outstretched limbs, over his face, and finally to the place where his heart had been. When he touched the pulsing, discordant knot of power, it shuddered. And so did the body.

More, for a second he could've sworn he saw the ghostly image of Saamal, alive and well, standing beside it.

"Fuck me. It *moved*!" Strike jerked Myrinne back a step and brought up his shield. The Nightkeeper magic sparked red-gold where it intersected with the dark-magic spell.

Saamal's body went limp as the dark magic drained away from the chest cavity, attracted by its opposite, dark to light, negative to positive.

"Back off," Rabbit snapped. "You're messing with the balance, and I can handle the dark stuff." What was more, he thought he knew what he was looking at, though not how the elder had managed it.

He was a little surprised when the king complied without argument, falling back and taking Myrinne with him. "Be careful," Strike said in quiet warning. "Iago knows you inside and out, literally. *This* could be the trap."

Rabbit shook his head. "I don't think so. I think the

old man used the magic to tether his soul to his body after death." If he concentrated, he could almost make out the ghost standing beside the corpse. "I think he sent the nightmare to summon me here, knowing I wear the hellmark but have no allegiance to Iago."

"If he had the chops for that level of magic, why didn't he reveal himself when you were here before?" Strike pressed.

"Beats the hell out of me." He had a few suspicions, though, none of them good.

With Strike out of range, the dark magic flowed back into its original pattern, and the power bundle in the old man's chest cavity began pulsing again. But it was far weaker than it had been before, as if the encounter with the Nightkeeper magic had nullified part of the spell. This time when Rabbit touched the knotted dark magic, the corpse didn't move.

"There's something going on here." He described the power flow to Strike, the way it kept pulsing in Saamal's chest, unfocused and losing steam. "I think he died before he could finish the spell. If I could just—"

"No fucking way," Strike interrupted. "So far all I've heard here is a bunch of wishful thinking."

"You saw the body move."

"I need more than that before I let you use dark magic."

Trust me, Rabbit wanted to say, but didn't, because he had a feeling he and Strike might've passed the point of no return on that front. But while he had betrayed Strike's trust by not telling him about the visit to Oc Ajal, he'd done way worse to Saamal and the villagers.

"You want proof? Fine. Keep your eyes on the left side of the body." Fixing his attention on the barely perceptible ghost image, he sent what little dark magic he had left into the wavering shape. Nothing happened. Then, slowly, Saamal's ghost became visible as a translucent shadow standing beside the open-chested corpse.

"Holy. Shit." Strike stared, jaw working. Then he nodded stiffly. "Okay. What do you need? You want an uplink?"

"Not with you guys. I want Michael." At the king's sharp look, Rabbit turned up his palms in a "What the hell else can I do?" gesture. "I need dark magic, not light, and he's the only one who comes close. Lucius said the old rituals used to split the *muk* into its dark and light halves, right? Well, I've got both bloodlines in me, and I wear both marks. I might be able to take Michael's magic, divide it into light and dark, and funnel the dark half into Saamal."

"*Might be,*" Strike repeated ominously.

Rabbit met his eyes and did something he almost never did. He said, "Please."

The king stayed silent for a long moment. Then he nodded. "Fine. We'll try it." He got on the radio and recalled the entire team, his body language stiff and annoyed.

While they waited for the others, Rabbit met Myrinne's eyes. She gave him a covert thumbs-up and the special smile she reserved just for him, which smoothed out some of the nerves that were digging into him harder by the minute. He sent her a wink of thanks. And as the others converged, he said a small, directionless prayer: *Please, gods, don't let this be a trap.*

He didn't think it was, but Iago knew him too well. Better, it seemed some days, than he knew himself.

"I need a ten-foot radius," he said. "Except for Michael. I need you in here." Quickly, Rabbit explained what was going on, and what he was going to try. As he did, Saamal's ghost faded entirely; he hoped to hell it wasn't all the way gone. When Michael came up beside him, he said, "I need you to boost me with the smallest trickle of *muk* you can manage." Which was a little like trying to plug a reading light into a nuclear power plant—it might work . . . or it might blow the lamp right the fuck up. And he was the lamp.

"You're sure about this?"

"Yes." *No.*

At a nod of agreement from Strike, Michael moved around behind Rabbit and gripped his shoulders, the way he did when he balanced Sasha's *chu'ul* magic. "You ready?"

Rabbit nodded. "Bring it."

Michael brought it, all right. Silver power slammed into Rabbit, searing from his shoulders to the ends of his fingers and toes and back again. Pain ripped through him and he hissed out a breath.

"Too much?" Michael asked, his voice rocky with the effort of squelching the power to a thin trickle.

"I'll deal." After the first sledgehammer blow the pain leveled off, then warmed to something closer to pleasure. Magic twined through Rabbit, the silver becoming braided strands of brown and red-gold, dark and light magic intertwined. "Okay," he breathed, peripherally aware that the others were fixated on him, waiting for him to do something amazing.

Well, he was godsdamned well trying.

Slowly at first, and then with growing confidence, he separated the strands with fingers of thought; he sent the light magic into the back of his brain, where his Nightkeeper talents resided. Then he put his hand once more inside Saamal's open chest cavity, where his heart should have been, and channeled the dark magic to that point.

For a moment, nothing happened. Then the dark power curled around his hand, taking the shape of his fist and becoming almost tangible. Within the bundled magic, he felt a flutter. A pulse. Another.

The throbbing gained in rhythm and intensity as he channeled more dark magic into Saamal. He could almost hear the pulses become a twofold beat: *lub dub, lub dub.* It was fucking working.

What was more, the ghost became visible once more as a dark shadow beside the body. And, as Rabbit continued to feed the dark magic into the half-finished spell, the ghostly image started drifting down to align with the corpse.

"Come on, old man," he said under his breath. "You must've stuck around for a reason."

"Ho-ly shit," Patience whispered from the other side of the fire pit, where she and Brandt stood shoulder to shoulder.

There was enough of his old crush left that he got a buzz off her gasp. But in the split second he was distracted, the magic built inside him too quickly, threatening his control. A shimmer of red-gold magic leaked through the connection, making the ghost writhe with a soundless scream.

"*Shit!*" Rabbit yanked back the light magic and tried to send it toward his talents, but his usual reserves were already beyond full.

"Let off some steam," Michael warned in a low voice. "You've got to keep the balance between light and dark."

"Right." He couldn't pour dark magic into the elder without bleeding off an equal amount of light magic. But where was he supposed to put it?

Fire, came the immediate instinctual answer. *Light this place up in a pyre that all the gods will see.* But the thought brought a twist of nausea and the image of the pole buildings burning with people inside. Smoke clogged his throat and sinuses, smelling of charred flesh. *No*, he thought. *Not fire.* Too much had burned there already. With his mind-bending blocked by the circlet, he was left with his smallest talent, that of low-level telekinesis, but what—

"Give it to me," Jade said unexpectedly. When Lucius no-fucking-way'd her, she waved him off. "Hear me out. There's a strange sort of pattern here, some sort of concealment spell. I can't get a handle on it, though. I need a boost to get a better look."

Rabbit held out a hand. "Free magic," he rasped. "Onetime offer, first come, first served."

At Strike's nod, Jade moved forward. The moment she took his hand, Rabbit felt a huge rush of relief as the light magic left him and headed for her, and the painful pressure inside him eased.

Then something strange happened: The air around them all took on a gleam of red-gold, then a hint of silver.

"Jade?" Strike said in soft warning.

"There's a cloaking spell permeating the village," she said, voice tight with effort. "It's not the normal sort of magic, but I think that I can reverse it if I just—" The light magic surged through Rabbit and then drained away to almost nothing as she leaned on their link. "There it is. I think if I . . ."

A psychic shock wave rolled through Rabbit, and both the dark and light connections winked out of existence. *Boom*, gone. Like they had never been.

"Jade, no!" he cried, but it was already too late. Whatever she had done, it had cut his connection to Saamal. He couldn't sense the dark-magic spell anymore, couldn't hear the *lub-dub* heartbeat that had been going strong only moments before.

But *something* was happening.

"What the hell?" Michael breathed, staring out

into the forests, where a shimmer of magic moved in the distance, working its way around the village, spiraling inward.

Rabbit turned to follow the movement, aware that the others were doing the same as the incandescence became more visible, skipping from one place to another, getting closer.

"It's coming from the bodies we found in the woods," Sven said. He pointed ahead of the moving shimmer. "The next one is right about there." Seconds later, magic flared near where he'd just indicated.

After that, the spell—or whatever the hell it was— entered the village, hazing the air around the burned-out pole buildings where human remains were mixed with char. The magic moved one to the next, ever inward, until it reached the men lying near the central pole building and the woman with the blood-spattered grindstone. When the shimmer cleared, the woman was taller and paler, with honey-colored hair where it had been dark a second earlier. The men too were bigger and burlier, and had lighter hair.

Before Rabbit could even begin to comprehend what he'd just seen, the shimmer coalesced around Saamal's body. The air around the corpse shimmered and shifted, and then the body *grew*, its limbs and torso elongating with strange, Gumby-ish plasticity, then thickening with ropy layers of muscle gone soft with old-man flab. The elder's face broadened and paled slightly, while the skin of his unmarked forearm darkened in a familiar pattern.

When the air stabilized, the dead man was well

over six feet tall, big and tough looking. And he wore a black quatrefoil on his inner right wrist.

"Fuck. Me," Rabbit said.

He turned away from Saamal, trying to stem the tide of grief, guilt, and anger. He'd found the right village, after all, but he hadn't realized it. How had the old man tricked him? How—shit. It didn't matter now, did it?

"You were right," Strike said, his tone indecipherable. "They were dark magi. They've been hiding up here all this time."

"Until I led Iago straight to them," Rabbit said bitterly. "They must've deserted from the Order of Xibalba and broken their links to the magic."

"Then who cast the cloaking spell?" Strike asked.

"I don't know. But why else would their marks be black if they weren't deserters?"

"You've got it backwards," said a rasping voice, coming from behind Rabbit.

The only one back there was Saamal.

Blood draining from his head, leaving him woozy, Rabbit turned and looked down at the body. *Oh, holy hell.* The spell had worked, after all.

The elder's eyes were lit with a parody of life. His body remained pale and motionless, his chest open and full of congealed blood, but the pumping throb of oily brown magic had returned his soul to his body.

But any victory Rabbit might have felt deflated at the sight of the terrible pain and soul-deep loss that clouded the elder's eyes. His soul might have returned to his body, but no amount of magic could undo the villagers' murders and the destruction of Oc Ajal.

Rabbit's chest suddenly felt as hollow as the empty splay of Saamal's ribs. He was aware of the others gathering close, of Myrinne gripping his shoulder in support, but those inputs were peripheral. He sank to his knees beside the dead man, started to roll the nearest mortar stone off him, only to stop when he realized that the stones were woven into the reanimation spell, that they were part of what was keeping him alive.

"I'm sorry," he said, the words emerging through lips that felt numb and strange, like they weren't part of him anymore. "I didn't mean to tell Iago where—" He broke off. "Wait. You speak English?"

Saamal's eyes narrowed. "*That's* what you want to know right now?"

"Christ, Rabbit." Strike crouched down in the elder's line of sight. "I'm Striking-Jaguar." He paused a beat, testing.

The elder glanced at Strike's forearm, then at the edge of the circular *hunab ku* visible beneath the sleeve of his dark tee, which marked him as the Nightkeepers' king. "Names aren't important right now, nor is rank. What matters now is that you listen to me, and believe what your ancestors would not. That is why I called the young crossover here." His eyes went to Rabbit. "And used the last of my power to keep my soul tethered beyond its mortality."

"Crossover? Oh, you mean half blood." Actually, Rabbit decided he liked "crossover" better. "Because

I can use light and dark magic." When the elder nodded shallowly, he pressed, "If you know who and what I am, then tell me about my mother. Who was she?" *Oh, gods.* His eyes tractor-beamed to the woman with the grindstone. "Was she here? Did the *makol* kill her? And why didn't you tell me who you were?" His voice rose, edging toward his boyhood tenor. "We could've brought you in, could've protected—"

Strike cut him off. "Let him talk. I'm guessing his clock is ticking."

"That is true, jaguar king. My time on this plane is limited." The elder closed his eyes, as if composing himself. When he opened them again, some of the grief and pain was blocked behind a warrior's focus. To Rabbit, he said, "I did not reveal myself to you because my people are your enemies, and vice versa. Or rather, we *were* your enemies. This village housed the last members of the true Order of Xibalba, users of dark magic and guardians of the sky barrier on behalf of the dark gods."

Rabbit didn't care about sides right now—he wanted to know what happened when Red-Boar visited the village, damn it. But he held himself in check as the elder described how the members of the order were the Nightkeepers' opposites, dedicated to preventing what they called the "sky demons" from tearing through the barrier and overrunning the earth plane during the end time.

Strike said bluntly, "No offense, but since there's no fucking way you're converting us, we don't need a philosophy lesson except and unless it pertains to what we're dealing with right now. Tell me about Iago. He's one of yours, isn't he? Or he was." The king was strung tight, his expression flat and unreadable.

"His father, Werigo, was one of us, yes." The elder's voice was thinning, but when Michael started forward, the old man shook his head. "No, *muk* wielder, no power on this plane can keep me soul-tethered after this spell runs out. Once I'm done, I'm done."

"So talk fast," Strike ordered.

Rabbit glared at him, but didn't waste time picking the fight. It was coming, though.

"Werigo became devoted to an offshoot sect of the order, one that was destroyed long ago because its goals diverged from those of the true Order of Xibalba. The members of the sect believed that our mandate wasn't to secure the barrier against the sky demons; it was to rule the earth ourselves."

"Who wants to bet this sect spun off to live with the Aztecs?" Lucius murmured.

"Just so," Saamal agreed. "Although the sect itself was destroyed during the conquest, its last leader— the Aztec god-king Moctezuma—hid key codices and ceremonial objects. Twenty-six years ago, acting on a dream he claimed was a vision from Moctezuma himself, Werigo dug up the cache and began subverting members of the true order over to his cause." A pause. "The dream came a few months before the magic ceased working."

Rabbit glanced at Strike. The king wasn't telegraphing shit, but it couldn't be a coincidence that

Werigo's prophetic dream had coincided with the ones that had set Strike's father on the road to the Solstice Massacre.

"Werigo was a hard, harsh man before the dreams," the elder continued. "He was the elder son of our leader, but when our father died, I—the second son—was made ruler instead of him. That festered. In the end, Werigo and his sons left the old village along with ten others. Anticipating that he would come after us when he grew strong enough—looking to take prisoners, sacrifices, and converts, much as the god-kings of old used to do—I relocated the village, and we learned to hide our true natures." Saamal paused. "He and his followers grew even harder and harsher, and became fanatically convinced that it was their duty to reincarnate Moctezuma and complete the Aztec conquest. They found us one solstice, and attacked. They killed everyone they could find, murdering the men, women, and even children who had been their friends and family. Only a dozen of us survived. . . . Eventually, we came here. To Oc Ajal."

Where they were safe, Rabbit thought hollowly, *until I showed up.*

As if he had heard the thought, Saamal zeroed in on him. "Werigo could have found us if he had truly looked. Since so long had passed, we thought he had decided we weren't important. We became so wrapped up in our own preparations for the end time that we were taken by surprise when his soldiers appeared today. We had grown soft and sloppy, and because of that, we lost the war before we even got a chance to fight. So now it's up to you."

"Do you mean the Nightkeepers, or me, specifically?" Rabbit almost whispered the words. He didn't bother correcting the elder's assumption that Werigo had been behind the attack. Father or son, it didn't seem important just then.

"The Nightkeepers serve the wrong gods. You are the crossover; you stand in both the light and shadows." The elder's voice sank to a windy sigh. "Three women went with Werigo when he left; two others were captured later. Your mother must have been one of them. I'm sorry, but I don't know which one."

Rabbit's throat closed. "I'm not sure I want to know more than that. We came . . . I came here looking for allies. I guess I've got my answer."

"Indeed. Now I'll give you three things you didn't come looking for. A triad, if you will." Saamal's lips lifted fractionally, though the effort was grotesque against the sagging backdrop of pale skin and eyes that glossed over as the life-magic failed. "First, I give you a warning. The *makol* stole a sacred knife that belonged to our father—an ancient war trophy that Moctezuma himself was said to have used in the first fire ceremony." Saamal's voice was almost gone. "Second, I give you a gift, one that I was led to by a dream of my own. There's an eccentric hidden beneath the center post of my house. It is yours. And third and last, I give you what has, for centuries, been a blessing among the members of the order. We say: *'May the crossover bring balance to all things.'"*

Rabbit's heart raced. There were a thousand things he wanted to ask the old man, and the sum total of them logjammed in his throat, leaving him silent save for the one thing he couldn't go without saying. He bent over, leaning close to Saamal as he whispered, "I'm so sorry I led them here."

The elder's eyes were opaque in death, his skin sallow and sagging, but he managed a grotesque parody of a smile. "The gods choose the hour of our passing regardless of our actions. If they had wanted me to live, I would still be alive. They want me to begin my journey now, so off I go. Do not take the blame for what others and the gods have done. Instead, remember the strength of your name. The rabbit not only saved the Hero Twins and their father; his is the shape of the shadow in the full moon."

Rabbit's throat went dry. "I know." One night when he was just a kid, Red-Boar had taken him up on the roof of the shitty apartment where they'd been staying, and told him how the rabbit-shaped shadow had gotten onto the moon, implying that was the origin of Rabbit's name. When Rabbit had asked later for a repeat performance, Red-Boar had claimed not to know what the fuck he was talking about.

The thing was . . . Jox hadn't known the story either, and Lucius hadn't been able to find it in the library. Ergo, it wasn't Nightkeeper. Yet Red-Boar kept the name and passed on the story.

What the hell was he supposed to take from that?

"Find the eccentric," Saamal pressed. "And find

your true balance, even if your actions contradict the beliefs of those who love you."

Rabbit didn't make the promise. Instead he touched his forehead and the spot over his heart. "Have an interesting journey, old man." The Xibalbans had believed that the nine levels of the underworld were a series of tests and competitions, and that a true warrior would fight his way all the way down to a seat at the ceremonial ball court of the dark lords—or, better yet, a player's position.

"Same to you, young Rabbit." Without ceremony or outward sign, the elder's soul made the transition. The flaccid lips went still and the last of the dark magic slipped away, leaving Rabbit kneeling beside the elder's corpse with his hand wet to the wrist with the old man's blood.

He stayed there for a moment, feeling . . . nothing. He was numb. Exhausted. Confused.

"Hey." Myrinne's face came into view as she crouched down beside him. "You okay?"

"I'm . . ." He trailed off, then shook his head. "I have no clue how to answer that."

She held out her hand. "Come on. Let's go find whatever he left you. Assuming the *makol* didn't get it."

"Right. The gift. Door number two." And shit, she was right. What if the *makol* had found it? Relieved to have something—*anything*—concrete to focus on, he let her pull him up, and they headed for Saamal's hut.

"Rabbit, wait," Patience called. "Don't go—"

In there, she would have said, he realized the moment he crossed the threshold and his eyes adjusted to the light, if not to the sight confronting him. *Oh, shit,* he thought frantically, remembering too late the noises he'd heard coming from the building in his vision.

Myrinne turned away, gagging, but Rabbit made himself stand and look.

The woman hung limply, trussed to the center post. Based on her clothing, he thought she had been one of the ones who had been grinding corn when he and Myrinne had first visited. He couldn't be sure from her face, though—not because the cloaking spell was gone, but because she had been horribly mutilated, sliced and slashed until the front of her body was more meat than skin. There was blood everywhere, and the air was thick with the smell of body fluids, death, and terrible fear.

Aware that the others stood there, some in the doorway, some just outside, he swallowed, trying to find some moisture to wet his mouth. "I heard her screaming. In the dream, she was still alive while they were—*shit.*"

He spun, got a hand over his mouth, and bolted. He made it to the edge of the forest, beyond the village circle and the stone archway. Then he puked violently into the undergrowth, retching until his stomach muscles hurt and tears streamed down his face. Then he stayed there, hunched over and clutching himself, for a long, long time.

When he heard someone come up behind him, he said, "That's in my blood. It doesn't matter if my mother followed Werigo willingly or if she was captured later. She was part of *that*. And my old man—" He broke off on a dry heave that hurt like hell. "He stayed with them; he had to have stayed. He kept their name for me, he kept *me*, but he didn't . . ." He trailed off. He didn't want to snivel that his father hadn't loved him, hadn't liked him, had barely tolerated him most days. But still. "How does that make any *sense*? He was a *Nightkeeper*, for fuck's sake! He was *the* Nightkeeper. How could he do that? And what the hell am I supposed to do about it? I don't want to be a half blood. I don't want to be the crossover, whatever the fuck that is. I just want to be a godsdamned mage." He stood and turned, opening his arms for a hug, assuming it was Myrinne who had come after him.

But it wasn't Myrinne. It was Strike.

"Shit." He turned the arms-out move into a swipe at his tear-soaked face and puke-fouled mouth, then drew back, jamming his hands in his pockets. "Want to take a swing at me? Go ahead. I could use a good pounding right now. Might make me feel better about—" He broke off as a faint breeze stirred the air, bringing him the smell of blood and terror.

The image of the woman's body hit him again, and his gorge rose. He fought it down this time, and lifted his chin in a dare. Tears sheened his vision, making the world shimmer. "Go ahead. What are you waiting for?"

Strike shook his head. "I didn't come out here to pound on you. I came out to apologize. I've been acting like a dick and it's not fair. What's more, it meant you couldn't talk to me about wanting to track down your mother."

Rabbit swallowed hard, taking a second to process the apology. Which just made him feel more like shit. "I should've told you anyway. You wouldn't have let me go, we wouldn't be here now, and none of this—" He swallowed the heave, knowing it was his body's way of wussing out of facing what he'd done. "None of this would've happened."

"Or maybe it would've happened a different way. We can't second-guess the gods—sky or Xibalban." Strike paused, grimacing. "But I wish this had happened differently. I wish I'd handled it better, wish I'd handled *you* better."

"Why didn't you?" Rabbit hadn't meant to ask. He'd told himself he didn't care, that he had Myrinne for support and Jox for the occasional piece of advice, so it didn't matter if three of the four people he'd grown up with—Strike, Anna, and his old man— were out of the picture.

But now, off alone with Strike after what they'd just been through, it wasn't about him and Strike the king, but rather him and the guy who'd helped raise him, and who'd been older by enough years to play a role that had hit halfway between big brother and father figure. And who had disappeared on him recently.

With it just the two of them, and him raw as hell, Rabbit could admit that it had mattered. It had mattered a shit-ton.

"Because you terrify me," Strike said finally. "I'm terrified *of* you. I'm terrified *for* you. And I'm afraid of what's going to happen to the rest of us if things go wrong with you. You're already the strongest mage of the bunch of us, and I have a feeling you haven't even started to tap what's in that head of yours. You're too fucking brave for your own good, and you've got the shittiest luck of anyone I've ever known. You put all that together, and it keeps me up some nights worrying about what's in your future. Two days, two weeks, two years . . . shit, I don't know what you're going to be doing two minutes from now, except that I know that whatever it is, you'll be giving it a hundred percent effort, for better or worse."

Strike paused, but Rabbit didn't say anything—he fucking *couldn't* say anything past the millstone that'd just landed on his chest.

After an awkward pause, the king shrugged. "So, yeah, I've been riding your ass. Jox's too, because he's ripping himself to shreds trying to keep it all together at Skywatch and making himself miserable in the process. And Brandt and Patience . . . shit. The team is coming together, but some of the people in it are on the edge, and I don't know how to pull them back. I—"

He broke off, jamming his hands into his pockets, his shoulders sagging from their usual "I can handle whatever the hell you want to chuck at me" squareness. "Fuck. And I've just turned what happened here into something about me, which I didn't mean to do. I just thought . . . I just wanted you to know that nothing that's been going on between the two of us has a godsdamned thing to do with who your mother was—or, hell, who your father was, what he did, or what he was thinking when he did it. You're you. I've known you most of my life. And . . . I love you. I just thought you might need to hear that right about now."

Forget not being able to talk. Rabbit couldn't breathe.

Strike stood there for another moment, looking uncomfortable as hell. Then he shrugged, shot a funny half smile that Rabbit remembered from a thousand times before, growing up, and turned away, heading back to the village center.

He'd gone two steps when Rabbit's feet finally came unglued and his lungs and throat started working again.

"Hey!" he called. And launched himself at his king.

Strike caught him on the fly and they hugged like they hadn't since . . . shit, Rabbit didn't remember. Since back before he'd gotten too cool to do crap like hug the big brother who wasn't really. They both ignored Rabbit's stifled sob and the way Strike hung on a beat too long, and when they separated, they both stared into different parts of the forest rather than at each other. But the air between them was clearer than it had been in weeks, maybe longer.

"We should get back," Rabbit said finally. "There's a shitload left to do."

But when they stepped through the archway together, he saw that the others had been seriously busy while they'd been gone. Either that, or he and Strike had been gone longer than he'd thought.

The bodies from the forest and village had been stacked beside the fire pit and layered with wood that had been stripped from Saamal's hut, leaving the structure's skeleton behind. The central pole was gone; a hole in the bloodstained sand marked where its base had stood.

Myrinne crossed to Rabbit and held out her hand. "Here."

From Lucius's tendencies toward verbal diarrhea when he was working in the library, Rabbit knew that "eccentric" was a catchall term for the small, flat objects the ancients had made from stone, imbuing them with ritual significance—and sometimes even power—through their choice of shape and stone. Some had holes so they could be worn as pendants or carried in pockets, while others had been sacrificed or buried in a house or village to ward off evil.

Leah, Nate, and Alexis each wore one given to them by the king, signifying that they were members of the royal council; those eccentrics were abstractly curving shapes that made Rabbit think of Chinese dragons.

The one that Myrinne held out, in contrast, was a flat, flared quatrefoil.

He stared at it. "Well, hell."

"Literally," she quipped, but her eyes searched his. "What can I do to help?"

"You're already doing it." He took the eccentric

and held it flat on his palm; it was heavier than it looked. He didn't see any markings on it, didn't catch any power buzz. It seemed to be nothing more than a carefully knapped piece of waxy gray flint. "Ten bucks says I slice myself every time I stick my hand in my pocket with this thing."

"You could wear it around your neck."

He was pretty sure she was kidding. "Yeah. That'll happen. Not." He wasn't even sure he should carry it day to day. "What if it—I don't know—attracts dark magic or something?"

"Like the hellmark doesn't already?"

She had him there. "I'm just wondering if I should leave it here. Nothing says I have to accept it. You heard Saamal—they weren't our allies at all, and they were operating on a whacked theology. I mean, sky demons? Seriously?" He shook his head. "No. Even if this branch of the order was threat-level yellow compared to Iago's, they opposed the gods." He rubbed a thumb over the eccentric, which had warmed in his hand. It was soft to the touch. Appealing. "I shouldn't carry it, or even keep it."

Myrinne thought for a moment. "How about you hang on to it for now and ask Lucius to check it out? Once you've got more info, you can make the call."

"Yeah." He nodded, exhaling. "Yeah, that'll work." He went to slip the eccentric into his pocket and was startled to realize he already had.

"They're waiting for you."

"I know." He was all too aware that Strike had helped the others finish their grisly work. Now he and the other members of the team stood loosely ringed around the large stacked pyre that contained the village inhabitants, and another, smaller one next to it, where Saamal lay on a crisscrossed pyramid of poles, with a brightly colored swath of fabric covering his gaping chest. Strangely, his color looked better now than it had at the end of the reanimation spell. Was that a sign that dark magic took a toll on the user?

Catching Rabbit's eye, Strike said, "You okay to do this?"

"No. But I'll do it anyway." Fire was cleansing. It was traditional. And although he'd never tested out the theory, he had a feeling that on some level, it tapped into both light and dark levels of the magic.

Before he started, though, he moved around the pyres and pulled Strike away a few paces. "I just wanted to run this by you." He showed the king the hellmark-shaped eccentric and went through his and Myrinne's thought process. "If you don't like the idea of me holding on to it, though, tell me now, because I'd like it to go into the pyre."

"Keep it. We found a cache of codices and a couple of modern notebooks in the elder's place. Lucius and Jade are going to go through them as soon as we get back. Maybe one of them will have something about the eccentric."

Rabbit hadn't realized he'd tightened up until the tension eased. "Okay. Good. That's good. Thanks."

"No problem," the king said, like it was no big

deal, but as Rabbit turned away, he caught Strike's almost imperceptible nod.

The thing was, he also caught Myrinne's fleeting scowl. She lost it the moment he turned back to her, but he was sure he'd seen it. That brought back some of the tightness, because he sure as shit didn't want to wind up caught between her and Strike. He'd let her jealousy ease him away from Patience—he'd even kind of liked that she'd cared enough to be territorial—but Strike was family.

"Myr?" he asked. *You're everything to me*, he wanted to tell her, *but you can't be the only person I care about*. At the same time, though, he didn't know if he could've coped just now if she hadn't been there.

She smiled, though the warmth didn't make it all the way to her eyes. "Time to do your thing, Pyro."

He nodded, feeling none of the anticipation that usually accompanied the prospect of fire magic. "Yeah."

He took his place in the circle, with his back to the stone archway that would long outlive its builders. He refused to call on the dark lords, but knew the villagers' souls wouldn't appreciate him praying to the sky gods. So in the end he blanked his mind of everything but the magic as he called fire . . . and finished burning Oc Ajal to the ground.

CHAPTER SIXTEEN

Skywatch

It was early afternoon before the teammates reassembled in the great room, showered, changed, and more or less recovered from the morning's ordeal. Physically, anyway. Brandt had a feeling that the Oc Ajal massacre was going to stick with all of them in one way or another.

Whatever had gone down between Strike and Rabbit had cleared the air between the two of them, but that didn't come close to offsetting the pall cast by the villagers' slaughter. The magi drooped, tired in body and soul, tended by somber *winikin*.

Sitting beside him on the love seat, Patience said, "I don't care who they worshipped. That was . . ." She trailed off.

"Yeah." Horrific, inhuman, vile, evil, and a hundred other words applied, yet none could fully encompass what had happened to the almost forty victims. There had been at least ten bodies in the village itself, and twenty-eight more in the surrounding forest, probably cut down as they had run toward the village, no doubt called by the screams.

Maybe a dozen of them had been kids, including twins a few years older than Harry and Braden; they'd been lying just beyond the elder's hut, near a pair of dead coy-dog pups.

At first, Brandt had tried not to wonder whether the woman in the elder's hut had been their mother. Then he decided their memories deserved his pain, so he let himself picture the boys trying to get to her, hearing her screams and calling her name as the *makol* shot them down. Or had the *makol* shot the boys and pups first, while their mother watched, and then dragged her into the hut, lashed her to that damned pole, and gone to work on her?

He could still smell the smoke and blood, as if it had leached into his skin and hair, permeated his soul. He hadn't known any of the victims. Hell, they were the *enemy*. But it was far, far too easy to imagine his family in that village. He kept picturing Patience in the woman's place, Harry and Braden lying in the dirt near those pups, Woody cut down defending his charges, Hannah sprawled facedown with a grindstone near her outstretched fingertips.

Even worse, he could picture the scene there at Skywatch, with bodies scattered in the mansion and out near the picnic area.

Was that how it would happen? Would the Night-keepers be cut down in their homes, ending the war before it truly began?

The villagers had hidden behind glamours rather than wards, he reminded himself. And they had been priests and acolytes, not warriors.

"So why kill them?" he said. "How the hell were they a threat to Iago?" When the room went still, he realized Strike had been talking, that he'd totally zoned out on the start of the meeting. *Way to engage, dickhead.* "Sorry," he said with a guilty look at Patience. "I was thinking out loud. I'll stop."

"Don't stop thinking," Strike said wryly. "You could, however, work on the timing."

He didn't seem that upset, though, probably because they were all feeling pretty damned fragile, and the exchange eased the heavy mood in the room. Not by much, but it was something.

After a raised-eyebrow pause to see if Brandt was going to jump in, Strike said, "It's a valid question. As far as I can see, there are three main answers that jump to mind: One, Iago wanted to finish his father's work by destroying the other Xibalban sect, and he didn't know where the village was until he got the info from Rabbit." He ticked off a second point on his fingers. "Two, he doesn't want Rabbit to get any further on his search for his mother. That's intriguing, because it suggests there's a weakness we don't know about, some way the other side of Rabbit's heritage could harm Iago."

Rabbit unbent from the elbows-on-knees slouch

he'd assumed on a couch next to Myrinne, expression pensive. "It's possible. Iago knew her. He *has* to have known her. The timing—"

"Hold it," Leah broke in using her cop voice, which was guaranteed to stop Rabbit in his tracks. "Promise me you won't dip into his head for the answer until and unless the royal council clears it and you've got spotters standing by. Better yet, promise *Strike* you'll wait until then."

A year ago, asking for Rabbit's promise would've been about as useful as trying to stop up the bathroom shower with a single finger—sort of effective, but not really. Now, though, he actually winced and thought about it for a second before he met Strike's eyes, and said, "I promise I won't connect with Iago to find out about my mother until you give me the go-ahead." Myrinne shot him a look, but didn't say anything.

The king considered that for a moment, no doubt looking for loopholes. Then he said, "Let's make this a fair trade. Once this solstice-eclipse is behind us and things—gods willing—settle down a little, I promise that I'll do what I can to help you figure out as much or as little as you want to know about that side of your family. Deal?"

Rabbit's eyes widened. "Deal."

Strike nodded. "Good. Now, last but not least on the list of 'possible reasons why Iago would send the *makol* to attack Oc Ajal' is because they were looking for something. Question is, did they find it or not? We can assume they were looking for the knife the elder mentioned—the Moctezuma connection is too obvious. But were they also looking for Rabbit's eccentric?"

Lucius said, "Unfortunately, the eccentric isn't showing up in the library, archive, or any of the outside searches I've done so far." He looked over at Rabbit. "I'll talk to some of the more out-there Aztec scholars I know, see if there are any rumors that might not've made it into the official press. My gut says that'll be a dead end, though. Eccentrics were common, but we know almost nada about what they actually symbolized or how they were used."

Rabbit shrugged. "Well, on the bright side, it doesn't come with a 'touch this and die' curse."

"At least not one the Xibalbans made public," Lucius agreed. "The knife, on the other hand, was pretty easy to find—or rather the first fire ceremony was."

Strike grimaced. "Yeah. Jox used to pull that one out when the Xibalban boogeymen stopped working. 'Knock it off or I'll use you to start the new fire,' he'd say. Usually worked too."

Jox flushed a little when the other *winikin* looked at him. "What? Like he said, it worked."

Carlos frowned. "Never heard of it."

"Me neither," Brandt muttered aside to Patience. "You?"

She shook her head. She wasn't the only one; the room seemed about equally divided.

Seeing that not everyone was up to speed, Lucius said, "There were several versions of the ritual. The basic theory was that every fire in the village—or, back in the day, the entire kingdom or the empire itself—was snuffed out simultaneously, plunging the world into darkness and essentially stripping mankind of the one big thing that separates us from the spirits and animals—the ability to use fire. Then the highest-ranking religious leader, whether a village elder or the emperor himself, would use flint and a sparker to start a new fire, and all the other fires would be relit from that one blaze. If we're talking about a village, everyone would snag an ember and go about their business. In cases where the ritual was commanded for a kingdom or the whole empire, runners would head in all directions. Each runner would light all the village fires on his route, then pass off his flame, Olympic-style, to another runner, and another, and so on. In this way, all the fires in the land were made fresh and new again." He paused. "One of the reasons to perform the ceremony was to encourage the sun or moon to return after an eclipse."

"Bingo," Brandt murmured.

Patience nodded. "We knew Iago would try to harness the solstice-eclipse. Maybe this is how he intends to do it."

"Which means all we've got to do is figure out how to stop him and keep Cabrakan where he belongs." Brandt exhaled. "No problem." Inwardly, he added, *And we've got to do all that without me retaking the Akbal oath.*

But that didn't sit right either. Not after what they'd seen in the village.

Lucius went on to describe the harder-core Aztec

versions of the ceremony, in which the new fires were started in the open abdominal cavities of living, eviscerated victims. He paused, clearing his throat. "There's one more thing. I wasn't going to mention it because we're all pretty raw right now, and I don't really see that there's anything we can do about it, but . . ." He took a deep breath. "The strongest of the new-fire rituals used children. Young boys, especially."

"Used them for wh—," Patience began, then broke off, her face draining of color. She grabbed on to Brandt like she was drowning, digging her fingernails into his skin.

He covered her hand with his own. His stomach clutched sourly, but he said, "The twins are safe. Iago knows they exist, but there's no way he can find them. Hannah and Woody are pros at staying hidden."

Lucius held up his hands. "Sorry. My bad. I was more wondering about the villagers."

"You think the *makol* took prisoners," Brandt grated.

Lucius nodded. "The Aztecs were big on it. They even used to set up mock battles with neighboring kingdoms, as a way of capturing each other's culls for use as human sacrifices." He paused. "We don't know how many kids were in the village. They might've captured a dozen, or none. There's no way of knowing."

Brandt shook his head, hating the thought, and what it meant. "Iago is escalating. He started with individual murders, and more often than not, he took the time to do something with the body, either posing it like the first old lady, or—" He broke off with a look at Myrinne, because his second example would have been the Wiccan who had raised her. "Then the kidnappings started—Sasha first, then Rabbit and Myrinne, Lucius. . . . We got all of them back, but Sasha and Lucius both saw other prisoners. Then last year, he started leaving his own people to die, first the human acolytes, then other Xibalbans. And now . . ."

"What happened today was different," Patience agreed.

"The profilers would call it overkill," Michael put in. And he would know.

"That's Moctezuma's influence," Lucius said. "We're not just dealing with Iago anymore. He's something different now, something far more powerful, far more violent."

Brandt tipped his hand in a 'maybe' gesture. "I'm sure that's part of it, but the pattern was in place before he summoned the demon." He had watched his fair share of crime-solving TV back in the outside world. "I think he's been learning as he goes."

"Iago was the second son," Patience said, catching on.

He nodded. "Think about it. Werigo was usurped by *his* younger brother—Saamal—so he probably harped on the 'trust no one, especially your little brother' theory when he was raising Ix." Adrenaline kicked deep down as it came together for him. "But then Werigo died and Ix found himself in charge of a group of dark magi and nasty-ass humans, feeling his little brother breathing down his neck. I'm betting

Ix wouldn't have given Iago any details on anything he didn't have to. So when Ix died, the information chain was broken. Iago didn't know all of the magic or plans." He paused. "I think that up until now he was making shit up as he went along."

"And now he's got Moctezuma helping him," Patience murmured.

"Yeah. Which means it's only going to get worse from here." Brandt tightened his grip on her hand. To Lucius, he said, "Unless you see a problem with that theory."

"Only that I didn't think of it first," the human said drily. Then his expression shifted. "The question is whether we can use it to—" He broke off at the burble of a digital tone.

Patience shot to her feet, fumbling an unfamiliar cell phone out of her back pocket. Flushing, she flipped it open and glanced at the display.

Her face went utterly blank, draining of color.

"Patience?" Brandt rose slowly, confusion turning into something far more uncertain as he connected. It was the phone she'd kept secret from him when they'd lived in the outside world, the one she'd used to talk to Hannah.

Eyes wide and scared, she turned the display so he could see the text. It read: *Put it on speaker.*

A heartbeat later, the main house phone rang.

CHAPTER SEVENTEEN

Heart hammering, Patience stared at the landline. Jox reached to punch the speaker button, then paused and looked at her. "Okay?"

She was badly afraid that things *weren't* okay. Why the text? Why the speaker? Why was Hannah contacting her at all? It had to be her or Woody; they were the only ones who had the private number save for Rabbit, and he was in the room. And Reese Montana, granted, but she wouldn't be calling after all this time. Which meant it was Hannah or Woody . . . and that knowledge held Patience all but paralyzed.

Good news or bad news? She didn't know, couldn't think, couldn't breathe.

"Do it," she told Jox, her voice barely above a whisper. Brandt took her hand and moved up behind her, his body warm and solid. The *winikin* punched the button and the phone emitted the faint snake hiss of live air.

She swallowed hard, then said, "Hannah? Woody?"

"They're here," a man's voice said, "but they can't talk right now. Someone else wants to say hello."

Patience's knees nearly folded as Rabbit lunged to his feet with an inarticulate cry of horror. But even without that confirmation, she knew. She *knew*. Her stomach lurched and her heart hammered into ovedrive. "*Iago.*"

Brandt's fingers closed on hers hard enough to hurt, but she barely felt the pain. Every fiber of her being was focused on the phone, on the hiss of connection and the rustles of movement on the other end.

Then a small, scared voice said, "Mommy? Daddy? Are you there?"

The world stopped as she stared at the phone. She hadn't heard the voice anywhere but in her dreams for the past two years, but she knew it instantly, intimately. *Braden.*

"Nooo." The whisper leaked from her lips, taking air and hope with it. This wasn't happening. It wasn't possible.

Only it *was* possible. And it was happening. *Please, gods, no.*

"*Sonofabitch!*" Brandt moved around her, headed for the phone. His face was dull red and etched with rage.

She grabbed his arm and tried to yank him back. It was like trying to stop a moving vehicle by pulling on a door handle—impossible—but she couldn't let him get to the handset. Training and instinct took over, and she spun, kicked out, and caught him with a foot sweep. By the time he'd regained his balance, almost beyond himself with fury, she had darted around him and put herself between him and the phone, arms outstretched.

"Don't," she warned in a low voice. "That's not Iago right now. It's Braden, and he's terrified."

She was shaking. Behind her, small breathing sounds came down the line, making her picture Braden clutching a phone and trying to be brave while Harry watched, wide-eyed. The image nearly killed her. But at the same time it brought her the strength to stare down Brandt, holding him off until some of the wildness left his eyes.

He let out a long breath, then stepped up beside her as she turned back to the phone. He took her hand, gripping hard. He was shaking. They both were. Voice almost breaking with the effort of holding it together, she whispered, "We're here, baby. Are you and Harry okay?"

"I'm here," said a second version of the same voice, this one softer and more hesitant, not from shyness but because Harry weighed each word so carefully. He added, "We're okay."

"Hey there, champ," Brandt said, using the daddy voice she hadn't heard from him in so long. Hearing it now nearly broke her. He continued: "You're going to have to help each other be brave. We'll be there soon." The promise was underlain with a threat aimed in Iago's direction.

"Are Hannah and Woody there?" Patience asked.

"They're in the other room, sleeping. When are you—" The heartbreakingly young voice shifted away, followed by a yelp of "Mommy!"

"Wait!" She reached for the phone, but stopped herself because it wouldn't do any good.

Brandt put his arms around her, holding her close. She leaned on him hard, but didn't take her eyes off the phone, knowing her babies and the *winikin* were on the other end.

In a low, dangerous voice, Brandt grated, "Talk to us, Iago. What do you want in exchange?"

"Who said anything about an exchange?" The Xibalban's voice was as oily as his magic.

"You didn't just call to torture us," Brandt said flatly.

"Didn't I? I'm getting a kick out of it, actually. Better yet is telling you that I wouldn't have been able to do any of this without you two. Ix lied and said he was going to the hellmouth down in the cloud forest that night. Once I knew which ruin he'd actually been at, it was easy to find the dark-magic entrance. I'll be there when the passageway opens. Me and the other members of your little family."

"Please," Patience whispered without really meaning to.

"Which is worse, I wonder—for me to have my brother vanish, leaving me with little more than spellbooks and lies . . . or for you to know that your sons and *winikin* are going to help me start the new fire and call an army?"

She swallowed a sob, refusing to give Iago the

satisfaction. But she couldn't speak, couldn't think, couldn't do anything but cling to Brandt.

Voice resonating with fury, he rasped, "Patience and I killed Ix, not the boys and the *winikin*. What's more, I'm a Triad mage. That's what you really want, isn't it? You want the power of the Triad backing up your magic. Even better, you want to take one of the Triad magi out of the equation. That's right, isn't it?"

"You're not a Triad mage yet," Iago countered.

"Your intel is dated," Brandt said without hesitating. When Patience frowned up at him, he glanced at Rabbit and tapped his temple, indicating the jade circlet that had—they hoped—cut off Iago's connection with his embedded spy. Then, hardening his voice to a *last chance, asshole* growl, he said, "Do you want to make the trade or not?"

"Four for one? I don't think so." A beat of silence. "You and wifey-poo together. Four for two."

Half a second before Brandt could no-fucking-way Iago's counteroffer, Patience said, "It's a deal. When and where?"

"Eight tomorrow night, on the other side of El Rey, near the palace." Iago paused. "Don't be late." There was a click, and the line went dead.

Silence filled the great room.

A shudder racked Patience. "Oh, gods." She let go of Brandt and staggered away, pressing the back of her hand to her mouth as vicious nausea ripped through her, nearly folding her double. "Oh, shit. I'm—"

She broke and bolted for the bathroom just past

the kitchen, cracked her knees on the marble flooring, and puked miserably in the toilet, hanging on to the seat and sobbing in between bouts. Then she was just hanging on to herself and sobbing, folded into a huddle on the bathroom floor. Brandt didn't try to get her up. He just sat on the bathroom floor to gather her against him and hold on tightly, rocking her as long shudders ran through his big body.

She clung to him as the first terrible wave of grief and fear passed, leaving her wrung and miserable.

"We'll get them back," he said, whispering the words into her hair, over and over again. "We'll do whatever it takes. I swear it."

And even though she knew he couldn't make that promise, she tightened her arms around him. "Thanks. I needed to hear that."

He stilled. "I didn't say anything."

They pulled apart, looking at each other, and then at their forearm marks. Her *jun tan* didn't look any different, didn't feel any different. But she had just heard him in her mind.

When they returned to the main room, Strike was waiting for them, face drawn. "I'm sorry," he said. "I swore to you that they would be safe off the grid. I was sure they would be . . . but he's stronger than any of us thought."

Patience swallowed the surge of bile that came at the thought that, in the end, the boys probably would have been safer staying at Skywatch. Exhaling against the pain, she said only, "Then we're going to have to be stronger than *he* thinks."

"He won't know what hit him," Brandt said, voice low with menace. But she knew he was thinking about what he had been saying about Iago only minutes earlier. Things like "serial killer," "monster," and "escalating."

Before, the Xibalban had been too unsure of his powers to attack them directly. Now he had no such qualms.

Strike said, "Based on the cement blocks and old radiation signs Rabbit saw through Iago's eyes, we think he's hiding in a bunker or a fallout shelter."

"Carter put together a list of possibilities," Jox reported from the kitchen, where he stood with a cell to his ear. "Jade cross-referenced them against power sinks, prioritizing Aztec and Mayan ruins, and got the list down to a hundred and twenty-four possibilities. It's going to take time to check them out."

"Too much time," Strike said.

"Maybe not," Leah countered. "Some detective work might help us narrow down the location."

Jox said, "Carter's also trying to run down the more distinctive tats you guys saw on the *makol* that attacked you, hoping we'll be able to figure out where Iago's doing his recruiting. No luck so far, though."

"I was thinking more along the lines of doing some investigating for ourselves." She turned to Strike. "Can you crack whatever box you set up and find out where Hannah, Woody, and the boys are living now?

If Iago grabbed them from their home, there might be evidence of where the *makol* were prior to the attack. That could lead us back to Iago."

Patience shuddered. When Brandt's fingers brushed hers, she grabbed on tight.

Strike tipped his hand in a yes-no gesture. "I can get the address, but it'll take some time. Lawyer one is going to have to ask lawyer two, and so forth, complete with a satellite-bounced password that changes every three days." He paused. "I really didn't want to know how to find them, in case . . . well, just in case."

"In case we had a major security breach, you mean," Rabbit said resignedly. "I'm grateful for your paranoia, because it means this wasn't my fault. Not like Oc Ajal."

He said something else, but Patience couldn't make out the words over the sudden rushing in her ears.

"Oh, gods," she whispered. Her stomach surged, knotting muscles that were already sore from retching, and felt like they were going to be at it again, real soon. *"No."*

Brandt tried to tug her closer. "What?"

"No." She dropped his hand and backed up a step, away from them all. "Gods, no. He didn't. He couldn't have." But he could have. And he had.

"Patience." Brandt got in her face and took her shoulders. "Talk to me."

She locked on to his gold-shot eyes and her heart broke. He would hate her. She hated herself. Gods. This was her fault for being weak, for being a liar and a sneak.

Voice shaking, she said, "In El Rey, Rabbit and I were directly blood-linked when Iago downloaded him. And I got a splitting headache right after." She swallowed another hard, hot surge of nausea. "He said he wouldn't have been able to do any of this without us."

"He was talking about the intersection," Brandt argued. "Even if he got into one of our heads through the blood-link to Rabbit, he *couldn't* have gotten the boys' location. None of us knew it." He took a step toward her, hands outstretched.

She backed away. "I—" She couldn't get it out.

His color drained. "No. Tell me you didn't." She would've given anything to deny it. When she didn't, his hands fell to his sides. *"Patience."*

"I knew." The words felt like they'd been ripped from the place where her heart used to be. "The address I found on Strike's laptop was out-of-date. I couldn't use Carter, so I went into the archived files and found Strike's report of his first meeting with Mendez, when the bounty hunter grabbed him. I wanted her name."

"You hired Reese Montana to find your boys?" Strike asked. He was staring at her like he'd never seen her before.

She knew the feeling.

"She found them within a few days and texted me the address. I memorized it, deleted the text, and started making plans to go see them . . . but when it came down to it, I couldn't do it. I don't know if it was my warrior's talent, rationality, or what, but

I finally admitted that you guys had been right. I couldn't risk it, couldn't risk *them*, just to make myself feel better. So I made myself forget the address and stop pretending that seeing the boys was going to make everything better."

"Oh, Patience." Brandt's voice was barely above a whisper.

"If I had thought there was even the slightest chance Iago would . . ." She trailed off. Forcing herself to meet his eyes, where the gold flecks were buried beneath dark anguish, she said, "I'm sorry." Her voice broke on the inadequacy of the words.

She was braced for his wrath.

She wasn't prepared for him to cross the few feet separating them and take her in his arms.

"We'll get them back," he said, voice low and determined, as much a vow as if he'd shed blood and sworn to the gods themselves. "You're not the enemy. Iago is."

Then he kissed her temple. And she lost it again.

Clinging to Brandt's solidity, she buried her face in his chest and wept silently, pushed beyond sobs to long, shuddering wails of tears, grief, and misery. Through it all, he held her, the two of them standing there, leaning on each other in the middle of the great room, as the others melted away.

He didn't say anything, didn't try to tell her it was going to be okay, that he was always going to be there for her, or any of the other platitudes they both knew he couldn't guarantee. He just held on to her and let her cry herself dry.

When it was over, when the storm of weeping had passed, leaving her headachy, wrung out, and dry mouthed, she held him a moment longer, pressing her cheek against the wet fabric of his shirt, and listening to the strong, steady beat of his heart. Then, finally, she pushed away and looked up at him.

His face was deeply etched with strain and wore the impassive self-control of a warrior, but he was looking *at* her rather than past her.

Her voice shook. "If I hadn't gone looking for them—"

He silenced her with a finger to her lips. "If I hadn't gotten stuck inside my own head, you wouldn't have needed to." He brushed his knuckles across her cheek. "But I'm here for you now, and we're going to get them back."

She let herself lean into him for a moment longer, thinking that maybe she could count on him this time. But if she'd learned anything over the past couple of years, it was that she also needed to be able to count on herself.

Easing away from him, she inhaled a shuddering breath, and focused. "I know where they were living as of six months ago. We can start there."

Under an hour later, Patience stood at the side door of a neat, unremarkable house in a neat, unremarkable suburban neighborhood, fighting the shakes as Rabbit worked on the lock. Brandt was beside her; the others were ranged behind them, a chameleon shield hiding them from view. But neither her teammates nor the shield spell could change whatever was waiting for them on the other side of the door.

She was trying not to imagine blood, but it painted her mind.

"The boys said the *winikin* were with them," Brandt said under his breath. "He said they were sleeping." He'd repeated it so often that it sounded like a mantra. She wasn't sure which of them he was trying to convince.

"Got it." Rabbit twisted the knob and opened the door, but stepped back to let them lead the way.

Brandt went in first, pushing past her like he wanted to shield her from whatever was inside. She was right behind him, though, nearly piling into him when he got halfway across the room and stopped dead.

She saw blue Formica, dark wooden cabinets, glossy black appliances, and a neutral tiled floor. The refrigerator was covered with cartoon-character magnets, newspaper clippings, and childish pictures drawn with more enthusiasm than skill. A Bose radio took up counter space and played jazz—one of Hannah's favorite styles—with the volume set low.

There was no blood spatter, no sign of a struggle. That wasn't why he'd stopped. His attention was locked on a framed photograph that sat beside the radio.

In it, the foursome had been caught midpicnic, laughing, with sandwiches and drinks spread haphazardly on a wooden table. Hannah's hair was shorter and had more highlights, but the purple pirate's bandanna and the lively sparkle in her good eye were the same. Woody's hair might've gained more threads of gray, but his casual dress and easygoing smile were unchanged. The boys were tall and lean for their age, with Brandt's intensity in eyes the color of her own. Braden, handsome and perfectly groomed, stared directly into the camera with a charmer's smile, while Harry looked into the distance with a dreamy smile, his clothing faintly rumpled, his hair sticking up over his ears.

"They're growing up." Brandt's voice broke. "And the *winikin* . . . gods, I miss them. I want them back, not just safe, but with us. For good."

Before, she would've given anything to hear him admit that, to know that he felt it too.

Now, she moved up beside him, leaned on him briefly, and pressed her cheek to his shoulder. "We're in this together," she said, meaning not just the two of them but the entire team.

His fingers brushed hers, caught, and held. He squeezed, then let go and nodded once, a short, businesslike chin jerk. "Let's do this."

The magi fanned through the house. Patience and Brandt took the upstairs, first checking the big, brightly painted master that held an odd mix of neatness and jumble that reflected the twins' personalities. She wanted to sit there and inhale the fragrance of crayons and the well-oiled baseball gloves that sat on a shelf, one splayed flat, the other with a ball carefully fitted into the pocket. Instead, she kept moving, touching Brandt's hand on the way by.

On the other side of the hall, the *winikin* had separate rooms, which messed with her mental picture of the four of them as a tightly knit nuclear family.

Standing just inside a neat room done in masculine neutrals but with Wood's distinctive flare in the velvet Elvis on the wall, she murmured, "Did something go wrong between you two, or does Woody snore like a chain saw?"

She hoped it was the latter. She wanted to believe they were happy.

"Maybe he couldn't sleep with all the purple," Brandt suggested from the next doorway down.

Patience joined him and glanced in. *Oh, Hannah,* she thought, her throat closing at the sight of purple and more purple—it was in the curtains, the bedclothes, and a small herd of stuffed dragons and dinosaurs on the bed, a profusion that went beyond garish to playful, and made her smile through a mist of tears.

"We should go." But although his voice was clipped, his eyes were dark with strain and grief, and he lingered for a last look in the boys' room, his shoulders bowed.

The team regrouped downstairs in the main room, where the TV was on, glasses of juice sat half-finished on a coffee table, and a remote-controlled robot marched listlessly in a corner, going nowhere, its batteries wearing down. There, as elsewhere in the house, there was no sign of a struggle, no hint of the *makol* having been there.

Brandt crouched down to turn off the robot, his big hands lingering on the remote, touching something his sons had been playing with—what, two hours earlier? Less?

Leah shook her head, frustrated. "Nothing. It's like they were ghosts."

Ghosts. Patience glanced at Brandt as the word sent a cool shiver through her, a reminder that Iago wasn't their only enemy and the first-fire ceremony wasn't the only threat. Time was running out on the Akbal oath.

He looked up at her, jaw set. "They'll be okay," he grated.

But the gold was gone from his eyes.

CHAPTER EIGHTEEN

December 21
Winter solstice-eclipse
Skywatch

For Brandt, the night passed in a gut-gnawing blur of fruitless research and burning frustration. He wanted to fucking *do something*.

But Lucius and Jade hadn't been able to find a way for him to renegotiate the Akbal oath, and the list of possible Xibalban bunkers was still too long, so the plans had shifted to staking out the dark-magic entrance and grabbing Iago and his prisoners on the way in. And in order to do that, they had to *find* the dark-magic entrance.

It had been Patience's idea for Rabbit to mind-link with Jade and attempt to blend her de-cloaking talent with his dark magic, in order to search for the second doorway. Brandt had been proud of her for the potential breakthrough . . . but he hadn't told her so.

In fact, he'd been avoiding her, because he didn't want to fight about the Akbal oath anymore.

He got her logic—of course he did. The Triad magic could hold the key to defeating not just Cabrakan but Iago as well. But the sticking point remained: He owed the gods a life. *Her* life.

She had argued that it was like the village elder had said: The gods made their choices as they saw fit. They didn't need his permission to take her. Which was true. But the Akbal oath was his burden . . . and his decision.

He wished Woody were there. He wanted to talk to the *winikin*, wanted his fucking family back together, wanted things the way they used to be. But the gods didn't give a shit what he wanted, did they? That much was patently clear.

Have faith. The whisper came in Wood's voice, shaming him.

Which was why, as the clock ran down into the last couple of hours before they would begin their stakeout of El Rey, he wound up in the mansion's circular ceremonial chamber, on his knees in front of the *chac-mool*.

The sun shone down through the glass roof, casting diminishing shadows on the stone-tiled floor and warming the fabric of his black tee and cargo pants as he scored both palms and let a few drops of blood fall into the shallow bowl atop the altar. Then, settling back on his heels, he folded his bloodstained hands together and tried to remember how to pray.

Gods help me, he thought, but instead of leaving him and heading for the sky, the words stayed trapped inside him, banging around in his skull. Frustration flared, but he tamped it down and tried again. "Gods help me." He said it aloud that time, so it couldn't stay stuck inside, but he didn't feel the bond he'd once felt, the click that told him the gods were listening. Because they weren't. Not to him, anyway.

Heart heavy, he cleaned off his knife and hands, rose to his feet, and turned for the door.

Patience stood just inside it.

Like him, she was dressed in combat gear. But where before he'd occasionally thought she made the outfit look like coed-goes-goth, the woman who faced him now looked capable, deadly, and determined. Which drove home something he had realized while arguing with her over the Akbal oath: She hadn't just gotten stronger as a person; she'd grown as a warrior. And that scared the shit out of him.

He wanted to ask her to stay behind, but couldn't. So he said simply, "Time to go?"

"Almost." She looked beyond him to the altar. "Any luck?"

He shook his head.

"I've been doing some more thinking about the Mexico City earthquake back in the eighties," she said, which was no surprise. She had spent a good chunk of the previous evening obsessing over the killer quake and the toll Cabrakan could take on mankind.

He knew it was her way of coping, just like the

oracle cards had started out as a way for her to beat her depression. But he didn't want to talk about the earthquake anymore. If Cabrakan got through the barrier, people were going to die. But he couldn't—wouldn't—sacrifice her.

"Can we please not do this again?" he asked.

Her expression darkened. "Hear me out."

"We're not going to agree on this one, sweetheart, so I don't see the point in continuing to argue."

"Because you've made your decision," she said flatly.

"I don't want us 'porting to El Rey pissed at each other." He reached for her.

She took a big step back. "You seem to be forgetting that it's not your call."

His frustration upped a notch. "It's my oath, my decision. And we both know that Strike won't order me to retake it. Not after he broke the thirteenth prophecy to save Leah."

"I was talking about me. Or are you so used to calling the shots for me that you can't wrap your head around the fact that I've got my own opinions now?"

"What the hell are you talking about?" He jammed his hands in his pockets so he wouldn't be tempted to do something else with them. "Look, I know you need to think about something other than the boys or you'll lose it. I get that. But let's not do this right now. We need to focus."

She flinched almost imperceptibly, but held her ground. "If you can't see that the lack of balance in our relationship is affecting your judgment—and potentially our ability to go after the boys and *winikin*—then you're the one who's not focusing." Her eyes softened. "Don't you get it? You don't get to decide what's best for everyone else, least of all me."

"For fuck's sake, I'm not trying to run your life. I'm trying to figure out how to *save* it."

"You don't get to make decisions for me. I'm not the kid you married anymore." She paused. "The way I see it, things started going wrong when I got my warrior's mark and entered full-on battle training. The more I started having opinions, and the more we were expected to work together as a mated warrior team, the more you checked out on me."

He clenched his teeth. "That was backlash from Werigo's spell, damn it."

"I wanted to believe that, I really did, but let's face the facts: You pursued me in Cancún even knowing that you shouldn't, and you're refusing to retake the oath now because all the signs indicate that I'll be the gods' choice. If you can ignore those imperatives, then you damn well could have done the same with feeling that you needed to push me away. It doesn't make any sense that you would go along with your subconscious unless it was telling you something you wanted to hear. Which means you wanted that distance."

"That's—" *bullshit*, he started to say, but broke off. "Can we please focus on getting our asses to El Rey and grabbing the boys and *winikin* before Iago gets them underground?"

She met his eyes. "The stronger we are, the better chance we have to rescue them. And, outside of you retaking the Akbal oath, the only way we can make ourselves stronger is to fully reopen the *jun tan*."

Finally, something concrete. He thrust out his hand, palm up. "Fine. Let's uplink and get it open."

But she shook her head. "You know it doesn't work that way."

Acid burned in his gut. "Then tell me how you think it *does* work. Give me something specific, damn it! I'll do whatever you want—just tell me what you need from me."

She met his eyes. "Accept me for who I am today, not who I used to be. Make me your partner instead of your backup. Trust me to take care of myself during a fight. And do everything you can to save Harry, Braden, and the *winikin*. Period."

His blood chilled. "In other words, retake the Akbal oath. You want me to prove that I love you by sacrificing you."

"If the gods want me, they'll take me."

"I can't—" He broke off, swallowing hard. This was why he hadn't wanted to get back into this argument. Because she wasn't wrong. But he didn't think she was right either. "Not yet," he said. "If it comes down to it, I'll say the words. But not now. Not until we're sure there isn't another way."

She wanted to keep arguing; he saw it in her eyes. Instead, she nodded. "Okay. I don't like it, but okay. We'll do it your way."

"It's not about doing things my way, damn it."

Her look said, *Isn't it?* He would've liked to think the words came through the *jun tan* link, but his forearm mark was cool, and for all the times she had accused him of being distant, now she was the one who seemed very far away as she crossed the circular chamber, knelt before the *chac-mool*, and bowed her head.

After a moment, he joined her there. But instead of a prayer, all he could come up with was, *Come on, Rabbit. Hurry up and find that fucking doorway.*

CHAPTER NINETEEN

El Rey

Rabbit was sweating as he and Jade quartered the ruins of the El Rey palace, which was little more than a stone-outlined footprint of where the big structure once stood. They were blood-linked, which allowed him to enter her mind despite wearing the jade circlet, and they were doing their damnedest to blend his dark magic with her sensitivity to concealment spells. Michael and Sasha trailed them, weapons drawn, and the shimmer of his chameleon shield concealed them from the *makol* sentries Iago had undoubtedly posted in the nearby forest.

The flop sweat sliding down Rabbit's back wasn't from the warm sunlight, or even his churning worry that this particular cardinal day was poised to go really fucking wrong. It came from the fact that using his mind-bend to slant Jade's talent toward dark magic was way too close to Iago's ability to borrow other people's magic. Rabbit didn't like the squick factor brought by the comparison . . . or the skirl of temptation that licked at the edges of his mind.

Saamal had called him the crossover, but what the hell did that mean? Was he supposed to reunite the light and dark into its ancestral form? Michael used only the destructive, death-dealing aspects of *muk*. If Rabbit could harness the full power of the magic, it could be a huge plus for the Nightkeepers. And—

And nothing, he told himself, aware that he was spinning into grand-plan territory, which tended to get his ass in trouble. *Keep your mind on the gods-damned job.*

"See anything?" Jade asked as they picked their way across a central courtyard that was outlined by crumbling pillars.

"Nothing. You?" They weren't sure which one of them would see the dark-magic shimmer, or even if their combined efforts would work.

"Ditto."

Glancing at the sky, Rabbit winced when he saw that the sun was a quarter of the way down to the dusk horizon. "It's getting late. I still think we should try—"

"You're not connecting with Iago. King's orders, nonnegotiable," Michael interrupted from behind them.

"But this isn't—" *working,* Rabbit started to say, but broke off when he caught a quiver in his peripheral vision, like a heat shimmer, though it wasn't that hot. He focused on the spot, which was near the palace's back wall. There, three large stone slabs were inset into the ground, each of them approximately the size and shape of a coffin.

The one in the middle was swirling with the greasy brown smears of dark magic.

"I see it," Jade whispered. "That's got to be the second doorway."

"Nice job." Michael pulled his phone and summoned the others, who were there in five minutes, materializing in a hum of red-gold Nightkeeper power.

Almost before they were boots down, Patience broke the 'port uplink and hurried toward the doorway team. Brandt followed a couple of steps behind her, grim-faced. Rabbit cut a sharp look between the two of them, not liking what he saw. Over the past few days, their unique *jun tan* link had begun resonating in his perceptions. Maybe the magic hadn't been as strong as it used to be, but he'd thought they were on the mend.

Now, they could've been strangers.

When Patience came up beside him, he whispered, "Did something else happen?"

"Just more of the same," she said, avoiding his eyes. "Don't worry about us. We're solid."

He knew damn well that was an overstatement, but she had been there for him after his old man's death, so he didn't poke at her now. Instead, he took her hand and squeezed it. "We're going to get them back."

She nodded, swallowing. "Thanks."

Out of the corner of his eye, Rabbit saw Myrinne's expression sharpen. She was at the back of the group, wearing black on black and carrying a jade-tip-loaded autopistol, having finally, after eighteen months, won her way fully onto the team. He sent her a finger-wiggle, but wasn't sure if she saw.

There wasn't time for more, because Strike and Brandt moved up on his other side, and the king said, "Okay, you two. Let's get this thing open."

Rabbit and Jade clasped hands once again, blending their magic so her uncloaking ability was skewed from light magic to dark, and got some extra oomph. As she cast the spell, the air over the coffin-shaped stone shivered and the dark-magic smear started swirling faster and faster, expanding with each revolution.

Then the magic solidified with a low-level *boom*, and a small stone temple appeared right in front of them. It was plain, square, and unadorned, and the end facing them was almost entirely taken up by an arched doorway that led to a set of stairs heading down.

Two Aztec *makol* stood just inside the doorway, looking startled as hell.

"Rabbit, down!" Michael barked from behind him.

Rabbit dropped to his knees. A split second later, death magic flared straight over his head in a killing stream of silver light that forked to hit the *makol* chest high. They died instantly in a flare of *muk*, becoming greasy piles of gray char that crumpled inward and collapsed with a hiss.

Rabbit glanced back over his shoulder and saw that Michael had turned ash gray himself. Sasha took his hand and summoned her *chu'ul* magic, working to level off the aftereffects. Although the assassin's power was lightning fast and worked against all but the strongest of their enemies, it took its toll. Michael wouldn't be good for too many more flat-out kills.

Which could be a problem, because the guards weren't a good sign.

Thinking to test for more of them, Rabbit stepped through the doorway and opened up his senses. And was instantly awash in power.

As if coming from very far away, down a long, echoing tunnel, he heard Strike say: "Fuck. Iago's already down there." There was a pause; then he said, "Rabbit, can you sense anything?"

He didn't answer. He couldn't.

Dark magic flowed all around him, through him, weighing his soul and making him want to gag at the same time that it skimmed over his skin, lighting his neurons and getting him hard. He loved it, hated it, wanted it, despised it. For a moment he was balanced. Then there was a surge, the scales tipped, and he leaned into the glorious flow of coppery brown magic, opened himself up to it, and—

"*Rabbit!*" Myrinne was suddenly in his face, shaking him. "Shut it down, now!"

It took him a second to focus on her, another to figure out what she was talking about. Then the gag response flared higher as the Nightkeeper half of him reasserted itself, beating back the lure of the dark power.

He shut down the connection, slamming the barriers down. His head echoed with sudden emptiness and he sagged against the wall, would've gone down without it. Scrubbing his hands over his face, he rasped, "Holy shit."

He'd never sensed the dark magic like that before, never felt like he could ride the wave to someplace incredible.

"Somebody get a shield over the doorway," Strike ordered. Then he gripped Rabbit's shoulder. "Talk to me."

"Let him breathe first," Myrinne snapped.

But Rabbit shook his head. "I'm okay." *Sort of.* "The hellroad is wide-open."

Strike cursed. "That shouldn't be possible this far ahead of the solstice." He paused. "Maybe it's something to do with the eclipse, or Moctezuma's magic."

"Or else Iago jump-started it with blood," Patience said, her voice barely above a whisper. Brandt reached out and took her hand, but although she leaned into him, the air around them remained still.

"Does he know we're here?" Brandt asked, eyes fixed on the staircase leading down.

Rabbit shook his head. "He's pouring all his power into keeping the intersection open. He doesn't know we took out the two *makol* up here."

Strike glanced at him. "What do you think? Can you still do it?"

When the kidnapping had nixed the plan of baiting a trap by letting Iago see specific things within Rabbit's mind, Jade had modified the spell in the other direction. Now Rabbit should be able to make his presence look like part of Iago's background mental pattern and—in theory, anyway—influence his thoughts.

There hadn't been any time to test it, though. "If he senses me, he's going to link up and take over," Rabbit warned, though they had been over the pros and cons a dozen times already. "You might not even know he's got me until it's too late."

"I'll know." Myrinne moved up beside him so they were shoulder to shoulder facing the temple door.

Strike nodded. "Do it."

Taking a deep breath and hoping to hell this shit worked, Rabbit slipped off the protective circlet. Although he'd had it for only a few days, his head felt seriously naked without it. *Deal with it,* he told himself, and got to work.

Disguising his thoughts beneath a layer of mental patterns that were as close as he could get to Iago's, he dropped the blocks and cracked open the hell-link. Between proximity and the power of the solstice-eclipse, the connection formed instantly. One second he was looking at Myrinne, and in the next, he was in a ceremonial chamber, looking out through Iago's eyes as the Xibalban raised Moctezuma's knife. And advanced on his first sacrificial victim.

As Rabbit tuned out and swayed on his feet, Patience gave a low moan and whispered, "Please, gods."

Brandt gripped her hand and got a return squeeze, but he didn't feel anything more than the press of her fingers on his. They were standing in the middle of El Rey, yet he couldn't sense the special buzz of magic that had been theirs alone.

She was blocking him. She had closed herself off, distancing herself when they most needed to be working together.

"Don't shut me out," he said under his breath.

She glanced at him. "I'm not."

But there was a barrier between them, one he didn't know how to breach. The Akbal spell wasn't the answer. He was sure of that much.

"I'm in," Rabbit said suddenly, his voice a low, effortful gasp. "I'll stall him as long as I can, but we need to move fast. He's already got his first sacrifice prepped." He fixed on Brandt. "It's Woody."

The world froze as the words rocketed around inside Brandt's head, in his heart, icing his universe. *It's Woody. . . . It's Woody. . . . Woody . . . Woody.*

Sudden heat raced through him, boiling the ice with mad, murderous rage. He lunged for the dark-magic doorway, lashing out with his warrior's talent and slamming aside Michael's sturdy shield spell.

"Holy shit," someone said; he didn't know which one of them it was. Didn't care. All he cared about was that he would have the strength of an eagle warrior when he went up against his enemy.

Patience was right on his heels, with the others behind her. When darkness closed around him, he called up light—not a weak and harmless foxfire, but a fighting fireball that pulsed red-gold and dripped sparks from his hand, searing stone and sand to glass where they fell. Talent magic hadn't worked beneath Chichén Itzá, but it worked here. Michael spread a chameleon shield over them, cloaking the light and noise as the others called their fireballs. The burning lights cast the smooth, water-cut tunnel walls blood-red as they raced down the twisting staircase.

Rabbit haltingly briefed them as they went: Iago and Woody were alone in the sacred chamber, but there were twenty Aztec *makol* on the far side, in the short stretch of the light-magic tunnel that had survived the cave-in. They were guarding Hannah and the twins, who were in an offshoot room Iago had discovered.

"They're all okay," Rabbit said, but the unspoken caveat was, *For now.*

Another twenty *makol* guarded the dark-magic entrance; the Nightkeepers would have to go through them to get to the chamber. And although Rabbit was working to prevent Iago from killing Woody while also keeping the Xibalban from sensing the incoming attack, the effort was costing him. He leaned heavily on Myrinne, and his words slurred as he said, "We're almost on top of them."

And then they *were* on top of them. Brandt whipped around a corner, caught sight of a double row of *makol* standing at some sort of parade rest, and slammed himself flat along the wall. The others did the same as Michael lunged to the front of the group, pulling Sasha with him. He slapped a chameleon shield across the entrance to the ceremonial chamber, which was just beyond the enemy squadron. In almost the same move, he unleashed a deadly stream of *muk*, hosing it from one side of the tunnel to the other.

The silver magic flared brightly, searing Brandt's retinas with the afterimage of Michael's face, etched with a terrible combination of exultation and grief as he wielded his death magic.

The *makol* died as they had stood. A couple in the back managed to get their buzz swords activated, but the magic died as quickly as they did.

When it was done, the silver *muk* drained away and the tunnel returned to fireball-lit darkness, with a glimmer of torchlight up ahead, past the ash-shadows that were all that was left of the Aztec *makol*.

Michael collapsed against the wall and waved them past. "Shield's down. *Go!*"

Brandt lunged past him, skidded on the ash, and surged through the doorway. His brain snapshotted the first frozen image: Woody lay strapped atop the crude altar, his head hanging off one end, his legs off the other, his arms out to the sides and his Hawaiian shirt open, his torso bare. Iago stood over him, holding a forearm-long knife that was made of carved stone and edged with gold. Its tip was stained with blood, and red rivulets ran from Wood's palms to drip on the floor.

But when Brandt burst in, Wood's head whipped up and his eyes snapped wide. *"Brandt!"*

Iago spun, his glowing green eyes going wide with

shock. That moment of surprise, coupled with a jerky hesitation that had to be Rabbit's work, was enough.

Roaring, Brandt unleashed a fireball straight into the Xibalban's face, which was unprotected above black body armor. The bolt hit hard and exploded on impact, napalming to engulf the Xibalban's head and upper body in flames.

Patience darted past Brandt, leaped in the air, and kicked the staggering Xibalban in the chest, driving him down and away from the altar. Iago roared and went down on the far side of the altar while she stood watching, her eyes bright with fury.

She looked every inch the capable warrior. The realization tightened something in Brandt's chest.

Then she turned to him, locking eyes. He saw the fierce lust for action that he'd seen in her from the very beginning, tempered now with her loyalties: to him, their sons, their *winikin*, their teammates. And something clicked deep inside him.

"I'll get Woody," she said, heading for the altar with her knife drawn. *"Finish the bastard."*

Was it close enough to the solstice for the head-and-heart spell to work on the powerful *ajaw-makol*?

Let's find out.

Baring his teeth, Brandt unsheathed his ceremonial dagger and headed for Iago. He lay still, curled up on one side. And he stank of charred flesh.

"Brandt!" Patience's cry was scant warning as the second group of Aztec *makol* erupted from the light-magic doorway and raced for Iago. Their buzz swords were whizzing, and they launched a salvo of the deadly blades as they came.

He got up a shield just in time, protecting Patience and Woody as well as himself, but it cost him: The *makol* got between him and Iago, covering their master and driving the Nightkeepers back with swords and flying blades.

With Michael's death magic depleted and Rabbit sagging on Myrinne's shoulder, too exhausted to command fire, the Nightkeepers let rip with a salvo of fireballs—or in Jade's case iceballs—and conventional jade-tipped bullets. The weapons barely made a dent on the solstice-toughened *makol*.

Brandt fell back to the altar, reaching it just as Patience finished hacking through the leather straps that had held Woody bound. The *winikin* lurched up and off the altar, and fell when his legs gave out. Brandt caught him on the way down, and for half a second just hung on to the slight, wiry man. "Damn good to see you."

Wood hugged him back, but said, "Hannah and the boys are up in the other tunnel."

In other words, *Fight now. We'll talk later.* It was typical Woody, and sent a burst of relief through Brandt as he released the *winikin*. Some things, it seemed, didn't change no matter what.

He caught Patience's eye and jerked his chin toward the tunnel. She led the way, followed by Woody, with Brandt forming the rear guard.

The other magi were fighting a battle of attrition against the *makol*. "Go," the king shouted. "We'll keep the exit open."

But then, without warning, a new group of war cries split the air and eight more *makol* soldiers, entirely unexpected based on Rabbit's psi-scouting report, poured through the dark-magic entrance.

"The sentries!" Brandt cursed, making the connection—the Nightkeepers might have made it past the outer perimeter of guards undetected, but now that stealth became a liability, as it meant the *makol* had reinforcements and the magi were surrounded.

He slapped a shield just inside the door, slowing the rush, but the *makol* attacked the shield with their buzz swords and he felt the spell give. It wouldn't hold for long. These bastards were *strong*.

And when they broke through, they were going to go after Hannah and the boys. Brandt saw it in their green-hued eyes, in the way they were wholly focused on the far doorway. *Gods.*

"I'm going up that tunnel." Patience's expression was fierce. "You stay here and keep the exit open. The others can't hold it without you."

The tightness in Brandt's chest increased a thousandfold. He grabbed her arm, felt her strength, but also her softness. *No*, he started to say, but the word died in his throat when he saw the look in her eyes— not weakness or a plea, but a challenge. A warning.

Love me for who I am, she had said. *Make me your partner. Trust me.*

Brandt froze. They hadn't been fighting about the Akbal oath, after all. It'd been about him trusting her to make her own decisions. Maybe she had said that, but it hadn't registered. Now it did.

Woody shot a look from Brandt to Patience and back again, and shook his head. "Don't try to do everything yourself," he said, as he'd said a hundred times during Brandt's teenage years. "You're not a fucking island."

"Shit." He wanted to kiss her, hold her, put her behind him, protect her with every last breath in his body. Instead, he tossed her his extra ammo clips and spare flashlight. "Tell them I'm on my way. Tell them . . . tell them that I love them."

Her eyes flashed and a fierce smile lit her face, a brief oasis in the midst of battle. "I will."

"Go!" he barked as the shield spell gave and the *makol* reinforcements rushed the chamber. And, as she bolted across the room and into the tunnel, he said under his breath, "Gods, please keep them safe."

But as Wood yanked the autopistols off his belt and fired into the onrushing *makol*, and Brandt spun up his magic, he was all too aware that his prayer had stayed on earth. He was still cursed.

He just hoped he hadn't cursed all of them in the process.

Patience raced up the dark tunnel with her heart hammering so loudly in her ears that she couldn't hear her own footfalls, couldn't hear anything but the *lub-dub* of joy, excitement, and terror. Joy that Brandt had finally trusted her to do something other than watch his back. Excitement at the prospect of seeing Harry, Braden, and Hannah. Terror at what she might find up ahead.

She turned a corner and saw torchlight coming from an irregularly shaped doorway. Killing the flashlight, she went invisible, then advanced soundlessly with an autopistol at the ready.

When she reached the doorway, she crouched low and eased her head into the opening. What she saw on the other side stopped her heart's *lub-dub* in its tracks.

In the plain, unadorned room lit by a trio of torches, a single Aztec *makol* stood guard, facing the doorway but unaware of her invisible self. Behind him, Hannah sat with her back against the wall. The boys were plastered up against her, one on each side. Hannah had lost her bandanna, they were all dirty and bedraggled, and tear tracks marked all three faces.

But they were alive. Intact. *Thank the gods.*

Her heart started beating again, flaring relief through her veins. She must have gasped or made some small noise, because the *makol* snapped to attention, barking a string of unfamiliar words as it activated its buzz sword. But it looked around wildly, unable to pinpoint her as she skirted the room and got behind it.

Patience saw Hannah and the boys flinch away from the *makol*'s agitation, saw their confusion, their weary fear. Her chest hurt; her eyes stung. She wanted to hold them, touch them, tell them she was there and everything was going to be okay. Instead, she slapped a shield spell over them, and shouted, "Stay down!"

The second the shield spell took hold, the *makol* spun, locking onto her magic and launching its blades in a smooth, deadly move.

She dropped and rolled, still invisible, and called a fireball, launching it almost before it fully formed.

The glowing red-orange energy pulse slammed into the creature's chest and detonated, instantly wreathing the thing's body in flames.

It screamed in pain, a too-human sound that made her heart clutch, not because her enemy was suffering, but because her sons were seeing it.

Wanting it over with, she slammed a second fireball into the thing's head, vaporizing half its skull with grim purpose. *Head and heart.* When it toppled, she followed it down and said the banishment spell.

The *makol* crumbled to greasy ash.

And she was alone with her sons and *winikin*.

Hannah's eye was locked on the air above the ash pile, slightly to the left of where she actually was. The boys were both staring straight at her, brows furrowed, as if they could sense her but weren't sure of their perceptions.

"Patience?" Hannah asked, the single word carrying wary hope.

"Yes." The word was almost a sob as she dropped the invisibility spell and rose to her feet. She had meant to cross the short distance between them, but once she was up, her legs refused to carry her.

She could only stare as Braden uncoiled himself, his eyes getting very big as his mouth shaped the most beautiful word in the world. "Mommy?" The first one didn't have any sound, but when she hiccuped on a sob and nodded, he shouted it, "Mommy!"

He launched himself at her. Harry was a split second behind him.

She had just enough presence of mind to drop the shield spell that had protected them, and cast a new one across the doorway, sealing them in.

Then they hit her one-two, like automatic fire, driving her back under the impact, and she couldn't think about anything but them. Finally. In her arms. Their whippet-lean bodies were an alien contrast to the toddler sturdiness she remembered, yet her heart knew them instantly.

Her legs gave out and she thumped inelegantly to her knees, then gathered them close and pressed their tear-streaked faces against hers, their bodies into hers. She was shaking—maybe all three of them were. Then Hannah dropped down opposite her, and they clung together.

Thank you, gods. Thank you, thank you, thank you. She wasn't sure if she thought the words or said them, didn't care, cared only that she was holding her sons again, and being held by her *winikin*.

For a long, shuddering moment, she let herself be at peace.

Then, knowing the fight wasn't over yet, she broke the huddle and drew, back, keeping contact with Hannah and the boys as she did, trying to take in the reality of them, the small changes.

She had only seen Hannah bandanna-less a few times in her life, and up close the scarred flesh and partly covered socket were discomfiting, but the strangeness lasted only a few seconds before Patience's brain readjusted and she saw only her *winikin*. The one constant in her life.

"Is Woody okay?" Harry asked. It was the first sound he had made since her arrival.

"Your daddy and I got him away from Iago," she said. Which was the truth, but what was the situation now? Her pulse accelerated once more.

She tried her earpiece but got only static, which left her with precious few options, all of them bad. Letting her warrior's talent lead the way, she got to her feet. "Come on. We're going to hide further up the tunnel."

The pyramid's collapse had blocked it as an escape route, but anything was better than staying where Iago expected them to be.

"Will Daddy be able to find us?" asked Braden, his blue eyes wide and worried.

"Always." She squeezed their joined hands, healed deep inside by the feeling of the small fingers in hers. "He wanted me to tell you that he loves you very much."

"Is he coming soon?"

"As soon as he and the others are finished with Iago and the rest of the *makol*," she said aloud. But when her eyes met Hannah's, she saw her own fear reflected back.

Worse, she thought she felt a faint vibration beneath her feet. She didn't know if it came from fighting magic or a miniquake. Wasn't sure she wanted to know. But as they headed up the tunnel, carrying a couple of the torches, moving away from the fight and toward the cave-in, she sent a whisper of thought toward the *jun tan*: *We're okay. But you guys need to hurry.*

The solstice was coming, and with it, Cabrakan.

Rabbit battled through his growing exhaustion and kept the fireballs coming, because the fucking *makol* kept coming too.

Any other time, he would've been totally jacked by the way Myrinne stood right beside him, expression fierce as she ran through her clips and knocked the green-eyed bastards back. Now, though, he was more panicked than turned on, because he could barely protect himself, never mind her.

His head was splitting, partly because of the power he'd pulled to cloak their initial attack, and partly because he hadn't been able to get out of Iago's mind fast enough when he caught on. The bastard had tried to slam the door shut, and Rabbit had only gotten out because Myrinne had jammed the circlet back on him, cutting the connection before it was too late. The pain of severing the link had been excruciating, though. The agony lingered, sapping his strength.

"Get that one," she said, pointing at a downed *makol* that was barely moving. "I'll hold the others off." She fired off two short bursts, one on each autopistol. Standing hipshot in her combat gear, with her hair in a long, dark ponytail pulled through the back of a black ball cap, she looked kick-ass sexy. And she fit with the team, after all this time.

He snapped off a sluggish-feeling salute. "Yes, ma'am!"

Reversing his gore-spattered knife, he went for the incapacitated *makol*, steeling himself for the messy chore of finishing it off before it managed to regenerate. He crouched down by the bullet-riddled body, set his knife to its neck, and—

"Rabbit," Strike bellowed, "*move!*"

Obeying without stopping to look or think, Rabbit flung himself to the side, rolled, and came up with an autopistol in one hand, his knife in the other. He spun back at the sound of Myrinne firing and screaming, not in pain, but in anger.

She was unloading her clips at Iago, who was bearing down on him with gruesome fury. The Xibalban had regenerated to the point of having eyes, nose, and mouth, but his flesh was waxy and fire-ravaged, and his luminous green eyes were bright with rage.

Myrinne's bullets stopped short of him and pinged to the ground, the jade tips deadened by the *ajaw-makol*'s powerful shield magic. Strike launched a fireball and Michael followed with a thin stream of *muk*, but both bounced. The others were trying to get through to help, but the *makol* fought fiercely and with purpose: They were gradually bunching the Nightkeepers up against the altar, away from the doorways, trapping them together

In the split second it took Rabbit to see and react, Iago slammed a layer of dark shield magic around the two of them, shutting them off from the others.

Howling with rage and desperation, Rabbit buried his old man's knife in Iago's armpit, where the body armor provided thin entry. The knife came out slick with blood and Iago hunched, snarling. But he didn't back down, didn't slow down. He grabbed Rabbit's knife hand by the wrist and bore it back, twisting hard.

Wrenching agony flared, first in his arm and then in his head, as the touch link allowed Iago to override the protection of the jade circlet.

Little fucker, the Xibalban hissed inside Rabbit's skull. *Hope you enjoyed sneaking in here, because that's the last trick you'll ever play on me.*

Agony flared from the place where Iago gripped his wrist, his blood-wet palm centered over the hell-mark. Rabbit shrieked and bowed as something tore inside him, not muscle, flesh, or skin, but on the level of his consciousness, his magic, his very soul.

The Xibalban's waxy, burn-ravaged lips pulled back from heat-cracked teeth and his eyes changed, going from featureless luminosity to a hint of irises and pupils, all in glowing green.

In them, Rabbit saw Iago. He saw the god-king Moctezuma. And he saw his own death.

Then, past Iago's shoulder, through the greasy swirl of dark shield magic, he saw Myrinne. She had her hands pressed to the shield, though he knew it must be burning her with acid and electricity. Her face was etched with pain, and her lips shaped his name.

The sight brought a spurt of power from the deepest depths of him, one that flared hard and hot and whispered: *Kaak.* Fire.

It was his first talent, his best talent, the one that had come to him even before he'd earned his bloodline mark.

Wrenching his mind free, he shouted, *"Kaak!"*

Flames erupted from his wrist, searing Iago's hand and climbing his arm. The Xibalban jerked in astonishment. He recovered almost immediately, but it was just enough for Rabbit to push himself upstream along the agony into the other man's mind. Iago roared and grabbed onto his consciousness in the same hurtful grip he was using in the physical world. *Gotcha, you little shit!*

But on a far more basic level, Rabbit had *him*. Because while Iago was focused inward, Rabbit was busy disabling the Xibalban's shield spell.

For a split second, he saw through both his own eyes and Iago's, bringing a double-vision view of Myrinne's fierce relief as the shield went down, then her mad battle fury as she brought up her autopistol and unloaded the clip into Iago's face.

Rabbit screamed as pain slashed through him, coming from Iago's new injuries and the severing of their mind-link as the *makol* was flung away from him, breaking the touch link. Then the circlet's protection snapped back into place, cutting off the mental connection and slamming the air locks shut.

But a piece of him tore loose from his mind and went with Iago.

"No." He crumpled to the ground. *"No!"* He didn't know what Iago had taken, didn't know how bad the damage was; he knew only that he *was* damaged.

"Rabbit!" Myrinne dropped down beside him. She touched his face; her hands came away slick and red. He tasted blood, felt it prickling in his sinuses, suspected it was mixed with his tears. His head pounded; magic spasmed wildly through him, formless and hurting. Gods, what had Iago *done* to him?

"I'm—" *Okay,* he started to say, but even that one word was too much for him, sending his system spinning. Panic licked at him; if he passed out, Myrinne would be unprotected. She would be—

"I've got you," she whispered, leaning over him. Her expression was bare of the sardonic reserve that usually left him guessing at her true feelings; instead he saw her fear for him, her growing determination. "I won't let you down."

His senses fluctuated strangely, expanding and narrowed. He heard the Nightkeepers' shouts, the sounds of battle, and knew that the fight wasn't over yet. Far from it.

"Help them," he whispered. "We can't let Iago win."

Or he thought he said it aloud; he wasn't sure. All he knew was that as the gray closed in, his senses narrowed to a point, so all he saw was his own forearm, blood-smeared and blistered.

Shock hammered through him, sending him the rest of the way into unconsciousness.

His hellmark had gone from red to black. Iago had broken their bond.

CHAPTER TWENTY

"Brandt!" Woody bellowed over the chatter of jade-tipped ammo. "The tunnel!"

"I see him," Brandt grated, agony slashing through him as Iago's shambling form disappeared through the far doorway. He roared and unloaded a volley of fireballs into the *makol* lines, but they barely made a dent, just as they had done every other time he'd tried to break through and follow Patience up the tunnel.

The green-eyed bastards had the Nightkeepers pushed back to the altar and trapped against the wall. Rabbit and Myrinne were outside the *makol* line, but Rabbit was down, with Myrinne bent over him. Michael's death magic was shot and the other magi were sagging, their united shield magic flickering in and out.

They were fucking trapped. And Iago was headed for Patience and the boys. Brandt had sent her up there, and then he hadn't protected her six like he'd promised. And he was getting only static through his earpiece. *Please be okay.*

"I've got to get through!" he shouted to the others. "I have to—"

Suddenly, unexpected gunfire erupted from behind the *makol*, and the two creatures closest to Woody and Brandt went down in a bloody spray. Behind them, Myrinne was firing two-handed, blasting a hole in the line. "Go," she shouted. "Run!"

"Come on!" Brandt dragged his *winikin* through the gap.

The *makol* reacted quickly, spinning and firing point-blank. Strange, fiery orange shield magic flared to life and blocked the first attack, but then died off just as quickly as it had appeared. Out of the corner of her eye, Patience saw Rabbit slump back and lose his brief grip on consciousness.

But his shield had provided the distraction the other Nightkeepers had needed. They unleashed a deadly hail of magic and bullets, working to drive the *makol* away from Myrinne and Rabbit and bring the two into the Nightkeepers' faltering sphere of protection.

Strike bellowed, "Go. We'll be right behind you!"

Brandt bolted through the light-magic doorway and into the tunnel beyond, with Wood at his heels. Darkness swallowed them, but there was faint torch-light up ahead.

Moving silently, they approached an irregular opening that had been disguised as a water-worn depression in the tunnel wall. Brandt motioned for Wood to go low while he went high, and together they swung through the doorway.

The room was empty, save for a pile of greasy *makol* ash.

Woody gave a low groan. "They were sitting right there when Iago came for me." He indicated a scuffed spot. "There was one guard."

One guard. One ash pile. Which meant Iago was still out there, in search of the sacrifices he needed as the equinox approached.

Brandt jerked his head at the door. "If they're not in here, they're further up the tunnel. Come on."

They returned to the tunnel and started up in the direction of the cave-in. He tried to gather fireball magic as he ran, but he was tired, his power drained, and he managed only a weak gleam that quickly winked out. He stumbled on his bad leg and nearly went down.

Wood grabbed him, steadying him as they kept going. "Screw the fireball," the *winikin* said, voice rough with pain and exhaustion. "We'll use the guns."

"The jade-tips barely dented the regular *makol* down below," Brandt argued. "They're not going to do shit against Iago." They needed something stronger. Far, far stronger.

Like the Triad magic.

Despair slashed through him. "Wood, I—" He cut himself off, refusing to let the oath be the answer.

Gunfire split the air, coming from up ahead.

"Fuck!" Adrenaline hammered and Brandt took off at a dead run, with Woody right behind him. At the sight of torchlight around a corner, they got up against the wall. Taking high and low again, they looked around the edge.

"Give it up." Iago's voice rattled and slurred. He had his back to them; the torchlight shone on waxy, misshapen flesh that not even the *makol*'s regenerative magic had managed to heal. Blood-spattered and ragged, he gathered dark magic with jerky movements, holding on to a shield spell while he built a thick, greasy churn of fighting magic.

Opposite him, Patience bared her teeth. "I. Don't. Give. Up." Her dirty face bore the evidence of tears, but her chin was up, her eyes fierce. Behind her, Hannah and the boys were huddled together against a section of rockfall, protected by a shield spell that flickered and spat red-gold as it cut in and out. Patience stood guard in front of them with an autopistol in one bloodstained hand, her knife in the other, and shield magic crackling in the air around her.

Relief hammered through Brandt. They were alive. Whole. *Thank fuck.*

Braden's eyes locked on him and widened.

No, Brandt thought as loud as he could, hoping against hope that something would get through the bloodline link. *Pretend you don't see—*

"Daddy!" The word rang out over the crackle of magic.

Shit. Brandt threw himself around the corner with

Woody half a breath behind him. He tore magic from somewhere deep in his soul and launched a fireball just as Iago let rip with his bolt of dark energy.

The opposing powers collided and nullified each other. Magic detonated, the backlash slamming Brandt aside. He hit the wall hard and slid down.

The world tried to gray out, but he didn't let it. He dragged himself to his feet, surprised to realize that the magic had blasted him and Woody toward the rockfall, Iago away from it. The enemy mage lay farther back down the tunnel, protected behind a shield of dark magic that blocked off any hope of escaping while he was down.

But Brandt had ended up where he belonged: with his family.

"Daddy." Braden lunged at him.

He barely got his arms up in time to make the catch, almost went down under the impact, but he didn't care. He hugged his son tight, aware that Patience had cast a sputtering shield spell around the six of them. A second body thudded against him as Harry followed, clinging to his thigh, face buried in his body armor. He was shaking.

Brandt got an arm around him. "I've got you. I'm here. It's okay." The words poured out of him, promises he couldn't guarantee, but meant with every fiber of his being. He reached out blindly and caught Patience's hand, latching on. "We're going to get you out of here."

And they were running out of time.

"Go help Hannah," Patience urged the boys. Once

she had their attention, the *winikin* herded the boys to the farthest corner of the rockfall, where a tongue of debris created a bit of protection. There, they started piling rocks into a barrier. Woody was searching the area, scrounging the last of the autopistol clips.

Iago was still down and out, but the strong shimmer of dark magic surrounding him warned that the bastard wasn't dead.

As the clock ticked down in his head, Brandt took his wife in his arms, surrounding her, holding on to her, filling himself with her. *"Thank you."* Gratitude hammered through him. "Thank you for saving them. For not quitting on me."

"We're not out of this yet." But she turned her lips to his. "You're welcome. And thank you for trusting me."

Beyond the torchlight, Iago twitched and then stretched. Moving. Regenerating.

I can't take him. Brandt held her tighter, hating the truth. He was shot, with barely enough magic left to feed the faltering shield spell. There was no way he could muster an attack, or defeat an opponent who wouldn't stay down.

But then he caught Woody's eye, and the *winikin*'s voice whispered in his head. *You're not a fucking island.* Suddenly, though, the words resonated far more than they ever had before.

He'd been trying so hard to get everything right with Patience—*for* her—that he'd forgotten to be part of their team. "I *do* trust you," he said, pulling away to look into her eyes. "What's more, I need you."

Wariness flared, but she squared herself into a businesslike fighting stance. "For an uplink."

Something tore inside him, but the pain was followed by a strange sort of peace. "Not just for an uplink. For everything."

Faintly, below the level of hearing, deep inside his soul, he sensed the faintest hum of the magic that was special to them, to this place.

He tightened his grip on her hand. "I lost my parents and brothers, my two best friends. I don't want to lose you too. But if the gods take one of us, I don't want it to happen without me having said that I need you, and my life isn't right without you . . . because I love you."

Love. Her lips shaped the word, but her expression stayed wary.

"I'm not just saying that because we're cut off, because we're in El Rey, or even because it feels like we're a family again. This is real." He lifted their joined hands to his lips, then let go of her hand to pull his knife and freshly blood his palm. Magic flared through him and the hum in the air intensified. He held out his hand. "Link with me. Fight with me. And whatever happens next, believe that I love you. I loved you before as my wife and the mother of our sons. Now I love you as my mate and partner too." And to a mage, that was so much more.

Eyes misting, she took his knife, and bloodied her palm. As she returned the knife, she lifted up on her tiptoes to touch her lips to his in a soft kiss that brought equal parts heat and magic. "I love you too."

Then she took his hand, matching blood to blood . . . and the *jun tan* link opened wide.

Magic poured through Patience, coming from lust and love, from the feeling of being fully joined once more, after so long, with her husband. Her lover. Her mate. Her heart filled with the soaring power of it, the mad joy of it.

The shield spell protecting them from Iago solidified, shimmering red-gold and opaque.

The part of her that kept track of their failures tried to warn her that at worst he was using her feelings to strengthen his magic, or that at best it was just another fresh start. But deep down inside she knew this time was different. *He* was different. She could feel it in their magic, in the sync of their blood and power, in the echo of his thoughts within her.

For the first time in their relationship, he didn't just want and love her; he *needed* her as much as she needed him. And he was willing to risk loving and losing her. He was ready to take it on faith.

Faith. It had never really been about the Akbal oath, she realized. Or at least not the way she had thought. She hadn't needed him to retake the oath to prove that he trusted her to take care of herself. She had needed him to love her despite the curse, needed him to want her enough—*need* her enough—that he was willing to risk loving and losing her.

After that, it was up to fate and the gods.

"I think we've finally found our balance," she

whispered, staring up into eyes that had gone molten gold with love and magic.

He leaned in to touch his forehead to hers. "Stay safe. I love you."

"You too."

Then they separated and turned to face Iago, who had dragged himself to his knees on the other side of the shield magic. But although they weren't touching anymore, they were deeply linked, intimately aware of each other.

She glanced over to where Woody and Hannah stood shoulder to shoulder at the farthest corner of the rockfall, each holding an autopistol and wearing an expression of fierce determination. Behind them, the twins were partly protected behind the hastily piled wall of debris.

Hannah met her eyes square on. *You can do this,* the look said. *This is who you are.* She felt Brandt's unspoken wash of agreement. And the thing was, she appreciated their support . . . but she didn't need it. She knew who she was now.

Suddenly, Iago's voice carried from the other side of the shields, "Give it up. Drop the shield and I'll spare the *winikin.*"

"That wasn't the deal," Brandt called back. "You've got me and Patience. Let the others go." Inwardly, he sent, *He's got us cornered. He wouldn't make an offer like that unless he's weaker than he wants us to think.*

He used himself up regenerating, Patience agreed. But that didn't mean he wasn't still dangerous.

"You want to save your *winikin* or not?" Iago demanded.

Brandt hesitated just long enough for it to be believable. "Okay. Shield's coming down." *Ready?*

Ready.

Together, they spun up the *jun tan* magic and used it to shield the twins and *winikin*, then themselves. Beyond those shields, their battle magic painted the air a sparkling red-gold.

Now! Brandt sent.

They dropped the shield and Iago appeared, his molten-wax features distorted with rage and hatred, and haloed within a cloud of dark magic. Roaring his brother's name, he unleashed a bolt of power at them.

The magic wrapped around them, coating their shields, which groaned but held as they lashed back, sending a massive fireball hurtling at the Xibalban.

Iago raised a strong shield and the fireball spent itself harmlessly. But he let the shield wink out again as he built his next bolt.

Understanding slashed through Patience. *He can only handle one spell at a time!*

Hold the shields, Brandt said. *Reverse ours when I give the word, and then break right. We need to split his attention.* He sent a mental image of his plan. Which she thought might work.

Gods willing.

She nodded, sweat prickling at the drain of holding two shields, one around her and Brandt, the other protecting the *winikin* and the twins. *Stay alive,* she ordered him. *I love you.*

You too. Ready? . . . Go!

She dropped both of the shields and used all her power to create a new one that surrounded Iago in a sphere of reflective magic, just as the enemy mage unleashed a deadly energy bolt straight at them. The dark magic caromed off the shield and flew back toward Iago, who screamed as he disappeared within a coalescing cloud of brown hellmagic.

Patience held the shield, but it drained her, sapping even the *jun tan* power. The sphere lasted for only a few seconds before it dissolved beneath the dark-magic onslaught and Iago roared free once again.

She dove and rolled to the right. Brandt spun, lunged the other way, and let rip with a fireball.

Iago spun and, seemingly instinctively, slashed at the incoming fireball with Moctezuma's knife.

The red-gold magic flared and disappeared, leaving the knife glowing.

Oh, shit. The thought echoed through Patience and Brandt at the realization that the first-fire knife wasn't just a symbol. It had powers of its own.

Iago's eyes lit. Lifting the knife, he lunged for Patience.

She reeled back, scrambling to cast a new shield.

The spell failed. The *jun tan* magic was depleted.

Brandt shouted her name. A heavy weight slammed into her from the side, sending her flying into the wall.

Her head cracked against stone. And the world went dark.

"No!" Brandt saw Patience slide down the wall, limp and unmoving, saw Woody drop down beside her. The *winikin* had pushed her out of the way, but not soon enough. Iago closed on them both, raising the glowing knife. Denying what was about to happen, Brandt screamed, *"Patience!"*

He flung himself at Iago, slammed into the bastard's dark shield magic, and fought to push through the faltering spell, which flayed him raw, lashing him with harsh agony. Then he was through! He went in low, tackling Iago and sending him flying backward.

They went down hard together, grappling for control of the knife.

Iago had the strength of an *ajaw-makol*, but Brandt was desperate. He fought dirty, ditching his martial arts moves for the "fucking get it done" techniques he'd learned from Michael. He jammed his elbow in Iago's windpipe, grabbed his knife hand, and twisted so hard he broke the fucker's wrist. The Xibalban bellowed in pain and Brandt wrestled the knife from him, but the enemy mage got his other hand around Brandt's neck and squeezed hard.

"Screw. You," Brandt grated. He reversed the first-fire knife, which vibrated with trapped Nightkeeper magic, slashed it once across Iago's throat, and then drove the blade into the Xibalban's gut, angling high to slice through his diaphragm to his heart. As he did so, he started reciting the head-and-heart spell, hoping to hell they were close enough to the moment of solstice that he would be able to banish the *ajaw-makol*.

Iago's body arched and he gave a high, keening cry. Dark magic broke over them both, in a shock wave that was like being inside a thunderclap. Power surged as the Xibalban overrode the energy cost that normally prevented teleportation through rock.

'Port magic rattled and the bastard vanished.

In the sudden silence, Brandt knelt on the blood-stained stone, gripping the first-fire knife white-knuckled.

Failure drummed through him. He had beaten Iago. But he hadn't killed him.

"Son of a *bitch*!" Furious with Iago, with himself, he heaved the knife, which skittered across the stone floor and banged off the far wall.

"Brandt." Patience's voice brought his head up; the look on her face got him on his feet.

"What's—" He broke off at the sight of Wood lying halfway across Hannah's lap. The twins were glued to either side of Hannah, seeming unsure of whether they should pay attention to their parents or the *wini-kin*. Wood's eyes were closed, his skin sickly pale. Patience was leaning over him with her hands over-lapped, applying direct pressure to his upper chest.

Blood streamed between her fingers.

Oh. Shit.

Brandt stumbled over. "No. Oh, no. Please, no." The whispered plea bled from his lips in a jumbled almost-prayer. He dropped down beside Woody, his knees cracking into the stone, and took his *winikin*'s hand. "Shit. *Woody!*"

The *winikin* stirred and cracked his eyes. "Is Iago gone?"

"Yeah." Brandt had to work to get the word out. "He's gone."

Wood's eyes went to Patience, then up to Hannah and each of the boys in turn. His expression eased slightly. "You're all okay."

"We couldn't have done it without you." Brandt gripped his hand, voice going thick. "Hang on. We'll get you to Sasha. She'll take care of that scratch."

So much blood.

The *winikin* met his eyes. "Remember how I always said that you should trust your instincts, that you'd know what to do when the time came? Well . . . it's here."

Brandt froze. The air left his lungs, left the universe. "You don't know what you're saying."

"I know. I always knew." The *winikin* shifted painfully to put his forearm beside Brandt's, so the eagle glyphs lined up and the warrior's emblem matched up with the *aj-winikin* glyph. "I serve," Woody said softly. "Not just because it's my blood-bound duty, but because I love you, and because I believe that you're what this world needs."

"Oh," Patience breathed, closing her eyes so they spilled tears.

Emotions thundered through Brandt: guilt, grief, remorse, regret . . . and an aching sorrow for the years they had lost, the sacrifices the *winikin* had made for him. The one he was prepared to make now.

When a warm, quivering body pressed against his side, he looked down into Harry's face, suddenly seeing not just himself and Patience but also the parents and brothers he barely remembered. Yet at the same time, the features belonged entirely to the boy who slowly reached to touch his and Wood's joined hands, linking three generations.

On Woody's other side, Braden mirrored his brother, leaning against Patience and touching the place where her hands were locked over Woody's wound. At the *winikin*'s head, Hannah's single eye was awash, but her face was soft with acceptance. With, he thought, faith.

"Do it," Woody whispered. "Retake your oath. And remember that I love each and every one of you, whether in this life or the next."

Heart heavy, Brandt looped his free arm around Braden. Taking solace from the small, sturdy body, he whispered a brief, heartfelt prayer for his *winikin*'s next life, and then recited the oath that had been burned deep in his memory: *"Kabal ku bootik teach a suut."*

He lifted his head to meet Patience's tear-drenched eyes, and said, "As the gods once paid for my life out of the balance, now I repay that debt, three for one. A triad for the Triad."

Pain seared the numb spot on his scarred leg. He didn't look; he didn't need to. He knew that he once again wore the Akbal glyph.

Wood's breathing hitched, then hitched again.

Brandt was peripherally aware of a clamor in the tunnel that rose as teammates arrived, bloody and battered but alive, then fell silent when they saw what was going on.

Sasha pushed through and knelt beside Woody, but after touching him for only a moment, she shook her head. "I'm sorry. I'm too drained."

"It's okay. The sky is calling me," Woody said with a soft smile, his eyes going faraway. "Emmeline's waiting. She looks just like I remembered."

Brandt swallowed hard. "They couldn't marry because they were both fully bound *winikin*, but they were lovers when their duties permitted. She died in the massacre." And now Woody was seeing her. Brandt didn't know whether that was real or a trick of the mind. But as he watched Wood's face soften, his breath slow, he hoped to hell it was real.

The *winikin*'s lips moved. Brandt leaned in to get closer. "What?"

"Two years and one day from now, when it's all over, I want you and Patience to work on making the boys a little brother. Woodrow's a good name. It should stay in the bloodline."

"Yeah." Brandt's throat closed on the word. "You're right. It should."

He straightened away. Even before he saw Wood's eyes go glazed, he knew his *winikin* was gone. He knew it from the laxity of the *winikin*'s hand in his, from the sudden hollow emptiness in his soul . . . and from the burn on his calf, which said that the Akbal glyph was gone as quickly as it had appeared.

But even as the Akbal magic faded, another spun up to take its place. A big fucking something that stirred atavistic horror deep inside him, even through the numbing grief.

Son of a bitch. The Triad spell was back online.

"Woody—" he began, but the power closed in on him, shutting him down with a churning whirl of thoughts and memories that weren't his own. Fear flared, but he didn't keep it to himself this time. Instead, he met Patience's wide, scared eyes, and reached for her hand.

I need you. He wasn't sure if he said it aloud or not, knew only that she met him halfway.

Then the lights went out.

The barrier

The transition wasn't like any other Brandt had ever experienced. One moment he was in the cave, hunched over his *winikin*'s body. In the next, he stood in the gray-green mists, surrounded by dozens of strangers who were all looking at him, their faces lit with hope and welcome.

Oh, holy shit, he thought. They were the ancestors. *His* ancestors, his bloodline's strongest talents, who had been gathered into the *nahwal* and were now re-born, thanks to the Triad magic.

Their clothing came from a mix of eras, weighted heavily toward the eighteen and nineteen hundreds, as if the older souls had faded away over time. He couldn't process anything beyond that, though. He could only clear his throat and rasp, "Tell me what to do. We don't have much time." The solstice was approaching fast.

There was a stirring in the crowd, and two men pushed to the front.

Brandt's throat closed as he recognized his brothers, Harry and Braden. They looked exactly the same as they had twenty-six years earlier, at the time of the massacre. Exactly the way he had remembered them, though no longer bigger and older than him. Instead they were ten years or so younger, frozen at the moments of their deaths.

"Hey," he said, voice gone so thick with emotion that he couldn't get out anything better.

They didn't say anything, not in words. But the cool mist warmed around him, bringing a deep thrum of magic and a sense of awesome power hovering just at the edges of his consciousness.

Braden held out his hand in invitation.

Brandt hesitated. Then he heard Wood's voice whisper at the edges of his mind: *Have faith.*

He took a deep breath. Clasped his brother's hand. And became a Triad mage.

CHAPTER TWENTY-ONE

El Rey

Patience tried to catch Brandt as he fell. Instead she wound up pinned beneath him, with his head in her lap, in a position that was too close to the way Hannah had held Woody as he died.

She leaned over him, held on to him as her pulse beat so heavily in her ears that she could barely hear anything above the drumbeat throb.

"Please, gods, not now. Not like this." She was barely aware of whispering the prayer aloud as the others gathered close, Jade taking the boys off to one side while Hannah wept silently.

Then, without warning, the *jun tan* bond flared to life and Patience could see what Brandt was seeing, feel what he was feeling, as the skills, thoughts, and experiences of dozens of eagle warriors whirled through him in a maelstrom of power. But it wasn't the terrifying possession she had expected, the one the library had warned against. Instead, it was more like the downloading Rabbit had described, a transfer of information rather than the loss of free will.

What was more, it wasn't chaos. As she watched, mental images of high wooden filing cabinets materialized within his consciousness. Moments later, the glowing bits of information, which had been whirling madly around, all started sailing toward the cabinets, which thrust out their drawers to snap up the information, sorting the whirl by skill, spell, subject, and whatever other filing system Brandt's highly ordered brain could devise.

Understanding broke over her like the dawn. The sun god might have almost chosen Rabbit as the Triad mage, but whatever god had saved Brandt from the accident years ago had known the truth: Brandt had been destined for this all along. He was, for better or worse, perfect for the job.

His analytic, linear thought process, combined with the strength of an eagle warrior, had given him an almost terrifying ability to compartmentalize. And although that had caused problems before, now it would allow him to continue functioning as both a Triad mage and the man she loved. She hoped.

As if that was what he had wanted her to see, the filing-cabinet images shimmered around her, then dissolved, and she was back in her own body, blinking down at Brandt. Moments later, he stirred, groaning. He opened his eyes and looked up at her, his expression awed.

"Gods," he croaked, finally able to call on the sky deities after all these years. "All their powers, their talents. The battles they've fought. The things they've seen . . ." He trailed off, expression clouding.

"You can handle it," she said.

The full impact still seemed to be catching up with him, though. "If I can do almost anything an eagle mage has ever done," he said softly, thoughtfully, "how can I tell *what*, exactly, I'm supposed to do?"

"You're not alone." She gestured to their teammates, then to Hannah and their sons. "We're all in this together."

His eyes never left her face. "You're right," he said. "I'm not alone. And thank the gods for that."

They were going to be okay, she thought. "I think—"

A train-track rumble erupted beneath them, around them, cutting her off. The teammates braced as the tunnel shook and shuddered in short, rhythmic bursts, then in one long, drawn-out shimmy before the movement stopped.

There was dead silence for a moment, as the miniquake brought home an ominous fact: The magi might have prevented Iago from enacting the first-fire ceremony, but the threat of Cabrakan remained.

And the clock was ticking.

Brandt moved to where Woody lay, still and gray. Hannah sat beside him, the boys beside her. Patience joined them and burrowed in, needing to touch them, feel them, be reassured that they were there, they were okay, for the moment at least. Brandt, too, crouched to be with his family, and to reach out and touch his *winikin*'s face, stroke a hand along the gray-shot hair. "Woodrow's a good name," he said softly. "We won't forget it."

He reached for Patience and folded their fingers together, and she felt a surge of power, sensed a re-shuffling of the cabinets. When Sven started to say something, she shook her head and mouthed, "Wait. Let him work."

After nearly a minute, Brandt broke the contact and looked up at the others. "Okay. Triad-magic time. When I concentrate on the solstice-eclipse and Cabra-kan, I get two images from my ancestors. The first is a hand-drawn map of an island with four straight causeways leading to it and a bunch of buildings on the island, like a city, or maybe a sprawled-out pal-ace. The second is a painting from an old wall mural, or maybe part of a codex. There's a bunch of people standing near a broken wall that has a repeated eagle motif carved into it. They're holding hands beneath a full moon that's painted dark orange, like it's in full eclipse, and lines of red light are radiating away from them." He paused. "I think we need to link up right near that wall. Problem is, I don't have a clue where it might be."

"I do," Patience said. When he glanced at her, she said with some asperity, "I tried to tell you about it earlier."

"Sorry."

"I get a freebie on our next fight." There would be one, of course. But this time she wouldn't have to wonder if he loved her. She knew it—believed it—deep down inside. Feeling an inner glow at the thought, despite everything else, she continued: "What I figured out was that big earthquake in Mexico City wasn't just the year after the Solstice Massacre. It was less than two days before the fall equinox. What's more, there were two major aftershocks: a seven-point-five on the day of the equinox, and a seven-point-six exactly six months later, a few days after the spring equinox." When she paused, there was dead silence.

Then Brandt muttered, "Cabrakan was testing the barrier even back then."

She nodded. "I think so. Only the massacre had sealed it tight, and kept it sealed for the next twenty-some years, so Cabrakan couldn't do anything. Then, last spring, a five-point-nine tremor hit, followed by the one the other day. All under Mexico City." She paused. "I think there must be a weak spot in the barrier right there, maybe one that's specific to Cabrakan himself."

Lucius said, "Moctezuma reportedly sacrificed hundreds of thousands of captives, trying to appease the dark gods when the conquistadors arrived. That sort of sacrifice, along with the geologic makeup of the place, with the dry lake bed amplifying even the smallest tremor, could certainly attract Cabrakan. And the map fits: The city was originally an island in the middle of the lake, and the Aztecs built four causeways connecting it to the mainland."

Brandt turned to him. "Tell me you know where there's a wall of carved eagles in Mexico City."

Lucius nodded, suppressed excitement firing in his eyes. "Five centuries of Mexico City are layered over the top of Moctezuma's palace, but archaeologists started seriously excavating the site in the late seventies. One of the buildings found near the palace has been identified as the barracks of Moctezuma's warrior elite . . . who were called the Eagles."

"That's where we need to be," Patience whispered.

Gods willing, they wouldn't be too late.

Mexico City

The ruins of Moctezuma's palace—the Templo Mayor—were set up as a tourist attraction, complete with a museum and clearspan roofing that stretched across the excavated areas, including the warriors' barracks. Little remained of the original structure except for a long wall that had been intricately carved with bas-relief eagles, repeated over and over again.

The Nightkeepers had detoured to Skywatch in order to drop off Hannah and the boys and grab calories, which meant it was almost exactly fifteen minutes before the moment of solstice when their boots hit the ground near the eagle-carved wall.

The ground hit back.

The earthquake tossed the world around, making the surface beneath them undulate and heave. Out in the street things crashed and people screamed. The

Nightkeepers had materialized with Patience's magic in full force, rendering them invisible to any humans who might be nearby, but although the Templo Mayor and surrounding buildings were popular attractions, the place was deserted. The locals and tourists were far more concerned with either getting out of the city or hunkering down someplace reinforced to ride out the quakes.

Brandt landed and locked his knees, and when Patience nearly went down, he hooked an arm around her waist. They hung on to each other while the quake went on far too long, the earth rippling with unnatural liquidity.

"It feels like the barrier," Patience said against his chest, and she was right, except that instead of a soft, yielding surface and harmless fog, they were standing on stone slabs that threatened to crack and buckle, and there were steel girders all around them, arching overhead to support the flapping expanse of plastic.

"Hope the roof doesn't come down on our heads," he muttered. Even as he said it, a section of clearspan tore free and swung down in a ghostly flutter, to reveal the night sky. The stars seemed unnaturally bright in contrast to the eclipsed full moon. The moonlight was orange red, painting the carved eagles with light the color of old bloodstains.

The solstice-eclipse was almost on top of them. They needed to hurry.

Even when the tremor was past, the ground seemed to hum with a low, tense vibration that put Brandt on edge. The others felt it too; they muttered and traded looks as they started moving into place, forming an uplink circle with their knives at the ready. Rabbit didn't move, though. He stayed off to one side, bent over with his hands braced on his knees, breathing heavily.

Myrinne bent over him. "What's wrong?"

"I hope he didn't use himself up back at El Rey," Brandt muttered, low enough that only Patience heard him. "We're all dragging ass, and we've still got a demon to fight." Even without the hellmark, Rabbit was their strongest fighter.

"It's this place," Rabbit said, his voice sounding thick and strange. "Gods. What's *with* this place?"

"Violence," Lucius said. "According to some of Cortés's men, more than a hundred thousand skulls were displayed, and the carved idols in here were fed with hearts and covered with five or six inches of clotted blood."

"I can smell it," Rabbit grated. "Shit. I can *taste* it." But his color was getting better, his breathing coming back to normal. "Give me another second to finish blocking it out. It's not dark magic, really, or at least not the way I used to sense it. This is . . . pain. This whole place is soaked with pain."

"We've fought through pain before," Strike said grimly. "We'll do it again."

Working fast, the magi uplinked. Brandt joined the circle last, taking Rabbit's hand on one side and Patience's on the other. He felt his powers expanding and deepening, taking sustenance from the solstice-eclipse, the teamwork of the Nightkeepers, and wide-open *jun tan* bond that linked him and Patience, feeling vibrant and alive.

But it wasn't enough. The low-throated vibration of old pain and violence threatened to drown out the hum of Nightkeeper magic, and the ground shuddered beneath their feet. Worse, there was no sign of the streaming red lights his ancestors had shown him.

Brandt's chest went hollow as he forced himself to say it. "In the painting there were dozens of magi near the wall, and more in the distance. Hundreds, maybe." He paused. "What if there just aren't enough of us?"

The ground shifted beneath them. In the street, something crashed.

"We're going to have to be enough," Michael said bleakly. "We're all there is."

Patience squeezed Brandt's hand. "Try the Triad magic again. There has to be something more, something we're missing."

Needing the contact, he leaned down and pressed his forehead to hers, taking her warmth, her strength, as he concentrated on the inner question, *How can we fight Cabrakan?*

He got only the image of Patience's face, lit from within with love.

Panic and despair spiraled through him. He couldn't lose her. Not now. *Please, gods, help me out here.*

He saw Patience again, this time studying a spread of cards. And for all that he had come to accept that the Mayan Oracle wasn't the crock of shit he had once believed, it seemed odd that he would picture her like that.

Which meant it wasn't an accident.

Adrenaline kicked. "You're the answer," he told her. "You or—"

"Love," she interrupted. "Maybe love is the answer." She turned to Lucius. "Neither the Aztecs nor the Xibalbans use sex in their rituals, do they?"

"Not the way the Nightkeepers do."

She looked back at Brandt. "Which I'll bet means there isn't a dark equivalent of sex magic. What if we can use that to break through the layer of pain that's covering this place?"

"*Etznab*," he said, making the connection. At her look of confusion, he said, "Think about how our *jun tan* works: It creates a feedback loop that lets each of us mirror what the other is feeling. If we can do the same thing with power . . ."

Her eyes lit. "It'll amplify. Maybe even enough to override Cabrakan's dark magic."

Rabbit stepped forward. His eyes were stark hollows in his angular face, but intensity burned at their depths. "If you can show me how your *jun tan* works, I can transmit it to the others." He glanced at Strike. "Okay?"

Overhead, through the torn spot in the roof, the last sliver of white moon disappeared. "Do it," the king said implacably, his jaw set in a hard, uncompromising line. "We do whatever it takes. That's why we're here."

But it wasn't the only reason they were there, Brandt thought as he held out his hand to Patience. Because what was the point of the war if they weren't also fighting for the smaller, equally important parts of themselves? Love, family, a personal future . . . it was all worth fighting for.

It had taken him a long time to see that. Almost too long.

Patience took his hand and they closed for a kiss, with Rabbit tapping in via touch link. Brandt put everything he had into the kiss and their *jun tan* connection, not just giving her his body, strength, heart, and soul, but taking hers in return, until it wasn't his strength versus hers anymore—it was their combined power that fired his bloodstream and lit him from within with a level of power he'd never before experienced.

The magic came from the solstice-eclipse, and from the way the stars and planets were beginning to align as the end time approached. But it also came from him and Patience, and the new level of connection they had forged from the ashes of their old lives.

Thank you for not giving up on me, he sent through the *jun tan.*

He got a wash of love and acceptance in return, and a whisper of, *I might've given up on you . . . but I couldn't give up on us.*

And thank the gods for that.

He slanted his mouth across hers and took the kiss deeper, hotter, harder, until sex magic sparked and crackled around them and his body tightened with the need for privacy, the need to bury himself inside her. The need, quite simply, for her.

Red-gold power responded, washing from him to her and back again. His *jun tan* heated, activating; he could feel her pleasure and his own, along with Rabbit's discreet contact as he fed the *jun tan* pattern to the others, showing them the feedback loop. Then he felt the incremental increases in his power as the mated pairs came online, each adding their own distinctive flavor to the burgeoning mix of magic.

The power cycled higher and higher, until, without warning, a soundless detonation slammed into him and then out again, down through his feet and into the earth itself.

And the Nightkeeper magic took on a life of its own.

Brandt broke the kiss as the power surged beyond sex magic to something incandescent. It wasn't coming from the *jun tan* connections anymore; it was *using* them, flowing through them and drawing light magic from the survivors and the strength of their gods-destined pairings.

The ground heaved beneath them in a tremor that was far stronger than any of the others. A roaring noise welled up from beneath them, sounding less like a subway now and more like the cry of an angry creature, a demon trying to fight its way to freedom, bent on revenge and destruction.

Out in the street, the screams intensified, and Brandt heard the first few ominous cracks and rumbles of major structural damage. He flashed on the

TV images of the big earthquake: crumbled buildings, ash-coated figures, and child volunteers crawling through narrow gaps to pull babies out of a collapsed hospital wing. The threat of failure tunneled his vision. This wasn't going to work. They didn't have enough people, enough power, enough—

Focus! The word echoed in Woody's voice. *And for fuck's sake, have a little faith.*

The memory—or was it something else?—snapped Brandt out of his downward spiral. He blinked, clearing his mind of the noise out on the street, and the TV images. Within the relative calm that followed, an image formed: that of a huge lake with an irregularly shaped island rising out of the center, connected to the mainland by four causeways built up out of stone and rubble.

And he freaking got it.

"I'm not an island," he said, "but this piece of Mexico City used to be."

He opened his eyes to find Patience, limned in sparks of magic, staring at him in wonder. "Your eyes are gold," she whispered.

He caught her hands, using her to anchor him as he reached out with his mind and found the inner filing cabinet where he had put the scariest, most tempting and terrifying part of the Triad magic: his ancestors' powers.

The eagle magi had designed the pyramids of Egypt and Mesoamerica using math, physics, and arcane schematics painted onto fig-bark codices. Now their combined talents expanded his senses, letting him perceive the structure of the city around him. He sensed the buildings above the surface, their cracks and stresses, and the places where they had been shored up against earthquake damage. Beneath them, he perceived the layers that represented five centuries of habitation, with Moctezuma's capital city of Tenochtitlán at the very bottom.

He perceived the ghostly foundations of the ancient palaces, temples, and markets. More importantly, he saw where the causeways ran across the lake bed, two from the northern end of the island, one from the west, one from the south. The causeways had long been buried beneath the rubble that the Spanish had carted in to expand Mexico City beyond the island. But their structures were still there . . . and they were the only things holding Cabrakan in check.

The demon strained against them, drawn to the place where generations of terrible blood sacrifices had weakened the barrier enough for him to punch through during the solstice-eclipse, but held back by the four causeways, which had been built by the slave labor of captured Maya, and held the power of their sky gods.

The big earthquake two decades earlier had weakened the causeways, and the recent miniquakes had further crumbled their stone bases and compressed paving. One or two more good tremors, and the demon would be free.

Not on my watch, Brandt thought fiercely. He bore down, pulling power from his ancestors, his teammates, and Patience—his wife, mate, and partner. His forebears had once built vast cities from stone and the images in their minds. Now their knowledge, along with the combined magic of his teammates, gave him the power to rebuild the roads that anchored the center of Mexico City.

A spell whispered in his mind, coming in a man's voice that sounded oddly like flutes and drumbeats, and brought the icy chill of river water to touch his skin.

Brandt said the words aloud. And the world turned bloodred.

Power detonated. Fiery magic streamed out of him and blasted along where the four causeways had been, going from crimson to translucent as it passed the limits of the ruin. The ground heaved and shuddered, nearly pitching Brandt to his knees as Cabrakan fought back far below them.

The magic poured out, draining Brandt and making his head spin, but he kept going, pulling strength from the depths of his soul and beyond. And the causeways responded, beginning to realign into the form they had taken a thousand years ago. The changes were infinitesimal at first—a stone returning to alignment in one spot, a fracture sealing in another—but then the alterations mushroomed, gaining speed.

Brandt sensed Cabrakan's rage against the magi who had killed his brother and now barred him from the earth. The dark lord slammed against the earth beneath Moctezuma's palace, which had been at the center of the bloodshed and was now the weakest spot of all.

The ground yawed and threatened to shake apart. Something crashed down from above, but was deflected by shield magic.

"Thanks," Brandt grated, not sure who had set the shield, but understanding that the others were protecting him so he could concentrate everything he had on locking stone against rubble, rubble against sand.

Although the original causeways had ended at the island's shores, he continued inward, reinforcing Cabrakan's prison all the way inward to the Templo Mayor, which was the central point where all four causeways intersected, and where slave-built temples had been soaked in blood.

There, wielding the magic of love and family, of past and present, Brandt joined the causeways together, stabilizing the ground beneath Mexico City and sealing the demon into Xibalba.

And then, spent, he let himself fall, knowing that Patience would catch him and bring him home.

CHAPTER TWENTY-TWO

December 22
One year, three hundred and sixty-four days
to the zero date
Skywatch

Woody's funeral rites were planned for noon the day after the solstice-eclipse. His pyre was built at the edge of where the Nightkeepers' Great Hall had stood before the massacre. Red-Boar had been sent to the gods from that spot, as had Sasha's father. There had been zero discussion of setting up a second funerary site for the *winikin* even though the separation had been traditional in their parents' generations. *Winikin*, Nightkeeper, human . . . they were all teammates, all equally worthy of the gods' attention on their way to the sky.

Brandt, Patience, and Hannah did the bulk of the work on the pyre, with Harry and Braden alternately helping and getting in the way. To Patience, their perpetual motion and piping voices brought a sense of lightness, completion, and joy that she had so badly missed . . . and one she would yearn for when they left again.

But now, more than ever, they needed to stay hidden.

Iago's injuries would heal, and when they did, he was going to be *pissed*. She didn't want the boys anywhere within his reach. If she could have sent them to another planet, another plane, she would have. As it was, she was doing the next best thing: She was entrusting them once again to Hannah, and this time she wouldn't go looking for them, no matter what. She would love them best by letting them go. Even if it killed her to do so.

"There." Brandt stepped back, dusted off his hands, and stuck them in the front pockets of his jeans as he surveyed the work. Braden did the same, mimicking his father so they stood side by side, both with their hands in their jeans pockets and their shoulders slightly hunched beneath black T-shirts, staring at Woody's pyre with matching frowns.

Patience's heart turned over when Brandt glanced down, caught Braden's fierce scowl, and laughed out loud. It was a rusty-sounding chuckle, one forced through his grief for Woody, and his sorrow at knowing the boys would be there for only a few more hours. But instead of shutting all that away, he caught her eyes and shared it: the laugh, the grief, and the sorrow.

"You guys are going to be okay," Hannah said softly from behind her.

Patience turned to find the *winikin* sitting atop one of the nearby picnic tables, with Harry cross-legged on the picnic bench near her feet, watching his father and brother debate the placement of the three ceremonial sticks of ceiba, cacao, and rubber-tree wood.

Moving to sit on Harry's other side, Patience propped her elbows on the table and nodded. "You know what? I think so."

In another lifetime, when she'd been young and so caught up in being in love that she hadn't remembered to be herself, she would have been adamant about it, would've made sweeping statements about love at first sight and forever. Now she was far more cautious. But at the same time, now she knew what it took to make love at first sight last forever . . . and she had a partner who knew he had to meet her halfway.

As if he'd caught a hint of her thoughts through their vibrant *jun tan* connection, he looked for her again, sent her a "hey, babe" smile . . . and went back to consulting with his junior contractor.

Seeing the exchange, Hannah nodded firmly. "I know so."

Patience smiled, because she knew so too, and also because Harry gave them a disgusted look, muttered something about girl talk, and headed over to join the engineering debate.

"How about you?" Patience asked the *winikin* once Harry was out of earshot. "Are you going to be okay?"

They both knew she was really asking, *How upset are you over Woody? Did you lose a friend, a lover, or the one and only?*

Hannah's lips curved softly. Wearing a deep purple bandanna over her missing eye, along with a black, puffy-sleeved blouse, she looked particularly piratical, though Patience suspected she'd been trying to tone down her usual peacock hues to human-style mourning colors.

After a moment, the other woman said, "Woody and I worked together better as *winikin* than we did as lovers. We synced amazingly well when it came to raising the boys and making family decisions. In that regard, it was a perfect match. In the other"— she lifted a shoulder—"we kept each other warm sometimes, but he wasn't my one and only and I wasn't his, and that was okay with both of us." Her eye drifted in the direction of the mansion. "I'm sad about Woody, and I'll miss the heck out of him. He was a part of my life, and I'll remember him until the gods call me up to the sky . . . but my heart isn't broken."

"Are you going to be okay working with Carlos?" It had been decided that the ex-wrangler would go with Hannah and the twins, in order to share the workload that came with raising a couple of bright, active boys, and—unstated but understood—to provide redundancy in case something happened to her. He had raised Sven and his own daughter, Cara, and had helped Nate through his rough transition into the Nightkeepers. He was a good choice.

But perhaps, Patience thought, not the absolute best choice.

"Carlos is a good man," Hannah said. "A good *winikin*." Which wasn't really an answer. But before Patience could press her on it, the funeral procession emerged from the rear of the mansion and started heading in their direction.

Leah led the way, followed by most of the *winikin*. They carried the litter that bore Woody's body, which had been intricately wrapped with cloth and tied into a mortuary bundle.

Hannah frowned. "Strike and Rabbit aren't there."

"Jox either," Patience put in, though she suspected Hannah had noticed that first, then looked for Strike. She stood and started toward the procession. "Something's up." *Please, gods, not something bad.*

But Leah sent her an "It's okay. Stay where you are" wave, and when she got out to the pyre, she said, "Strike and Jox will be out in a minute. They said for us to set up without them, that they'd be here for noon."

As the *winikin* carefully placed the mortuary bundle atop the pyre, though, Patience noticed that Leah kept glancing back toward the mansion. When Patience caught herself doing the same thing, she made herself stop it, and focus on the ceremony.

Brandt, who had moved up to stand beside her in the loose ring of Nightkeepers, *winikin*, and humans surrounding the pyre, whispered, "Woody wouldn't mind. He'd be dying to—" He faltered, then swallowed and continued. "He'd want to know what's going on too."

"We'll find out when the time's right. This is for Woody." More, it was a way for the rest of them to say good-bye.

As they waited, Patience kept close tabs on Harry and Braden. Although they were far more aware of death than the average human, they were still five-year-old boys who had lost the man who had stood in for their father over the past two years. So far they seemed okay; Harry was watching the funerary bundle intently, as if trying to convince himself that Woody was actually inside. Braden was off near the steps leading to the training hall, fencing against an invisible enemy with a leftover piece of wood, but he kept darting glances at Hannah, his parents, and the pyre, keeping his own tabs on the members of his family.

The adults hadn't yet told the boys that they would be leaving after the funeral, but Patience suspected that on some level they knew. Hannah and Woody had always been very up front with them about why they couldn't live at Skywatch with their parents, and although the boys seemed to have bounced back remarkably well from their brief captivity, the experience—and watching their parents fighting to save them—had made a major impression. Patience ached that she wouldn't be there to talk them through the inevitable nightmares, and that they would all have to readjust to the separation. But the twins would have Hannah and Carlos. And each other.

Brandt took her hand, threaded their fingers together, and squeezed. *I'm here,* the gesture said. *I'm not going anywhere.*

And she believed him.

Hearing footsteps, she turned to find Strike coming up the pathway alone. Aware that he was instantly the center of attention, he said without preamble, "Anna regained consciousness earlier this morning." When an excited murmur started, he held up a hand. "Unfortunately, there seems to be . . . she's . . ." He cleared his throat. "The doctors don't know if the damage is permanent or if she'll improve with time. She's going to need time, rehab . . ." He trailed off, then said softly, ". . . prayers."

Leah crossed to him and leaned her cheek against his arm, just above his *hunab ku.* "She's a jaguar. She's too stubborn to give up."

He nodded. Voice strengthening with disgust, he said, "Her husband called to tell me he wanted to sign her over—those were the words he used, too, the fucktard—to me as her closest blood relative. He wants out."

"Gods," Brandt muttered. "He really is a dick."

"Give him what he wants," Lucius said flatly. His face was dull with anger and a disgust that mirrored Strike's own. "He doesn't want her. We do. It's as simple as that." Except they all knew that it wasn't that simple, because she didn't want them. Or she hadn't before.

But Strike nodded. "That's the plan. We'll move

her to a rehab facility in Albuquerque and go from there."

"I want to see her," Sasha said, voice thick with tears. "I might be able to help her now that she's conscious."

"I'll take you after the funeral." Strike paused, then looked over at Patience and Brandt, then beyond them to Hannah. "There's something else."

Patience's stomach clenched. What else could there be?

"What?" It was Brandt who asked, his grip tightening on her hand.

"Mendez is also awake. From the looks of it, he came around at almost the exact same time as Anna." He paused a moment to let the ripple of response die down. "Now, here's the thing. . . . He seems to have come back with not only the Triad magic but with a whole new perspective on life. According to him, when his ancestors got a look inside his head and saw what his *winikin* taught him—most of which was lies and twisted versions of the truth—they kept him under long enough to straighten out some major misapprehensions. I've got Rabbit confirming his story right now, but if it's true . . . well, let's say it'd be a far better outcome than I was expecting."

"What does that have to do with us?" Patience asked. Granted, it'd be huge to have Mendez work out, not just as a Nightkeeper, but as a second Triad mage. But that would impact the team in general, not her, Brandt, and Hannah.

"When we told him where everyone was, he asked if he could come out for the funeral. He doesn't want to take attention away from Woody, but he'd like to show his respect for Wood's sacrifice." Strike paused. "Either he's talking a really good game, or his ancestors did a hell of a job reprogramming him."

Patience looked up at Brandt. "Your call."

He nodded. "Yeah, let him come on out. Woody would like knowing there might be one more of us."

Strike palmed his cell and made the call. A few minutes later, Mendez appeared on the pathway, walking slowly between Rabbit and Jox, not entirely steady on his legs yet. Awake, he looked pretty much the same as he had when he arrived—huge even by Nightkeeper standards, with sharp features, a Mayan nose, and a punch of edgy charisma that was notable even among the magi—with the addition of a pair of pale hazel eyes that seemed to be trying to take in everything at once.

When the small group joined the funerary circle, Rabbit took a moment to look at the pyre and make a gesture of respect, and then sent the twins a finger-wiggle. Finally, he gestured to Mendez and said, "He believes what he's saying, and it checks out as far down as I can go."

Strike nodded. "That'll do for starters." To Mendez, he said, "Consider yourself on probation. I believe you're familiar with the concept." He and Mendez exchanged a long, charged look before Strike glanced at the others. "Okay, everyone . . . this is—"

He broke off, glancing back at the newcomer. "Mendez? Snake?"

After a pause, the big man said, "I go by Dez." His voice was surprisingly smooth for his bulk, more rich baritone than bass. He scanned the crowd. "It'd be ridiculous to say 'Don't let me interrupt,' so I won't. Instead, I'll say thanks for having me, and I look forward to meeting the rest of you after the ceremony." He was looking at Brandt as he finished, as if he had recognized him as another Triad mage, and from there made the connection to Woody.

Brandt tipped his head. "Glad to have you." Patience was pretty sure he meant it too.

For her part, she couldn't get past the feeling that there was something a little too easy about Dez's conversion. Then again, Triad magic was powerful stuff. She supposed it was possible.

As Strike had implied, they would let time tell on this one. Still, her fingers itched for her star deck. She wondered what she would get if she asked about Dez. Would he be the Chuen trickster, sent to shake them up, or would she draw the Oc card, which symbolized breakthroughs and new beginnings? Or something else entirely?

Strike began the funeral rites, and she focused on the ceremony as he invoked the gods and his kingship, and then ritually praised Woody for his strength and sacrifices, both those he had made in his life and the ultimate sacrifice of his death.

As Strike spoke, Harry and Braden joined the circle, fitting themselves between her and Brandt.

Braden kept looking up at Brandt to see if he was doing things right. Harry, on the other hand, had his eyes fixed on the mortuary bundle.

What do you see? Patience wanted to ask him, certain somehow that he was perceiving something more than human-normal. She wished she could spend longer with him, with them both, but that time would come. *One year, three hundred and sixty-five days*, she thought, only then realizing that she had started to count, not to the zero date, but to the day after that, when the new cycle would—gods willing—begin and life would go on.

When the time came, Brandt held out the torch to Rabbit, who lit it with a quick burst of fire magic and stepped away. But Brandt waved him in. "Get your ass in here. You're part of the family."

Rabbit's quick surprise was followed by a rare smile. He nodded and stepped into the group as Patience, Hannah, Harry, and Braden all added their hands to the torch Brandt held. When Rabbit too was gripping the torch, they together touched it to the edge of the pyre. The fire caught and spread quickly, with Rabbit giving a little pyrokinetic encouragement. Within minutes the whole thing was ablaze, driving back the circle of mourners.

The gray smoke spiraled up into the sky, twining tendrils of gray amid puffy winter clouds. Two tendrils crossed, darkening for a moment. When they parted again, an eagle flew where there hadn't been one before.

"Did you . . . ?" Patience trailed off.

"Yeah. I did." Brandt glanced at his forearm as if just realizing that he was now the only person on the earth plane who wore the mark of the eagle bloodline.

"*Oh.*" Hannah's soft exclamation drew their attention back to the sky, where a dozen other eagles suddenly winged out of a cloud and bore down on the lone eagle. They split to surround the single bird, and then the thirteen eagles flew together, arrowing up into the sky, into the clouds . . . and disappearing.

"That didn't just happen." Patience's voice was thick. "Eagles don't flock. They're loners."

Brandt slipped an arm around her waist and leaned into her. "Not today, they're not."

It was a long time before anyone said anything else.

Then, too soon, it was time for Hannah and the boys to hit the road. She had insisted on taking one of the Jeeps rather than having Strike 'port them, staying off the magical radar from the very beginning. She and Carlos planned to ditch the vehicle by nightfall; Sven would track the GPS the following day and retrieve the Jeep . . . and Hannah, Carlos, Harry, and Braden would be in the wind. Gone.

Most of the teammates said their good-byes on the way back to the mansion, including Rabbit, who had to snuffle back tears as he hugged the twins goodbye. That left just Patience and Brandt to accompany Hannah and the boys out to the looping driveway at the front of the mansion, where Carlos was going to meet them with the Jeep.

While Brandt took the boys a few steps away and crouched down, talking to them earnestly, Patience threw her arms around Hannah. "Take care of them," she whispered. "And *you* take care too. Be good to yourself."

"I will. I promise." Hannah hugged her back fiercely. But when they parted, the *winikin*'s eyes glittered with a mixture of hurt and anger. "He didn't say good-bye."

Patience nodded. "I know." For all that Jox had followed Hannah with his eyes when she wasn't looking, he hadn't spent any real time with her. Worse, he'd made only a brief appearance at the funeral, and he'd slipped away once the good-byes started.

Granted, the royal *winikin* had a heavy burden of responsibility to his blood-bound charges and as the leader of the *winikin*, and he'd had to prioritize those duties over Hannah. But as far as Patience was concerned, their situation might suck, but that didn't give him the right to be cruel.

"You should go after him," she said. "If nothing else, you could corner him, kiss the hell out of him, and have the satisfaction of imagining him pining after you for the next two years."

One corner of Hannah's mouth kicked up. "I tried that a long time ago. It didn't help."

The Jeep cruised around the corner of the garage then. Seeing the vehicle, the twins strangle-hugged Brandt and bolted for Patience.

Faced with the reality she'd been trying not to

think about, she sat on the paved pathway as her legs practically gave out. She opened her arms to her sons and gathered them close, trying her best not to clutch too hard and freak them out more than they already were. When they drew away, faces solemn and swimming with tears, she said to Braden, voice cracking, "Promise me you'll behave for Hannah and Carlos?"

He nodded. "I promise."

"And you'll look out for Harry?"

"Of course." His look of offense cheered her immeasurably.

She turned to Harry. "Promise me you'll get in trouble every now and then? Not big trouble, but some little, fun trouble."

His too-serious eyes glinted. "I promise."

"And you'll look out for Braden?"

"Of course."

"You're sure you've got them straight, right?" Brandt asked from behind her. "I'd hate to think you mixed them up."

Her laugh came out as a sob, but she was grinning through her tears as she held back a hand for him to help her to her feet. "I never mix them up." Okay, almost never. But as Brandt pulled her vertical and urged her back against his strong, warm body, she felt better for having laughed, and the twins looked far less tragic than they had moments earlier. In fact, Braden was starting to glance at the Jeep.

"Okay, guys." Carlos climbed down and pushed

the driver's seat forward so the twins could get into the back, where he'd installed a pair of kiddie seats. "Last one in is a rotten . . . er, something."

Braden was the first one to break away and head for the vehicle. Harry followed soon, though. He shot several looks back at Patience and Brandt, but then faced forward and climbed in. Carlos strapped them in, then slid the seat back into place. Leaving the door open, he approached Hannah, looking distinctly wary.

"Do you have everything you need?" she asked diffidently.

"Change of plans."

Hannah stared at him. "Excuse me?"

"I'm not going." Carlos jerked his chin toward the mansion's front door. "He is."

Jox stood there with a knapsack slung over his shoulder and a resolute expression on his face.

"*Oh*," Patience said as her heart thumped a couple of times and her eyes filmed with a new wash of tears at the thought of Hannah and Jox finally getting a chance to be together after more than twenty-five years.

Hannah stared at him with an expression that bordered on horror.

After a long moment, she blurted, "Is that all you're bringing?"

He lifted a shoulder in a casual, knapsack-burdened shrug. "I've always traveled light . . . except where it came to you."

Her eyes filled. "You *rat*. I thought you weren't speaking to me. I thought . . . damn it, I don't know what I thought. But it wasn't good."

"I couldn't say anything until I told Strike I wanted to leave. He . . . it wasn't easy, not for either of us. Then I had to talk to Rabbit. And now . . ." He glanced back at the mansion where he'd been born, the one he'd renovated from top to bottom and run as his own kingdom for the past two and a half years. The one that represented humanity's single hope for survival, even if humanity didn't know it. "Now I'm ready to leave. That is . . . if you'll have me?"

"But, but—" Hannah went speechless for a few seconds as a tear tracked down her face. Her voice dropped to a disbelieving whisper. "What about the war? What about the other *winikin*? Who's going to run things around here?"

Jox came down the rest of the pathway to join her in the semicircular drive, stopping a few feet away. "The war won't be won or lost by a single *winikin*, but you and Woody already proved that one person *can* make a difference when it comes to protecting the next generation. As for the other *winikin* and keeping this place on an even keel, they'll manage. If they can't put together some sort of a workable democracy, with Strike as the buck-stopper, I've left instructions. One way or the other, they'll be okay without me."

"But . . ."

When she didn't say anything else, just stood there looking scared and confused, he said softly, "I know

I've put my duties ahead of you for way too long, that maybe it's too late for us. But I'm asking you to let me come with you. This doesn't have to mean we're dating, or courting, or, hell, so fucking crazy about each other that we can't keep our hands to ourselves." A distinct gleam entered his eyes as he said the last part. "We can take our time. Whatever you want. Just say you'll bring me with you. I can be a good *winikin* to the boys. I'll teach them, protect them, love them like they're my own. And I'll put you equal to that, with nothing above you three, I swear it. I—"

She launched herself at him and cut him off with a kiss. He rocked back under the impact, and his hands stayed out to his sides for a few seconds, as if it had been so long since he had kissed someone or been kissed that he couldn't quite remember what to do with them.

Then his arms folded around her, and they merged, for a moment, into a single unit.

Carlos walked past them, back into the mansion, whistling tunelessly. Patience blew out a happy, relieved breath. "Well. That was a long time coming."

"Really?" Brandt asked, looking honestly shocked at the turn of events. "Where have I been?" When she glared at him, he held up both hands. "Don't answer that."

"*Men,*" she muttered, but she was grinning faintly, and her smile broadened as Hannah and Jox separated, both looking more than a little awestruck.

Then it was time for more good-byes; Patience climbed halfway into the Jeep to kiss and hug each of the boys again, and then hugged Jox, and then Hannah. As they parted, Hannah said, "Keep that card close to your heart, sweetling."

Patience nodded. "I will. I promise."

Brandt finished with the boys, kissed Hannah's cheek, and did the manly handshake-backslap thing with Jox. "I owe you one," Brandt said with a pointed look at the backseat.

Jox nodded. "I'll collect in a couple of years, gods willing. I'm toying with the idea of rebuilding the garden shop that Rabbit torched; I never got around to putting the property up for sale right after the fire, and then the market tanked. So I still own it." One corner of his mouth kicked up. "If I decide to rebuild, I'll be looking for a good architect."

"You've got one," Brandt said firmly, then echoed, "Gods willing." He waved them into the Jeep, and then joined Patience as she moved back toward the covered entryway.

As they crossed the drive, she caught several flashes of movement from various windows as the inhabitants of Skywatch waved to Jox, Hannah, and the boys. It was the single unmoving figure in an upper window of the royal quarters that caught her attention, though.

Strike stood staring down, his body etched with weary resignation. "He looks so sad," she said softly.

Brandt followed her eyes. "I bet you never thought you'd feel bad about the idea of him being cut off from his *winikin.*"

"A lot has changed over the past week."

"You're telling me." He went silent as the Jeep fired up.

They turned back, their hands twining together, as the vehicle rolled toward the gate in the perimeter fence surrounding Skywatch. Together, they lifted their free hands in a dual wave. Magic washed over her skin as someone inside the mansion dropped the blood-ward to let the Jeep through the perimeter. The vehicle cleared the main gate; brake lights flashed, and Jox tapped the horn in a cheery *beep-beep* . . . and then he drove away, following the dirt track that led away from the compound.

"See you in two years," Patience whispered.

Brandt pressed a kiss to her temple, leaning into her hard enough to let her know that the kiss was as much for him as for her. "*We'll* see them in two years."

Neither of them said "gods willing." It seemed too much like a lack of faith.

Instead, as they stood together, watching the Jeep dwindle to a dust cloud, he said, "What card was Hannah talking about?"

Patience's heart lightened, just a touch. "I did a one-card reading, asking about the day after the zero date. I pulled the Kan card, which represents the iguana. It's the one card in the entire star deck that I've never pulled before, ever, even though it should be my bloodline totem. It represents two things." She paused, smiling softly. "The first one is hope."

"I like that one." He gave her a one-armed squeeze. "What's the second?"

"Fertility." Aware of the shiver that ran through his

big frame, she grinned. "I was thinking . . . Woodrow is a good name."

"Yeah." His voice went rough. "Yeah. It is."

They stood like that a moment longer, even though the dust cloud was gone. Then, in unspoken consent, they turned and headed back into the mansion. Arm in arm. Together.

GLOSSARY

Below are some Nightkeeper terms and their meanings. Pronunciation-wise, most of these words sound the way they're spelled, with two tricks: First, the letter "x" takes the "sh" sound. Second, the letter "i" should be read as the "ee" sound. Thus, for example, "Xibalba" becomes "Shee-bal-buh." For more information on the Nightkeepers' world, excerpts, deleted scenes, and more, please visit www.JessicaAndersen.com.

Entities

Banol Kax—The lords of the underworld, Xibalba. Driven from the earth by the many-times-great-ancestors of the modern Nightkeepers, the *Banol Kax* seek to return and subjugate mankind on the foretold day: December 21, 2012.

Kinich Ahau—The sun god of the ancient Maya. Each night at sunset, Kinich Ahau enters Xibalba. With the aid of two huge black dogs called companions, the god must fight through the underworld to reach the dawn horizon each morning, beginning a new day.

makol (ajaw-makol)—These demon souls are capable of reaching through the barrier to possess evil-natured human hosts. Recognized by their luminous green eyes, a *makol*-bound human retains his own thoughts and actions in direct proportion to the amount of evil in his soul. An *ajaw-makol*, which is a ruling *makol* created through direct spell casting, can create lesser *makol* through blood sacrifice.

nahwal—Humanoid spirit entities that exist in the barrier and hold within them all of the accumulated wisdom of each Nightkeeper bloodline. They can be asked for information, but cannot always be trusted.

Nightkeeper—A member of an ancient race sworn to protect mankind from annihilation in the years leading up to December 21, 2012, when the barrier separating the earth and underworld will fall and the *Banol Kax* will seek to precipitate the apocalypse.

Order of Xibalba—Formed by renegade Nightkeepers around 600 A.D., the order was believed to have been destroyed. However, the order survives, and is now led by a powerful mage named Iago.

winikin—Descended from the conquered Sumerian warriors who served the Nightkeepers back in ancient Egypt, the *winikin* are blood-bound to act as the servants, protectors, and counselors of the magi.

Places

El Rey—A small Mayan ruin located in the middle of the Cancún hotel district. Although not considered a "major" ruin by most Mayanists, it has deeply buried secrets.

Skywatch—The Nightkeepers' training compound is located in a box canyon in the Chaco Canyon region of New Mexico, and is protected by magical wards.

Xibalba—The nine-layer underworld, home to the *Banol Kax* and *makol*.

Things (spells, glyphs, prophecies, etc.)

barrier—A force field of psi energy that separates the earth, sky, and underworld, and powers the Nightkeepers' magic. The strength of the barrier fluctuates with the positions of the stars and planets; the power of the magi becomes stronger as the barrier weakens in the years leading up to 2012 . . . in theory, anyway.

jun tan—The "beloved" glyph that signifies a Nightkeeper's mated status.

library—Created by farseeing Nightkeeper leaders, this repository supposedly contains all the ancient artifacts and information the magi need to arm themselves for the end-time war.

Solstice Massacre—Following a series of prophetic dreams, the Nightkeepers' king led them to battle against the *Banol Kax* in the mid-1980s. The magi were slaughtered; only a scant dozen children survived to be raised in hiding by their *winikin*.

skyroad—This celestial avenue connected the earth and sky planes, allowing contact between the Nightkeepers and the gods. Since Iago's destruction of the skyroad, the gods have been unable to directly influence events on earth, giving sway to the demons and tipping humanity's balance dangerously toward the underworld.

Triad—The last three years prior to December 21, 2012, are known as the triad years. During this time, the Nightkeepers are prophesied to need the help of the Triad, a trio of übermagi created through a powerful spell.

writs—Set down by the First Father, these delineate the duties and codes of the Nightkeepers. Not all of them translate well into modern times.

The Nightkeepers and their *winikin*

coyote bloodline—The most mystical of the bloodlines. Coyote-Seven, known as Sven, can move objects with his mind and wears the warrior's mark. His *winikin*, the senior statesman Carlos, also watches over Nate Blackhawk. Carlos's daughter, Cara Liu, is supposed to be serving Sven. Instead, she has returned to the human world.

eagle bloodline—A bird bloodline, and therefore connected with the air and flight. The current members of this bloodline include Brandt, his wife, Patience (who has the talent of invisibility), and their twin full-blood sons, Harry and Braden. On the king's order, Brandt's and Patience's *winikin*, Woody and Hannah, have taken the twins into hiding.

harvester bloodline—Although the harvesters most often worked behind the scenes, the bloodline's last remaining member, Jade, is a spell caster with warrior-level talents. She and her human mate, Lucius, are the guardians of the Nightkeepers' vital library.

hawk bloodline—Also connected with air and flight, this bloodline can be aloof and unpredictable. Nate Blackhawk, the surviving member of this bloodline, was orphaned young and trusts few. He is a shape-shifter whose potentially destructive power is kept in check by his love for his mate, Alexis, and the steady guidance of his *winikin*, Carlos.

jaguar bloodline—The royal house of the Night-keepers. The members of this bloodline tend to be loyal and fair-minded, but can be stubborn and often struggle between duty and their own personal desires. The current members of the jaguar bloodline include the Nightkeepers' king, Strike, and his sisters, Anna and Sasha. Strike is a teleporter, Anna a seer who denies her talents, and Sasha a wielder of the life-giving *chu'ul* magic. They are protected and guided by the royal *winikin*, Jox. Strike's mate and queen, Leah Daniels, is full human, a former Miami-Dade detective who now leads Strike's royal council.

peccary bloodline—The boar bloodline is old and powerful; its members ruled the Nightkeepers before the jaguars came to power. The last surviving member of this bloodline, Rabbit, lives with the stigma of being a half blood, and commands wildly powerful magic. His human lover, Myrinne, is at times a questionable influence.

serpent bloodline—The masters of trickery. Newly released from prison, Snake Mendez has not undergone any of the proper ceremonies, yet already wears his Nightkeeper marks and commands some of his powers. His *winikin*, Louis Keban, is seriously unstable.

smoke bloodline—Often seers and prophets. However, the surviving member of this bloodline, Alexis Gray, has shown neither talent. Instead, she wielded the power of the goddess Ixchel, patron of weaving, fertility, and rainbows. With the destruction of the skyroad, she has lost her Godkeeper connection but remains a fierce warrior.

stone bloodline—The keepers of secrets. The members of this bloodline are known as great warriors, although the last surviving bloodline member, Michael, is a master of the shield spell as well as the killing silver magic called *muk*. His *winikin*, Tomas, and his mate, Sasha, combine to keep him balanced when the deadly magic threatens to tip him toward darkness.

Earthly enemies

Iago—The leader of the Order of Xibalba, Iago is a mage of extraordinary power, capable of "borrowing" the talents of other magi. Iago hopes to gain additional power by allying himself with the might of the bloodthirsty Aztecs through the soul of their mighty god-king Moctezuma.

Do you like bad boys, big magic, and high stakes?
Then don't miss the next sizzling installment in
Jessica Andersen's Nightkeepers series,

STORM KISSED

Dez and Reese's story is coming to you
from Signet Eclipse in June 2011.

Cancún, Mexico

Reese Montana had always thought wedding venues were tacky as a rule, but this one took the freaking multitiered, pink-frosted cake.

As if the velvet sombreros and striped serapes plastered on every available surface of the hotel lobby weren't bad enough, when she followed a series of cringe-inducing signs to the wedding chapel, she found the entryway decorated with what she suspected was meant to look like an ancient Mayan temple, but came across as papier-mâché gone horribly wrong. Inside the chapel, a faux-stone archway took the place of the usual flower-and-lattice bower, the aisle was lined with fake palm fronds, the rank-and-file chairs were wearing parrot-hued slipcovers, and the rollaway screen behind the main stage was painted with an art student's version of Chichén Itzá in its heyday, with the city intact, the temple ruins unruined, and people thronging in the foreground, staring at the stone archway with creepy, goggle-eyed intensity.

Thank Christ the room was empty. It was bad enough Reese was semicrashing. Be worse if she laughed her ass off during the "I dos."

"Not exactly what I was expecting," she murmured. Then again, it was her own fault that the moment she had opened the FedEx to find a plane ticket to Mexico and a request for her to come talk about a job, her brain had gone to a tropical fantasyland far from Denver's drab gray winter. Hell, it was probably just a run-of-the-mill deal for an aging paterfamilias who had lost track of a kid and was feeling depressed about it amid the sib's wedding prep. Typical locator gig.

But it still paid better—and was way safer—than her old job.

Following the low drone that said "The party's over here," she crunched across the fake leaves, tucked herself into the shadows, and took a look through the back door, to where a couple of dozen bodies thronged in an open-air dining area.

She stilled as the sight in front of her refused to look run-of-the-mill.

Twenty or so people, a fairly even mix of men and women, were knotted together on one side of the room, the men in decent suits, the women in an eclectic mix of high-end, with no rent-a-tux'd groom or

Barbie-doll bride in evidence. Six of them were small and compact, their gestures quick, their eyes always on the move. Overall, they weren't too far off from ordinary.

The rest, though . . . whoa. Not ordinary.

All in their late twenties, early thirties, they were uniformly huge—in height and muscle, with zero flab—gorgeous and somehow *glossy*, like the overhead lights bounced off them differently from the others. They drew her eye, made her want to stare . . . and brought a pang.

So did the realization that they all moved like fighters.

Suddenly, accepting the anonymous invite south of the border started seeming less like an adventure and more like a dumb idea. But even as her new self said she should do a vanishing act, the woman she used to be planted her feet, because what if they were trying to locate someone worth saving? She'd seen it before. Hell, she'd *been* it before.

You can't help everyone, she reminded herself. But she stayed put and checked out the setup as her pulse kicked up a notch.

The stone patio was surrounded by a high vine-covered fence, and the overhead latticework was decorated with a gazillion fairy lights that failed to disguise the fact that the hotel was smack in the middle of a bunch of other hotels. There was only the one door, which didn't make sense. Crowds like this always had an exit strategy. Unless she'd misread them? She didn't think so.

She should walk away. Call Fallon. Let the pros handle things.

Instead, glad that she'd gone with her first instinct and stopped at a local pawnshop to buy a piece on her way to the hotel, she stepped out of the shadows and into the light.

Within seconds, every one of them had marked her—their eyes flicked to her, then to one another, and there was a subtle shift in the room as some jackets got twitched aside and other bodies got out of the line of fire. But they didn't draw down. Disciplined or cocky? She didn't know.

She held out her empty hands as her pulse upshifted another gear. "I'm not looking for trouble. I was invited." Sort of.

A pretty blond-and-blue off on one side glanced at the big brown-haired man beside her, and said, "We didn't invite you." Okay. Bride and groom weren't the prospective clients. Didn't look like newlyweds either. Renewing vows, maybe? Or was this whole thing a setup? She didn't know, but she wasn't moving away from that door.

"I invited her," said a big guy on the other side of the room. When he spoke, the others gave way a little, telling her that he was the boss of this outfit. He was built like a bouncer, and had shoulder-length hair and a jawline beard that made her think of a Renaissance fair. And he was vaguely familiar, but not from her present life.

Oh, shit. Again, her new self said to run. Again, she stayed put. "Do I know you?"

He gave her a once-over with brilliant blue eyes. "Where's all the leather?"

She was wearing glossy silver-toed boots, trim black pants, and a subtly studded blazer. "Dog's TV show turned it into a cliché." Which was too bad. She had liked her old working outfit. "I've still got the thigh-high boots if you're interested."

"He's not." A smaller blond-and-blue moved up to his side and shot her a look.

Reese knew that look. Fallon had hit her with it often enough. "You're a cop."

The ID eased her nerves a degree. Granted, there were cops who crossed the line, but fewer than the TV made it seem. More, she wasn't getting the "bad guy" vibe off this crew, and although her instincts weren't infallible, they had a pretty good record. So who were these guys? A task force working the wrong side of the border? If so, why did they need her? And why not go through channels?

Unless they had, and Fallon had told them to fuck off. That, she could believe.

The cop nodded. "And you're the bounty hunter."

The others relaxed a smidge and the bride's mouth went round in surprise. Reese stayed focused on the big guy in charge. "I used to be a bounty hunter. Now I'm strictly private." She paused. "You'll have to help me out here. Where do I know you from?"

"Three years ago, in a burned-out warehouse in Chicago."

"Three—" She broke off as her stomach knotted on a sharp stab. Keeping the poker face that had saved her life more times than she wanted to count, she nodded and breathed past the pain. "Right. Strike. I remember."

Would've been better if she could forget. She still had nightmares where she was back in that warehouse shell, breathing stale smoke as she crept up on the two men, one dangerous, one an unknown who had a gangsta name but wore normal duds and showed up in a rented minivan. With the other, more deadly hunters closing in faster than she had anticipated—a warning that she had already wasted too much time trying to eavesdrop on the meeting—she had nailed the dangerous one from behind with her souped-up Taser and had her two quasi bodyguards drag his ass back to lockup. Not letting herself think about what she had just done, she had chased the other guy—this guy—back to his rental, labeling him harmless.

Okay, she thought, forcing herself away from the past, *I was wrong about the harmless part.* Because her instincts told her that the man facing her now was dangerous in his own right. Either he'd changed, or he'd been playing her before.

What the hell was going on here? And why did it have to be *that* grab?

Doesn't matter, she told herself. That part of her life was over. *Not going back there.* Shifting the small black carryall she had looped over one shoulder, she cleared the way to get at the .38 she had tucked at the small of her back. "I don't do find-and-grabs anymore."

Strike's eyes didn't waver. "All we need you to do is locate him. We'll take care of the rest."

She should turn him down. Hell, she shouldn't have come out here in the first place. She was just starting to hit her stride back in Denver, and this crew had "questionable" written all over them, with too many things not lining up. But it was the questionability that had her sticking. She knew what it felt like to be lost. Now she tracked down the lost and reunited them with their friends and family . . . or if they were better off lost, she helped them stay that way permanently.

"Tell me about the target," she said.

"It's the same guy you bagged out from under me that day in the warehouse: Snake Mendez."

He said something else, but she couldn't hear him over the roaring that suddenly filled her head as her heartbeat revved. *Mendez. Oh, Christ.* She had to lock her knees to keep from sagging as it all tried to come rushing back—memories, pain, betrayal.

Keep breathing. She couldn't go there again. Not now, when she was just starting to put her shit back together.

More, there were too many questions. How much did this guy know? Who was he working for? Why the wedding charade?

Let Fallon handle that. You get your ass out of here. Clinging to her poker face, she retreated a step toward the doorway. "Mendez is dead." She practically choked on the words. "Last year in Chicago. The Varrio Warlocks got him." Although his parole officer had sworn he'd been playing it straight, he had died as he had lived: trying to run the world one city block at a time. *Got to get out of here.*

"Wait." Strike took a step in her direction. "Don't go."

"You don't need me to find a dead man." Another step back put her in the doorway.

"He's alive."

She froze, going cold and numb. "Bullshit." The word was little more than a whisper, poker face or not. "The VWs claimed the kill."

"They lied. Dez has been working with us in New Mex for the past year, but he took off on his own two days ago. We want you to track him down."

"He . . ." She trailed off as the numbness grew teeth and bit in.

Dez. The nickname had been reserved for the inner circle. Which meant . . . Baby Jesus, she didn't know what it meant, except that this guy had inside knowledge, and he—and his crew—reminded her of Dez. They were all big, gorgeous, glossy. They could almost be . . . Oh, shit. Related. *Oh shit, oh shit, oh shit.* Suddenly her heart was trying to hammer its way out of her chest and she couldn't catch her breath.

Those were just stories. Fairy tales. Not real. Never real.

Right?

Strike crossed the room, stopping an arm's length away. "I've seen you work, and my PI says you're still the best. I'll pay all expenses and triple your normal rate, no bullshit, no questions. Just find him for us and report back." He stuck out his hand. "Deal?"

She took his hand, but instead of shaking, she gave a yank so his sleeve rode up. On his inner wrist, he wore five glyph markings done in stark black. She stared at them as panic slashed through her—it was all too much.

Mendez wasn't alive. The stories weren't real.

And she shouldn't have come.

She dropped his hand and backed up another step so she could see the mural of Chichén Itzá in her peripheral vision. "I . . . can't help you. I'm sorry."

Then she did something she had done only a few other times in her life.

She turned and ran like hell.

JESSICA ANDERSEN

NIGHTKEEPERS
A NOVEL OF
THE FINAL PROPHECY

*First in the acclaimed series that combines Mayan lore
with modern, sexy characters.*

In the first century A.D., Mayan astronomers predicted the
world would end on December 21, 2012. In these final years
before the End Times, demons from the Mayan underworld
have come to earth to trigger the apocalypse. But the modern
descendants of the Mayan warrior-priests have
decided to fight back.

**"Raw passion, dark romance, and
seat-of-your-pants suspense, all set in
an astounding paranormal world."**
—#1 *New York Times* bestselling author J. R. Ward

Also Available
Dawnkeepers
Skykeepers
Demonkeepers

Available wherever books are sold or at
penguin.com

S0014

Ever wonder how to find out about all the latest romances from New American Library?

nalauthors.com

- See what's new
- Find author appearances
- Win fantastic prizes
- Get reading recommendations
- Sign up for the romance newsletter
- Chat with authors and other fans
- Read interviews with authors you love

Penguin Group (USA) Online

What will you be reading tomorrow?

Tom Clancy, Patricia Cornwell, W.E.B. Griffin,
Nora Roberts, William Gibson, Robin Cook,
Brian Jacques, Catherine Coulter, Stephen King,
Dean Koontz, Ken Follett, Clive Cussler,
Eric Jerome Dickey, John Sandford,
Terry McMillan, Sue Monk Kidd, Amy Tan,
J. R. Ward, Laurell K. Hamilton,
Charlaine Harris, Christine Feehan...

You'll find them all at
penguin.com

*Read excerpts and newsletters,
find tour schedules and reading group guides,
and enter contests.*

Subscribe to Penguin Group (USA) newsletters
and get an exclusive inside look
at exciting new titles and the authors you love
long before everyone else does.

PENGUIN GROUP (USA)
us.penguingroup.com